T0279331

THE SALVATION CYCLE

BOOK TWO

DAWN BREAKER

JODI MEADOWS

HOLIDAY HOUSE   NEW YORK

FOR EVERYONE WHO WANTS
TO MAKE A DIFFERENCE.

PROLOGUE

This was her beginning:

A gateway on the cusp of closing, a barrier raised high, and an immortal soul torn in two. One piece stayed with her. The other was placed into a mortal body.

Still asleep and unaware, Nightrender was sculpted into a weapon of devastating glory. She bore great wings, meant for battle as well as flight. She could burn away evil with merely a touch. And she required very little in the way of sustenance and shelter.

Nor did she need love.

It was best, her makers believed, if she did not grow too attached. Mortals lived such short lives, and Nightrender would exist forever.

Only one companion would be a constant: the shard of her soul, re-incarnated throughout the ages. She would always fight to save that piece of herself—and the world it lived in.

In addition to strength and purpose, her makers granted her all the history and understanding they had accumulated over the millennia, all the martial knowledge she would require to fight their ancient enemies.

For she alone would stand between mortal beings and the unrelenting dark.

Finally, as the opening between worlds narrowed and time grew short, her makers created the Relics. One hundred of them, painstakingly built and imbued with numinous power: a black sword and crown, three standing stones meant to summon this newly built Nightrender, and other tools intended to defend the world from rancor and further unknown dangers.

With but minutes to spare, Nightrender's makers bade her open her eyes. Awaken. Then they retreated from the world.

The gateway closed.

Nightrender was alone.

From the very moment she drew breath, Nightrender knew her duty. She steeled herself to begin her fight for Salvation, with only a mortal shard of her soul and the knowledge of *ninety-nine* Relics to help her.

In the first ages after the Shattering, humans were active in their own defense, mounting enormous expeditions to charge into the Malice and wipe out every rancor within.

Songs rose across the land—tales of battle, death, and glory—with Nightrender at their hearts. Paintings emerged as well, of stately queens wearing Black Reign—the obsidian crown crafted by the Numina themselves—and handsome kings bowing before Nightrender, a red sky and the dusty chaos of battle behind them. (As if Nightrender would have paused to pose for a sketch when she could have been cleaving rancor in two.)

They fought, everyone united, laying siege after siege against the Rupture—the gateway between the mortal plane and the Dark Shard—but no matter how long a campaign lasted, the Rupture spit out more rancor. It was an endless fountain of terror.

The war seemed hopeless. Over time, people lost heart. The great armies vanished.

Rather than fight rancor, the three kingdoms found excuses to fight one another. But though they were enemies, they agreed that none would use malice against the others. To do so would be a violation of the highest order. With Nightrender grimly observing the agreement, the Winterfast Accords were written and signed, intended to last forever.

Life went on. For thousands of years, kings and queens summoned Nightrender to drive back the darkness, trusting her to save Salvation as her makers had commanded. Each kingdom continued to train armies of Dawnbreakers—Nightrender's elite soldiers—preparing them to march into the Malice and fight alongside her. It was a great and deadly honor.

But that, too, came to an end.

For a rancor king passed through the Rupture, an unprecedented horror. Such monstrosities could not enter the mortal plane of their own accord. They had to be summoned by name, drawn through the aperture between worlds by immense power and sacrifice.

Worse, all who fought a rancor king were subject to the law of conquest:

To kill a rancor king was to *become* a rancor king.

So Nightrender could not kill him, but she *could* send him back—back to the darkness of the demon plane. And she was on the cusp of doing so when she learned the truth: he had been summoned by mankind's rulers. They had broken the Winterfast Accords.

Possessed by a newly forged link with the rancor king, one created in the bloodletting of battle, Nightrender had abandoned her mission to exorcise him and flown to all three kingdoms, one after another, slaughtering the kings and queens in their keeps.

Better to sever the blight before it festered.

After the Red Dawn, mortals sought to magically excise their misdeeds from her mind—cutting the event right out of her.

Thus, her second beginning.

All her existence, Nightrender's memories had been a map of stars. Constellations built over centuries spanned the sky of her mind, stretching into infinity. Each moment of her life was recorded, from her first awakening to her last. She could recall every battle and setback and triumph she had ever experienced.

But the magical injury made by mortals spread, an untreated infection branching wider and hotter, consuming memories as it expanded. Hundreds and thousands of moments vanished. With a single cut, huge swaths of her inner sky were made blank, without even a trace of the light that had once been.

Eventually, Nightrender feared, there would be nothing left but this lifetime.

Nothing left but this moment.

Soon, the world would lurch into a new age: one where Nightrender, champion of the three kingdoms, hero of the people, Sword of the Numina, was capable of failure.

This was her ending.

1.

RUNE

Rune breathed in red.

He breathed out red.

Red was thick on the air, filling his lungs. Dirt and blood covered his torn armor. Grit gathered between his teeth. With every inhale, he felt the slime of corruption coating his insides.

Nothing was clean in the Malice.

But Rune—he hardly noticed. He stalked a circuit around his cell, shoulders hunched and fists flexing, while the last hours—days? weeks?—raced through his mind. He wasn't sure how long he'd been here. Time lurched and stumbled in the Malice. It could have been eternity.

He hated that he was here, a hostage meant to buy an armistice between the Nightrender and her ancient, unkillable foe: Daghath Mal.

It was a false truce—one that would break eventually. But until then, Rune was trapped.

This captivity was a sacrifice he'd made willingly. At the time, it had seemed like the only option. It *still* seemed like the only option, but burn it—Rune was needed at home. In Caberwill, where his mother had just been killed, slaughtered by a rancor. There were rites. A funeral. Perhaps a spare moment for his own grief?

He had a whole *kingdom* to tend to.

Sisters.

And a wife.

There was the war with Ivasland as well . . . although given how his army fared when a malsite erupted in its camp, it was hard to say whether Caberwill could continue the fight.

Burn it all. He needed to get back home. He was *king.*

A caged king.

His cell didn't even have a door. Or windows. (It'd had both, briefly, but they'd disappeared.) And though he'd thoroughly inspected every inch of it, there was no crack, no escape: the walls, floor, and ceiling were all made of unyielding bone. Human femurs and ribs glittered in the omnipresent red light.

He knew whose bones they were, too. Dawnbreakers.

Rune stopped in his tracks, biting back a tide of hopelessness. He had to be strong. The Nightrender wouldn't let him stay here forever. She'd said as much.

You are my soul shard. I would see you free.

Her soul shard. The knowledge burned through him, just as bright and hot as before.

It had come like lightning. In the thick of battle, when their eyes had met across the throne room, Rune had spoken her name. Her *true* name.

Medella.

She'd been fiercer after that. Deadlier. No longer hampered by whatever dark magic had made fighting excruciating for her before. But even that hadn't been enough to save Rune's men. They had died one by one until only he was left, Daghath Mal's talons at his throat.

Thus, the truce.

Slowly now, Rune resumed his circuit around his cell.

He'd had a lot of time to think about what had changed—why he'd been unable to remember the Nightrender's name until that moment, why he hadn't known they were bound together—and the only answer he could fathom was this: whatever had damaged her memory had also affected him. It was a deep, soul-level wound that had smudged out the knowledge of her name.

But when he'd hurtled into the Malice to help her, he'd healed it. He had chased the pull of his soul to hers, and it had brought him clarity. Focus. Her secret name.

And a kiss.

He shouldn't have done it. He was already obligated, and besides, a soul shard wasn't meant to be a lover—merely a companion, a friend. But he'd touched his lips to hers and kissed her anyway.

And she'd kissed him back. Then she'd...thanked him? He had no idea what to make of that.

You are my soul shard. I would see you free.

She would. He believed she would come for him the moment it was possible. But in the meantime, he was stuck here, unable to do *anything* but pace. He needed to be useful to her. Somehow.

"Burn everything," he muttered.

The cell began to tremble as a section of the wall dilated open, revealing a red-lit hallway.

Rune's heart kicked as he backed away, half expecting a rancor—or worse—to enter. But the passageway beyond was clear.

No, that wasn't right. There was...something.

He tilted his head, trying to listen. The castle was silent, and yet it wasn't. What he heard—what he felt—was the opposite of noise. Like a voice yawning up from the deep—except the voice was nothing, and it made everything else nothing, too.

With a physical jerk, Rune wrenched his mind back, focusing on the thrum of his heartbeat and the scuff of his boots against bone. He cleared his throat just to hear the sound.

The opening in the wall remained, all the bones pushed aside, red mortar squeezing out in thick, wet clumps.

Well, he'd been searching for an exit.

The Malice wanted him. He knew that. It would rot him from the inside out if he didn't fight it. And if he failed...it would corrupt him. Eternal subjugation to the Dark Shard.

If he lived, but left this place with malice in his heart, he would never be the king he wanted to be. Nor the man.

Rune knelt, reaching into his boot, letting his fingers touch the dark feather he'd sheathed there, given to him by the Nightrender herself. But he didn't withdraw it. Not yet. Not while he was being watched by this malignant nothing. It was just...he needed the reassurance that it was there, the Nightrender's parting gift.

"What would you have me do?" he murmured.

The opening waited.

Rune tensed his jaw, watching, but nothing else changed. It seemed the rancor king had decided to loosen his leash, allowing Rune to roam. If he dared.

Rune dared. He would explore. He would learn. And he would do whatever it took to destroy Daghath Mal when the time came.

Whatever it took.

He breathed in red.

He breathed out red.

2.

HANNE

"They're calling for your head, Your Majesty."

This was unfortunate news, but Hanne didn't take her eyes off her game. She was winning. Barely. She couldn't let this report, no matter how unsettling, distract her when victory was so near at hand.

"They're saying that you're responsible for the events at Silver Sun."

Careful not to muss the bandage on her hand, Hanne drew a card. Four. *Burn it.* She needed a queen or king to take her piece over the finish line.

Still, she moved her small golden bell forward four places, opting not to bluff her way farther—not right now, when she wasn't sure what her face was doing in reaction to the declaration that Embrian peasants wanted her dead.

The parlor was quiet as Hanne's opponent—her cousin Nadine Holt—drew a card. Nothing about Nadine's expression so much as twitched as she moved her emerald hound across the board, placing it one spot ahead of Hanne's bell. "How do they think Hanne could possibly be responsible? She was here with us when that awful machine detonated."

Maris Evans, the lady-in-waiting who'd brought the message in from the aviary, placed a basket of curling strips on Nadine's side of the table, along with an opal-handled magnifying glass. Piece by piece, she pulled out the letter to be read as a whole.

Cecelia Hawkins and Lea Wiswell, Hanne's other two ladies-in-waiting, hurried over to align the strips according to the coded numbers in the left corners. The papers were small—light enough for a dove to wear around its leg—and sealed with the tiniest drop of wax. The letter was written in Embrian micro-code, known only to members of the royal family and their most loyal staff. By necessity, that included the four ladies-in-waiting Hanne had brought from home.

Once the papers were ordered correctly, Nadine peered at the coded writing through the glass. She raised an eyebrow at Hanne. "It's from your royal mother. The people are saying you are the one who came up with the design for the mal-device. They're saying that when Ivasland was struggling to finish it, you went there personally to build it yourself, and that getting trapped in a malsite was a ruse."

"Oh, of course. I built it with all my extensive mechanical training." Hanne rolled her eyes and read a strip for herself, the tiny dots and lines and circles glaring up at her.

We formally request aid to defend Solspire against the angry mobs....

"Really." Hanne snorted. "Mother wants my help, does she now?"

"Consider it a compliment, Your Majesty." Lady Sabine Hardwick, an elderly Embrian woman, put her knitting on the windowsill before standing and stretching out her spine. The cracks were audible even from the other side of the large parlor. "Queen Katarina never asks for help. That she is requesting it from you is a sign of her respect."

Sabine might think she knew Katarina Fortuin after years of serving her, but *Hanne* knew her mother. The queen of Embria was not paying Hanne a compliment. Every interaction was a command, a test, or a dismissal. This was the former.

"Back to the game." Nadine tapped the deck of cards. "It's your turn, Hanne. Draw, or I will claim victory."

"My life is in danger, you know." Hanne pinched the top card between her fingers to draw. Four again. *Really?* That left her two places before the finish line. Hanne moved her bell ahead five places. The next card—however poor a value it showed—would grant her victory.

Nadine drew without calling Hanne's bluff. "Your life has been in danger since before you were born. Find a different excuse for losing this game." Then Nadine moved her hound right past Hanne's bell—and across the finish line.

Hanne barely restrained herself from stamping her foot. "I think you cheat."

A smile curled up the corners of Nadine's mouth. "Are you calling my bluff?" She tipped the card but didn't show its value.

"No." Wrongly calling a bluff on a winning move doubled a loser's payout when playing for money. Hanne and Nadine were only playing for fun, but the etiquette still mattered. "I'm saying you *cheat*. No one should win *all* the time. It's a game of chance as much as skill. Unless Sardin truly favors you above all others." Sardin was the Numen of Luck, a popular choice among thieves and gamblers.

"There's no way to cheat at Mora's Gambit. You make the moves your card allows, or you bluff your way farther along the board and pray your opponent hasn't already seen the card you're pretending to have drawn. For example, moving five places when all the fives had already been drawn from the deck."

"Wait—"

With a prim smile, Nadine gathered the cards and quickly shuffled them, her face a mask of innocence. As though there were no way to arrange a deck to benefit one player over another. Next time, Hanne would have Lea or Maris shuffle. Both of them were terrible at shuffling.

"Your Majesty. Nadine." Sabine's tone wasn't quite scolding, as no one *scolded* a queen, but she managed to sound exasperated without crossing any lines. "Recall the aforementioned letter."

"Yes!" Hanne swept the golden bell and emerald hound off the board and dropped them into the wooden box that held the extra pieces. "Let's recall that. The people are calling for my head, as Maris so kindly phrased it."

Maris paled. "That was the way your mother phrased it, Your Majesty."

"None of us should phrase it like that again," Sabine said sharply. "It is unbecoming of young ladies to make light of such things."

That came dangerously close to criticizing *two* queens, but Hanne let it pass. She looked again at the slips of paper.

It wasn't a long message, by Queen Kat's standards. Only twenty-three strips, with a few duplicates in case a bird were shot out of the sky, or killed in a sudden spike of malice as it flapped its way across the continent.

With the magnifying glass pinned between both bandaged hands, Hanne read through the entire note.

Johanne, my little dove—

After the unforeseeable tragedy at Silver Sun, the common people have declared that you, my beloved daughter, are somehow to blame for the malice device. Not only do they claim that you are responsible for the concept and design, but that you yourself went to Athelney to finish it when the incompetent Ivaslander scientists could not.

It is absurd. Your father and I deigned to receive the leaders of this little uprising, but after so many baseless claims—that you were not actually trapped in a malsite, but off gallivanting with Ivaslanders—we were forced to decorate the gates of Solspire with their heads. Unfortunately, new leaders have arisen and because of your actions, they are calling for all our heads.

I'm afraid this may be an actual rebellion, one our army isn't equipped to handle at the current moment. There was, unfortunately, a mal-device thrown into our army's camp as they marched toward Ivasland to join with Caberwill in battle, and a significant number of our men were transformed into livestock by the uncontrolled dark magic. Dead livestock, now. The country people butchered many of them for food.

We formally request aid to defend Solspire against the angry mobs. They are unusually hardy, and their numbers will only grow stronger as more join them from all corners of Embria. Remember, they blame you. You must help us settle this.

With regards, your adoring mother,
Queen Katarina Fortuin of Embria

P.S. Opus and Grace: Faster than we'd agreed, but even so, effective.

Really? Queen Kat should have known better than to bring up the plan, even in code.

It had been simple: unite Caberwill and Embria by marrying Rune, and quickly use that alliance to punish their common enemy in the south. Ivasland deserved it, given their breach of the Winterfast Accords. Once Ivasland had been dealt with, Hanne would remove the queen and king of Caberwill—over the course of years, not days—and then, after she had pushed out an heir of her own, remove her husband and any remaining competition until no one remained to challenge her.

Hanne would be not just *a* queen, but *the* queen.

The Queen of Everything.

But events had happened far more quickly than she'd anticipated. Ivasland had sent an assassin, leading to King Opus's untimely demise. Then the rancor king had sent one of his minions, leading to Queen Grace's untimely demise. Finally, Ivasland (again) had sent a mal-device to the camp where Rune and his army were bedded down, leading to Rune's sudden disappearance on the road south.

It had been fast. Much too fast.

She slammed the magnifying glass back on the table. "Burn these."

Cecelia nodded emphatically. "I couldn't agree more, Your Majesty. Burn them all. Every last one of those traitorous peasants. How dare they blame you for their problems?"

"No, I mean— Well, yes, that, too." Hanne grabbed a handful of papers and dropped them back into the basket. "But mostly burn the letter. The last thing we need is to learn the hard way that Caberwilline maids double as codebreakers." If anyone from Caberwill saw this missive, Hanne would be just as dead as the previous king and queen.

"Ah, yes. Of course, Your Majesty." Cecelia swept the last of the papers into the basket, then tossed every incriminating drop of ink into the fireplace.

"I'll go to the aviary to make sure there aren't more duplicates coming in," Lea said.

"Sabine, you're certain there are no spy holes in here?" Hanne asked. "No hidden spaces?"

"Quite certain, but I will check again if it eases your mind." Sabine wasn't actually one of Hanne's ladies-in-waiting. No, she was her spy mistress, her unofficial protector. But as far as the rest of the court was aware, Sabine was simply a grandmotherly figure, an adviser of sorts.

"Thank you," Hanne said, because Nadine was always telling Hanne that people liked to be thanked for their work. "Has there been any word on my package?"

Sabine shook her head. "The delivery will happen on schedule, I assure you. Our man will return with the package within the week. Should he fail, he will throw himself into a malsite as penitence. Any kind you choose."

"Very well. Keep me informed."

"Of course, Your Majesty." Sabine retrieved her knitting bag and headed toward the bedroom, her ruby-colored dress swishing. "Come along, Cecelia,

Maris. It's time to prepare Her Majesty for the council meeting this afternoon. Gown and makeup. That's your job."

"Yes, Lady Sabine." Both girls sent quick curtsies Hanne's way, then followed Sabine.

This council meeting would be Hanne's first official meeting as queen, and she intended to make it memorable: Because she, Johanne Fortuin, was a conqueror.

Here she was, in the chambers of the queen of Caberwill, surrounded by all the finery her new subjects could muster. All she needed now was for Rune to return and finish the job of making an heir, and then her place would be secure.

Hanne went to the balcony door and stepped outside, Nadine following.

The thin, sharp air of Brink greeted her. Her gaze slid down the sheer walls of the castle, through the north yard, and beyond the outer walls to where the city spread out before her. From this height, Hanne could see all the way down the main thoroughfare, the streets branching off it in wild, unplanned dashes and loops and curls. The buildings were all stone, built—like the castle—from the mountain on which the city perched, part of a jagged, imposing range.

Beyond Brink, the road was a series of switchbacks, until the land settled into a lush piedmont where farms squared off the countryside, and the Brink Way spun into the distance.

"It's not as pretty as Solcast." Hanne tilted her head. "But I'm beginning to see the charm in it."

"It's a stark sort of beauty," Nadine agreed. "Severe but lovely, like a honed blade."

A blade that might cut them, if Hanne didn't do everything exactly right.

"How you will respond to your mother's request?" Nadine asked.

Hanne sighed. "I *shouldn't* allow peasants to kill my mother and father. It would set a bad precedent. The peasantry might come to believe they can just dispose of rulers they don't like. Or worse—they may wish to *choose* who rules!"

"Indeed. Commoners hardly know what they need. Such a system of governance would never last." Nadine glanced west, toward Embria, toward home. "But we mustn't forget—it's you the peasantry wants most."

"Royals are dropping left and right. I don't intend to become another victim." Wind whipped her blond hair, which shone bright and gold in the morning light.

"But how many troops would be needed to quell such a rebellion?"

"You're my official adviser now. Advise me."

"Unfortunately, your mother neglected to give a full account of conditions there. How many rebels? How many soldiers and royal guards? Has the palace staff turned against them, or do the servants remain loyal?" Nadine shook her head. "How should we know what to send?"

An uncomfortable urge to defend Queen Kat rose in Hanne. "Someone who's never had to ask for help doesn't know what kind to ask for."

"I will write back to ask the relevant questions." Nadine's mouth pulled into a line. "I suppose you'll need to discuss troops and supplies with the council. I don't like that you have to request anything so early. Not something like this."

Hanne gazed at her cousin. Nadine, every Numina bless her, seemed to believe that sending troops to rescue the Embrian monarchs was Hanne's only option.

Nadine continued. "After Ivasland ambushed Rune's army with the mal-device, Grand General Emberwish will be hesitant to send the remainder of his men anywhere."

"I believe it is *my* army now," Hanne said.

"Yes, of course. But remember that Caberwilline generals—for the most part—care about their soldiers. As individuals."

"How exhausting."

"Indeed." Nadine rubbed her temples. "And with that in mind, recall that the grand general was *there* when the malice machine detonated. He saw those men die. He feels accountable for his men and what happens while they're under his command. It wouldn't surprise me if he felt personally responsible for Rune's absence as well."

Hanne nodded thoughtfully. "Certainly I can find a way to use that against him."

"Certainly," Nadine agreed. "And what Ivasland did to the Embrian army was even worse. Well, not worse when it comes to losing royalty—that is deeply unfortunate for Caberwill and for you personally. But worse from a military perspective."

A shudder worked through Hanne. Thousands of men turned into beasts—then carved and eaten by greedy peasants. No consideration of what the shredded uniforms or tents meant; no curiosity about why there were suddenly so many steers roaming—just hunger, hunger for *meat*.

Meat made by malice, with malice still inside it.

And it was in those peasants now.

"It will be delicate," Nadine went on, "forcing the Crown Council to understand that Embria is instrumental in defeating Ivasland. Caberwill cannot do it alone. We must assist them."

"I'm considering not sending troops."

Nadine looked sharply at her. "Why?"

"If the peasants succeed in capturing my parents, then I am queen of Embria."

"If the peasants succeed in capturing your parents, then *they* are in charge of Embria. They will never bow to you if they believe they have the ability to rule."

Hanne gritted her teeth, but perhaps Nadine was correct.

Still, Hanne needed the Caberwilline army at the *Malstop*—not in Solspire. Burn it, she needed the *Embrian* army at the Malstop, but apparently that wasn't going to happen.

She sighed and looked toward the great dome in the center of Salvation. It touched every kingdom. They were *all* responsible for stopping what lay inside, though only she seemed to care. (Never mind that she had only decided to care recently, after her encounters with rancor, her terrifying vision of the Dark Shard, and the barrier growing so thin and weak that it actually *flickered*.)

For years, she had believed her purpose was to bring peace to the three kingdoms. Now she understood that Tuluna the Tenacious, the patron Numen of Embria, had loftier plans.

"When the Malstop falls, I will need warriors. As the bulk of Embria's forces are . . . gone . . . Caberwill's men will have to do."

"When the Malstop falls," Nadine echoed softly. "Yes."

"That is the real threat," Hanne insisted. "I must prepare to face it."

"The Nightrender should do it."

Hanne shook her head. "The Nightrender won't save us. But I will."

You will change the world, my chosen. The voice in the back of Hanne's head was sweet and cool. It belonged to Tuluna, who guided Hanne's steps, who whispered to her that she could be anything she dreamed.

"If anyone can, it's you." Nadine flashed a tight smile and bumped Hanne's shoulder.

Hanne basked in the surge of warmth that was her cousin's unwavering support. "Nevertheless, your counsel is prudent. In spite of this rather large setback, Embria still controls incredible wealth. It can hire and train new soldiers, soldiers we will need. I shall ask Grand General Emberwish to send troops to Solspire."

"And Embria can provide resources, too: weapons and rations," Nadine agreed. "Armies need money. Soldiers must eat."

Hanne immediately wished her cousin hadn't said *eat*, because she was, again, imagining the Embrian soldiers and their unhappy fates.

"Now you just have to make these arguments to the Crown Council," Nadine said.

Hanne groaned. She and Nadine were always coming up with good ideas for how to run the world, but someone forever stood in their way. Hanne's parents, when Hanne had been just a princess in Embria; and now the Crown Council, even though *Hanne* was the queen. It seemed wildly unfair that she should still be held back by all these politics.

Hanne could handle the grand general. Men with swords were wont to find reasons to use them. But Duchess Charity Wintersoft and Earl Rupert Flight were going to be problems. Charity controlled the purse strings, as she was the treasury chancellor, and would be unlikely to support more spending even with Hanne's promise that Embria would repay this favor tenfold. As for Rupert, he was the information chancellor, and his spies likely had numbers for how many peasants were banging down the doors of Solspire. Which would be useful information to have—if it were only *Hanne's* information. Rupert opposed her presence in Caberwill and would use it against her.

"I'd better get dressed." Hanne started to turn, but Nadine touched her arm.

"Some of your subjects have noticed you up here. You should give them a wave." She motioned to the castle yard below, and the city beyond the gray stone wall and open gate.

"But my hands." Hanne nodded at her bandages.

Nadine smiled gently. "All the better. What you did was incredible. You killed a rancor and avenged poor Queen Grace. I've heard whispers that some call you their Dawnbreaker Queen."

Hanne jerked around to glare at Nadine. "Why? I have nothing to do with the Nightrender. I'm certainly not part of her army."

"You killed a rancor right here in Honor's Keep," Nadine said. "They have only one word for mortals who can do that."

Hanne would have preferred a word not so closely associated with the Nightrender. It was that creature's fault that Hanne had been trapped in that malsite to begin with; if the Nightrender had only done her duty four hundred years ago, clearing the world of malice, none of this would be happening now.

Still...in slaying a rancor, Hanne *had* done something extraordinary. She was accustomed to Embria, where the people feared their rulers. But in Caberwill, they wanted to love them. They wanted to feel protected. Defended.

Hanne could do that. She could be what they wanted and more. Their new queen. Their beautiful queen. Their Dawnbreaker Queen.

"Fine. Let them love me."

So even though she was still wearing her dressing gown, even though her hair was a golden riot in the wind, Hanne moved toward the edge of the balcony. Immediately, common people noticed. They pointed at her, shouting for others to look as well.

Hanne could imagine the history books, the way they would describe this moment: the foreign queen caught on the balcony for a private talk with her lady, followed by a warm greeting to her new subjects.

As more faces turned upward, Hanne held aloft the black glass shard that hung from a heavy gold chain around her neck. It was the snapped-off spike from her obsidian crown, the very weapon she'd used to kill the rancor and saw off its head. This was the reason for her bandages; the obsidian had sliced into her palms, and the rancor blood had seared her skin. But nothing could have prevented her from finishing the job. No person. No fear. Certainly no pain.

Now the shard was smooth and clean, all the blood scrubbed from its slick facets. She'd worn it every day since killing the rancor, and kept it beside her bed at night.

Gradually, the hum of voices from below grew into a roar. But not, Hanne realized, a roar of approval. They were *booing*. Jeering.

"She doesn't belong here!" a man called. "Send her back!"

"Embria doesn't want her. Haven't you heard the rumors?"

"Put her back in the malsite!"

A cheer rose up—agreement. Others began to shout about *which* malsite they'd choose. Someone else suggested sending her to Ivasland. "She works for them anyway!"

Fury boiled through Hanne. How *dare* they talk about her this way? How *dare* they pretend they were any better than her? They were but *insects*—necessary, but disgusting, disease-ridden. Hanne, though. Hanne was a queen, Tuluna's chosen, the bringer of peace.

As the voices of the common people crescendoed, Hanne's fingers and hands and arms began to tremble. Her heart raced faster. Her vision swam, flashing red in the corners.

Burn them, she thought. *Burn them all.*

If they refused to love her, they would learn to fear her.

Suddenly, the mountain—the very cliff Brink sat upon—gave a great shudder and lurch.

And then all Hanne could hear was screaming.

3.

RUNE

Nothing made a sound.

Footfalls, breath, even the drum of his heart: all of it happened in that awful, disorienting silence. As though nothing he did was real.

He'd tried to ignore it, and he almost could: he was so caught up in turning a corner here, reaching the end of a hall there. He'd intended to map the castle, making himself useful for the Nightrender when she returned, but its structure was bizarre. Doors and walls wouldn't stay put.

Within minutes of leaving his cell, he was lost.

He pressed on, moving randomly and as quickly as he dared, certain that—at any moment—a rancor would strike from the shadows.

Rune was prey in this predator's keep.

Certainly, this castle was meant for a king, with vaulted ceilings, wide archways, and thick columns. But the rooms Rune hurried past were empty. No plush rugs. No grand furniture. There was no clear purpose for any of the various chambers. Daghath Mal's castle was simply a large space made into smaller spaces.

It did have Daghath Mal's own version of art, though surely no mortal king could take pleasure from such monstrosities. Rune passed bleached-white skeletons artfully arranged in gruesome poses: men slaughtering men, rusted swords at one another's throats. Other skeletons were part human, part animal: giant antlers, horse bodies, bear skulls. Most made no sense at all.

Silently, the castle shuddered. More red mortar oozed from the skeletal walls.

Rune's stomach twisted as he hurried on, the hallway expanding and contracting beneath his feet. Red air shivered around him. Walls convulsed, and several times he thought he saw them shifting in the distance, as though leading him somewhere, creating a path.

And then he reached a dead end.

There was nowhere to go but back, so he pivoted—straight into another dead end. Trapped.

He went absolutely still, feeling the great thud of his heart against his ribs, the air squeezing from his lungs. Slowly, he turned a full circle. Were the walls...getting closer?

Yes.

Bones swallowed bones as the trap narrowed, a box closing. The walls pressed against his shoulders. He could reach up and touch the ceiling.

Rune couldn't breathe. Couldn't think. Couldn't move. All he could do was watch. The castle would crush him.

"I'm sorry, Medella," he whispered hoarsely. "I wanted to help you."

And then, like a clap of thunder, *sound.*

It was cacophony, at a volume so intense that Rune nearly fell to his knees. The wall in front of him sliced open, and Rune hurled himself through—into a red-lit chamber the size of a cathedral.

Behind him, the wall closed with a terrible rumble. If he'd hesitated, he'd be dead now.

Rune released a long breath, but he wasn't out of danger. He'd arrived somewhere worse.

Hundreds of red crystals lit the chamber, as in the throne room where the Nightrender had fought Daghath Mal. But this space was much larger—and so much more terrible, for it held an immense sphere, black with scarlet sparks that danced across its surface. It was hard to judge how big the sphere was in the vastness of this chamber, but Rune had the impression that it was huge, the size of a water wheel.

And he knew what it was.

The Rupture.

It was more awful than he could have imagined, seeping dread and despair. He watched in horror as a bubble of darkness protruded from the sphere, shimmering like oil. It elongated, pinched off, and, with a sickening *splat,* landed on the floor.

At first, Rune thought it was only slime, some kind of inter-planar pus. But as it settled, angles emerged from its surface, sharp like knees or elbows.

It wasn't a bubble at all. It was a larval sac with a creature inside—one that stretched the sac's substance so thin it split open.

A rancor—fresh from the Dark Shard—tore free.

Instinctively, Rune recoiled. It was repellent. Raw muscles; double rows of pointed teeth; ribs protruding from a barrel chest; long, strangely jointed limbs. When it looked at him, it was with cold black-and-yellow eyes that sat recessed above the hole where its nose ought to have been.

Double tongues flickered out of its mouth.

Run. Run. But there was nowhere to go. The room had no exit. None besides the Rupture.

"Grand, is this not?" Daghath Mal's voice echoed through the chamber, drawing the rancor's eager attention. "I am rebuilding my army quickly."

The rancor king flickered into existence beside the Rupture. He was an enormous creature, alabaster white with great bat-like wings and bright veins of red. He had the same skull-like face as his subjects, with lips permanently peeled back to reveal bloodred gums and far, far too many teeth. Powerful. Utterly revolting.

Daghath Mal looked at the Rupture for a moment, considering, and then thrust a clawed hand inside. The limb vanished, but the muscles in his arm constricted, as though he'd clenched his fist around something.

Then he *pulled*. And the Rupture *grew*.

A horrible wave of sickness blinded Rune. He doubled over, his stomach twisting. He heaved, but nothing came out.

Then Daghath Mal released whatever he'd been holding, and the Rupture snapped back to its former size.

Rune sucked in a breath to clear his head.

"Right now," Daghath Mal said, "the Malstop is putting pressure on the Rupture, keeping it small."

This oozing sore on the world should never be described as *small*.

"When the Malstop is gone, I will pull the Rupture wide. My armies will pour through like water."

That couldn't happen—could it? The Malstop couldn't just disappear. The old magic that powered it would always maintain the barrier.

Unless...

Rune's stomach turned. "You said 'when.'"

"Don't confuse conversation for confession. I will not reveal anything to you." Daghath Mal knelt beside the newly arrived rancor, peering at it as a general might a soldier. "No, I simply wanted to show you what your time in my domain will buy."

Gooseflesh prickled over Rune's arms. "Chaos."

"Peace." Daghath Mal plucked a black strand of slime off the rancor and flicked it away. "Humans respond only to fear, and so fear is what they will receive. Imagine a world cast into eternal night and endless winter. The only light *my* light."

Without sun, the plants would die. Farms would wither, livestock would fade, and people would starve. What happened in Small Mountain—that would be *nothing* compared to the catastrophe of Daghath Mal's long night.

"If you try to rule us," Rune growled, "we will fight back."

Daghath Mal laughed. "You haven't tried very hard these last four hundred years. You've avoided me, avoided this place. You've made matters worse at every turn. You would slaughter one another throughout eternity if left to your own devices." He shook his head. "But I will save you from that fate. You will discover the peace of fear, the peace of obedience, the peace of punishment. Under my rule, you will learn to love me."

Impossible.

"So you let me out of my cell to talk at me, is that it?" Rune had been told many times, by many people, that he was *quite bothersome*, and if bothering the rancor king was the only thing he could accomplish here—then he'd do it.

Daghath Mal smiled. "I wish to talk *with* you. King to king."

"To what end? What do you hope to gain?"

"Everything. First I want to be free of this prison. Then I want the world." A low chuckle rumbled through the space. "But I wouldn't expect *you* to deliver it. After all, your Nightrender asked many favors of you, and you denied her." Daghath Mal paused, almost thoughtful. "I would have given her anything she asked for."

"You would have made her a monster."

"I would have made her a *queen*." Daghath Mal stalked toward him, bat-like wings flaring. With every motion, he flickered in and out, like this world didn't want him. "What I saw in her—you could not imagine. Her fury. Her fire." An angry edge cut into his tone. "But she spurned me. No matter how I helped her, what insights I offered, she pretended I was nothing but a gnat in her mind—a dark, intrusive thought she could will away."

Rune stiffened. "What do you mean?"

"Ah. She didn't tell you." A bloody smile rippled across the rancor king's face. "I have heard and seen and felt everything she has. Everything. I have been in her thoughts."

Chills prickled Rune. This beast had seen through the Nightrender's eyes?

"I knew everything that was in her mind," Daghath Mal continued. "Even her lost memories. Her fear of forgetting. All those thoughts about you..."

Rune wanted to be sick. This abomination had intruded into her private self. It was so violating.

"Do you want to know what she thought about you?" Daghath Mal stepped closer, framed by the Rupture's dark glow. "Do you want to know how desperately she wished that you were not her soul shard?"

Not her soul shard.

She hadn't wanted him. Rune's chest cracked open.

It shouldn't have hit him so hard. He should have expected that she would prefer someone less complicated, someone more capable. Someone *worthy*.

But he couldn't despair. He had to *become* worthy.

"Go burn yourself," Rune hissed. The rancor king was trying to get a rise out of him. And, all right, he was succeeding. But Rune was determined to prove a challenge. "Burn your army. Your sick castle. Your red world. Your Dark Shard. Burn all of it."

Hot air rippled off the rancor king; a deep growl reverberated through the chamber.

Rune pressed on, not caring how his voice shook. "Burn your ugly face. That vile breath. And your delusion that she would *ever* be your queen!"

Suddenly the beast was mere inches from him, nauseating heat rolling off his grotesque body. Instinct told Rune to flee, or freeze. But not fight. There was no part of him that believed he could fight the rancor king and live.

The air shimmered. The beast's arm flickered out; his taloned hand wrapped around Rune's throat.

Yellowed claws dug into Rune's skin, just shy of breaking it. It was the angle Daghath Mal held him at that was of more concern; one swift snap and Rune would be dead.

But if he died, the Nightrender could freely return—the truce would be broken. She could destroy the rancor. She could send Daghath Mal back to the Dark Shard. Salvation would finally be safe from this Incursion. Perhaps he *should* hope he died.

"That is the difference between us," Rune rasped. "I know I'm not worthy of her. You are unable to admit the same."

Rage filled the beast's red eyes. Those membranous wings stretched wide, blocking everything from sight.

There was only this.

The beast.

The rancor king.

The unkillable foe.

Blackness fogged the edges of Rune's vision. His breath came short, tight. For a moment, he wondered if this was it—death.

Strange. He wasn't scared.

The Rupture shuddered. Daghath Mal dropped Rune and backed away.

"No," he murmured. "I will not risk her ire. Not yet."

Rune's heart pounded as red air came rushing back into his lungs. His sight returned, though it swam for several seconds. "You're a coward." His voice scratched. "You're afraid to face her in a true battle, one where she is not held back by anything—not even a soul shard."

Teeth flashed. Another rumble vibrated the room.

But Daghath Mal didn't lose his temper again. "Go," he said, waving a clawed hand. "My hospitality is at an end. You can wait for her in the wilds."

Behind Rune, the wall groaned open. It was not the castle beyond, but the red wasteland of the Malice. Still, Rune didn't think twice; he rushed through, gulping down dry, dusty air.

"Just be mindful," Daghath Mal warned with a low chuckle. "It isn't safe for mortals. None of mine will touch you, but there are *other* dangers."

The wall closed, trapping Rune outside. However terrible his cell had been, its protection was gone. Now he was exposed.

And the moment Daghath Mal's army was rebuilt, Rune's life would come to an abrupt end. It was impossible to say how long he had left.

So he had to get his bearings. He had to *move*.

Rune scanned the red wilderness: the bone castle stood on a tor, a deep earthen depression encircling it like a moat. He could just make out the vast blue dome of the Malstop overhead. And there, in the distance, were the remnants of a path.

Well, it was a direction.

He had no supplies. No weapon. But he did have information: Daghath Mal would not simply wait for the Malstop to disappear; no, he had a plan to remove it.

Perhaps, now that he was closer to freedom, Rune could find a way to send that message to the Nightrender.

He took a shaky step forward. Dirt plumed around his boots, coating them like rust. Then he took the next step, and the next. And at last, he ran from the castle as fast as he could.

4.

HANNE

The world crumbled around Hanne. The mountain roared. Screaming, wailing everywhere. Hands reached for her.

"Run!" Nadine shouted.

The balcony floor swayed under Hanne's feet. She followed unsteadily as Nadine led her inside. Visions of the entire balcony cracking off the castle pursued her—she could imagine the stone crashing to the inner ward, shattering on impact.

Hanne tripped.

Instinctively, she reached out and grabbed the doorframe. But that, too, was unsteady, and the sudden pressure against her injured palm made fire race through her. She shouted, staggered, but Nadine held her up as the quake made the floor jump again.

The seconds stretched longer. Hanne had the uncomfortable feeling of moving slower than the rest of the world, of time slipping in and out of its usual rhythms. And beyond the roaring in her ears, she could hear the scrape and rumble of stone; the cries of Caberwillines; the tiny fractures in reality, little pops and gasps, joined by lights flickering on the edges of her peripheral vision.

Hanne squeezed her eyes shut as hard as she could, but that only allowed another image to fill her mind: an enormous rancor, as white as bleached bone, with scarlet lines veining its body and great bat wings. The beast looked at her. It smiled. Its mouth pulled back farther than should have been possible, revealing row after row of dagger-sharp teeth.

The rancor king.

Yellowed claws reached for her. Hanne struggled to get away, but as in a dream, she couldn't move. So she screamed. But her scream was silence, as if sound had all been stripped away, swallowed whole.

And then the shaking stopped. Time went back to normal. Hanne opened her eyes to find that she'd dropped to her knees.

Nadine knelt before her, holding her shoulders. Cecelia, Maris, and Sabine were rushing through the parlor, asking Hanne if she was all right; their voices were hollow and distant. A shimmery halo of light surrounded everyone, as though they didn't quite exist in the world.

As though *Hanne* didn't quite exist.

She trembled as her ladies helped her to her feet. Strange that their hands didn't pass right through her. How odd that she didn't drop through the floor and into the mountain.

"Your Majesty? Are you—"

"Give her a moment. She's had a fright."

"I heard the people outside. How dare they—"

"I will have the worst offenders identified and punished."

Hanne blinked, forcing herself to focus on Nadine's worried face, her frightened green eyes. As always, Nadine grounded her.

"I need space." Hanne tried to keep her voice steady, but a faint tremble found its way in anyway. "And"—she held up her bandaged hands—"something for the pain. I grabbed the doorframe without thinking."

Truthfully, the pain was not nearly as bad as it should have been. She'd slain the rancor only days ago. The gashes were still fresh.

At least, they should have been.

Maris jumped up to fetch tea and new bandages, while Nadine helped Hanne to a nearby chair.

"Are you all right?" Nadine asked quietly.

"I will be."

"Thank Nanror," her cousin breathed.

Hanne wasn't sure the Numen of Mercy had anything to do with her, but she forced a smile. "Did the people see me fall? They cannot hold me as weak. Caberwillines despise weakness."

"I don't think anyone saw," Nadine said. "They were too busy looking out for themselves. But what happened? You looked . . . like you were somewhere else."

Hanne closed her eyes. "The Dark Shard is intensifying its attacks upon me."

Nadine's eyes went round. "What do you mean?"

"As you said, I am the Dawnbreaker Queen. Perhaps this has always been true—and why the rancor chased *me* into the malsite. Perhaps that is why it coerced *me* into assisting Ivasland with the mal-device—something I never would have done without this threat to my very soul." Hanne pressed her hand against her heart. "The Dark Shard seeks to destroy me."

"I know," Nadine said. "But you had no choice. You did what was needed to survive."

"Just now," Hanne whispered, "I saw something. Not a rancor. A rancor *king*."

"A king." Color drained from Nadine's face. "The rancor you killed—the one that killed Queen Grace—it spoke of a king, did it not?"

"It did." Hanne swallowed a knot of fear. "It said the king was called Daghath Mal."

Nadine pressed her hand to her mouth. "I feel we should not speak that name. What if you summon it?"

You are safe with me. You are my chosen. Tuluna, as always, comforted Hanne.

I trust you, Hanne thought, but even so, she found herself fearful of the Dark Shard, what it could do to her, what it *would* do if she was not vigilant.

Nadine's voice dipped even lower. "Hanne. *How* did you see this? How is the Dark Shard reaching into your mind to show you these things?"

Hanne shook her head. "I don't know. But because of what I am . . . Daghath Mal is watching me. Threatening me. He knows I aim to strengthen the Malstop, and he intends to prevent that."

A worried scowl twisted Nadine's face. "Perhaps if you focused on the realm, he would lose interest. The council, the throne, the war: those concerns are more than enough to occupy any monarch." Nadine touched Hanne's arm. "Why do *you* have to put an end to Incursions and the Malice forever? Let someone else do it."

"I cannot," Hanne said. "I am the one. I must be."

Then Cecelia and Sabine were there, and Maris returned, carrying tea and bandages. As they took care of Hanne's injuries and reassured her that the jeerers would meet justice, she did her best to pay attention and nod along.

But her thoughts kept fluttering back to the vision of the rancor king and Nadine's question: Why couldn't *someone else* do it?

Stay the course, Tuluna whispered. **I am guiding you.**

Hanne knew that. A powerful queen—a conquering queen—did not leave this kind of work undone. She had promised the world peace. How could she do that if she did not deliver peace from the Dark Shard as well as peace among the kingdoms?

The earthquake was a warning. The king from beneath knows of your ambitions. Your enemies will do anything to stop you.

Yes. That was it.

As her ladies buzzed about and her guards came in to check on her, Hanne turned her gaze toward the fireplace, where flames consumed the last pieces of Queen Kat's note. "Write back to my mother," Hanne said abruptly. "Find out the numbers we discussed. Demand a short—and speedy—reply that requires only a few birds. I don't need to read another of her novels."

"Yes, Your Majesty." Nadine bowed her head, cheered now that the discussion had shifted back to politics.

Nadine tried to understand. Truly. But she hadn't been in the malsite with Hanne. She hadn't seen the rancor slaughter Queen Grace in the sunroom. And she didn't have Tuluna guiding her.

The war against Ivasland was vital to the survival of Embria and Caberwill. That was accurate. But it was the war against the Dark Shard that truly mattered. Hanne understood that now.

And when the Malstop fell and monsters poured forth, the world—Nadine included—would understand as well.

They would see the truth of their plight. They would see that there was only one way to peace.

Hanne's way.

5.
NIGHTRENDER

She dreamed that the world shook, that the mountains reached higher and the valleys plunged lower. She dreamed that the rivers ran backwards, returning to the safety of snowcaps and glaciers. She dreamed that the Malstop cracked open and malice spilled across Salvation in waves, reality splintering apart.

She dreamed that time ran riot across Salvation; some plants swarmed toward the sun, bright and green and hungry, while others withered, turning brown and brittle and finally to dust. In coastal villages, babies grew into toddlers before their mothers' eyes—and then older still, until they died of age in an afternoon.

She dreamed that people turned into trees, and trees turned into people. Flames burst into being atop candles, burning away all the wax at once. Darkness spread across the world, blocking out the sun and stars. A land without light. Eternal winter. Hunger. And sorrow.

Across Salvation, people cried out to the Numina for help. None of those cries reached the Bright Land, however, for the way there was blocked, the gateway closed so long ago.

Honeyed sunlight slanted into Nightrender's eyes, spilling across her face and throat and chest as afternoon deepened. Heat spread through her, a gentle touch.

She was alive.

"What is the last thing you remember?" The voice was a soft, hollow tenor, familiar and strange all at once. It was Known, one of the ghostlike figures who maintained the Soul Gate, along with the other, whom Nightrender called Unknown. They looked similar, the maintainers, both vaguely human with eyes the same blue as the Malstop, but she'd never had trouble telling which one was which. They were constants in Nightrender's world, where mortals died so quickly. Friends, of a sort.

So she was alive. And she was safe.

"Coming through the Soul Gate." Nightrender's throat was dry, raw, leaving her voice like crackling autumn leaves. "Allowing Rune to become Daghath Mal's hostage. A terrible truce."

Nightrender tilted her face away from the light. She could still see Rune's terrified expression as she left him alone in the rancor king's castle. It didn't matter that they'd had little choice but to agree, or that he'd urged her to go, or that she'd left him as well equipped as she could.

She had abandoned her soul shard to the rancor king.

"I fear the Malice will corrupt him." Nightrender could hear the low hum of the Malstop nearby, the only barrier between Salvation and unrelenting evil. And Rune was on the wrong side of it. "The malevolent energy will burrow into him, driving its roots deep until he is as twisted and wild as a rancor. My soul shard will become unrecognizable."

Known spoke kindly. "Soul shards were never meant to go into the Malice. Why was he there?"

"He didn't know." Nightrender tried to swallow a dry knot in her throat, but coughed instead. When the fit subsided and she opened her eyes, Known raised a steaming cup.

"Drink." They held the cup to Nightrender's lips and tilted.

It was chicken broth, full of salt and bubbles of fat, with shredded carrots and thin slices of meat. Nightrender sipped until she could speak again, then pulled away.

"You were saying Rune didn't know he is your soul shard." Known tilted their head, watching her with those pale eyes.

"My soul shard always remembers my name," Nightrender said. "Rune did not. I thought it kinder to let him believe he was merely the only man brave enough to summon me when no others would. But I knew. Not from the start, but soon enough."

"Did you take him into the Malice yourself, even knowing what he is and how he could be used against you?"

Nightrender shook her head. The muscles in her neck ached, but slowly the stiffness was working itself out. "There was a portal. It opened into the throne room of Daghath Mal's castle."

"Daghath Mal is the rancor king you spoke of?"

"Yes."

Known looked down at her, their face as pensive as ever. "It seems that Rune made his own choice."

"He would have made a better choice if he'd known what he is," Nightrender insisted.

"Are you certain?"

Nightrender glanced down. Rune so desperately wanted to be worthy, to do the right thing, to save everyone. Soul shard or not, he would have come after her if he'd believed he could do some good.

And he had. He'd remembered her name. The blazing light of that sudden connection had sliced through the cord that tied Nightrender to Daghath Mal, excising him from her thoughts. Without the darkness present in her mind, Nightrender had been able to fight to her full ability. She had killed dozens of rancor—hundreds, perhaps—reducing Daghath Mal's army so sharply that he needed the truce as much as she did.

"Can you sit?" Known moved aside.

Haltingly, Nightrender pulled herself up, mindful of her wings, which always needed to be arranged just so. The left one still hurt, but not as badly as before. As for her other injuries, well, she would live.

"Do you know where you are?" Known sat beside her, the cup of soup still in their small hands. They offered it to Nightrender.

After another drink, she looked around. There were four rows of perfectly made beds, each with a small nightstand and washbasin beside it. "An infirmary."

"Yes. This is my tower." Known rose from the bed and removed a bundle of white cloth from the nearest nightstand. "I'll take you to the washroom, if you'd like to clean up. I suggest you do." Known looked meaningfully at Nightrender—quite the feat for a face that didn't usually display emotion.

"It's only a little gore." Nightrender gazed down at her torn and bloodied armor, the fabric clawed apart. Slowly, the numinous cloth was mending itself; the damage to it must have been even more severe than Nightrender had realized before, if it wasn't yet finished. On top of the damage, a fine layer of red dust covered everything, like rust.

"It's disgusting." Known motioned for Nightrender to stand.

Nightrender drained the last of the soup and left the cup on the nightstand before attempting to rise. When she did, dizziness gripped her. She swayed, but caught herself on the bedpost.

Gradually, her sight returned. She would have to be careful. Blood loss. Pain. They affected her as well as mortals, although she'd rarely suffered the consequences for very long.

"This way." Known led her across the room, down one of the central aisles between the empty beds.

"Tell me why you have an infirmary here."

"It's practical." Known looked over their shoulder. "Your focus is understandably on leading Dawnbreakers into the Malice, but some do return through the Soul Gate."

Some did, true. Most just died in the Malice, their bodies never recovered.

"Those Dawnbreakers require immediate attention. This space provides that. We once had help. Physicians, nurses. But there's no one now."

Unease turned in Nightrender's gut. "I should have known this was here."

"You did." Known paused in front of a closed door. "After victories, you used to visit your surviving Dawnbreakers."

Nightrender had no memory of that. None at all.

A chill swept through her.

She had been forgetting things. She knew that. Sometimes, she could feel when they vanished, like a word balanced on the tip of her tongue before it fell the wrong way. Mostly, however, she had been able to sense the gaps, feel the shape of what had been lost.

But now . . . Now the gaps were so big she could no longer sense the edges. She had no idea how much of her past had been taken. Nightrender lifted her fingers to her head, as though she could feel the absence like a wound.

Known's face was gentle with sympathy. "We saw the cut in your mind. The one mortals made hundreds of years ago, when they carved away that awakening. I wish we could have fully healed it and restored your memories, but the only thing we could do was slow the erosion and prevent others from disappearing as quickly."

"You could not cure me."

"The damage was too severe. Perhaps four hundred years ago we could have done more." Known spoke softly: "Should you go back to sleep in Winterfast, the magic there will preserve what is left of your memories."

Nightrender's heart twisted. It was better than nothing, but it seemed she would always be *less* now. Less knowledgeable. Less capable. Less complete.

"I don't want to forget anything else," she whispered.

"I'm sorry."

"Daghath Mal offered to restore my memories. He had access to them before they vanished from my mind."

Known inclined their head. "You said no."

"I couldn't have said yes." But she'd wanted to. Daghath Mal had spoken to all her fear and anger, dangling the promise of her past before her.

"You could have," Known said, a slight tremble in their voice. "But you would have been his, and the world would have crumbled before you."

Nightrender wanted to know what more Known knew about it, but the maintainer had already turned away and opened a door, leading her into a bath area. It was large enough for attendants to help a wounded person wash: a huge tub with a faucet, a standing stall nearby, and a counter with grooming supplies.

Known placed a bundle of clothes on the counter. "I assume you don't want my help."

Nightrender stepped back, her wings flaring. "I do not."

A faint, fleeting smile touched Known's face. "I'll return soon." Known stepped through the door again and started to pull it closed.

"You use doors," Nightrender said quickly. "And you hold things." She'd never seen them use doors or hold things before. At least not that she could remember.

Known paused and canted their head. "Yes."

"It was an observation," Nightrender clarified. "Not a question."

"Of course not." Another smile flickered across Known's face, and then they were gone.

Alone, Nightrender sat on the edge of the tub and began peeling off her armor. Rancor blood had burned her skin, leaving red welts. Gashes looked worse in the stark light of the washroom. Something dark and sludgy dripped from her hair.

Known had been correct: disgusting.

Gingerly, she stepped into the standing stall and turned the knob. Hot water blasted down, beating against her body, making dried blood run rivulets down her stomach and arms and legs. Dirt spilled from the black strands of her hair and disappeared down the drain.

It hurt, this assault of water, but in the way exercise hurt, or anticipation. Even as her sodden wings drooped under the weight of water, she soaped and scrubbed and soaped again.

Exhaustion weighed on her. She was so *tired* of fighting, of waking to find the world was—once again—on the verge of catastrophe, and all the people who'd had a hand in bringing about that catastrophe suddenly needed her help to fix it.

She wanted to be finished with it, to move on and just *live*, but she couldn't imagine what that end looked like.

It didn't matter. Such a day would never come.

6.

HANNE

"I heard there hasn't been a serious earthquake in Brink in almost a hundred years." Lea ran the comb through Hanne's windblown hair. "Apparently there are tiny earthquakes all the time, but most people don't feel them. I'm told sometimes the hounds whine or bark, and people occasionally find that their belongings have shifted, but mostly no one notices."

"How did you hear all that?" Cecelia leaned in close to Hanne's face, patting rose-paste blusher on her cheeks.

"I have my ways." Pink-faced, Lea glanced toward Sabine. The older woman was sitting by the dressing room window, her knitting needles flashing in the sunlight. When Sabine didn't look up, Lea leaned in and lowered her voice. "All right, one of the boys in the aviary likes to talk to me."

"He likes to *talk* to you." Maris giggled as she finished rewrapping Hanne's bandages. "I'm sure that's all."

By now, Lea's cheeks were bright red. "That's all I will allow. He's an aviary boy, after all. A servant."

"Even the lowliest of servants can hold great value. He's an asset." Sabine had excellent hearing, something the younger ladies consistently forgot. "Don't compromise future marriage prospects, but get closer to him. Make him think you like *talking* to him as much as he likes *talking* to you. From now on, you'll be the one to collect Her Majesty's correspondence."

The flush drained out of Lea's face as she nodded. "Yes, Lady Sabine."

"He may not be able to give us the content of anyone's messages," Sabine went on, "but he will know who is receiving them, and how frequently. Perhaps he'll even know from where they've come. All of that is valuable to us."

Poor Lea, Hanne thought. The girl should have known better than to bring it up in front of Sabine; the old spy mistress viewed everyone as an asset. She had eyes and ears everywhere, and a mind to make these ladies-in-waiting just as cunning one day.

Lea was the softest of the ladies Hanne had brought from Embria, the one most prone to daydreams. She didn't yet understand that happy endings were an illusion, meticulously crafted by people like Sabine, Hanne, and Nadine.

"Well," Lea said, after a minute of uncomfortable silence. She had moved on to another length of Hanne's hair and was almost finished combing out all the tangles. "Sparrow also said that—"

"Wait." Cecelia picked up another jar of cosmetics and a mink-fur brush. "This boy you like—this boy who works in the aviary—is named *Sparrow*?"

Lea's face flushed bright red once again. "It's hardly his fault!"

"I agree." Nadine looked up from the small writing desk where she was making a few revisions to Hanne's council speech. "Caberwilline parents are *so* cruel. Why would anyone do that to a boy they claim to love?"

"It's absurd," Maris agreed. "But go on, Lea, tell us all what your bird boy said."

As conversation flittered about the room and Lea resumed binding Hanne's hair into an artful knot, Hanne focused on her face in the mirror. With her eyes shaded dark gold, and crushed pearls brushed across her cheekbones, she looked otherworldly. Polished.

"If we get an aftershock, you should fall into his arms!" Cecelia laughed. "Then you could come back and tell us all about it."

Hanne kept her expression neutral, so as not to encourage them. But truthfully, she didn't care if they talked about the earthquake (or boys). Early reports indicated that no one had died, and there'd been no obvious structural damage, so this was really the most exciting thing to happen since the wedding.

At last, the ladies were finished with Hanne. Lea inserted the final pin into Hanne's hair with her quick, gentle hands, and Cecelia arranged all the undergarments to be put on before the gown.

"You look beautiful, Your Majesty," Maris said. "Radiant."

"I do," Hanne agreed. "You've all done very well. The Crown Council will be impressed, I'm certain. They won't be able to look away."

Which was the intention. In Embria, before allowing a marriage to proceed, noble families considered what the offspring might look like, diligently consulting charts of dominant and recessive traits. (Of course, wealth and class suitability were also given due attention, as well as how clever a child might be.) But at home, in the world Hanne had grown up in, people used their best features as elegant weapons, distracting their opponents from whatever it was they wanted to hide. Higher taxes? Smile more. The crown wanted to claim a forest for personal use? Dazzle away any dissent.

Everyone trusted beauty. It was instinctual.

Then...there was Caberwill. While home to many reasonably attractive people, this kingdom hadn't yet figured out how to use that to forward their political ambitions. Instead, they bred for strength and size, for physical prowess. Sometimes, that led to happy accidents like Rune Highcrown, who had both the physical presence Caberwill society desired as well as the appealing sort of face an Embrian could admire.

We'll make beautiful babies, Hanne thought. Beautiful and smart, like Hanne, but strong like Rune. Assuming Rune ever came back.

"Perhaps I should announce that I'm pregnant." Hanne stood, allowing her bandaged hands to slip toward her abdomen.

The dressing room went completely quiet, all the giddy chatter evaporated.

"Your Majesty?" Lea was clearly suppressing a grin. Her eyes were round and hopeful. "Is there happy news?"

"No," Hanne admitted, pretending she didn't notice the way Lea slouched. "But an heir on the way would help to legitimize me—and my presence at council meetings."

"I think it would be wise to wait." Nadine leaned back in her chair, her expression thoughtful. "No one would believe that you actually know yet. It hasn't been long enough. Only a few days."

Hanne sighed.

"Perhaps you might consider finding someone else in the meantime." Sabine looked up from her knitting. She was always knitting. Whenever someone asked what she was making, she said simply that it didn't matter, she only liked to keep her hands busy. But rumor had it that she'd used those very needles to kill a man once. "That way you will have a contingency plan, in case King Rune never returns."

"But what of the gentleman?" Lea asked. "How would his silence be assur— Oh."

Sabine had paused her knitting and was contemplating the points of the needles.

Hanne let her hands fall to her sides. "I will consider it if my courses run next month."

"We shouldn't wait too long," Sabine cautioned. "Otherwise, you'll face questions about the timing. And finding the right man will take some effort. We'll need someone who looks enough like His Majesty, but who, of course, won't be missed when it's over."

Hanne nodded noncommittally. It wasn't that she felt any particular loyalty to Rune, especially since he wasn't here, but bringing anyone else into orbit came with risks. Even if Sabine disappeared him once Hanne was pregnant, there was still all the time before that, when a strange man might be caught in her rooms.

Was it worth the gamble? Rune might yet return. That alone would make her position secure.

Nadine pushed up from her desk and brought a sheet of paper to Hanne. "I've added a few words to touch on the earthquake."

Hanne scanned the lines of Nadine's neat handwriting. "There's nothing in here about the Incursion."

"I took it out."

Once again, the room went silent, this time with discomfort.

"Why?" Hanne struggled to keep her tone neutral, but she knew she had failed when Lea drew herself back.

Nadine, however, pulled herself up taller, as though she'd anticipated this. "Because the Crown Council doesn't believe we are experiencing an Incursion."

"A rancor just killed their queen. I was trapped in a malsite. These facts are undeniable." Hanne threw the sheet of paper to the floor. "Even the burning *Nightrender* is here. Somewhere. *She* says there's an Incursion."

"As your adviser, I must tell you that it's unwise to focus your first Crown Council address on this, Your Majesty." Nadine's voice sounded stiff. Hanne hadn't been aware that Nadine *could* sound stiff until now. "You already face too much resistance. The council is against you. You are a foreign queen. Your husband is missing. And they didn't care for him to begin with."

Hanne clenched her jaw.

Nadine pressed on. "If you bring up your campaign against the Malice, they will view you in the same light as they viewed Rune. That was what *he* did, and look where it got him."

There was a faint, terrified gasp from one of the other ladies.

"I see." Hanne looked from one lady to another. "Do you all feel that way?"

"I wouldn't presume," murmured Lea. "I am not an adviser."

"Nor am I." That was Cecelia. Maris, too, shook her head.

"Sabine?" Hanne looked at the older woman. "Do you agree with Nadine?"

"You are the queen, and you should address the council as you see fit." Lady Sabine picked up her knitting again. "However, Nadine's intelligence is correct. The council does not respect King Rune. They suffer his rule only because of his blood. I would advise you to set yourself apart."

Burn Rune. Burn him right to the Dark Shard.

"Become invaluable to them," Sabine went on. "Indispensable. Unfortunately, I fear that will be difficult if you immediately begin addressing them regarding King Rune's priorities."

"I know it is important to you. It should be important to the council as well." The gentleness in Nadine's voice made Hanne's skin prickle. She was speaking as though Hanne were a breakable thing. "But they are not with you—not yet."

Hanne sucked in a shallow breath. Her heart thudded. "Are *you* with me?"

Nadine's eyes widened, and for the first time in this discussion, she looked truly shocked. "Yes. Of course."

Permit no dissent. *You* are her queen.

Hanne stared at her cousin, her confidante, her closest friend. It had always been the two of them against the world. Nadine had *never* defied Hanne.

Before now.

A memory fluttered through her mind—that same night she'd arrived in Honor's Keep, when she'd told Nadine all about the malsite, the rancor, Ivasland. Nadine had told her something, too. She had told her that Earl Flight had suggested *she* should marry Rune, if Hanne was gone.

Nadine had nearly become queen of Caberwill.

No, Hanne thought. *Nadine is not trying to undermine me. She is not trying to take what is mine.*

Nadine would never.

Would she?

Cecelia, Maris, and Lea all shifted uncomfortably, their glances dancing back and forth between Hanne and Nadine. Sabine's needles never stopped flashing in the sunlight.

Hanne broke the silence first. She took command. "I intend to move forward with my observatory project. It's the only way to fix the Malstop—and to end the Incursions."

"Of course." Nadine blinked. Then blinked again. Her pulse fluttered faster in her throat.

She does not want you to pursue this.

She will not get in my way, Hanne thought. *She will do as I instruct.*

Be certain, my chosen.

Hanne wanted to be certain. She hated this doubt, the crack forming between them. She'd always depended on Nadine's loyalty. Never had she questioned it. But now . . .

A sharp knock sounded on the outer door. Without waiting to be ordered, Maris hurried to answer it. In a moment, everyone could hear the murmur of low, urgent voices from the parlor.

"It doesn't sound good." Lea bit her lip.

"I bet it's something to do with the earthquake," Cecelia said. "Perhaps one of the water pipes burst and we won't be able to wash again for three days."

"It's no use speculating," Sabine chided.

Only a moment later, Maris came rushing back into the dressing room. "Your Majesty, the Crown Council has already assembled!"

"But it's too early." Hanne turned her glare on Nadine. "You said we had another quarter hour."

Nadine squared her shoulders. "They've intentionally assembled early. They mean to cut you out of their discussion."

"Dress me," Hanne ordered. "Immediately."

With Nadine at her side, and Captain Oliver—her principal guard—just after them, Hanne stepped out of the queen's chambers, into the royal wing of Honor's Keep. Hanne had donned a formal gown, this one bright shades of blue, with sparkling gemstones sewn into the bodice. It was a masterful creation that commanded attention and showed off the golden tones of her hair.

Bloodwood wainscoting ran along the walls, with striking paintings of Highcrown ancestors and the royal crest displayed wherever possible. Light globes glowed from iron sconces, illuminating the bearlike men who'd sat upon the Caberwilline throne.

"I will discover who began this meeting early." Nadine strode next to Hanne. "They will regret disrespecting you like this."

Hanne only gave a sharp nod. She suspected it would not be that difficult to identify this person. But Nadine was eager to earn back Hanne's confidence after that mess of a speech.

Burn it. The speech. It was still lying on the floor in Hanne's dressing room. She hadn't had time to memorize it.

Well, she wasn't going to need it anyway.

They hurried past the king's chambers, where Rune would live if he ever returned. Then the crown prince's chambers. Then suites meant for other royal children, including the Highcrown princesses.

Currently, the door to their rooms was thrown open. Maids bustled in and out, cleaning up after the girls.

The council chamber was just ahead, with guards posted outside the door.

Hanne had only been to the council chambers a few times, but she knew all of the members by sight. She had spent a significant portion of her wedding day with these people, thanks to the attack on Small Mountain.

Urgency spurred her faster, and by the time she stood before the guards, she could hear the raised voices coming from behind the closed doors.

"Let me in," she commanded.

The two guards stared past her as though she wasn't there.

"You will allow Her Majesty entry," Nadine said, "or you will spend the rest of your days in the dungeon. Oh, I wonder what condition the dungeon is in after the earthquake. Terrible, I'm sure."

"I suppose we will soon find out." Captain Oliver reached for the weapon at his hip.

The guard on the left broke first.

"I'm sorry, Your Majesty," he said. "Our instructions are to keep the doors locked until the meeting is over."

"Who gave you those orders?"

"I'm afraid I cannot say." The man looked uncomfortable, as well he should. "And I cannot disobey."

"In Embria," Hanne commented, "the response to sedition is entire families being arrested. It's impossible to know what kind of ideas spouses share after dark, or if such treachery is hereditary. Those poor children. But we can't be too careful, you understand, and I believe the Embrian practice to be correct in these matters. Oliver, arrest them. And then arrest their families. Even the little babies."

Hanne wasn't actually certain that an Embrian captain—even one such as Oliver—could legally arrest Caberwill citizens, but that seemed like a problem for another time.

The second guard—the one who hadn't spoken before—lurched for the door and hauled it open. "Forgive us, Your Majesty. We were only following orders."

Orders only mattered when Hanne was the one giving them.

She swept inside the council chamber, and the din of voices stopped.

With a smile that could cut glass, Hanne strode past the secretaries and aides and royal guards, until she stood at one end of the long council table, in the space reserved for the queen.

One by one, she looked down the line of councilors. There were the three who'd attained their positions by rank—the grand general, grand priest, and grand physician—and the three who'd been elected by the guilds. And, lastly, on the far end of the table, were Rupert Flight and Charity Wintersoft.

She'd known they would be a problem, but she hadn't anticipated the trouble starting even before she had a chance to speak. Or that they would do *this*.

Seated at the head of the table, in the space between Rupert and

Charity, were two younger girls, both impeccably dressed—by Caberwilline standards—and sitting with a rigidity that betrayed their discomfort.

Princess Unity and Princess Sanctuary. Rune's sisters.

Their governesses and guards stood at watchful attention along the back wall, jaws clenched with unease.

"Ah." Charity looked up at Hanne. "We were just discussing you, *Your Majesty.*"

Anger seethed within Hanne, and red flared in the corners of her vision. "I see. Gossip." Her tone was ice.

Someone—one of the aides around the room—let out a small snort of laughter.

"Perhaps," Hanne said slowly, "you will be so kind as to tell me why you've begun the council meeting early—without informing me—and why you've brought Princess Sanctuary and Princess Unity here. We're to discuss war and retribution. Let them go back to their studies."

"Oh, but this meeting directly affects the princesses." Charity pushed a dark curl over her ear. "You see, we were just discussing which of the Highcrown princesses will be queen."

7.
NIGHTRENDER

When Nightrender had dressed in the soft white clothes Known had provided, she returned to the infirmary. The maintainer was on the far side of the room, pulling sheets off the bed where Nightrender had slept.

Her head was clearer than it had been in a long time—four hundred years, perhaps. Where the dark voice of Daghath Mal had lurked before, now there was only clean space. The tether between them had been thoroughly snapped.

Because of Rune.

Nightrender closed her eyes and exhaled slowly. She tried not to wonder what he was doing right now, but it was too late; she could too easily imagine rancor bearing down on him, how hard he'd try to fight, how he would inevitably lose.

But Daghath Mal wouldn't let Rune die, that much she believed. If Rune was dead, then the rancor king had nothing to hold over her, no way to control her.

"Your armor?" Known asked.

"In the washroom. Drying. The worst of the damage is nearly healed."

"Good. Do you need more soup?" Known bundled the dirty sheets into a tight ball. "Or more sleep, if you'd like. Choose any other bed. Someone got blood on this one— Oh." Known's gaze drifted beyond her. "You've never had to clean up after yourself before, have you?"

Nightrender followed their look to see water and towels and streaks of blood strewn across the tile. "No."

Known sighed. "I suppose when you've been worshipped as a demigod all your life, there's always someone to perform those mundane tasks for you."

Nightrender had spent her life cleaning different kinds of messes, often with kindlewater and a spark of numinous fire, followed by an inferno of holy purification. "Tell me how long I was unconscious."

"You came through the Soul Gate two days ago." Known placed the bundled sheets on the foot of the bed. "We had to carry you in here."

From the window, Nightrender could just see the Malstop, a crackling wall of white-blue energy. Rarely was she given the opportunity to simply look at it, but it was beautiful in its way. Ancient and powerful.

"When you came through the Soul Gate, you said that the Malstop is under attack." Known kept their voice soft. Gentle. "This attack is worse than the others?"

Nightrender nodded.

The Malstop was always under attack. There were always rancor throwing themselves at the barrier, letting it burn them until they died. Even the very air inside corroded the shield, endlessly peeling away at the inner layers of energy.

"One of the mortal kingdoms has developed a device that contains malice—at least for a short time."

"Ah." Known's shoulders sagged a little. "That machine violates your Winterfast Accords, doesn't it? Will they be punished?"

Nightrender thought of the alliance, the deadly focus both Caberwill and Embria had fixed on their southern neighbor. "Yes," she said at last. "But Ivasland is not alone in breaking the Winterfast Accords. All three kingdoms took part in summoning the rancor king four hundred years ago."

Known nodded faintly. "And you believe there is a connection between the rancor king and this...malice machine?"

"It is surely not a coincidence that this machine came into existence now, when Daghath Mal is at his greatest strength and has gathered an enormous host." Nightrender shook her head. "But how everything relates, I do not know."

The only thing Nightrender was certain of was this: If the Malstop fell, rancor would pour across Salvation unhindered. Darkness would spill like ink across the map, leaving nowhere for humanity. Salvation would fall to the Dark Shard, just as every other continent on this planet had so long ago.

"I must do something," Nightrender murmured.

Rune had told her to find Queen Johanne, but what good would that do? They needed to mount an assault on the Malice, the scale of which had not been seen in thousands of years, yes—but even if Queen Johanne agreed to provide armies, that wouldn't solve the problem of a *rancor king*. Nightrender could only weaken him, not kill him; to kill him was to become him.

It seemed hopeless.

"What is the last thing you remember?" Known asked.

"I told you before: coming through the Soul Gate." But that wasn't all that had happened. "Wait. You put your hands on me. You and Unknown touched my head and my heart and—"

And a new memory had burst into existence. Like the birth of a nearby sun, it had appeared first as a hot white light that speared the midnight sky, blazing brighter and brighter until it washed out other stars, and even all the world around it. This memory was the only thing that Nightrender had been able to see, at least until she'd collapsed against the white flagstone at the maintainers' feet.

"You gave me a memory." Her heart thundered in her chest. "Different from how Daghath Mal gave them to me." Those had been ruddy and imperfect, while this was blindingly pristine.

"We unlocked it," Known said. "Daghath Mal could only share memories of your memories—copies. This memory was always within you, but hidden. Not even the mortals' cut would have touched it."

Nightrender swallowed hard. "Tell me how you did this." Her voice rose as the implications of their mind manipulation became clear. "No one should have access to my memories, not without dark magic. Perhaps you intend to force some sort of connection to me, whisper into my mind as he—"

"Stop." Strength poured through Known's voice. They seemed more solid suddenly, less ghostlike; their eyes, too, shone a brighter blue. Power crackled off them in sharp spears, bright and hot and pure.

With a faint gasp, Nightrender stepped backward until her wings brushed the nightstand behind her. "Tell me what you are." Her whisper was hoarse.

"You know what I am." Known stepped toward her, reaching out a luminous hand. "Medella."

Nightrender stared at the maintainer. Her heart became thunder in her ears. Her breath turned shallow. Her eyes watered from the brilliant form before her. "Numen."

Known did not move.

"But you left this plane thousands of years ago. All of you."

"Not all." Known lowered their hand. The light around them dimmed.

"But you did." Nightrender's hands curled into fists. "You left me."

They *had* left. This was some kind of test, a trick. Known and Unknown could not be Numina.

Because if they were, then Nightrender had been abandoned not only by the Numina who left for the Bright Land ages ago, but by these two—here—who had simply never told her what they were.

She was their weapon. Nothing more.

Nightrender turned away from Known. Her eyes were heavy and her face felt hot, but she wouldn't show the way this hurt. Not to Known. Not to anyone.

After thousands of years—after her memory had been hacked open and bled dry—Nightrender couldn't actually recall what Numina looked like. Or sounded like. Even some of their names had vanished from her mind.

"Once—" Her voice was rough. She cleared her throat. "Once, I believed some Numina might have remained on the laic plane. But I gave up that hope. If you're truly Numen, tell me why you would stay behind." Nightrender clenched her jaw. "Tell me why you would remain when you could have returned to the Bright Land with the others. It would have been better there."

"It would have," Known agreed. "But as the aperture was closing, we were chosen to remain here, to maintain the Malstop—and keep watch over you."

Nightrender straightened her spine. Keep *watch*? She had been built, a soul spun with their own hands, given knowledge and strength and an *overwhelming* sense of duty. And still they had not trusted her.

"No one could have predicted how long we would be here," Known went on. "I had hoped the gateway would be closed for only a short time, that everyone would return and we could put an end to this eternal war between the light and dark. Instead, we've been trapped here, the same as you."

"No." Nightrender turned, her wings lifting, her fists clenching. "You had this place. Your towers. Your duties. You even had *me*. My Dawnbreakers. But mostly, you had each other—someone who understood you on a fundamental level. Numen to Numen. Meanwhile, I was the one fighting this endless war. I was the one *created* to fight it so you could leave and forget about this place." Nightrender swallowed a knot of anger. "I was *alone*."

Known only stood there, their light faint and flickering.

"Say something!" A headache formed between Nightrender's eyes as she blinked and blinked again.

"What would you have had us do?" Known asked.

"You could have *helped* me." Nightrender's voice broke. "Tell me— Tell me where you were four hundred years ago, when Daghath Mal's rage took me over and I slaughtered every member of every royal family in every kingdom. Tell me why—just days ago—you didn't do anything when I came to your gates without an army. Tell me why you allowed me into the Malice on my own, to be shredded and brought before a rancor *king*."

Rune had been right. Numina didn't care. They'd abandoned this world. Even those who'd stayed weren't *really* here.

"Twice I have faced the rancor king. Twice I have failed." Nightrender turned her gaze outside—toward the Malstop. Her voice fell, soft and contemplative. "Some mortals believe that they are always dying, that from the moment they're born, their bodies are in a constant state of decay, hurtling toward death. I never understood this. I could hear the life in them, smell the smallest pieces of them multiplying—*living*."

"But now?" Known asked.

"Now I understand the way they must feel—shedding old skin and hair, eyesight weakening, endurance flagging. Minds fading." Nightrender lowered her gaze. "I grow more diminished every moment."

"Can you *grow* diminished?" Known's tone was thoughtful. "Can you grow *more* diminished?"

Anger tightened its grip around Nightrender's heart. "I am losing my entire past! I cannot defeat the rancor king. And you have been hiding your true nature from me all these ages. Do not distract me with—with linguistic contradictions."

"I am sorry."

Nightrender's jaw tightened.

"Perhaps we should have revealed ourselves to you. But I am not certain what difference it would have made. We, too, are cut off from the Bright Land, our own abilities reduced. And we have given *everything* to the Malstop, to maintain it, to strengthen it. We have given everything to you and your Dawnbreakers." Light shifted—Known drifting toward her. "We didn't expect to be here for so long. And we had hoped—like you hoped—that perhaps we weren't the only ones. But if there are others, they have yet to present themselves. And so our power continues to wane. One day, it will be gone."

And what would happen to the Malstop then? Nightrender shivered. "Tell me you have a plan to stop Daghath Mal."

"You are the plan." Known gazed steadily at Nightrender. "And we are your allies. There's a reason we unlocked the memory. You wanted another option, and you'll find it. If you *look*."

"Oh." Nightrender pulled back, searching the stars across her mind.

And there it was.

For a moment, it was too hard to look at, too bright and shining. But when she could see clearly, the memory—the knowledge, really—washed through her, and she finally understood why Known kept asking what she remembered.

"Tell me why I didn't know about this before," she whispered.

"It had to be hidden, saved for the most dire of circumstances," Known said. "You will be able to use it only once."

Nightrender's jaw flexed. She had fallen so far. But she could still make this right. "Tell me where it is."

"I do not know," Known said. "It's in three pieces. That is all I can say."

Three pieces... three kingdoms. Nightrender would start with Queen Johanne, as Rune had asked.

Hope stirred in her chest. There was a chance. Narrow, but possible.

"Be careful. Daghath Mal doesn't know about it, but rancor will be drawn to the pieces once they're exposed. You won't be able to hide this for long."

Nightrender gathered her sword and baldric and slung them over her white clothes. Then she started for the washroom to retrieve her armor.

Somewhere in the world, a weapon existed—a weapon so powerful that it did more than simply kill: it destroyed the very essence of its victim, shattering every individual part so that nothing remained.

This weapon was humanity's hope.

She could simply end the rancor king. Forever.

8.

HANNE

"A new queen." Hanne arched an eyebrow. "Why, Duchess Wintersoft, are you planning to have me killed?"

The council chamber went completely quiet. On the far side of the room, the princesses shot each other uneasy looks.

"Careful," Charity purred. "With talk like that, some people might begin to think you're paranoid. It wouldn't be the first time a Fortuin went mad under the weight of the crown."

Hanne kept her voice low and even, a warning. "You're the one insisting I'm not queen. There are only so many ways to end my reign. Are you a murderer, Charity?"

Perhaps it *was* unwise to bring up assassinations right away—no need to give anyone ideas—but Hanne could defend herself. Sabine and Oliver would throw themselves in front of a sword to protect Hanne. Maris had been tasting Hanne's food since they were young. Cecelia checked all of Hanne's clothes and bedcovers for powders or any other potential hazards. So if they were going to come for her, they would have to be craftier than all of Hanne's ladies and guards.

"There are other ways to be rid of an unwanted queen," Charity said smoothly. "No murder necessary."

"The council has the power to deem a ruler unfit." Rupert Flight shot Hanne a pointed smile. "Provided there's another heir to take the throne, we can remove an illegitimate monarch."

So they intended to rip the throne out from under her. Usurp her.

They could *try.*

"Illegitimate," Hanne breathed. *"Illegitimate."* She leveled her glare on Earl Flight. "I am Rune Highcrown's wife. I am one half of the living alliance between our kingdoms. I *am* the queen of Caberwill."

"Only so long as you are married to the king of Caberwill," Rupert said. "His Majesty *is* missing, and the kingdom cannot go without a ruler—a ruler born into the Highcrown line."

Hanne kept her voice cool, dispassionate. "This council has a history of hasty decisions. Now you are telling me that you have no desire to hold the kingdom for Rune's return. Instead, you will become regent to a princess who has not yet reached her majority. But what, I wonder, do you plan to do with King Rune when he returns to find you warming his throne?"

Everyone looked uncomfortable. Princess Sanctuary let out a sudden, gulping sob. One of the governesses touched her shoulder.

"We all know that Rune disappeared into a malice portal during Ivasland's attack on our army. Of course, we worry for those who were taken from us." Hanne's eyes cut to the grand general, who sat stoically in his seat. "However, two-thirds of those who went through such portals have already been safely recovered—or are on their way home now. We are sure to be reunited with more of the missing."

The grand general nodded. "That is our hope."

"Including our king," Hanne said softly. "Unless—in spite of the incredible odds of his survival—you believe he is dead."

On the other end of the table, tears shimmered in the eyes of both princesses. They blinked and blinked, refusing to cry in front of the Crown Council.

An uncomfortable quiet settled on the chamber as people shifted their weight or glanced at the floor. A few looked guiltily at Sanctuary and Unity.

"Oh, Charity." Hanne turned back to the duchess. "Did you fail to explain to the princesses that our dear king is most likely *alive*? Or is the regency that precious to you?"

Guilt needled between Hanne's ribs as the girls' faces paled, realizing they had been lied to. Why should she feel guilty, though? She had never been coddled. She was doing these girls a favor by opening their eyes to the simplest truth of all: No one could be trusted.

Hanne pushed away the uncomfortable feeling of moral deficiency and rallied her far more comfortable feeling of moral superiority. "How can you claim to care for them when you use them in this way?"

"Their Highnesses understand their duties as Highcrowns," Charity countered. "They have always known one of them might rule someday, however painful the implications."

"How dare you do this to them," Hanne said quietly. "Haven't they suffered enough? Yet instead of offering hope for Rune's safe return, you tell them they've lost him, too."

Hanne shook her head, as though thoroughly disgusted. And she was.

She hadn't realized it until this moment, but Charity Wintersoft dragging these girls here was abhorrent to her. The princesses had already been through so much, and here were these councilors, trying to put one of them on the throne—trying to rule a kingdom through a child.

It *was* disgusting. Besides, this was *Hanne's* kingdom now.

Charity drew herself up tall. "Regardless, a Highcrown must rule Caberwill."

"And so one shall." Hanne put on her most beautiful smile. "We have so many serious matters to discuss today—wars, earthquakes, rumors, foreign aid, and, apparently, the duchess's rather transparent ambitions to make herself regent—but I suppose now is as good a time as any to deliver the happy news."

"What happy news?" asked Professor Lelia, education chancellor.

Hanne pressed her palms against her abdomen. She hadn't wanted to play this particular card so soon, but the council was moving to remove her from power more quickly than she'd anticipated. "I hadn't thought to announce this to you just yet, but I am pleased to inform you that I am pregnant with King Rune's child—the heir to Caberwill."

Quiet gasps filled the council chamber. A few members sat up straighter, as though to get a better look at her—hoping, it seemed, to see into her and judge for themselves whether she was pregnant.

Swan Brightvale spoke up first. "You couldn't possibly know yet."

"Of course I know. The king and I share a special bond."

Noir Shadowsong leaned forward on her elbows. "Your Majesty, many young ladies believe such things, but—"

"*Furthermore*"—Hanne bit back a satisfied smile—"do recall that Rune was in Embria for weeks before we came to Brink to be married in your temple. We spent hours together every day as the marriage terms were decided. We have always had an exceptionally passionate relationship...on and off the negotiating table."

Noir lifted her elbows from the council table. "This is quite...scandalizing, Your Majesty."

"But not unprecedented," Hanne said as sweetly as she could manage.

"And with that in mind, is it any wonder that my husband went to such lengths to free me from the malsite, going so far as to summon the Nightrender? We are, after all, ardently and energetically in love."

Several of the councilors cringed.

"I know my husband lives. And I know this child will be strong and clever, the best of both our lines. Should you attempt to remove me from the throne, you put your own legitimacy as a governing body at risk."

"I've heard enough." Dayle Larksong pressed both wrinkled hands to the table and pushed himself up. "The laws of succession are clear. If Her Majesty is indeed carrying a child, we the Crown Council must hold the throne for that child—whether or not King Rune lives. And I believe he does. I will vote to hold the throne for our rightful king."

That was good. Definitely in Hanne's favor. But Dayle was the easiest of the councilors to persuade—he truly admired and believed in Rune. He was the *only* one.

The room was quiet for a moment. Then Stella Asheater, the grand physician, lifted her eyes and said, "I second the grand priest. I have my reservations, but things will become clear soon enough, and we must move on to the business of running the kingdom. As Her Majesty said, there was an earthquake not one hour ago."

Hanne bit back a smile.

Swan nodded. "I agree. It's time to move on."

"You would," Noir muttered. "Everyone you represent has gotten wealthier since the treaty with Embria."

"There are plenty of agreements in place that benefit the industrial quarter, too," Swan sniffed. "We all know iron is in higher demand. Not to mention fine wools."

"What is your vote, Noir?" Dayle asked.

Noir glanced at Charity, her eyes narrowing. "I vote to hold the throne for the king. He has surprised us before."

One of the secretaries snorted. Someone else shushed him.

"Lelia?" Dayle looked at the education chancellor, then the grand general. "Tide? Surely you two have opinions."

Professor Lelia sighed. "The kingdom needs stability. For that, King

Rune's return would be the best. Monarchies in transition are weak, as history shows us. Regardless, it seems an heir is on the way. So I will not support elevating one of the princesses just yet, although"—Lelia glanced at them—"I do believe you are both quite qualified for the position."

Sanctuary and Unity both lowered their faces demurely.

Everyone looked at Tide Emberwish, the grand general. They all respected him. (Embria had long been on the receiving end of Tide's campaigns, so Hanne's respect for him was the kind of respect one has for an adversary: grudging, patiently waiting for a mistake.)

Tide took a deep breath. "The protection of the realm must take precedence in these times of"—he nodded toward Lelia—"instability. I would not risk our alliance with Embria. Queen Johanne must remain so, for the time being."

Charity gave a small grunt of frustration.

Hanne simply nodded. Inwardly, however, she was glowing at this victory, and she knew Tuluna was satisfied as well. The council—the majority, anyway—was with her, however reluctantly. She would hold the throne another day.

"Very well." Rupert's tone was conciliatory, but his expression suggested that this fight was far from over. "If the council accepts Queen Johanne as the rightful ruler of Caberwill, I will not stand in the way."

Charity's eyes narrowed, but after a moment, she gave a prim nod. "I, too, accede to the majority's will." She turned to the princesses. "My apologies for taking up your time, Your Highnesses."

Sanctuary stood first, then Unity. "Numinous blessings on all of you," said the former. "We are happy to serve the kingdom and council in whatever way thought best."

They were good, Hanne thought. Perhaps they could be useful.

"If I may." Hanne addressed the young princesses. "I'd like for both of your ladyships to stay. It is my hope that neither of you need take up the burden of the throne, but should the worst befall us, you must be trained for it. Are you amenable to that?"

Hanne *had* intended to kill them. In the future. But with the king and queen dead so quickly after her arrival, she needed to bide her time. Not to mention she disliked the idea of murdering children.

Although they would not always be children.

The girls looked at each other, their heads tilted in unspoken communication. Then Sanctuary said, "Yes," and they both sat down once again.

That was wise, Tuluna murmured. **Lead them to your side. Appear to care for their well-being. They will not usurp you if they love you.**

"Very good. Now we can get to the point of this meeting: the kingdom." Hanne took her seat—the queen's seat—and addressed the full council. "Our first priority must continue to be King Rune. I know the malice portals are constantly monitored for signs of him, but we may need volunteers to go through some." Hanne looked at Tide. "Is that something you wish to handle, Grand General?"

He nodded. "I am doing everything in my power to find His Majesty."

"Good." Hanne turned to Noir. "As for any damages caused by the earthquake...?"

"It's being taken care of, Your Majesty." Noir consulted her notes. "I've deployed surveyors throughout Caberwill to get a more complete picture of the damage. Strange, though. There were no signs of this earthquake coming. No shocks or rockfalls..."

It was astonishing how close people could get to the truth of the Incursion before pretending, once again, that it wasn't happening.

"I knew you would have it under control." Hanne laid her bandaged hands atop the table. "Now, Ivasland. We cannot ignore their continued aggressions. They have struck industry and agriculture, and now the Caberwilline army—all using malice. Their flagrant disregard for the Winterfast Accords simply cannot be tolerated. And the ease with which they murder—or attempt to murder—Highcrowns must be punished in the most serious way."

Everyone nodded, and across the table, Unity took Sanctuary's hand.

"I want the princesses' guards doubled. Your best men, Grand General. And continue their combat training. They must be able to defend themselves." That was one thing about Caberwill that Hanne admired: there was no need to hide this sort of training from the public, and no shame in a woman carrying a sword.

"Certainly." Tide looked at the princesses, that guilt back in his eyes.

"As for our efforts against Ivasland, we must strike them, and strike quickly.

They cannot be allowed to continue activating their terrible machines." She would never forget the unapologetic way Queen Abagail had talked about the device, as though she couldn't *wait* to use it against her enemies to the north. And she hadn't. The moment the machine was ready, Small Mountain had been decimated, followed immediately by Silver Sun.

Rupert Flight looked straight at Hanne, a wicked gleam in his eyes. "Yes, *Your Majesty*. Tell us about the terrible machines."

Hanne's skin prickled. *He knows what I did in Ivasland.*

A sick feeling turned over in her stomach as she recalled a visitor coming to Rune's quarters late one night—a visitor she now understood had been Rupert Flight. Rune had been upset when he'd returned from the hall, his beautiful brown eyes dark with anger and confusion, so she'd admitted the truth—how the rancor had threatened her, tortured her, controlled her. Rune had been so very understanding. He'd *wanted* to understand.

But no one on this council would care what an impossible position she had been in. They would only see their enemy once more. All her work would be undone.

"Ah, Earl Flight." Hanne smiled again, keeping her voice level even as her mind whirred. "You must be referring to the absurd rumors against me—the ones planted by Ivaslander operatives. Say what you will about Abagail and Baldric, but their ability to deliver false information and have it be believed—no matter how ludicrous—is exceptional. Unfortunately, this fairy tale seems to be causing some trouble for my parents just now."

"Yes," said Tide, "I've heard that the situation in Solcast is deteriorating quickly."

Hanne nodded solemnly. "You are correct. The common people simply do not understand the intricacies of politics—and they are so easily swayed by foreign disinformation campaigns." She shot a glance at Rupert, letting everyone know that *he* was also deceived.

The grand physician leaned forward. "Please explain this disinformation. What is it?"

Hanne nodded accommodatingly, then spoke plainly: "I stand accused of building the mal-devices that detonated in Caberwill and Embria. *Me*. As though I could have."

"Indeed?" The grand physician tilted her head, then glanced at Rupert. "Is this Ivaslander propaganda?"

"My sources were clear," Rupert said coldly. "The Ivaslander who planted the device at Silver Sun was heard by my agents to identify Queen Johanne as a key member of the development team. We could call it nonsense...but I am told the Nightrender confirmed her involvement."

Hanne sighed with just the right blend of annoyance and patience. "Chancellor, I understand that your sources are sacrosanct to you, and I'm sure you believe them, but when could I have performed this task? While I was waiting for the marriage treaty to be finalized, constantly under the eyes of everyone in Solspire? Or perhaps while I was trapped in the malsite, terrified and starving? Or perhaps while I've been here, guarded every moment of the day?" She shook her head with an exhausted laugh. "I don't even have the type of knowledge such a task would require. But of course that doesn't matter when it comes to conspiracies. Facts are no fun."

"Did the Nightrender truly give a confirmation, Rupert?" Lelia asked. "Why?"

Down the table, Charity nodded in agreement. "Yes, what of the Nightrender?"

The Nightrender could die in the dark for all Hanne cared.

"I cannot speak for her," Hanne cut in. "What I can assess is this: my own people are angry that I've allied with Caberwill, so they are willing to believe that I have also allied with Ivasland. They are convinced that I support everyone *except* Embria." Hanne let herself sound exasperated. "That is the genius of these attacks, isn't it? They play into people's fears, their emotions. One cannot fight mass hysteria with logic."

"It does sound rather far-fetched," Stella murmured.

"Perhaps Rupert's spy misunderstood," Noir said. "Or misrepresented what was *actually* said."

"It's difficult to say," Swan agreed. "Unfortunately, the Nightrender isn't here and we cannot ask her for more information. However, given the timeline, this all seems unlikely—to say the least."

"Additionally," Lelia said, "*why* would Her Majesty help to build something that would immediately be used against her? It doesn't make sense."

The councilors continued on like that, dismantling every argument for themselves. Two, however, did not join in. Rupert and Charity.

Hanne cleared her throat, and the discussion faded. "The more immediate issue is this: a faction of rebels has my parents under siege in Solspire. While restoring order in Solcast isn't strictly part of the terms of the alliance, it would send a strong message of unity—to both of our kingdoms and to Ivasland. Let them see us work together."

"You want the Caberwilline army to march on Solcast and put down the rebellion?" Swan raised an eyebrow. "Do you understand the expense?"

Tide frowned deeply. "And what of the Embrian army?"

So this particular news had *not* reached Caberwill. "Livestock."

A beat of confusion passed through the room. Then Lelia said, "Your Majesty, I believe the phrase is *cowed*."

"The Embrian army I fought would never be cowed by commoners," Tide muttered.

"No," Hanne said quickly. "The Embrian army is—was—incredibly brave. But they were ambushed with a mal-device in the same way the Caberwilline army was. Instead of malice portals, however, they were—"

"Cowed." Tide was suddenly very pale. Everyone, in fact, looked rather ill. "Ivasland must pay."

Hanne agreed. Ivasland was costing Hanne entire armies now, and she needed warriors more than ever. If there weren't enough people to battle the rancor, humanity would be lost.

"More men will need to be trained," Hanne said. "In Embria, yes, but here as well. Both armies must grow if we are to have any hope of defeating Ivasland."

And the rancor king.

She almost said it out loud—named their true enemy—but when she glanced at Nadine, her cousin shook her head. Very well. Hanne would not press the council about the Malice. Not today. Especially when they had nearly deposed her only half an hour ago.

She let her gaze travel across the table to Rupert and Charity.

She'd bought herself some time, but they would certainly attack again. Hanne had to be ready.

If only Rune would turn up. Where was he?

9.

RUNE

The Malice was endless.

His hunger. His exhaustion. His desperate thirst.

Also endless.

Rune kept running, fighting to ignore the stitch growing in his side, the burn in his lungs, every piece of his body that begged him to stop.

His determination was endless, too. He *would* get a message to the Nightrender. Somehow.

The castle was a dark and angry blot behind him, black against the crimson sky. He put as much distance between himself and Daghath Mal as he could. He wished he had wings. He wished he could fly.

But the longer he ran, the more exhausted he became, until he tripped and fell, his head spinning. Dirt and dead grass plumed into his face, making him cough and spit against the bitter taste.

For a while, he didn't move. He just lay there in the dust, listening to the receding thunder of his heartbeat, the hiss of his lungs finally pulling in enough air. His burning muscles shuddered.

Rune cursed his overtaxed body. As his eyes began to clear, he pushed himself up and twisted to see what had tripped him.

It was a bone, its ends still buried, the central length of it visible where wind had blown away the dirt. His toe had gotten caught beneath it. Dazed, hardly in control of himself, he wrapped his hands around the exposed part and pulled. Dry earth grumbled and gave way, and then—he was holding on to something that had never belonged to a human.

It was as long as his whole arm, and just as wide. The bone was curved slightly, though not because it was broken. Whatever it had belonged to had been huge.

A rancor? For its size, the bone was not heavy, but it was strong. Could it fly, perhaps?

He used the bone as a crutch to push himself to his feet again and, relatively clear-eyed after his unintended rest, he looked around.

The castle behind him. The immense red sky above. The hills and valleys around him. The dark mountains in the distance, strangely reminiscent of Caberwill's proud range.

Closer in, there were scraggly, shadowed trees—not of any species he knew. These grew spikes rather than leaves, and their trunks were split in two, like legs. When he blinked, they seemed closer than before.

His heart kicked. He squinted, needing to be sure. The movement could have been his imagination. It probably was.

Then, directly in front of him: footprints. He hadn't noticed them before, too focused on moving, but now he couldn't miss the line of impressions in the dirt. Boots. Human? Or human shaped?

They led in a twisting path away from the castle.

Slowly, his whole body protesting, Rune reached into his boot and withdrew the Nightrender's feather for the first time since she had given it to him.

The feather was long and straight, with a narrow outer vane and rigid barbs on the inside. A primary, perhaps, or a secondary, although he was no expert in wing anatomy. Either way, it seemed perfect for flight. The shaft was stiff and hollow—and sharp on the broken end—and the edges of the barbs were like razors. He'd seen her kill rancor after rancor, not just with her sword, but with her wings as well.

And though the color of her wings had always appeared midnight black, the feather glimmered faintly in the ruddy light, nearly iridescent. It was striking. Deadly.

"Beautiful," he whispered.

As he held it to his chest, warmth rushed into him. The fog burned out of his thoughts and he imagined he felt . . . something. Heat. Clarity.

Somewhat restored, he tucked the feather back into his boot and fixed his grip on the long bone. It would serve as a walking stick. Or, if necessary, a weapon.

The spiky trees were closer now, their shadows taller than they should have been. And wider. And toothier.

A full-body shudder ran through Rune. He stared at them a moment longer, but they refused to move while he was watching.

When he started walking again, he kept his pace slow. Deliberate. And he made sure that he could always see the trees from the corner of his eye, even as he followed the boot prints.

Perhaps these were *her* prints. Perhaps they would lead to the Soul Gate—the way out—assuming she had already escaped this place.

And if she hadn't... perhaps they would lead him straight to her.

Time did what it wanted in the Malice, jumping and skittering, sometimes running backward. The sun was never in the right place, and not once did the stars make an appearance. With no sense of direction, Rune followed the tracks all the way until they stopped.

She wasn't here.

Instead, a single pair of eyes glared out from the shadows beneath a small ridge, glowing faintly scarlet. They were low to the ground; the creature was crouching.

The tracks Rune had been following led directly to this red-eyed thing. Disappointment burned, but he should have known better than to hope.

Gradually, the shadowed creature began to unfold itself, and Rune's mind spun toward the possibility that he'd stumbled into a rancor. He brandished the bone as the creature stepped into the angry sunlight, revealing itself.

It was human.

Mostly.

Sagging gray skin. Patchy, matted hair. Fingernails that curled into filthy claws. A man, caked with dirt and blood, his eyes red and reflective, his dark veins crawling over his skin, twisting and writhing even as Rune watched.

He was corrupted. He hadn't been fully human in a long time.

"Stay back." Rune's voice was rough with warning. "I don't want to hurt you."

The man squinted at him, taking in the bone, Rune's threatening manner. A word ground out of him, almost impossible to understand, as though his mouth was full of rocks.

"Caberwill!" The man sprang toward him.

Rune was almost too slow to respond. Almost.

He slammed the bone into the man's stomach, and then—as the man staggered backward—Rune kicked him the rest of the way to the ground. Unfazed, the man wrapped those clawed hands around his ankle and pulled.

Rune landed flat on the ground, the bone rolling out of his hand just as teeth sank into his leg.

With a wordless shout, Rune jerked his captured limb and kicked the man's face. Bone crunched under his heel, and blood spouted from the man's nose.

Rune scrambled away, hefting the rancor bone once more. "I said I don't want to hurt you!" A faint flutter of unease passed through the back of Rune's mind. What if the man was rabid? What if the bite became infected?

The man growled and scrambled to his feet. Blood dripped from one of his fingertips, where a nail had ripped off, but he didn't seem to notice. "Caberwill!" The word was even more unintelligible now, with his broken nose. He ran straight for Rune.

Rune had no time to think, no time to argue. He drew back the rancor bone and struck the man square between the eyes.

There was a loud crack as bone met skull. The man stopped and staggered backward, and before he could attack again, Rune swung the bone once more and struck him on the back of the head.

The red, unfocused eyes dimmed as the man fell into a heap on the ground. When he didn't move for a moment, Rune glanced around the area; the fight had been brief, but noisy.

The spiky trees were closer, their branches now stretched toward him. A shallow riverbed filled with black sludge ran between Rune and those trees, but whether that would hinder their advance, he didn't know. Perhaps the trees *liked* sludge.

A deep, gravelly groan drew Rune's attention back to the stranger. He wasn't dead. But he wasn't moving.

Cautiously, quietly, Rune raised the rancor bone and stared down at the ex-man. He should do it quickly, mercifully. He should bring the bone down on the man's head so hard that his breath stopped. Because eventually, Rune would have to rest. Eventually, Rune would have to sleep.

Rune glanced at the trees. They were closer.

Sleep was a fantasy.

His muscles trembled with strain. He told himself to do it, to remove the threat, but his arms wouldn't cooperate.

He couldn't.

Not with the bone.

Slowly, without taking his eyes off the man, Rune crouched and lowered the bone to the ground. Then he pulled the feather from inside his boot. It was sharp enough to do the job quickly. Quietly.

This close, Rune could see that the man wasn't much older than he was. A year or two, perhaps. Bubbles of blood popped with each breath. His heart was slowing. It wouldn't take much to finish him. Just a flick of the feather across his carotid artery.

"What happened to you?" Rune whispered.

Well, obviously he'd been here too long. He'd been twisted by the Malice, the same fate Rune would suffer if he stayed here.

This was Rune's future, red eyeshine and all.

Some battles are fought solely for the sake of resisting.

Rune glanced over the man's body again. He wore a ragged uniform, Rune realized, one of Ivaslander origin, but its style was old. Very, very old. "How long have you been here? How did you *get* here?"

As far as he knew, the last person to pass through the Soul Gate was the Nightrender. And before that—the Nightrender again. Four hundred years ago. With an army.

Which meant this man was a Dawnbreaker.

A *real* Dawnbreaker.

Rune tightened his grip around the feather, and a moment of clarity rushed him. He realized, all at once, what he'd been about to do: bash a man's head in, or slit his throat.

But this man was *ill*, not evil. Corrupted by malice—trapped in *the* Malice for four centuries. Perhaps Rune's own darkness wasn't as far off as he had thought. Perhaps this was how it began.

"*You must fight it,*" the Nightrender had said. "*You must be strong.*"

Rune's shoulders dropped a little. If every moment was a battle he must win, he was already losing.

"I'm sorry," he whispered.

A hand shot up and wrapped tightly around Rune's wrist. The Ivaslander's eyes flew open and he screamed, low and inhuman.

Rune tried to yank his arm away, but the man was strong, his grip unwavering as he pulled Rune's hand closer to his mouth.

"No," Rune gasped. "No—!"

Then he did the only thing he could: he drove the razor-sharp tip of the feather into flesh, just above the man's collarbone.

Lightning snapped between them, and a cold sliver of ice slid through Rune's heart. *Magic.* Rune yanked the feather back and scrambled away as fast as he could.

The Ivaslander was still screaming—shrieking now, really—his words completely unintelligible but his agony undeniable. Sympathy pained Rune, in spite of himself.

But as he looked closer, the dark veins receded from the man's face. His skin warmed to a living color. His red eyeshine faded. Whatever had happened to him . . . it was reversing itself.

Suddenly, the sunlight shifted. Deep shadows stretched long over the ground, reaching for him.

Burn it. The trees.

They'd crossed the sludge, and now they were almost upon him.

Then a shadow surged across the ruddy ground, all the way to Rune's boot. It thumped, a physical contact that should have been impossible.

Rune jerked away. "Stop shouting," he told the Ivaslander, making his voice low and strong. "Stop shouting. Right now."

His pulse ached against his throat; his head throbbed in time with his heartbeat. Prey knew when predators were about.

Rune thrust the feather at the Ivaslander's throat. "Shut up right now or I'll kill you." He didn't mean it—or perhaps he did, it was impossible to tell anymore—but it worked. The man went silent, and Rune withdrew the feather.

"Who are you?" the young man rasped, exhausted.

Rune glanced toward the trees, the hairs on the back of his neck prickling with alarm. "I'm a Dawnbreaker." Even though it didn't feel true. "I can help you." He lifted the feather, letting sunlight play off the barbs.

Hope lit in the man's eyes. "Is she here?"

Rune kept his expression neutral. He wanted the man to cooperate, but it would be cruel for him believe the Nightrender was here. Most likely, he thought she was near—and that Rune was four hundred years old as well. "We have to go. Can you get up?"

The Ivaslander touched his nose, then the stab wound under his collar. His hand came away with blood, although not as much as there should have been. With a short nod, he sat up.

Rune grabbed the rancor bone, sheathed the Nightrender's feather, and helped the man to his feet.

The man, clear-eyed for the first time, looked beyond Rune, at the trees and their shadows. "Thorns. They're after you."

They were closer than before. *Much* closer.

Soon, Rune and the Ivaslander would be surrounded.

"Run."

10.

NIGHTRENDER

Beautiful.

Nightrender was flying when the word rang through her. A tone. A bell. A familiar voice.

"Rune."

She halted and slowly turned in a circle, scanning the golden afternoon sky—even though there was no way that Rune could be up here. For one thing, he couldn't fly.

Nothing happened again for several more minutes. She started for Brink again. Then it hit.

Sharp pain made her gasp. It started small, like a needle prick, but just as she decided she could ignore it, the pain blossomed and *something* siphoned out of her. Something bright and numinous, integral to her very being.

"Wait!" Nightrender grabbed at the air, trying vainly to put the trickle of bright light back inside of her, but it was insubstantial; her fingers passed right through it. Agony exploded inside her, graying her vision, making her wings give out.

A heartbeat later, she was falling, wind rushing past her ears.

Bursts of color reeled around her, blurs of green and brown and bright pale blue. She was spinning, tumbling end over end, and the needle in her soul drilled deeper.

Nightrender shouted and clawed at the air, but she could hardly tell up from down. There was only this terrible feeling of plummeting—

Abruptly, the pain vanished. Her vision cleared and her sense of direction returned just in time for her to register the upper boughs of a tree right beneath her.

She flared her wings, catching air. She forced herself higher, until blue sky surrounded her again.

Oriented, more or less, and her wits gathered, she flew to the ground and landed properly, in a small clearing just south of Brink. From here, she could see the mountain that cupped the city in its palm, although the capital and Honor's Keep were on the opposite face—not visible from here.

Nightrender tucked in her wings and knelt in the grass. She felt as though something physical had been removed from her.

Perhaps she should go back to the Soul Gate. Perhaps the maintainers could look at her. Fix her. It seemed possible this was somehow connected to whatever they'd done to her memory. Or, perhaps, it was the price of snapping her connection with Daghath Mal.

No. She wouldn't go to them for help.

They'd hurt her by keeping her ignorant of their true natures. And perhaps she wasn't meant to possess the ability to feel that way, but she felt it, nonetheless. It ached, that sense of betrayal. To go to them, she would have to have no other option.

Hopefully, it wouldn't happen again.

Except—there'd been the voice. Rune's voice.

"Rune." Nightrender stood and glanced around the clearing, but there were only trees and birds, bugs crawling through the grass, and shadows deepening as the sun lowered itself in the sky. "Rune," she said again. If she could hear him, surely he could hear her.

But there was no reply.

Her heart sank as she turned herself north, toward Brink, and began walking; she needed to make sure she wasn't going to drop out of the sky again before she risked flying.

"It seems possible," she said to Rune, even though he clearly couldn't hear her, "that this problem is connected to my others. It could be the cut to my memory has spread to my soul. Perhaps my soul is . . . leaking."

That was a disturbing thought.

"If this is, somehow, my soul bleeding away, then perhaps I will die. Perhaps it won't matter that I'm losing my memories, because I won't be here to miss them."

Sorrow squeezed her heart.

But she'd heard Rune's voice. How?

At least she could be certain he was alive. And he had her feather. It was the best she'd been able to offer in the moment. Now she could do more.

She would find an ally, one in a position to help her discover the weapon's location. Quickly.

Which meant, unfortunately, Queen Johanne.

11.

HANNE

It was nearly midnight before Hanne had time to think about the Crown Council again. The day had been exhausting, filled with meetings and dinners, but at last she sat in her dressing room once more, all her ladies fluttering around her.

"If we were in Embria, I'd have my enemies removed the old-fashioned way. Suddenly and permanently. They could be here one day and gone the next, not a trace to be found." Hanne gazed into the mirror while Lea brushed her hair, letting the golden waves fall free over her shoulders. "Their whereabouts could be a mystery until some beautiful day, long after I have brought peace to all three kingdoms, a maid decides to do a deep clean of the dungeons. And oh, what's that? The rotted corpse of a horrible man no one can identify? Must be Rupert Flight."

All the ladies giggled.

"Sadly, such disappearances are frowned upon in Caberwill." Nadine shuffled through her notes from the various meetings they'd attended. "And investigated, which is a more important consideration."

"Would anyone know if Earl Flight disappeared?" Cecelia poured rosewater onto a white cloth, then dabbed Hanne's forehead. "Or would they assume he lost his pin? It's the oddest thing, but his face is so boring, I don't actually know what he looks like."

"It's his gift," Maris said. "He goes unnoticed. I heard that people used to walk right into him before, simply because they didn't notice him. They say at night he becomes completely invisible. It's why he has to wear the pin."

"So we take the pin," Lea suggested. "Then we have only Charity to deal with."

"She is the opposite of invisible," Maris muttered.

"Our first step is to remove them from the Crown Council," Hanne said, restoring order to her ladies. "Their attempts to undermine me make ruling more difficult. I already have enough to do without fighting them every step of the way."

"We'd need to replace them." Nadine lowered her notes. "I have two candidates in mind. You already know them: Prudence Shadowhand and Victoria Stareyes."

Slowly, Hanne nodded. Both women had been on Lord Bearhaste's list of potential supporters within Caberwill. Lord Bearhaste was dead, of course, slaughtered by a rancor in the Deepway Woods. But Nadine had recovered his notes and begun the work of meeting with everyone he'd named, even though Hanne was believed to be dead.

Truly, Nadine had supported Hanne under the worst possible conditions. Which was what made her reservations now so hard to bear.

"I like Prudence for information chancellor," Nadine said. "She doesn't have the network Rupert has, but we can supplement with Lady Sabine's."

"I remember her," Sabine said. "She has the right instincts for a spy mistress. She's always watching."

"I agree. And Prudence's network will grow, given time," Hanne said. "Everyone must start somewhere. As long as she's with us."

"She will be," Nadine said. "I've been sending business to her family's logging operation since our first meeting. And once the revolts in Embria are ended and the fires put out, people will need considerable timber with which to rebuild their homes and stores.

"As to my selection for treasury chancellor, the Stareyes family and the Wintersoft family have long been rivals. As a future countess, Victoria is well-suited to the position."

"Good. I'd like to meet with both of them again—to be completely sure before we bring them in"

"I will arrange it," Nadine said. "Now, on the subject of bringing people in: your *announcement* at the council meeting means that we must move swiftly to find an adequate gentleman. Or you will need to tragically lose the child in the next few months—before you would be expected to show."

"Find someone for me." Hanne stood. By now, her face was clean and her hair was loose. "I would have liked to give you more warning, Nadine." It was as much of an apology as she could muster.

"You did what you needed to," Nadine said. "They had you backed into a corner."

Cecelia gave an angry little sigh. "It would be so much better if King Rune would just come back. That would solve at least half your problems."

Not *quite* half—there was still the Malstop and rancor king to deal with—but a good number of them, certainly.

"Indeed," Nadine said. "Now I will begin—"

A knock sounded on the main door.

"But it's midnight," Lea protested.

"A queen is a queen at all hours." Hanne motioned for Maris. "See who it is. If it isn't actually urgent, tell them to come back tomorrow."

While Maris hurried to follow orders, Hanne checked herself in the mirror again. Dressing gown. Loose hair. Fresh face. Well. She wasn't *as* presentable as she would have liked. She looked younger and softer. But perhaps if she wore a crown . . .

Maris rushed back into the dressing room. "It's the Nightrender! She demands an audience with you."

Anger flashed through Hanne. How dare anyone *demand* an audience with her. Especially the Nightrender. The *audacity*.

However . . .

"Is she here?" Hanne strode toward the door, her dressing gown fluttering behind her. "Is that creature here right now?"

"No, Your Majesty. She sent a messenger."

Hanne paused at the parlor door, thinking through it. She hated the idea of her—a queen and an heir—going *to* someone like the Nightrender. The Nightrender should come to her.

Then again, did Hanne really want that carrion crow creeping through the halls of Honor's Keep, barging into the queen's chambers? No. Hanne certainly did not want the Nightrender to feel she could come and go as she pleased.

She turned to her ladies once more. "Pin my hair again. And dress me in a simple gown. I will go see her."

Every single one of Hanne's ladies stared at her.

"You will?" Nadine's expression twisted with bewilderment.

"Yes. As we were just discussing, I need Rune back. And if anyone knows where he is, it's the one who kept pulling his puppet strings: the Nightrender."

"Where are you taking me?" Hanne asked.

The messenger's voice was tight as he led her—and Captain Oliver—down an empty hall, lit only by fading light globes. "The Forsaken Tower, Your Majesty. That is where the Nightrender resides when she comes to Brink."

What an ominous name. Fitting, however, for one such as her.

"There are three keys to the tower," the man went on. "One for each ruling monarch, and one for the heir."

Hanne had indeed acquired a key when she'd been quickly coronated a few days ago, but no one had explained what it was for. She'd just placed it in a box in her room, assuming it was one of those strange Caberwilline customs, like wearing black to every event.

The messenger hauled open the heavy door at the base of the tower. It squeaked on its hinges and dust fell from the frame. "Currently, the tower is unlocked, as the Nightrender is awake."

Because *Rune* had unlocked it.

Because *Rune* had summoned her.

Because *Rune* had not sent her back to Winterfast Island as he'd promised his parents he would.

Anger tightened its fist around Hanne's heart. Rune broke so many rules where the Nightrender was concerned.

But she kept these frustrations to herself as she followed the messenger up the spiral of stairs. The space had been cleaned recently, but there were permanent stains left by dust and dead things decomposing.

At the top, they emerged into a single room the width of the tower. Maps hung along the walls, some marking major battles between the kingdoms, others depicting malsites. And there was a big ugly rock with a figure scratched onto it. A strange thing to keep here, but . . .

A memory tugged at her, something from long ago, something she couldn't quite pin down. Darkness, fear, and a strange green light—that was all that she could conjure. As for how it related to the rock? She didn't know.

Do not concern yourself with it right now. You must focus on this moment. Face the Nightrender.

Hanne stepped toward the rock. If she could just place it—

My chosen. There was a warning undertone in Tuluna's voice. **Focus.**

Hanne tore her gaze from the stone and looked back at the messenger, who'd dropped into a low bow.

"I will wait at the base of the tower for you, Your Majesty." He backed out of the room before she could ask him any questions.

"Shall I remain here, Your Majesty?" Captain Oliver asked.

Hanne glanced around the room again. The Nightrender wasn't here, but presumably she wanted to speak in private. "Go with the messenger. The Nightrender will not harm me."

Her bodyguard scowled but obeyed, leaving Hanne alone in this chilly old room. The light globes were dim, drawing the space deeper into shadow. But Hanne was not afraid. This was only natural darkness. It couldn't hurt her.

The balcony door opened, admitting a gasp of cool air.

The Nightrender stepped inside, her wings brushing the doorframe. She was ridiculously tall. Imposing. A weapon made flesh. Against the soft glow of the sleeping city, she was a black silhouette of simmering violence.

The door clicked shut and the Nightrender turned to Hanne. For one panicked heartbeat, Hanne wished she hadn't sent Captain Oliver away.

Tuluna will protect me, she thought. *I am Tuluna's chosen.*

"Queen Johanne." The Nightrender's voice was softer than Hanne recalled. Deeper, too. She looked weary, even as she stared down at Hanne—halfway *through* her, in that unsettling way she did.

For one bizarre moment, Hanne wanted to tell the Nightrender to call her Hanne, but she shook away the impulse. They weren't friends. They would never be friends. Plus, there was something exciting about the Nightrender having to use her title that she liked. Even this ancient creature was finally forced to admit that she, Johanne Fortuin, was above her.

"Lady Nightrender," Hanne said in her most courteous voice. "Welcome back to Honor's Keep. Where have you been? What happened to your wing?"

The Nightrender lifted her left wing a fraction, glancing at it with a trace of annoyance. "It was injured. It will heal."

That wasn't much of a story. But fine. Hanne didn't actually care anyway.

The Nightrender stepped around a small table and studied Hanne, those dark eyes eerie and unreadable. "I went to the Malice. I killed rancor and eased the strain on the Malstop."

Hanne *had* noticed that the Malstop appeared more solid than before. That was good, but it didn't change Hanne's plan. The Malstop *would* come down: that was a fact, one she was planning for. "What of the rancor king? Did you stop him?"

The Nightrender narrowed her eyes. She went completely still, not even her black feathers rustling. Then: "No. I could not."

Hanne tightened her fists—as much as she could, given her bandages. "You should have. Why did you come back here if you didn't finish your work?"

"The law of conquest."

"I don't know what that means." But the words tickled something in the back of her head, strangely familiar.

"To kill a rancor king is to become a rancor king."

Frisson passed through Hanne. She knew those words, understood them. But she couldn't remember why.

The Nightrender tilted her head, inspecting Hanne. Judging.

Hanne struggled to steady her breathing. "If you won't kill him, then what is your plan? You do have one, don't you?"

"Of course. I will fight the darkness until my last breath." The Nightrender reached over her shoulder and touched the hilt of her sword, as though re-assuring herself it was still there. "It is what I was made for."

Well. She wasn't doing a very good job at it, was she?

All of this was the Nightrender's fault. The deaths. The violence. The breach of the Winterfast Accords. If only she had done her duty four hundred years ago, none of them would be in the position they were now.

"Why did you want to see me?" Hanne demanded. "I'm very busy, you know. Being a queen."

The Nightrender took a globe off the wall and shook it until the chemicals mixed. Light splashed over her face, making the shadows around her eyes and cheekbones deepen and shift as she replaced the globe in its sconce. She made a show of studying the newly lit maps. "After the mal-device detonated in Small Mountain, I cleansed the earth and burned the remains of everyone who was slaughtered there."

Hanne set her jaw. "It's your duty."

"And then I went into the mine at Silver Sun to battle the risen dead. I purified the depths, so that miners could return to the dark places where their neighbors had been eaten by the very earth they burrowed through."

A faint shudder ran through Hanne. "Whether the malsites are new or old, they are your responsibility."

The Nightrender lowered her wings and inclined her head. "Indeed, they are. And I will destroy them—as well as the new malsites produced when the Malstop flickered. But I am displeased by your part in this."

Hanne began to sweat. She could halfway *smell* the tower where she'd met the malicists: the dirt of Athelney, the chemicals, the desperation. "You don't know what you're talking about."

"I know that you violated the Winterfast Accords when you helped finish the mal-device."

"I didn't have a choice." The words were out before Hanne could stop them. "The rancor would have killed me. Sent me to the Dark Shard. It got in my *head*—and it showed me what that world is like. I couldn't— I couldn't."

Her hands were shaking. Her jaw was trembling. When she blinked, all she could see was the starless sky and that glasslike shard.

The Nightrender was looking at her, an almost curious expression crossing her face. Then it was gone. "I would have chosen humanity over my own safety."

"I'm not you."

"You're a queen. Therefore, you must always put others above yourself." The Nightrender flexed her wings before tucking them behind her again. "Because of your actions, Small Mountain is gone, and there will be food shortages in Brink this winter. Unless your predecessors prepared stockpiles in case of an Incursion, the people of your new home will starve. However, as the Highcrowns continually denied there *was* an Incursion, I believe you will find those storehouses empty."

Unease worked through Hanne. It was true. She'd already had the old caches inside the mountain searched, but her people had found only dust and stale air.

"Furthermore, the Embrian people march against your family in Solcast. Hundreds of rebels—"

"Thousands."

"Thousands are sieging Solspire as we speak, rather than farming or black-smithing or any of the other jobs mortals must do. The occupants of your palace will soon starve. And here you are, pretending any of this would have happened without your influence."

Fury ignited through Hanne, so hot and bright that white flared across Hanne's vision and she rocked back on her heels. "I'm taking care of these problems. I have a plan to end the siege on Solspire. And to feed Brink."

"I'm sure you do," the Nightrender said.

"What's *that* supposed to mean?"

"I own my failures," the Nightrender said. "You should own yours as well."

"I thought mortal affairs didn't concern you."

The Nightrender's black wings lifted, making her loom larger over Hanne. Threatening. Her sword was there, visible over her shoulder. In the back of Hanne's mind, she wondered if it would hurt, or if the cut would be so swift that she wouldn't have time to feel it.

The Nightrender's eyes bore into Hanne's, terrifying and ancient.

But Hanne had seen worse things. She'd faced two rancor. Of course, this was the thing that killed rancor.

"You are forgetting another consequence of finishing the mal-device."

A knot wedged in Hanne's throat. It almost hurt to speak around it. "What do you think I've forgotten?"

"Rune Highcrown." Something changed in the Nightrender's expression. It was fleeting, and if Hanne hadn't been staring so hard she would have missed it. But it had been there.

Her own face must have given something away, too, because the Night-render gave a slow, single nod. "You need him back. To legitimize your position here."

"Do you know where he is?" Hanne asked.

The Nightrender didn't answer right away. Finally, she said, "Yes."

Was that guilt in her tone? Could the Nightrender feel such a thing?

Hanne narrowed her eyes. "Where?"

"He is where the portal sent him."

"Yes, but *where*?"

"Your men believe he is dead," the Nightrender said, as though Hanne hadn't asked anything. "The spheres drifting across the ground, the place where King Rune disappeared into one. Someone has planted a half-masted flag there."

Hanne wanted to be sick. It was one thing to hear such speculation from commoners and councilors. Those could be squashed, dismissed, challenged. But the Nightrender wasn't as easy to ignore.

"Well, is he dead?" She was losing her grip on this exchange, but she would have to worry about that later, when the most powerful creature in Salvation wasn't holding Hanne's future hostage—and accusing her of selling out humanity.

"Tell me why you want Rune."

"You know. You already said. Legitimacy. Without him, I lose everything." Hanne sucked in a breath. She hated this hot, unsteady feeling. She hated being on the defensive when she was always the one to attack, to strike fast, first, and repeatedly.

"Tell me something else," the Nightrender said. "Tell me if you love him."

"Will my answer change anything?" Hanne asked. "For you, I mean. You clearly have some kind of fascination with him."

The Nightrender was quiet a moment. Hesitating? "I simply want to know."

"Then no." Hanne saw no reason to lie about it. "I don't love him. I chose to marry him for the betterment of both our kingdoms—and to put an end to Ivasland's aggressions. That's all."

The Nightrender nodded, her mouth pressed into a pensive line. "Very well. To answer your question: King Rune is alive."

Hanne felt her shoulders drop in relief. "You're sure?"

"He asked me to see you. To get your help."

Of course he needed help. But she needed his help, so she would do whatever it took to get him back. "Very well. Where is he? What does he need?"

She was halfway to imagining her wayward husband stranded on a mountaintop somewhere far away, requiring a warmer coat and perhaps skis, but the Nightrender's expression was so grim that Hanne discovered new depths of dread within her.

"Rune is trapped in the Malice. The rancor king has him."

12.

NIGHTRENDER

There were too many things Nightrender didn't know.

Such as: How had Queen Johanne become aware of Daghath Mal? How had she participated in the construction of the mal-device? And—more important—how had that been arranged, if Queen Johanne had been coerced into it, as she claimed?

"Rune is in the Malice," Queen Johanne murmured, her face falling. Her eyes unfocused. And for a moment, it seemed she went somewhere else—into her mind, into a memory, into something dark and dangerous that had left an invisible scar. "How could he be in the Malice?"

"The portal." That should have been obvious, but sometimes shock made mortals need things explained in small words. "Unfortunately, it was one-way."

"How do you know? Did you see him?" A faint laugh escaped Queen Johanne. "I suppose you must have seen him if he asked you to find me. So you saw him in the Malice, but you didn't rescue him. And now he's trapped in that wretched place with the rancor king?" Queen Johanne's face reddened with anger. *"Why didn't you save him?"* Her glare raked over Nightrender, hatred hot in her blue eyes. "He's a person! He's trapped in there. With *rancor*. How could you just leave him?" She was shaking, her small body barely containing her rage.

Was it an act? Was she really so indignant that Nightrender should have done more to help Rune because he was a *person*—when the queen herself had condemned thousands of *people* to similar fates?

Nightrender made her face like steel. "I would have carried him out over my shoulder if that had been possible. But the rancor king—he is an old and clever foe, with legions at his whim. As for Rune, his guards had all been slaughtered and the rancor king had his throat. He is a hostage. Should I return to the Malice, Rune will die."

Queen Johanne's jaw tightened; her eyes were wide and round. "You should have—"

"I could not have."

"You should—"

"You weren't there." Nightrender pushed strength into her voice, trying to make Queen Johanne understand. "Rune is still alive, I swear it."

"How do you know?"

"I would sense his departure from this world."

Queen Johanne laughed. "You sound like a peasant girl. They're always talking about how they would *know* if their paramour had died in the cave-in, or in the fire, or at sea. They never do."

It seemed unlikely Queen Johanne had spent all that much time talking to peasant girls.

"Go back into the Malice," Queen Johanne commanded. "Kill a few more rancor. And bring Rune back to me."

Anger twisted in Nightrender. "You would condemn the king to death."

"What do you need?" Queen Johanne pressed. "An army? I can get you an army."

Nightrender scoffed. She'd heard that promise before. "Rune is my summoner, my Dawnbreaker, and my soul shard. If I could not get an army out of him, I would certainly not expect one from you."

"Your soul—" Queen Johanne set her jaw. "You shouldn't claim what you can't keep."

"Then mind your words when you call yourself queen."

Red flushed Queen Johanne's throat and cheeks. Fury burned in her eyes. "You don't know anything about me."

"I've seen rulers like you before, obsessed with power, terrified of what will happen when they lose it. It's nothing new, nothing special. You're no different from every insecure monarch before you." She shouldn't let this girl get under her skin, she knew, but Queen Johanne could do so much good—if only she put her mind to it.

"I *am* different," Queen Johanne seethed. "I *am* special. I've been chosen."

Chosen? An alarm rang in the back of Nightrender's mind. A warning. She lowered her voice, cautious now. "Tell me why you believe that."

Silence. Narrowed eyes. Then: "What is a soul shard?"

"It is nothing to you."

The queen turned inward for a moment, then gave herself a small shake. She smiled. "You're right. It is nothing. You may call him whatever you like, but he is my husband, my king, and the father of my child."

Child?

Nightrender listened, but she heard only the wind groaning around the castle, the mice chewing old plaster. If the young queen was pregnant, there wasn't yet a heartbeat.

But perhaps it was true. It was Rune's duty, after all. She should be happy for him, not remembering how—just by that table—he'd (drunkenly) offered to help her comb her hair; the gentle way he'd touched her face on the balcony; the surge of longing she'd felt when he kissed her in the Malice . . . just before she'd left him.

She should not think of those things again. Ever.

So Nightrender bit back a rush of hot emotion. She put away the guilt. She returned to the moment.

"Congratulations. You must be relieved."

The queen's eyes clouded, as though she were thinking about something, but it didn't seem . . . right. "Does it hurt your feelings?"

Another wave of suspicion crested inside Nightrender. Rune had asked her to seek out Queen Johanne for help, but something was deeply wrong here. She could not broach the weapon she sought, not when every instinct warned her against it.

"I must go," Nightrender said. "I should have anticipated that you would not help me."

"You haven't said what you wanted!" Queen Johanne protested. "Even though I've given you my offer. A whole army. As many men as you would like. You do like armies, don't you?"

"And I have given my answer. I will not return to the Malice."

The queen's eyes darkened. "I'd hoped we could be allies."

That was most certainly a lie.

But Nightrender had hoped for something similar. They both wanted an end to this Incursion—or so the queen claimed. But the mal-device, the insistence that Nightrender should return to the Malice regardless of the consequences—those were warnings she could not ignore.

Nightrender's gaze dropped to Queen Johanne's hands, both wrapped in bandages. They carried the odors of antiseptic and blood. "Tell me how you were injured."

"I killed a rancor." Queen Johanne touched the obsidian shard at her throat. "So you see, I don't need your help. I don't need anything from you. If you're not going to fetch Rune for me, or do whatever it takes to get him back safely, you're no champion of mine."

"That is impressive," Nightrender said softly. Even trained Dawnbreakers struggled to kill rancor, so if Queen Johanne was capable of such a feat, she was much more formidable than she appeared.

"It is." Queen Johanne pulled herself up taller. "Now go. I don't want to see you in Caberwill—or Embria—again." With that, she took up a light globe and went down the stairs.

Nightrender listened to the footfalls, to the distant murmur of voices, and to the hiss of glass sliding into a sconce. There was no talk of preventing Nightrender from moving about the castle.

Well, even a queen didn't actually have that authority. Nightrender observed no borders.

It was a shame this meeting had been fruitless. She'd hoped—at the very least—she might hear a hint to the weapon's whereabouts. Something only royals knew, like the summoning shrines. But the entire conversation, she'd had a crawling sensation that she was being tested—tempted. Like the queen had been trying to tease out Nightrender's next steps.

I need that weapon, Nightrender thought.

If the queen wouldn't help her, then there was only one other person she could try.

13.

RUNE

"Run!" Rune shouted again.

Immediately, the Ivaslander took off, perpendicular to the trees' shadows, and disappeared down a steep slope. But Rune was too late. Too close to the shadows. Too slow to move.

A tree's clawed shadow snaked across the red earth and grabbed his ankle; another wrapped around the bone. As one, both shadows jerked him toward the trees.

Rune's knees dragged over the ground, and the rancor bone rolled out of his grasp—away from him. More shadows wrapped around his waist. Though it was only shadow, the pressure was tighter than a vise.

Then everything stopped.

Rune had been towed beneath the trees. This close, he saw the branches were claws, the wood knots were blank eye sockets, the trunk holes gaped like mouths. As long as he stared up, the trees were absolutely motionless.

But he had to blink.

In an instant, they shifted closer.

Desperately, Rune tried to hold open his eyes through sheer force of will, but dust kicked up as he struggled to untangle himself from the shadows. His eyes watered and—

A mistake. The instant he took his eyes off the trees, they were upon him: a dozen twisted crooked limbs, thorns slick with something brown and viscous. A sickly sweet odor turned Rune's stomach.

His vision blurred and his eyes stung, but he forced himself to look up, to stare *hard* at the spiny trees as he wrenched himself out of their grasp. Cloth ripped, and thorns cut into his skin, but he refused to flinch as he freed himself and felt around for the rancor bone, finally closing his fingers around it.

He swung it in front of him just as he blinked again. His eyes were *burning*.

The bone struck something solid: a branch cracked and one of the trees howled.

He climbed to his feet and lashed out again, aiming for the smaller twigs that made up their claws. The wailing came whenever he blinked, and they moved in stuttering bursts. Soon, limbs encircled him, gripping him, pinning his arms to his ribs. He gave a short, choked-off shout as the trees' spines dug deep, piercing his armor and skin. Warmth bloomed where blood flowed, and he was forced to close his eyes against the pain. His joints popped as the trees constricted—

"Open your eyes!"

It took great effort to obey the voice, with pain searing his body and pounding in his skull, but he forced his eyes open—and saw that there was a bristle of thorns just before his face.

Some predators went for the throat. This one went for the eyes. If he couldn't see, he couldn't stop them.

Rune forced his eyes to focus beyond the thorns—so that he looked at the trees themselves. They were so close that their limbs tangled and their trunks pressed together.

The man's voice came again from somewhere behind Rune. "Keep watching them!"

Wood crunched. Cracked. The man grunted. Slowly, the pressure on Rune began to ease, but his eyes were burning in desperation.

"Blink now," the man said.

Rune did—several times. His eyes satisfied, he called back, "Done."

Another grunt. Then came a huge crack, and Rune dropped to the ground, thorns ripping free.

Using the rancor bone, Rune pushed against the branches, breaking off bits that had been—moments ago—trying to kill him. When he had enough space to move, he scooted backward, coordinating blinking with the other man.

Then human hands were on his upper arms, dragging him completely free of the trees. Twigs, thorns, and entire branches littered the ground.

Without speaking, Rune and the other man hurried backward, several long strides away from the trees and their shadows.

"You came back."

"I wanted to keep running, but I couldn't—" He cleared his throat. "I couldn't leave another Dawnbreaker. Even if you are Caberwilline."

Rune's whole body hurt. He wanted to lie down and finish bleeding out. Instead, he took several more steps away from the trees, leaning heavily on the rancor bone. "Don't worry." His voice was tight. "I'm not exactly fond of Ivaslanders."

"Noted." The Ivaslander retreated with him, backward with his gaze on the trees. But now that they weren't coordinating their blinking, spurts of howling and shrieking rent the air as the trees discovered their broken limbs, fallen branches, missing prey. They stuttered closer, ready to chase once more. "We can't stay here."

Rune agreed. But he wasn't sure how long he could remain on his feet. The puncture wounds were bleeding freely, likely drawing more predators.

Still, he took another measured step backward, away from the trees, away from their shadows. The Ivaslander followed.

"Breaking the line of sight won't be enough," the Ivaslander said. "They will pursue until they catch us. Or until we go somewhere they cannot."

We.

Rune's teeth itched at the very idea.

But he was injured, and the Ivaslander clearly knew more about the Malice and how to survive.

He dragged in a long breath. Then: "So where do we go?"

The Ivaslander's tone was dark. "The Storm."

That sounded unpleasant, but perhaps—once he wasn't being hunted down by man-eating trees—he could find a way to send a message to the Nightrender about Daghath Mal's plan for the Malstop. "All right."

The Ivaslander looked up and around, as though trying to judge direction. Then he set off. "Walk backward and watch the Thorns while I lead. That should slow them long enough for us to reach the Storm."

Leaning heavily on the rancor bone, Rune walked backward after the Ivaslander. Every so often, the man called out instructions—*step left* or *careful of that hole*—but for the most part, they walked in silence. Even so, Rune could feel the pressure of questions building inside his new companion, but the Ivaslander didn't voice them, so Rune didn't offer answers. Not yet.

Minutes bled together. Sweat poured down Rune's face and chest. His legs burned, and a pinch grew in his side. He'd always been fit, but he was injured, and the Malice was draining; he could feel it leeching away his energy. It made his vision tunnel as he focused on shoving his feet across the dry red ground, trying not to fall. If he dropped, he wasn't sure he'd bother getting back up.

The spiky trees were but dark smudges on the horizon by the time the Ivaslander spoke again. "What's your name?"

"Rune." The Highcrown family had been prominent—if not yet royal—four hundred years ago. If Rune gave his surname, it was sure to be recognized and cause additional tension. Better that this Ivaslander believed him to be a Caberwilline commoner. "What's yours?"

"Thoman Summerhill." Ivaslander surnames were towns or cities—wherever the person was born—so Thoman sharing this was a small measure of trust, but not much of a risk.

Rune chanced a look over his shoulder. A huge boulder the size of a house sat ahead of them—a tempting place to sit and rest in some shade. "I need to catch my breath," Rune said. "And try to stop bleeding."

The Ivaslander—Thoman—glanced back at him. "Not there. We have to keep going. You can see the boulder's tracks when we pass."

As they moved around the boulder, Rune did indeed see its tracks: a long, twisting line in the red dirt. He couldn't guess when it moved, but like everything here, it surely had no problem obliterating two unlucky men.

They walked in silence for several more hours, taking turns watching the trees while the other navigated around brush or up small hills. During the stretches Rune got to face forward, he could see *something* looming the distance—a darkness splashed across the sky. *The* storm, he hoped. He needed to sit and tend his wounds—not that he had anything to tend them with. All his various pains began to blur together. He was a man made of agony.

"How—" Thoman's voice caught. When Rune risked a glance over his shoulder—to where the Ivaslander was walking ahead of him—the man dragged his long, curling fingernails down his face, scraping lines into the muck. "Before. When you found me. I don't remember much. Just feelings, dark and angry. So angry. And afraid. But now I feel"—he tugged at a lock of filthy hair—"clearer. I can think again."

Rune nodded.

"How did you do it?" Thoman touched the place where Rune had stabbed him. "There was pain, then..." He shook his head.

Rune paused. "She gave me one of her feathers. Do you remember? I used it on you."

Emotion flashed through the Ivaslander's eyes. "Is she here? Has she returned for us?"

"She isn't here."

"I dreamed that I saw her. She was flying overhead." He pointed upward, finger tracing a path through the sky. "She was going to the castle, but they got to her first. Rancor. The ones with wings dragged her down. The ones without wings—some had bows, and they tried to shoot her down. I ran to yell at her for—for leaving me. But she was already gone."

"That wasn't a dream." Rune stepped over a twisted tree root. "She was here. Now she's not."

"I don't understand. Where did she go? Did— Did they kill her?"

"She's injured, but alive." Rune tightened his grip on the rancor bone. "I'm sorry. I can't tell you any more than that."

Thoman grunted. "Typical Caberwilline."

Rune shot a look over his shoulder. "Excuse me?"

"You heard me." Thoman turned around again. "We may fight together as Dawnbreakers, but you're still from Caberwill. I know how Caberwillines and Embrians think, what you do to people from Ivasland: you withhold things. Things we need."

"Considering Ivasland *kills* people from Caberwill, my not telling you much shouldn't come as a surprise." Rune glanced back at the trees. They'd come closer while he and Thoman had been talking.

"Ivasland does what it must in order to survive." Thoman's hands curled into fists. A few of his nails snapped from the pressure. "Ivaslanders have always had less than you. But we've done more. We educate everyone. We ration food. And even with a smaller, poorer army, we train and deploy just as many Dawnbreakers. We pull more than our weight. The royal Athelneys do their best by their people. Meanwhile, the Askas work common Embrians to the bone—and then blame *us* for their misery. And the Skyreaches..." Thoman shook his head. "Your monarchs only want warriors, not thinkers. Any excuse to engage in battle. Any excuse to raid border towns and take what little we have."

Red fogged across Rune's vision, and for a moment, the only thing he could see was the Ivaslander assassin emerging from the shadows, the gleam of the blade as it cut his brother's throat, the utter shock and silence in the hall outside the family chapel as Rune's brother dropped to the floor. Just like that, Rune had gone from spare to heir.

And then the news only days ago—when his guards and mother came bursting into his room to relay the news that his father had been killed by an Ivaslander assassin, and that he was now king.

Rune had vowed to make Ivasland pay. At every turn, they'd brought more harm to him and his kingdom. He wouldn't be *here* if not for Ivasland. And Thoman! Well, he may be a Dawnbreaker, but he was an Ivaslander first.

"How many times did your king send his armies against defenseless towns?" Thoman pressed. "How many times did he steal our scientific advances, our—"

Faint rumbling sounded. When they looked up, the trees were closer, just strides away from where they were standing. The faces in their trunks were angry masks. Branches stretched outward, reaching.

"Burn it," Rune muttered. Fortunately, the shadows fell in a different direction. . . .

But even as he thought it, the sun shifted. The shadows moved. Though shorter now, they were aimed straight at Rune.

Heart pounding, Rune took several long strides backward, putting more distance between himself and the trees. If they caught him again, he wouldn't be able to fight them off.

Thoman did the same. "They're injured," he said. "Enraged. They were hunting before, willing to wait for you to tire. But now that we've hurt them . . ."

"They just want revenge." Rune's voice was rough as he continued retreating. The trees flickered, shifting in the split seconds Rune and Thoman blinked at the same time. "Are we almost to the storm?"

"We can run and hope it isn't raining."

Rune wasn't certain he *should* run, considering his many injuries, but an electric buzz of adrenaline worked through him. He could do it. He had to.

By now, they'd put more space between them and the trees—several body lengths, at least. "All right," Rune said. "I'm ready.

As one, they turned and ran toward a ruddy darkness. Clouds gathered in the sky, an ominous rust color, swollen with rain. Rune hurried toward it, this place that killer trees would not follow.

Rumbling, crunching, grinding: the trees were following, chasing their prey. Shadows stretched, brushing Rune's heels. When he could, he glanced over his shoulder to stop them—to buy himself and Thoman another second to get to the storm.

"We're close!" Thoman was ahead, running hard, spinning rocks and pebbles as he hurried up an incline.

It was one of those rocks Rune stepped on, one that was still moving down the slope. He slipped, and in an instant, he was on his knees, grit digging into his palms, the rancor bone rolling away from him. "Thom—"

He struggled to climb up, but blood slicked his hands. A shadow brushed against his boot.

Desperately, he rolled until he was sitting, looking at the trees again. They were nearly upon him, frozen now—until he blinked. The moment he did, he would be dead.

"I'm looking," Thoman called. "Move. Run. Now."

Rune heaved himself up, losing more blood in the process, and took up the rancor bone before he ran for the storm, mere steps away.

There was no mistaking when he'd reached his destination. A black line marked the boundary. The ground crackled beneath his boots. And when he turned—a shadow held the Ivaslander's ankle.

The trees frozen, Rune grabbed Thoman's arms and yanked him free—into the storm.

They tumbled over, just sitting and breathing for a moment. The trees were still, partly because they were being observed, and partly because they'd lost this chase. During the moments they could move, they shifted angrily.

"Thank you," Rune softly. "For noticing I wasn't behind you anymore."

Thoman shrugged. "I hate you. You're Caberwilline. You have—" He cleared his throat. "It doesn't matter. We are natural enemies, but . . ."

"We can't be enemies here." Rune groaned as he took in the gashes on his hands and knuckles. That last burst of energy had dulled the pain, but now it was back. There was no part of him that didn't hurt.

"Agreed." Thoman heaved himself up. He looked exhausted, but it was disconcerting how young he appeared—the age Opi would have been, if Opi had not been killed. "Come on," Thoman said. "We can't stay out in the open."

"Because of the storm?" Rune climbed up, keeping an eye on the trees as they watched hungrily.

"Yes." Thoman scowled. "The Storm. Capital S. And we don't want to be caught in a downpour."

"Why—" Rune's voice was hoarse as something dark and viscous dropped from the clouds. It hissed when it hit the ground; a tendril of smoke spiraled upward. This rain was not water. "Burn it." Quickly, he scanned their surroundings for a likely shelter. Scrub, grit, a shallow channel where this not-rain would run. "There!" He pointed toward a large outcrop of rock. From here, he could just make out a shallow space beneath the shelf of stone.

Thunder crashed and echoed all through the Malice. Rune almost dropped the rancor bone as he tried to cover his ears, but Thoman had already started running again. Rune tightened his grip on his weapon and followed as more raindrops fell, sizzling against the earth—and him. His face. His arms.

Suddenly, he understood why the trees wouldn't come here: the Storm would burn them into a dark pile of smoking sludge.

Rune threw himself toward the hollow—before the Storm killed him, too.

14.

HANNE

"Of course Rune chose her," Hanne grumbled. The thought had stayed with her all night, nipping at her every second. She'd hardly slept. "Of course he did."

Nadine glanced up from their game of Mora's Gambit. Nadine was winning. As always.

Hanne pulled a card from the deck. Five. She rested her fingers atop the tiny black-dyed glass crown, eyeing the board. (The glass crown was new to the game, created for her by the castle's jeweler in commemoration of her killing the rancor.) After a moment's consideration, she moved the crown seven spaces forward.

Nadine studied Hanne's face. "You're bluffing. Show your card."

"Burn it," Hanne muttered. "How did you know?"

"Your face." Nadine smiled primly as she took Hanne's crown and moved it back seven places from where it had started—the same as Hanne's bluff. "You seem very upset."

"Rune willingly ran through a portal and got himself trapped in *the* Malice. He did that to himself. And he did it for her, knowing we need him here."

Nadine sighed. "What will you do about it? Complaining to me isn't going to bring Rune back."

"I know," Hanne said, "but it makes me feel better."

Wait. Hanne narrowed her eyes at her cousin. Had Nadine always called Rune by his given name? Perhaps she'd started sometime after Rupert suggested Nadine might marry Rune?

Nadine pulled a card from the deck, giving nothing away as her eyes flicked to the value, then to the board. She moved her teacup forward seven spaces—straight across the finish line.

"No!" Hanne grabbed the card out of Nadine's hand. It was, in fact, a seven. She slumped and tossed the card onto the table. "I think you've stacked the deck."

"You wouldn't have so much trouble if you bluffed better."

"No one *ever* knows when I'm bluffing. Except you. How is that?" Hanne wanted to pout, but a knock sounded on the door, and Maris peeked in.

"They're here," said the lady-in-waiting.

"Thank you, Maris." Hanne stood and smoothed her skirts. "How do I look?"

Nadine didn't hesitate. "Like a queen."

Hanne nodded, fingering the pendant that rested against her chest—the shard of the obsidian crown. It comforted her, having it there, even though many would argue that it was an ugly piece.

Well, sometimes power was not pretty.

"I wish . . ." She stopped. It was too easy to confide in Nadine. She always had, after all. It was as natural as breathing.

Nadine waited.

"I wish I felt like a queen." Hanne kept her eyes trained down on the game board. "I wish it felt real."

Nadine touched her elbow, as comforting as ever. "It's only because everyone keeps questioning you. They're trying to make you doubt yourself. You're Embrian. They don't trust you."

"I need to make them trust me."

"And you will. One person at a time." Nadine motioned toward the door to the parlor. "Prudence and Victoria are out there because they want to trust you. They do already, in their way. They were among the first I spoke to when I arrived in Brink."

Cautiously, Hanne listened.

"We had breakfast the morning after I got here. I told them all about how brave you were, how you drew that rancor away from me and onto yourself. Hanne, it would have *killed* me. I owe you my life."

A knot tightened in Hanne's throat. "That's not—"

"And that's exactly what I told Prudence and Victoria. They know what you did for me—and what you've done in Brink." Nadine nodded pointedly at the shard of Hanne's obsidian crown.

Hanne took a shaking breath and nodded. The pressure was getting to her, the stress of knowing everything she had to do—and that she was the only one who *could* do it. Nadine understood that.

"I'll need to deal with Rune," Hanne murmured. "He is alive, and the Nightrender knows where he is. She may tell others."

"It would be better if he were dead."

Hanne considered this. "You think?"

"Better for you. If he should survive, if he should escape—he could tell the Crown Council that you lied: you aren't pregnant and you didn't sleep together in Embria."

"He wouldn't tell anyone. I'm holding his throne, too."

Nadine pressed her mouth into a line. "Well, if you want him, perhaps we can send a company of soldiers through the Soul Gate. Perhaps they can bring him back, since the Nightrender refuses."

Hanne wasn't sure how the Nightrender could simply refuse to get someone she called her *soul shard*, whatever that was. How hard could it be to fly into the Malice, get Rune, and fly back out? Would the rancor king actually *know* if the Nightrender went in there to rescue someone?

"I will get Rune back when the Malstop is down. I'll send a small company—our best men—to retrieve him and bring him home before the Malstop is reinstated."

"Do you know how long the Malstop will be out?" Nadine bit her lip, shifting her weight away from Hanne just a tiny amount.

"A little while." Hanne wished she could say exactly how much time it would take for the Malstop to reinstate, but Tuluna hadn't told her. It was possible Tuluna didn't know, either, although the idea of Tuluna *not knowing something* seemed truly impossible.

"I dislike losing the Malstop, even for a few moments." Nadine picked up the cards from the discard pile and began shuffling. "Who knows what will happen? Certainly people will die. New malsites will be created. Rancor will roam free. And— And the people."

Yes, some people would die. Perhaps a lot of people. That was inevitable. But in the end, when the Malstop came back clean and strong and whole, more would be saved.

"I'm sorry," Hanne said. "I wish I could give you better answers. But the Numina are on our side. Tuluna guides our steps."

Worry passed over Nadine's expression. "Of course."

Is she with you?

Yes, Hanne thought. *Yes, Nadine is always with me.*

Be certain.

Hanne wanted to be certain.

So Nadine had reservations. She disapproved. That didn't mean she would sabotage the plan.

Did it?

Nadine stood and smoothed her dress. "All right. We'd better see Victoria and Prudence."

Hanne nodded, and together they went into the parlor, where Cecelia was serving tea to the two Caberwilline ladies. "Lady Victoria Stareyes," Hanne said warmly. "Lady Prudence Shadowhand."

Both women stood and curtsied, offering quick greetings of "Your Majesty" and "How radiant you look today."

After graciously accepting the compliments, Hanne took a seat at the tallest chair and sipped her tea. It was hot and sweet, just how she liked it. Fortified, she began. "I suppose you know why you are here."

They exchanged glances. Victoria said, "We are both aware of your dispute with Charity and Rupert."

"Of course, we would not presume to know why you'd want to speak to *us,*" Prudence added quickly.

Usually, Hanne enjoyed delicate language, testing others, making them work for her good graces. But she still had a headache from last night, and—moreover—she didn't like this silent tension with Nadine.

So she wasn't in the mood to make these Caberwilline ladies squirm. Not today.

"Now that I am queen, I will remove Rupert and Charity from the council. They have been fixtures at the table for too long. My predecessors were unwilling to weather the political storm that would result from elevating someone new to treasury chancellor and information chancellor, but I am not. Their experience is, of course, highly valuable, and I'm grateful for their years and *years* of service, but the kingdom must move forward."

Prudence inclined her head. "I agree, Your Majesty." She slid her gloved finger down the handle of her teacup; she always wore a dark glove, black or gray, as her surname was Shadowhand and, apparently, she didn't want anyone to forget. It was a little on the nose, at least to Hanne's way of thinking, but if this woman would be loyal to her, she could do whatever she wanted, sartorially speaking. "Earl Flight has a wide network of informants, but he doesn't *appreciate* them."

Hanne nodded. "If someone else were to reach in and...grasp Rupert's network, that would cripple him—and whatever schemes he's concocting. But one would have to be sure of any turncoats. Lives are at stake."

Prudence mirrored Hanne's nod. "Indeed, Your Majesty. But how did Lady Holt put it? 'In Caberwill, loyalty is rewarded; in Embria, it is demanded.' If you select me for information chancellor, I would have Rupert Flight eyeless and earless within"—she glanced at Nadine—"two years."

"Make it one," Hanne said, "and the job is yours, once the new council period begins."

Prudence was quiet for a moment, perhaps reassessing her plans. But then she nodded. "Yes, I can do that."

Hanne didn't care if Prudence literally cut off Rupert's eyes and ears. She just wanted him out of her life. "Be careful. He must not have any warning that it's coming."

That was the problem with conspiring against the spymaster: there was a very good chance he'd learn of the conspiracy.

"And you?" Hanne turned to Victoria. "Charity may not be as deeply entrenched in her role as treasury chancellor, but she is powerful. She controls massive wealth, mines and mints, hundreds of business contracts..."

"Not for long." Victoria flashed a winning smile. "I'm prepared to *acquire* her best contracts through whatever means necessary. My entire family will support this effort. You must know our reputation."

"How wonderful."

"I've also had new tunnels opened in my iron mine, and sizable quantities of metal are already being extracted—iron being necessary for war, I believe, and I'm quite happy to sell it to the crown at a discount. I can also arrange for a portion of my holdings' harvests to be sent here to Brink, to fill our caches."

Hanne sat up a little straighter. The Nightrender had made her feel wretched about not being able to feed Brink this winter, but *here* was someone who was actually working to solve that problem.

"Good," Hanne said. "Be certain that your contract offers are generous. It wouldn't do for anyone to think the new queen of Caberwill won't pay for what she wants."

"Indeed." Victoria smiled again.

Hanne finished her tea. "I knew you were each special when Nadine was so enthusiastic about us meeting. You were such good company to her while I was indisposed—such good friends. And now, good friends to me. We truly represent a fine example of what this alliance can be."

Both Caberwilline women smiled.

"Moving forward, toward peace, is no easy task," Prudence said, "but I believe we can achieve it. Together."

"It is assured." Victoria smiled again.

She smiled a lot, Hanne thought, but it was a good smile. That had been Charity's problem—well, one of them: she was unfriendly, too high reaching, and too conniving, and she did nothing to disguise it.

Hanne stood, and the others followed immediately. "Thank you for your company this afternoon," Hanne said. "I wish I could stay to talk more, but I'm afraid I have another meeting I must make. If I could put it off, I would...."

"Of course," Prudence said. "You're queen. You have a very busy schedule. We are the ones who are grateful for your time."

After a flurry of niceties, and an invitation to a lavish dinner soon, the future councilors exited the room.

Hanne waited a few moments until they were gone. Then she raised her voice. "Sabine?"

Lady Sabine came out of the other room. "Your Majesty."

"My package has arrived?" Hanne asked.

Sabine nodded. "Yes, but she's quite angry."

"That is to be expected." Hanne ran her fingers through her hair. "Let's go."

Hanne, along with Sabine and Nadine and Captain Oliver, left the queen's quarters and started out of the royal wing.

Nobles glided throughout the halls, most going about their business, but there were always a few people who wanted to stop and talk with Hanne. She allowed them to take up some of her time as they asked about her dress (designed and sewn by her personal fashion mistress), gushed about how brave she was to face down a rancor (Hanne played humble), and advise her against eating soft cheese if she wanted a strong baby (Hanne did not have her guard murder them for the unsolicited advice, but she thought about it).

Eventually, they reached the dungeon stairs. With no eyes to see them, they descended damp stone steps, one after another. The passageway was narrow, meant to prevent large groups of prisoners from escaping all at once into the castle. Evenly placed globes lit their way.

In silence, they went down three flights of stairs before they finally reached the dungeon proper, a large space carved deep into the mountain, cavernous in height and depth. The cells were grated holes in the floor, lampposts mounted over each one.

Nadine approached the edge of one and peered down. "She isn't in one of these, is she?"

"Of course not." Sabine motioned toward closed double doors, taller than three men standing on one another's shoulders. "She's in the machine room for now. That's where the water pumps and hoses and such are kept."

"Are there any other prisoners here now?"

"Not currently, but expect to have—hmm—half a dozen commoners arrested for threatening you. To make an example of them." Sabine led everyone to a small access door beside the larger pair. Inside, water pumps took up most of the space, with cabinets and other mechanical items everywhere else.

In the center, roped to one of the giant pipes, was a girl. She had short dark hair, dirty with sweat and dust, and wore a familiar gray uniform. It, too, was filthy and spotted.

Dark eyes looked up and widened with recognition. "Hildy."

"It's Johanne Fortuin, actually. But I'd like for you to call me Hanne." She paused. "It's good to see you again, Mae."

15.

NIGHTRENDER

The numinous temple of Brink was old and grand, all stone spires and glass windows.

Nightrender had been here many times before, most recently to observe the wedding between Rune Highcrown and Johanne Fortuin. That wasn't a happy memory, particularly given how the day had ended—with her cleansing a nascent malsite and burning all the dead of Small Mountain—but it did mean that she easily found her way to the royal reading room, the same place she'd discovered Rune studying old Dawnbreaker texts.

She tucked in her wings as she took in the polished bloodwood, the large table, and the walls of bookcases. There was where she'd explained soul shards to Rune, and where she'd deposited the bag of rancor-summoning materials, giving him a way to ask his father for help in the true war.

So many things had gone wrong since then.

A small gasp. A crash. The scent of wood polish flooded the room as a young maid who'd been cleaning now dropped to her knees, hurrying to gather broken shards of glass. "I'm sorry, Lady Nightrender. Forgive me. I didn't hear you come in—"

"Do not apologize." Nightrender swept across the room, pulling a pile of rags from the cleaning cart as she went. "I'll get the glass. You sop the oil."

The maid's throat worked as she took the offered rags. She looked as though she couldn't decide whether to run for her life or obey.

"I won't hurt you," Nightrender said softly, plucking the shards of glass from the oozing mass of polish. She dropped them into the cup of her palm. "I did not mean to frighten you. I assumed this room would be empty."

"You— You didn't frighten me, Lady Nightrender." The maid worked at the spill.

Nightrender glanced up at the young woman, her black hair pulled back into a tight bun, her uniform soft and gray and neat. "I understand if I do."

"No, no." The maid shook her head.

Nightrender sighed. She hated that this woman felt she had to lie, felt she had to appease her in that way. "Tell me your name," she said gently.

"Draft, Lady Nightrender."

"Draft. Like a draft from a window."

"Like the draft of a composition." Draft went to fetch more rags. "The last few kings were Opuses, you see. I suppose my parents hoped I'd amount to something special, too, even if it had to be at a lower rank."

"I see." Caberwilline parents were so cruel. "Perhaps they hoped you might take an interest in music."

"Perhaps. But if I could choose, I'd mind the library," Draft went on, a little bolder now. "I love looking at the books when I have a spare moment. I like to imagine all their secrets."

"Most librarians here are priests."

Draft nodded. "Most. But not all. Perhaps..." She ducked her face. "I'm sorry. I shouldn't babble at you."

Nightrender didn't mind if it meant the poor maid wasn't terrified. "It's good to have dreams."

"Thank you, Lady Nightrender. I appreciate you saying so."

Nightrender picked the last of the glass shards out of the mess and wrapped them in the cloth. "After we've disposed of all this, I'd like to meet with Dayle Larksong."

"The grand priest? Of course!" Draft jumped into action. "I'll bring him straightaway." She soaked up the last of the polish and dumped all the rags into a separate bin, which already held a mound of filthy cloths. "Is there anything else I can get for you? Food? Something to drink?" She glanced meaningfully down at Nightrender's hands. "Something to clean yourself up?"

Nightrender stopped in the middle of wiping her hands on her armor. "Yes. Please." Her armor would clean itself eventually, but presentability seemed to matter to Draft.

Several minutes later, the maid had wheeled her cart out of the reading room, and Nightrender was in one of the small washrooms nearby. There was barely enough room for her wings in this space, and the faucet released only a trickle, but there was a stack of folded hand towels and soap.

She glanced into the silvered glass mirror. Hollow cheeks, smudged with oil and dirt. Black eyes, rimmed with heavy black lashes. And hair, dark and windblown.

It was the same as she'd always looked in the mirror—well, cleaner than usual—but just like that, a memory of looking at her own face snapped away.

Nightrender shuddered. The degradation had slowed, but she was still losing herself, bit by bit, moment by moment.

Quickly, she washed her hands and arms, combed some of the wind from her hair, and then made an attempt to rinse some of the oil off her armor. That only made it worse.

By the time she returned to the reading room, Draft had come and gone, leaving behind a ewer of water, empty glasses, and a loaf of warm bread. Nightrender poured some water and cut an end off the bread, then sat in the chair where Rune had sat just days ago. She imagined she could still feel the heat of his body. But she couldn't. She couldn't even hear him. Not right now.

He was alive, though. She was certain.

A soft rapping sounded on the doorframe. Dayle Larksong stepped in, something between a smile and grimace on his wizened face. "Lady Nightrender," he said. "How can I help you?"

Nightrender abandoned her water and half-eaten bread. "I seek a weapon."

The old man's eyes flickered to the sword on her back.

"A different weapon," she clarified. "A forgotten one."

"I see. The temple library has many books that describe ancient weapons. If you can tell me what type of weapon it is—"

Nightrender shook her head.

"Or what era it was forged—"

"Many thousands of years ago."

"Or who made it—"

"Numina."

Grand Priest Larksong stared at her. "Has anyone seen this weapon since its creation?"

"Not to my knowledge. It is a Relic, like Beloved, my sword, or Black Reign, the crown Queen Johanne wears. Ninety-nine Relics were known to me. I've just learned of a one hundredth."

"Did you? How did you learn of it?"

Nightrender remained quiet.

"Ah. Well. If you were unaware of it, then even our oldest catalogues of Relics wouldn't list it." He sighed and faced her. "A hidden weapon, though. What does it do?"

"It destroys." Nightrender stepped around the table. "A rancor king has come through the Rupture. Perhaps your old texts describe them."

"Yes." Grand Priest Larksong paled. "In texts that are very old indeed. Few living have read them. The horrors they describe are not something one easily forgets."

Nightrender swallowed a knot.

"But rancor kings cannot come to the laic plane on their own. They don't fit through the Rupture in the same way as their soldiers. So how—"

Nightrender leveled her gaze on him and waited. He would figure it out, she was certain.

His hand fumbled at the yellow silk around his throat, finally wrapping around a pendant of crushed obsidian. "He was *summoned*. Not with the simple materials such as you brought before, but with power. Real power. Royal power. Four hundred years ago."

Nightrender nodded. "Kings can only be summoned by kings."

"I was right, then," he murmured. "The Red Dawn was punishment for the actions of our ancestors. You enacted divine justice."

Her jaw tightened. "What I did was wrong."

"And the rancor king? Have you killed him?"

Nightrender was growing to hate this question.

"I have not," she said. "Not four hundred years ago, and not four days ago. To kill a king is to become a king. I would have become a terror upon this world, destruction incarnate." Nightrender fought the urge to glance toward the Malstop through the window. "He lives. King Rune is his hostage."

The old man gasped. "Then we must save him! Rouse the armies. Send everyone in Salvation into the Malice to rescue him!"

Now people wanted to follow her into the darkness? Now, when a single life was at stake? But when it was merely the whole world in peril? Nothing. No one was interested.

Humans were the most complex opponent she had ever faced.

"As much as it would please me to march into the Malice and set him free," Nightrender said, "I will not return there without this weapon."

"You could throw the rancor king back into the Rupture," Grand Priest Larksong pressed. "You don't have to kill him. You just have to send him back to where he came from. You know this, my lady."

Nightrender shook her head. "That was what I tried four hundred years ago." She decided to skip all reasons she didn't succeed. "And now the Rupture is concealed, so even if I wished to, I would have to find it. I cannot both search for the Rupture inside a strange castle while *also* battling the rancor king while *also* preventing him from killing Rune."

The grand priest was quiet for a moment. "Is the rancor king capable of killing you?"

"I am immortal. Not invulnerable." Once again, she was reminded that she was a weapon—the Sword of the Numina. A weapon. Not a woman. "It would be very difficult to kill me," she continued softly. "But one such as the king from beneath could do it."

The grand priest's fingers tightened around his pendant.

"This weapon will destroy the rancor king," Nightrender said. "It will completely unmake him."

"Why would such a powerful weapon be hidden? Why haven't you been using it for centuries?"

"It isn't needed against every adversary. And imagine such a weapon falling into the hands of mortals. The wars you wage against other humans are already disastrous. With that weapon, a kingdom could truly annihilate its neighbors. A ruler with that weapon would be unstoppable.

"Or, imagine the weapon in the rancor king's possession. There would be no hope for humanity, no way to end such suffering." Nightrender shook her head. "No, it was for your own protection that this was hidden until now, when it is most needed."

"All right. I'll help you find it," Grand Priest Larksong said firmly. "I suppose we should start looking for anything that discusses Relics. Certainly, even if there's no direct mention of a hundredth Relic, there must be some clues. If you were ever meant to wield it, it can't be *impossible* to find."

Nightrender followed the grand priest out of the reading room and down the hall into a massive chamber. Bookcases lined the three-story walls, every shelf full of leather-bound volumes. Yellow-green light illuminated the library; hundreds of glass light globes sat in mirrored sconces or hung like lamps, all kept faithfully lit by a young girl who climbed ladders and scurried up and down the wrought iron staircases.

"Surely you've seen the library before, Lady Nightrender." Grand Priest Larksong waited while she appraised the space.

"Of course. But it never fails to amaze me, the way mortals keep knowledge pressed onto paper and tucked onto shelves. It seems so... fragile."

"It is," he admitted. "And I take my duty to defend it most seriously." He motioned for her to follow to the nearest stair. "This way. Anything we might need will be in the restricted sections."

They went down a long hall lined with doors leading to restricted rooms. The labels on these doors were small. *Royal Diaries, Numinous Records,* and finally *Nightrender.* Her sigil—a light slashing across a new moon—was drawn next to it.

The grand priest pulled a key ring from the folds of his robes, picking through the keys until he came to one with Nightrender's sigil engraved into the metal. It fit into the lock, and a moment later the grand priest heaved open the *Nightrender* door.

Her eyes adjusted to the darkness immediately. And she gasped.

The bookcases. The displays. They were empty.

Not *completely* empty, but the shelves held more dust than books. There were so few. This room hardly had a reason to exist.

"I know." Grand Priest Larksong gave the glass globe by the door a quick shake, letting light bloom across the space. "So much was lost after the Red Dawn. I'm told these shelves used to be bursting with so many books that aides made stacks along the back wall. I've found three reports of book-related injuries from this room alone."

Nightrender dredged through her memories for an image of the complete collection, but even though she was certain she'd been here, there was nothing.

"I want to look through everything. And the other collection, the one about Numina. Any other ancient history you have." Perhaps she would write to *all* the temple libraries and have them prepare their collections for her as well. It was possible the other kingdoms hadn't purged quite so thoroughly.

"Of course," Grand Priest Larksong said. "Will you use the royal reading room? I can have everything brought to you."

"No. I will work here." This place was hers. And it was secret—or as secret as any place could be. She didn't want anyone else to know what she was looking for. "And have Draft brought to me."

"To clean?" Grand Priest Larksong raised an eyebrow. "These rooms aren't part of her normal rounds."

Nightrender let herself smile a tiny bit. Not too much. That tended to frighten people. But it was clear that the grand priest was a decent man; he hadn't needed to ask who Draft was. He cared for the people who worked for him. No wonder Rune liked him so much.

"I don't want her to clean." Nightrender paused and glanced around the room. "I want *someone* to clean. But I want Draft to assist me."

"She doesn't have the proper credentials, Lady Nightrender. Draft is a maid."

"But you, the grand priest of Caberwill, have the authority to give her a different job, should you desire. And to teach her."

She could see the uncertainty on his face, the consideration of how many ranks Draft would be skipping, the arithmetic of denying this request. At last, he nodded. "Very well, Lady Nightrender."

"Good." With another faint smile, Nightrender turned back to the room she meant to reclaim as her own. "It's time to get started."

16.

RUNE

Fire seared Rune's skin as the acidic rain intensified, but he didn't stop moving. He pushed himself uphill, after Thoman, and finally tumbled into the small shelter he'd spotted before: a hollow under a shelf of rocks.

He groaned as he drew his knees close to his body, tears half blinding him as he scooted farther under the shelter, wedged the rancor bone in beside him, and began to wipe the liquid off his skin.

"Use your clothes," Thoman said. "Don't rub. Dab it with the cloth."

Rune's hands shook as he slid one arm out of his sleeve, then gently pressed it against his face. The beaded slime soaked into the wool, dulling the worst of the burn. "What is it?" His voice was rough with pain.

"Ichor. Some call it rancor spit." Thoman shook his head. "I don't know what it really is, but it'll eat through you."

In the distance, lightning splintered the red sky, but instead of bright, blinding white, it was black—as black as a sky without stars. Thunder rolled across the world.

"It's not lightning," Thoman said when the rumble had passed. "And it's not thunder."

Rune glanced at him.

"It's a break in our reality, a brief window into the Dark Shard. That sound you hear, the noise your ears interpret as thunder—it's the endless chaos of rancor. You just hear it as thunder because that's something your mind can comprehend."

A shudder worked through Rune. "Amazing to find a nightmare storm in a nightmare wasteland."

"It's not the worst thing you'll find here."

Rune thought back to the Rupture, that oozing sore upon the world, festering and leaking reality-destroying magic. "I know," he said quietly.

"I can tell you're new." Thoman leaned his head back on the rocks. "You wouldn't have paused to see what the ichor did if you'd been here very long. You would have known about the Storm. Also, I don't remember you."

"And you know all your fellow Dawnbreakers?" Rune needled.

"Of course not. But you're from Caberwill, and you have a noble look about you. That's not a compliment."

"Mm-hmm."

"Ivasland has a long tradition of everyone applying to join the Dawnbreakers, if they can. Embrian nobility, no. Mostly never. Caberwill, sometimes. I always pay attention."

"You're right," Rune said after a minute. "I'm new. I arrived through a mal-site that coagulated into portals. One led here. Into the castle."

"Malsites?" Thoman's gaze darkened. "No . . . She was clearing them. How long have I been here?"

Rune hesitated. Then he whispered, "Four hundred years."

Thoman turned to watch the rain, his face unreadable.

Rune wanted to ask how he was even alive after all this time, but he knew things didn't work the right way here. Time. Distance. Death, apparently. Which begged the question: How long had *Rune* been here compared to the rest of the world?

His hand slid down to the feather before he'd even thought about it, scraping his thumb along the broken edge of the shaft. It hurt, but it made him feel better, as though he were closer to her. "I need to get a message out," he said. "To the Nightrender."

Thoman shot him a look. "If there were a way to get a message out, don't you think I'd have done it four hundred years ago?" He laughed humorlessly. "Even for *messages*, there's only one way in or out: the Soul Gate."

Embarrassment heated Rune's face. Of course Thoman would have sent a message if it were possible. "Then we should go to the Soul Gate. *We* could get out."

Thoman scoffed. "It won't open for the likes of us."

"Why not?"

Memory deepened Thoman's voice. "When she ordered us to leave the castle, some of us resisted. We refused to abandon her to that monster. But in the end, we had no choice. It was a fight every step of the way back to the gate, and I watched Dawnbreakers die one after another. I still don't understand how I made it."

Rune's heart softened with sympathy. "I know how that feels," he admitted. "Everyone who came in with me is dead. Rancor ripped them apart right in front of me." He hadn't known most of those men very well, but John Taylor—well, John had been the closest thing he'd had to a friend in the last two years.

"During the retreat, we saw the Nightrender fly overhead and thought she would meet us at the gate. But when we arrived, the portcullis was down. We yelled and begged them to open it, but the iron never lifted. Then rancor were on us and we had to run. By then the malice was already in us. There was no chance of the gate opening."

Rune lowered his eyes. He wanted to ask what happened after that, where the rest of Thoman's company was, but he already knew they were dead. "So you're saying the Soul Gate won't open for just anyone."

Thoman nodded. "It opens only for those with a key—or the Nightrender herself."

"What kind of key?"

"I don't know. My captain said she gave one to him—to all the captains—that would open the gate in an emergency retreat. But he died at the gate, trying to put it into the lock. We went back once. We searched everywhere, but there was nothing. It was just wasted time. Whatever the key was, it's long gone, and they won't open the Soul Gate without it. They may not even know anyone is there."

"Who is *they*?"

"The people who work the Soul Gate." Thoman sighed and looked out at the rain. "I don't know anything about them. I didn't even see them when I came in. I was looking up at the Malstop as it pulled open like curtains, a burning red sky on the far side. I was terrified—I thought I'd die here. And in a way, I have. I never considered this fate, not once: that I would be trapped here for four hundred years while everyone I knew lived and died, and all their descendants lived and died. But here I am. I don't know how you brought me back with the Nightrender's feather, or how you got it, but I do know this:

"I'm still corrupted. I'll never make it through the Soul Gate. There's no way out of the Malice. Not for me. If I'm lucky, I'll die here, and if you're smart, you'll be the one to end me."

They waited out the storm in uneasy quiet. Rune was exhausted, but he didn't dare sleep. The Ivaslander's eyes drifted shut after a while, and if he wasn't sleeping, he was doing a good job pretending.

Perhaps he truly was enjoying his first peaceful rest after four hundred years of waking nightmare.

But Rune couldn't. His gaze swung between the steady rainfall, the sleeping Ivaslander, and the feather shaft peeking out of his boot. Finally, he drew out the feather and cradled the length of it in his hands.

Even in the strange red light, dimmed by the torrent of ichor, the feather was arresting. It was perfect midnight when he held it one way, a sky of dark rainbows when he shifted it another way. Like the Nightrender, this feather hid its true beauty behind the sharp edges. But one only had to look a little deeper to see that there was more.

He traced his forefinger up the central spine, allowing himself a moment to feel the barbs, like silk and steel all at once. It seemed impossible a feather such as this should exist, that it should enable a girl to fly, but here it was, a piece of her in his hands.

Warmth filled him suddenly. The soft, sweet heat eased the sting in his face where the rancor spit had burned his skin and soothed the punctures from the trees.

Rune sneaked another glance at Thoman. Still sleeping.

"What was that?" Rune murmured, tilting the feather to inspect it again. There was no answer, of course. Feathers couldn't talk. But slowly, the hollow ache in his stomach faded, and the fog of exhaustion in his mind lifted. "Did you . . . do that?"

But again, there was no response beyond the effects on his body and mind. The longer he held the feather, the better he felt able to resist the Malice's corruption.

"Thank you." He touched the flat of the feather to his chest, just over his heart, and imagined that she was here with him, that they were huddled in this hollow together. They would sit in easy quiet, no need for words. Not when the tips of their fingers were touching. Not when he shifted his hand toward hers, and she was already reaching back. Not when the sides of their bodies were pressed together, and his arm was around her waist, and her cheek rested on his shoulder. He wasn't sure where her wings would be in all this—around them both? Tucked in?—or how he would avoid getting sliced open, but it was his imagination, so it worked.

Not-thunder rolled across the hills, vibrating through the rocks. Rune sighed. The Nightrender wasn't here, and even if she had been, he wouldn't have been brave enough to reach for her hand, let alone hold her.

Melancholy filled him. He supposed she hadn't been made for things like that anyway. Touch. Affection. People were not supposed to fall in love with her. Not even soul shards.

He didn't know what kind of wretch that made him, that he could imagine the curve of her cheek beneath his hand, or her short gasp of surprise if he dared kiss her again. Burn it, what kind of wretch was he that he *wanted* those things?

His body felt tight and achy, uncomfortable here in this shallow space with no place else to go.

Without warning, a tremendous crack of darkness opened in the sky. The yawning blackness screamed at him—terrible, tortured noises from another world. For a dreadful moment, Rune could see into the Dark Shard.

Twisting towers rose to meet a starless sky. Rancor flew and fought one another. And there was something else—something immense and crushing and devouring—

The window to the Dark Shard closed just as quickly as it had opened. The overwhelming din ceased, leaving an odd and uncomfortable quiet. Even the hiss of not-rain hitting the battered earth had lessened; the downpour was letting up.

"It's horrible, isn't it?" Thoman stared out across the Malice, his face without expression. When had he awakened? "Those cracks, I mean. What you see when you're close enough to look right into them."

Rune gave a jerky nod. "I don't know how you've survived it."

"I didn't." Thoman's voice was quiet, just under the patter and hiss of the dying storm. "You saw me. It got into me."

"Do you . . . remember everything?"

"I wish I could forget." Thoman's throat jumped when he swallowed. "I've done terrible things to stay alive. I wish I could cut out those years—centuries—and go back to the way I was before. When I believed I was a good man."

Rune turned the feather around in his fingers, wondering what the Nightrender would think. Her memories were precious to her, even the bad ones.

"It's coming back. The corruption." As the clouds parted, Thoman held his hands into the light. His skin was graying, his veins darkening.

Rune looked between Thoman and the feather, hesitating, even though he knew what he had to do. Then he forced the shaking out of his hands before he held up the feather. "I want it back as soon as you're finished."

A reverent look fell across Thoman's face as he reached for the feather.

"Careful." Rune twisted his hand so that Thoman could take it by the shaft. "The edges are sharp."

"What do I do?" Thoman gazed down at it resting across his palm, the purity of its darkness overwhelming.

"I don't know. Things just happen." Emotions swirled through Rune. Possessiveness, foremost; she had given that feather to *him*. Then jealousy that someone else could look at this piece of her the same way he did; he'd been the only one for so long.

But the people had *loved* the Nightrender in Thoman's day. Trusted her. Revered her. This man had been part of a world that Rune had always wanted to live in.

Hope drained out of Thoman's eyes as he gazed down at the feather—and then handed it back to Rune. "It won't work for me. I'm broken. Unworthy."

A sense of kinship knifed through Rune's heart. He didn't want it. Thoman was from Ivasland, a natural enemy. But the longing in his voice made Rune wonder if they weren't that different after all.

When Rune took the feather, warmth rushed into him, washing clean his mind and clearing the red haze from his thoughts. Perhaps . . .

Tentatively, Rune laid the flat of the feather against Thoman's wrist himself. Right away, the gray flesh turned a healthier shade, and the veins softened until they were just hints of blue beneath light brown. Thoman leaned back against the rock wall in relief.

"She gave it to me." Rune tucked the feather back into his boot. "That's why I have it. It was a gift."

A gift, essential to his survival here. The key to it, in fact.

He recalled the way she'd slipped the feather into his hand, the way she'd gazed at him, as though imploring him to understand something important. Vital.

Could the feather be the key? Or, perhaps, *a* key? If only the Nightrender could open the Soul Gate, didn't that mean *she* was the key? She could have given Dawnbreaker captains something as small and innocuous as a fingernail or a piece of hair, anything that fit into the lock.

Thoman wore an aching look. "She favors you. Most of us—we never got to know her. She did insist we all introduce ourselves to her. She said she always wanted to look her Dawnbreakers in the eye and know who we were, but there was nothing personal or lasting. Besides our devotion—our willingness to die for her."

"Things are different for her now." Rune peered out of their shelter. The rain had completely stopped. For now. "Do you remember the way to the Soul Gate? I want to go there."

"It won't do us much good, but yes, I can show you the way." Thoman pulled himself out of the hollow. "We need to go quickly, before the rain starts again."

Rune followed, grabbing the rancor bone on his way. "I'm ready." Suddenly, he didn't care that he couldn't get a message out. He had something better:

A way to get *himself* out.

17.

HANNE

"We are not friends! And I will not calm down!" Mae's voice was halfway to a screech. "You had me abducted from my home, hauled across two kingdoms, and then held in the maintenance room of a dungeon!"

Hanne sighed. Her personal guards had spirited the malicist up from the dungeon and into an abandoned tower, where the two of them stood alone. It was an old observatory, now packed with workbenches, cabinets, and boxes full of every material Hanne could recall from her time in Ivasland. The floor and walls were freshly scrubbed, and a lower room had been outfitted to use as sleeping quarters. It was all *intended* for Mae, but Mae was hardly in a cooperating mood.

Hanne tried again. "Allow me to expla—"

"Not to mention that you lied about your name!"

"Well, of course I lied." Hanne laughed a little, but that only served to make Mae angrier. "I wasn't trying to die. I know how Ivasland is toward foreign royalty."

"You had me taken from my home!"

"Yes." Hanne fought to keep her tone level. "But let's not obscure facts: you were being detained there. Seven men guarded you at all hours."

"And now I'll be detained *here*."

Hanne shrugged. "I will treat you better than Abagail and Baldric would ever dream. They were deciding whether or not to have you killed for your involvement with the star rebellion—and my escape. But I'll let you go once you've helped me."

"Yes, I'm sure—you'll let me go right off the edge of the roof." Mae narrowed her eyes. "You still haven't said what you want help *with*."

The image disturbed Hanne: lovely Mae splashed out on the paving stones below the tower. Certainly, Hanne's hands weren't bloodless. But she would never do that to Mae. "I would never do that to you."

"And do you think being dragged from Ivasland to Caberwill was *fun*?"

Mae pressed. "With your soldiers? I swear I saw one of them drink light-globe fluid."

"You may have. They aren't the brightest. Well, one might be brighter now."

Mae snorted. Then quickly scowled.

Hanne bit back a smile. "Anyway, the machine room wasn't *so* bad. It wasn't a cell."

"You try being surrounded by shoddy Caberwilline engineering without your tools."

"I'm sorry that you were bored. And that my soldier drank light-globe fluid in front of you. If it doesn't kill him, I'll have the cost deducted from his pay." Light globes weren't free, after all.

"Good."

Hanne made her voice gentler. "You know Abagail was going to have you killed, don't you?"

Mae bit her lip. "Perhaps."

"She *was*," Hanne insisted. "Bear and Barley"—those were the other malicists who'd worked on the mal-device—"are dead."

"*What?*"

"Heart failure and a cart accident, officially. But my sources tell me that Abagail visited with Bear after morning verses. They had tea. Later, Bear's heart stopped."

Mae pressed her palms to her own heart. "You think—?"

"I *know*."

"And Barley's cart accident?"

"He was called to the royal residence one afternoon, escorted by half a dozen men-at-arms. He should have been taken secretively, but *somehow* word got out that one of the malicists was being transported—and the star rebellion converged on his location. There *were* carts involved, but it certainly wasn't an accident."

Mae's shoulders slumped. "How could Queen Abagail do something like that?"

"Easily. You think she hasn't done things like that before? Ask anyone in Caberwill what happened to their crown prince—the one before Rune, I mean. Ask them what happened to their king." Hanne paused. "Again, the one before Rune, obviously."

"That sounds like Rune is up to something," Mae muttered.

"Rune is incapable of being *up to something.*" Hanne shook her head. Rune was a beautiful and obedient fool. And burn the Nightrender for not going to rescue him. "Abagail arranged those deaths. You know it. She was only waiting to remove you because she hoped to use you against me. But she cannot harm you here. She doesn't even know you're in Caberwill. You're safe."

"I don't *feel* safe." Mae jumped as the door creaked open.

Nadine stepped inside. "Captain Oliver just finished another sweep of the halls. The tower is secure."

"Good." Hanne turned back to Mae. "See? No one knows you're here."

"And where *is* here? What is this place?" Mae glanced around the tower room. "It's only marginally better than the machine room."

"It's an observatory," Hanne said. "It's for observing."

"Indeed." Nadine swept across the room to unhook a latch and push a section of the wall along runners. The wood rumbled as it moved, revealing a leaded-glass window. Cracks spiderwebbed across it, but the intended view was obvious.

The Malstop. Crackling blue energy crisscrossed the curved surface.

Nadine stood partially silhouetted by the pale blue glow. "If you want a view without the glass, you can go outside. There's a walkway that wraps round this room. And there's a trapdoor"—she pointed toward the ceiling—"that leads to the roof if you actually want to look at the stars. It's all yours."

Mae looked around the room again, taking in the telescopes and equipment as though seeing it with a fresh perspective. "Perhaps this isn't *such* a bad place to be trapped."

Hanne smiled. Finally, Mae was seeing reason. "You'll have a small staff to help you."

"Help me do what?" That suspicion was back in Mae's tone now, but it warred with the curiosity. That was the thing about scientists like Mae: they loved to work.

"I need you to build something for me: the same machines that you were building for Abagail. Twenty-four of them."

The observatory went quiet, save for air hissing through the cracks in the glass.

Emotions played over Mae's face, worry and fear. "If I refuse?"

"You won't." Hanne was confident.

"I agreed to make the mal-device for Queen Abagail because I hoped she would use it wisely." Mae hugged herself, her gaze sliding toward the windows. "But she made everything worse. She used my work to hurt people."

Of *course* Abagail had used the machines to hurt people. Mae had known she would. But Mae had—in the way good people sometimes did—deluded herself into believing she could control what became of her work. And she had convinced herself that the end justified the means—that everything would turn out well somehow.

"If I made them, you'd just use them against Ivasland."

"No, I wouldn't." Hanne stepped forward, urging Mae to hear the truth in her words. "I swear I would not use the machines against Ivasland. I would not break the Winterfast Accords by using malice against any other kingdom or person."

"I don't believe you."

With anyone besides Mae, Hanne would have given in and threatened her. *Make the mal-devices or else,* followed by a pointed look at the cracked windows. But Hanne wanted to convince Mae. Persuade her. She wanted her to do this willingly.

So she did what had worked with Rune: she told the truth. "When I go after Ivasland, it will be the old-fashioned way, with mortal soldiers armed with maces and bows. It will be as fair as any war ever was." She sucked in a long breath. "I will not be a queen who uses malice against my enemies. Before I went to Ivasland, I was trapped in a malsite. To everyone else, it was only a day. But to me—it was weeks. I was all alone. And I thought that I would die of old age before I was rescued."

"How did you get out?" Mae whispered.

"That's a story for when we're closer." Hanne kept her voice soft. Gentle. "But understand this: unlike Abagail, *I* know the true nature of malice. I have experienced it firsthand. I am not Abagail." She was so much better than Abagail Althelney. "I intend to use these machines to *fix* our world. I want an end to malsites and malice—and an end to *the* Malice, if such a thing is truly possible. I want to *save* Salvation, not bury it. I want *peace*, not war."

By the window, Nadine was nodding.

Mae looked between them, and at last she said, "I need to know exactly how you plan to use the machines. I don't want to be part of another Small Mountain or Silver Sun."

"I've already said you won't be." Hanne swept around to the nearest cabinet and pulled it open. "Everything is provided. Metals, chemicals, protective equipment—whatever you need."

"Why me? You could have had anyone do this."

"I could have tried. And I did. Some of my people have been working"— Hanne shut the cabinet she'd opened—"but they're not you. They don't understand the machine in the way that you do. You were my best option, and I always make sure I get the best." Hanne shifted her weight. "And I missed you. I wanted to see you again."

Mae's expression softened. "You could have sent a dove."

Hanne shrugged. "Abagail would have eaten it."

Again, Mae snorted in a surprised little laugh. "Indeed."

Hanne crossed the room and touched Mae's arm. "Will you help me?"

Mae stilled, looking at Hanne's pale fingers against her gray malicist uniform. Her voice was soft. "Aren't you married to Rune Highcrown?"

"Does that bother you?"

"A little." When Mae lifted her eyes, a small jolt of energy ran through Hanne. "I'd imagined that if I ever saw you again, we might be able to revisit our . . . discussion in the alley."

A *discussion* during which they had kissed.

"Who says we can't?" Hanne smiled. "Such discussions would have to be in private. But I'm willing. If you are."

Mae gazed at her for a long time. "Very well. I'll make your machines."

That was a huge relief. Mae had treated it like a choice, and Hanne had allowed her to feel it had been one. After all, it was (almost) voluntary, with all the help and courtesies one could wish.

"Good," Hanne said. "I want you to get started first thing tomorrow morning. For now, take a look around, enjoy your privacy, and I'll acquire anything else you need. Everyone who comes here will be in my personal employ, loyal first to me. Do you understand?"

Mae looked like she wanted to ask why this was all so very secretive, but perhaps, after working for Abagail, she was used to keeping her mouth shut. She nodded.

"I won't do anything to violate the Winterfast Accords," Hanne said again, more softly. And she wouldn't. The Winterfast Accords did not cover resetting the Malstop.

Stay the course, Tuluna whispered. **Stay true to our plans.**

I will not fail you. But the unease remained. She needed to be stronger. Humanity needed her to be stronger.

With everything settled, Hanne had her researchers brought up and introduced to Mae. "Mae will be taking over this project," Hanne said. "She is the expert when it comes to these devices, so heed her. And remember, this project is completely secret. There will be guards stationed throughout the tower to monitor progress and, of course, your discretion. There will be random searches and interviews as well. This is not because I don't trust you—"

It was absolutely because she didn't trust them.

"But because I want us to be transparent with one another. This is a matter of utmost importance, as you know."

They all nodded. And just like that, everything was going Hanne's way.

For a full two minutes.

Then Mae said, "Hanne, we're missing the most important ingredient."

"What is that?" Hanne frowned over the crowded tables and overflowing cabinets. "We should have everything."

"I don't need it just yet, but I will in the next few days."

Worry gnawed at Hanne. "What?"

"Malice."

18.

RUNE

Hunger gnawed at Rune, mostly because he *should* be hungry. He didn't remember the last time he'd eaten. Before the mal-device detonated at the camp, certainly. Had he eaten lunch that day? He'd eaten breakfast in Brink, before leaving with the army. But now he couldn't remember if he'd eaten lunch.

"What do you do for food around here?"

"I eat anything I find." Thoman glanced at him. "Plants, mostly. Insects. Rocks."

"Rocks? You liar." Rune picked up a pitted red stone and turned it over in his hands. He half expected it to sprout teeth and hiss at him, but it was just a normal rock. He tossed it to Thoman. "Look, it's lunch."

"Hilarious." Though Thoman did give the rock a healthy sniff. "Too salty."

"I suppose this isn't a question for polite company, but you're hardly polite, so: How are they coming out the other end?"

Thoman tossed the rock over his shoulder and gave Rune a dark look. "They don't come out."

Rune swallowed. "Ever?"

"Not so far."

"I'm not sure which Numen to swear to. Ulsisi? Nanror?" Those were the Numen of Pain and Mercy, respectively. "Is there a Numen of Digestion?"

"They're one of the Unknown Numina, I assume. People were probably too embarrassed to pray to them, so their name was forgotten."

"It seems like that's a Numen more people *should* pray to."

"Oh! Gardiar! The Numen of Rocks."

Rune nodded. "Good idea. But how do you word that? *'Sorry I ate so many rocks? Please let them pass smoothly'*?"

Thoman snorted. "Perfect. With a prayer like that, I'm sure I'll be fine."

They continued on, joking about rocks and trading stories about the worst things they'd ever eaten. Thoman kept winning.

If not for the fact that they were in the Malice—they were regularly reminded by the need to go around giant pools of a viscous red substance—Rune might have enjoyed it. He couldn't remember the last time conversation had been so easy with anyone, certainly not someone his age. Even with the Nightrender, a huge part of him was always just *longing*, wanting to be close to her, knowing that he shouldn't.

In a dark-humored sort of way, Thoman seemed to enjoy pointing out all the strangeness of the Malice, directing Rune's attention to a geyser that spewed molten ore, or a large patch of shadow that had once swallowed a rancor whole.

"What is the shadow?" Rune asked. "Is it a creature?"

"I think it's just a shadow. A hungry one." Thoman stared at it for a moment longer. "I considered going in there once."

He didn't have to say why.

It was impossible to tell how long it had been; the sun moved in erratic patterns across the sky. True darkness never fell. Secretly, Rune was glad for that. This place was horrible enough during the day. Nighttime would certainly be worse.

"My veins are turning black again," Thoman said after a while.

When they stopped, Rune drew the feather. A rush of warmth filled him, burning away malice trying to gain a foothold in him, too.

Thoman held out his hands, palms up, and closed his eyes while Rune used the feather. Same as before, the corruption retreated. "How much longer do you think that will work?"

"I don't know. But hopefully we'll be out of here before it runs out."

Thoman gave Rune a dubious look—like he didn't believe they could escape—but he started walking again. "What's happened since I've been gone? You said things are different for the Nightrender now."

"A lot of things are different."

"Do our kingdoms still hate each other?"

"More than ever."

Thoman gave a soft snort. "At least we're consistent."

Rune swept his gaze across the red world before him. It was still, with deep shadows and a scarlet haze. "I wish—" He hesitated. "I wish we weren't so consistent. I believe there is only one war that we must win. This one. Against the Dark Shard. I'm ashamed that I have not always acted in service of that belief." His voice caught. "When it counted, when the Nightrender asked me for help only I could provide—I let her down."

"Why?"

Rune pressed his mouth into a line. "Because I was torn between my duty to her, to the world—and to my parents and kingdom."

Thoman nodded in understanding. "My parents didn't want me to join the Dawnbreakers. They were afraid I wouldn't come back. They were right." His next words were barely audible over the crunch of their footfalls and the groan of the wind. "They're dead now."

A pang of sympathy hit Rune. The raw emotion on Thoman's face was hard to look at. It made him human. He'd had a family, once. For the first time in hundreds of years, he could grieve them.

"Did you have any siblings?" Rune asked.

"A sister." A smile lifted the corner of Thoman's mouth. "She was a pain. Always getting into my books. She was a good student. Better than I. She wanted to be a physician. I hope she succeeded."

Rune chuckled. "I have two younger sisters. I've never been close to them, but I want to fix that when I get home."

"What are their names?"

"Sanctuary and Unity."

Thoman cringed. "What were your parents thinking?"

"They couldn't help it. My mother—" Rune's voice caught. "Her name was Grace. Virtues are very fashionable these days."

"And being a Dawnbreaker? Are we still— Do people still care about us?"

Rune shook his head. "There haven't been trials in four hundred years. And the Nightrender's reputation—it's not good."

"So you hinted. Just tell me, though. What changed for her?"

Rune paused and leaned on the rancor bone for a moment. "I don't want you to think differently of her."

Thoman leveled his glare on Rune. "I deserve to know."

Well, Rune couldn't argue with that, so as they continued walking, he told Thoman about the Red Dawn.

When he was done, Thoman's brow furrowed. "If everyone was too afraid to summon her, even with the malsites festering for hundreds of years, how is she awake now? Who summoned her?"

"I did." Rune hesitated, but he'd already told Thoman so much. He might as well tell him the rest. "My fiancée had become trapped in a malsite—chased there by a rancor. I saw only one course of action that might free her and save our alliance."

"Alliance?" Thoman's expression turned guarded. "A political betrothal?"

"An alliance between Caberwill and Embria." Rune stopped moving and met Thoman's eyes, begging him to see that this wasn't personal—not against him, anyway. "Against Ivasland."

"Of course." Thoman scowled. "So after all this time, Caberwill and Embria have finally decided their mutual hatred for us should win. And what role do you play in this? How important are you?"

His heart was pounding, but it was too late to stop now. "I'm Rune Highcrown. When I married Johanne Fortuin, she was the crown princess of Embria, and I the crown prince of Caberwill."

Thoman took a step backward, paling.

"And after an Ivaslander assassin murdered my father, I became king of Caberwill. Assuming Hanne has been able to hold our thrones, I still am."

Thoman stared at Rune for several long, uncomfortable seconds. Then, without a word, he turned on his heels and continued in the direction they'd been going.

Rune's stomach dropped. He should have lied. They'd almost been friends. Almost. They'd come so close to setting aside their differences in favor of their similarities.

But Rune, simply by being who he was—*what* he was—had ruined it. Just like he ruined everything good in his life.

He took a long, aching breath. And then, when Thoman was far enough ahead, he started forward once more.

"The Soul Gate is there," Thoman said hours (or days?) later. He pointed toward the mountains rising before them. "Just between those towers."

Rune nodded stiffly.

Now that they were so close to the Malstop, he could almost see the other side: the abandoned guard towers, just suggestions of bent stone behind the crackling barrier. But the towers Thoman was pointing at were solid and straight—and they were much closer, tall and proud on the rocks. He couldn't see the tops of them. How high did they go?

"Those are the Towers of the Known and the Unknown," Thoman said. "That is where the people who open and close the Soul Gate are."

Rune didn't know anything about them. As far as he understood, no one was ever assigned there.

"I've been thinking," Thoman said, still not looking at Rune. "You said Ivasland assassinated your father. But that's not why Caberwill and Embria united against us."

"No." Rune hesitated. "Ivasland assassinated my brother, too. My elder brother, who was crown prince before me."

Thoman was quiet for a moment. His expression was pensive. "I can't imagine Embria cared about that enough to form an alliance."

"They didn't." Rune swallowed the tightness in his throat. Would talking about this ever get easier? "But Embria didn't want their own heir assassinated, if that was a tactic Ivasland was taking up. Better to protect each other."

"It's hard to imagine my king and queen employing *assassins*."

The royal Athelneys of Thoman's time had been a different family, and perhaps they'd been better people than Abagail and Baldric. But Rune doubted it.

"No, the true reason Caberwill and Embria formed the alliance was because Ivasland was breaking the Winterfast Accords." Rune had to speak plainly. Honestly. "We didn't know how, exactly. That was a closely guarded secret. But now we know that they were building machines capable of transferring malice from one location to another. Small Mountain is gone—just completely gone. A mine in Silver Sun started eating the workers. And it's how I ended up here: one of those devices was detonated where my army was making camp; it created portals to different parts of the world, including here. When I saw the Nightrender fighting the rancor king in one of them, I ran through. Some of my best men came with me. They're dead." That last word came out raw; his throat was too dry.

Everyone he cared about—they all died.

It's me, he thought for the hundredth time. *The people I care about die.* But he couldn't just stop caring about people, could he?

Thoman was staring at him, disbelief and horror written across his face. Slowly, he shook his head. "That cannot possibly be true. Ivasland would never—"

"They did." Rune's jaw clenched. "The Nightrender confirmed it."

And Hanne, he'd discovered, had played a role in helping to finish the machine's design—though she'd been coerced into it.

"I don't see how that's possible. The Ivasland I knew—"

"Is gone," Rune said. "The Red Dawn reshaped the world. Every kingdom lost its rulers. There was fighting, chaos, struggles."

"Ivasland values knowledge. Our rulers would not obscure any truth."

"No? They hid the development of the mal-devices." Rune sucked in a breath, then made his tone gentler. "I'm not trying to goad you. They're your people. Ivasland is your kingdom. I understand your loyalty. But Ivasland is not infallible. Rebel forces are gaining power in Althelney. And it's my under-standing that Embria will soon be dealing with a similar problem—if they aren't already."

It was hard to say, given he didn't know how long he'd been here.

"This is so difficult to believe," Thoman murmured. "But you arrived here somehow. Not through the Soul Gate. If you'd come through it, you wouldn't need my help to find it again."

Rune nodded.

"Which means you arrived as you say." Thoman's expression was grim. "You could be lying about the device. You clearly hate Ivasland enough... perhaps with cause. But unless Caberwill and Embria have greatly invested in education and invention, it seems unlikely they could produce anything like it."

"That stings a little," Rune admitted. "Our education chancellor works tirelessly to ensure everyone has access—"

"What I'm trying to say is: I believe you. I don't like it. But I do believe you."

It was a huge concession. Ivasland propaganda was very effective on their population. Rune had heard about the morning verses, the strict rules, and the university that was essentially a massive church to their patron Numen, Vesa the Erudite.

"If we get out, I don't know what I'll do. How can I go home when everyone I love is gone, and my kingdom has fallen so far?"

"You don't have to decide right now. First we need to escape, then get to Caberwill. I have no idea if there's still a war or not. Or of my wife's condition."

Guilt prickled him. He'd barely thought of Hanne at all. Perhaps the Nightrender had managed to find her, as Rune had suggested. Perhaps they were working together.

A terrifying possibility.

"Perhaps my knowledge—my historical knowledge—would be useful. I could help reinstate Dawnbreaker trials in all three kingdoms." Thoman pushed forward again, toward the towers. "I want to help make up for the wrongs of my country."

Rune lengthened his stride to keep up. "You aren't responsible."

Thoman shook his head. "That's not it. I want to have a place in the world again. And do some good in it."

"You'll have one," Rune promised. "If there is a world after this."

"It's really bad out there, isn't it?"

"Yes. So let's focus on reaching the Soul Gate." Rune motioned toward the mountains. "Tell me exactly what we can expect."

Thoman steeled himself before he spoke. "There's a tunnel that runs through the rocks. On either side of that tunnel, there's an iron portcullis. The Malstop runs between them."

"What about the lock?" Rune asked. "Where is that?"

"Directly in front of the actual gate. Just a few paces away. But it won't open the gate without a key."

"I can get us through," Rune said. "She favors me, remember? You said that. The gates will open for us." He couldn't bring himself to tell Thoman that the feather was the key—or, at least, that he *thought* the feather was the key. What if he was wrong?

About the feather *or* Thoman.

Unlikely as it was, he couldn't ignore the possibility that Thoman might steal the feather and try to escape without him. Or—worse—he could be a spy for Daghath Mal, "helping" Rune navigate the Malice all the way to the Soul Gate, only to take the feather and set the rancor king free.

It was unlikely, but not impossible.

After what felt like another short eternity, they came to the path that started up the mountainside—to the Soul Gate. It was wide enough for an army, but much of it had been reclaimed by scrub and brush. No army had been here to stamp down the overgrowth in hundreds of years.

As the path became steeper, a mix of stairs and switchbacks, a low thrum rose in Rune's ears like another heartbeat. It made the hairs on his arms rise, made his brain itch. He jammed his thumb into one ear and tried to rub out the noise.

"That's the Malstop," Thoman said knowingly. "Have you ever been this close to it?"

"Only once, when I was young. During a tour of the kingdom, my father took my brother and me to ruins called Alee—leftover from when the Malstop went up. But the noise didn't seem this loud."

"Perhaps the sound is different when you're inside it."

Yes, they were surrounded by it. Caught in its heavy pressure of magic.

His head was throbbing by the time they were halfway up the path, and his thinking echoed. No wonder Thoman hadn't come back here. Twice, they paused so that Rune could use the feather on them, just in case, but the low buzzing never eased.

At last, they came to the final switchback. Aside from the noise of the Malstop, the hike had been quiet, even uneventful. Rune shot Thoman a suspicious look, but the other man didn't seem to notice. His expression was measured as he gazed up at the towers—then as his hand snaked out and grabbed Rune's wrist, hard enough to bruise. He yanked both of them behind a screen of rocks.

Thoman's voice was low and urgent. "Something's wrong."

Carefully, Rune peered over the rubble. There wasn't much: a dry stretch of somewhat level path, a stone pedestal, and opposite that, a massive mountain tunnel, too dark to see into.

But there was a building, too: a squat tower made of brush, mud, and dead spiny wood. Thoman hadn't mentioned that before. Its architecture didn't match the elegant towers of the Known and Unknown, and it was set back into the rocks, not quite hidden, but not quite obvious, either. Rune judged it to be three or four floors high.

He lowered himself behind the wall again. "What is that?"

"New." Thoman's voice was so quiet that Rune had to lean in. "It looks like a watchtower. Anyone coming through the Soul Gate would be spotted immediately. One of those winged rancor could probably report to the king's castle before a Dawnbreaker army even got through the tunnel."

A shudder seized Rune. Had the Nightrender seen this tower on her way into the Malice? Or had she been so frustrated with humanity—so angry with *him*—that she hadn't noticed it?

He brushed his thumb over the end of the feather. A small spark flew out of it, white-blue and blinding.

"We must assume there are rancor in it," Rune muttered.

Thoman nodded. "They will prevent us from attempting to leave through the Soul Gate."

"How many do you think there are?"

Grunting a little, Thoman pushed himself up and twisted to look, counting under his breath. "I see three on the top floor."

Burn it all, Rune thought. "All right. Then I suppose we're going to need a distraction. How is your aim?"

19.

HANNE

"This was a bad idea," Hanne said as the carriage rolled through the mountain tunnel. Though hundreds of light globes hung along the chiseled walls, the dark still crept in, full of terrifying possibilities. After all, the Malstop had flickered recently. Globs of malice could have landed *anywhere*—including this well-trafficked tunnel. A malsite could be forming in the deepest parts of the mountain, its infection seeping through the layers of stone.

It could be on the other side of that wall, in fact.

Hanne shuddered at the thought.

"You knew this would be part of the process," Mae insisted, dressed in her work clothes.

"Of course." Hanne crossed her arms and looked at the women with her. Mae, across, and Nadine beside. Captain Oliver was there, too, for protection, but like a well-trained guard, he didn't speak unless directly addressed. The rest of their party—those working on the machines, mostly—followed behind in separate carriages. "I just didn't realize I would be required to go as well."

Nadine rested a hand on Hanne's arm. "I could have gone without you. We can always turn around."

"No!" Hanne shot Nadine a frown. "I would never send you into a malsite by yourself. We do it together, or not at all."

In spite of this unwelcome excursion to secure malice for the machines, she was pleased with the progress of the devices. Production, as far as she could tell, was going quite well. But the work *needed* malice. The nearest malsite to Brink was the one formed when the Caberwilline army had been shattered by portals—the malsite Ivasland had created with *their* machines.

It was guarded at all hours; only the highest-ranking people could gain entrance, which meant Hanne—or one of her most trusted ladies and advisers, like Nadine.

But Hanne would never let Nadine go to a malsite on her own. Partly because she couldn't bear to imagine her favorite person in a *malsite*—and partly because Nadine was still not fully in support of this project.

Oh, she followed orders, but always with that faint, disapproving frown, the suggestion of judgment.

All great queens are tested, Tuluna said.

The greater the queen, the greater the tests. Clearly.

"Are you sure you'll be able to collect malice here?" Hanne asked.

"You know I can't give you a firm answer until we get there," Mae said. "If it's bipermeable, like the ever-burning forests, then yes. But if it's more like your time slip— Oof. Sorry."

Nadine had—lightly, probably—given Mae a quick warning kick. They didn't talk about the time slip.

But Mae had a point. Malsites fit into two categories: bipermeable and unipermeable. It described the pellicle, the soap-bubble-like barrier that kept the malice contained, and whether or not a person could pass through that pellicle both ways . . . or one way. Hanne had been trapped in a unipermeable malsite. That characteristic made it impossible to collect malice for their machines. They needed a bipermeable site.

As for the portal malsite, it was unclear what type it was. Too new. And if it was the wrong type, then they'd have to seek out the nearest ever-burning forest or nightmare town.

Finally, the carriages emerged into a thinly wooded piedmont. The air was drier here, with a dusty quality that Hanne immediately associated with Ivasland, even though they were still in Caberwill. This was the less fortunate side of the kingdom, with somewhat poorer weather and fewer resources, thanks to the mountains disrupting rainstorms. They survived through rivers of snowmelt and clever irrigation.

At last, the forest gave way to a clearing—and the malsite. Yellow ribbons hung from trees, drifting in the wind. The tinkling of bells filled the air, deceptively peaceful.

Hanne's heart raced, beating painfully against her ribs. Her breath came short and fast as she caught the odors of ammonia and rot. No. She wouldn't show fear.

Oliver exited the carriage first. Along with Hanne's other personal guards, he walked the perimeter of the malsite, staying clear of the yellow ribbons. After speaking to a few men-at-arms, he returned.

"It's secure, Your Majesty. Whenever you're ready."

"I'm ready now." She didn't intend to spend any more time in this place than absolutely necessary.

One by one, Hanne, Nadine, and Mae slipped out from the carriage. Several of the soldiers watching the malsite gave Hanne strange looks, a mix of respect and curiosity and disgust. Because she was queen, she was here, and she was Embrian. In that order, she assumed.

"Get your team working," Hanne instructed Mae. "We don't have much time."

"Let's go!" Mae called to the researchers. "Weft, I want you to test the levels of ambient malice outside the yellow line, then inside—all the way up to the portals. Cable, start unloading the equipment."

"Does it have to be the autumn equinox?" Nadine asked as Mae continued away from them. "It's only a few days away, and the machines still need to be filled and placed. I don't see how we can make that deadline."

"We will. Tuluna will provide a way." Time *was* short. If only it hadn't taken so long for her people to get Mae out of Ivasland. "The equinox is not negotiable. It has to be when light and dark are equal."

"I would have done it during the summer solstice," Nadine muttered. "The longest day of the year."

"The solstice is already passed," Hanne snapped. Then she made herself softer. "Sorry. The burden of this task is getting to me. But I will be victorious."

Nadine's expression shifted from hurt to understanding all at once. "Of course. And with the Crown Council period coming up—there's also the urgency to remove Rupert and Charity from their posts and install Prudence and Victoria."

"Yes," Hanne muttered. There was so much to do. "I feel they are scheming something."

"I'm certain they're aware of your plan to replace them." Nadine motioned for Hanne to walk with her; they stayed outside the yellow line. "They're desperate to cling to power. But don't worry. Sabine has eyes on them at all hours. And Prudence's people have both Rupert and Charity under surveillance as well. So that's two spy networks watching them."

They were both very well aware that there was plenty of overlap in Sabine's and Prudence's networks, but Hanne nodded, because Nadine was trying to comfort her and she wanted Nadine to believe it was working.

"Now," Nadine went on, clearly sensing that she'd gotten Hanne into an agreeable mood, "you don't need to enjoy your time out here, but you do need to make the most of it. First, exercise a little. You've been cooped up in meetings too much."

Well, that was hardly fair—

"And you'd be wise to introduce yourself to some of these soldiers. Thank them for the work they're doing. This malsite has the potential to be an incredibly strategic tool if we use it right."

Hanne forced her eyes up to take in the malsite at last. Beyond the yellow line, the large clearing was filled with drifting spheres, all a faint green, all showing different scenes inside. A snowy mountaintop, a forest, a dark cellar.

"It's safe to walk among the spheres, Your Majesty," said one of the soldiers posted near where Hanne and Nadine were heading. The insignia on his gray uniform indicated that he was a lieutenant. "The spheres move, but not so quickly that you couldn't get away from them with a brisk stride."

"Thank you, Lieutenant." As she and Nadine drew closer, Hanne glanced at the name sewn onto the uniform. "Lieutenant Crosswind. Tell me about your work."

The handsome young man smiled. "We mostly stay out here, watching for anyone coming upon this malsite. We have posts in trees, barricades on the road, and traps set throughout the woods. No one gets through here unannounced."

"That's very good, Lieutenant Crosswind." Nadine let out one of her smiles, the kind that made people trust her implicitly. "Can you tell Her Majesty how many of these portals you've catalogued?"

Crosswind flashed a thoughtful frown toward the portals. "Roughly half. They move, so it can be difficult to keep track, but the rips on the other sides are all stable, so we've been able to leave markers. A scratch on the wall or tree, a flag in some places. Whatever the destination calls for."

"Would you show us some of the portals?" Nadine gave that smile again, and Crosswind immediately nodded.

"I'd be happy to. Your Majesty, my lady, right this way." He motioned them across the yellow line.

Hanne's heart raced back into action, hitting so hard she wasn't sure how she remained standing. More than anything, she did not want to go into the malsite. Just the thought of it filled her with hot, formless dread.

But even as her feet stayed planted on the safe side of the yellow line, Mae and her malicists were already moving into the clearing, taking measurements and making notes. Nothing happened to them. They weren't swept up into one of the portals, lost forever like foolish Rune. And they didn't disappear into another current of time.

Then Nadine was following Crosswind into the malsite, and Hanne lurched into motion.

Gripping the obsidian shard at her throat, Hanne kept up with her cousin (and her cousin's new admirer), half listening to their conversation.

"Most of the portals we've investigated lead into the wilderness," Crosswind was saying. "But we've come across a few that direct into homes or shops. Many of those have been blocked off from the other side."

"Of course," Nadine said. "If a rip appeared in my house, I'd cover it, too."

Hanne forced herself to keep up. Nadine made it look so easy, just walking around the malsite like it was an afternoon stroll. It was an act, of course; Hanne could see the tension in Nadine's shoulders, the tilt of her head. But she was fooling Crosswind and commanding attention, giving Hanne space to gather herself.

It wouldn't last long, though. Queens always drew attention. There were always eyes on Hanne.

Nearby, Mae was questioning some of the other soldiers. "The portals move in here, but they never cross outside the yellow line?"

The soldier nodded. "They simply change direction."

"Like they're bumping against something?" Eagerness shone in Mae's eyes. If she was frightened about being inside a malsite—one no one yet understood—Hanne couldn't tell.

"Yes, I suppose."

"Wonderful!" Mae bent to write something in her notebook. "That tells me that we're in a bipermeable malsite, not a collection of smaller, unipermeable malsites. This is perfect. What else have you observed about the behavior of the portals?"

As the conversations went on and Hanne walked farther into the malsite—and nothing bad happened—she let herself start to relax. If not for the reek of ammonia and rot, if not for the portals drifting in the breeze—images of their destinations shimmering inside—she could almost forget where she was.

Her hand slipped down from the obsidian shard pendant. The pendant wasn't her only obsidian today—it never was—but it was the piece that made her feel safest, seeing as how it had sawed off a rancor's head with relative ease. She had rings, brooches, and earrings. Nadine, too. All their obsidian was probably affecting Mae's readings, but as long as they were able to capture some of the malice to add it to the titanium bulbs, that was all Hanne cared about.

As Nadine and Crosswind moved ahead, Hanne began allowing herself to look deeper into the portals.

There was a hilltop, overlooking a small town with steep roofs and a gentle river running through it. The sky showed the deep blue of early morning, while here, the sun was fully risen. As Hanne walked around the sphere, she could see around the rip on the other side, where the glow of the Malstop was visible over the trees, and the sun rising behind it.

Embria. She was looking straight into Embria.

A small laugh escaped her. How novel to look at somewhere so far away, to see what was happening there in real time. She'd understood, intellectually, the strategical possibilities before, but seeing it was something different. Not only was this place incredibly useful in the war against Ivasland, but it could be valuable for trade and travel. If one ignored the fact that it was made from malice—and if one set aside the violence with which it had gotten here—it actually seemed kind of wonderful. Magical.

Head brimming with inspiration, Hanne went from portal to portal, noting the flags and stones and other markers that had been placed on the destination side. Some of the portals that led into buildings had signs nailed to the far walls, or words scratched into the wood—things like *Leave Us Alone* or *Way Is Blocked*—but those were few. Crosswind had been correct that most of the portals led outside.

"Oliver," she said, standing before one portal. The destination side was a nighttime forest, lit only by eerie, glowing wisps, and lightning strikes in the clouds above.

"Yes, Your Majesty?"

"Do you think we're seeing another continent right now?" She moved around the sphere to get a look in all directions. It was just wisp-lit forest as far as she could see, with no sign of civilization. "Could this be one of the old lands?"

"It could be," Oliver agreed. "I don't see a marker. Perhaps no one has gone through it yet. It would be dangerous, heading somewhere the time of day is so clearly different, with no sign of the Malstop."

Hanne glanced around until she spotted a sword rack. "Get one of those swords for me. And something with a flag. Oh, and a ribbon."

"Our flag or their flag?" Oliver was Embrian, after all, even if he currently resided in Caberwill.

"Either. Whichever you find first." Because she was queen of one, and future queen of the other.

A few minutes later, Oliver returned with the requested sword, a yellow ribbon, and an actual Caberwilline flag. "I couldn't find one of ours."

"It'll do." She took the sword and dug it point-first into the ground, then threaded the ribbon through the flag grommets. With the leftover length of ribbon, she fastened the flag to the sword hilt and guard, and tied the strongest knot she knew.

When she was finished, Oliver asked, "Would you like me to do it, Your Majesty?"

Hanne shook her head. "I'm queen. I should be the one."

She pried the sword from the ground beneath her and hoisted it above her head. "I, Queen Johanne Fortuin of Caberwill and Embria—and one day Ivasland, too—hereby claim this land." Then she hurled the sword into the portal.

It was a good throw. The sword flew true, in spite of not being made for this sort of thing, and the point drove into the ground on that faraway land. It stuck. And as a breeze kicked up, the flag snapped open, lit by the eerie wisps and flashes of lightning high in the sky.

"There." Hanne lifted her chin and smiled at one of her flags waving somewhere unknown. "If everywhere outside of Salvation wasn't covered in darkness"—perhaps literal darkness, she realized with some horror—"I would send someone there to explore. It would be quite the adventure. Who can say what kind of supplies they'd need? There's geography and climate to consider, food and water...."

She stared into the portal for a while longer, imagining such an expedition, imagining *she* were exploring forgotten worlds on the other side of the planet.

Of course, it could never be Hanne. A queen couldn't go about exploring when she was needed at home.

You are a conqueror, Tuluna murmured in the back of her mind. **Just because you can't explore it doesn't mean you can't go claim it, once you know if you even want it.**

Tuluna had a good point. *Perhaps one day, once I've brought peace to Salvation, I can bring peace to the rest of the world.*

She gazed deeper into the portal, imagining herself a light strong enough to burn away the darkness there.

Dawnbreaker Queen.

Yes. She liked the sound of that very much.

Then, with a bright weightlessness burning in her chest, she turned toward another portal. Everything on the far side of this one was red, deep and pulsing.

The chamber beyond was grand, with vaulted ceilings and immense gemstones set into the walls. It was the stones that cast that horrid red light, and—as Hanne stepped around to adjust her view—in that light she could see that the walls weren't brick and mortar, nor wood panels. No, the walls were made of bones.

"What is this place?" Hanne murmured. "Another land fallen to darkness?"

"It must be," Oliver agreed.

This, certainly, was more along the lines of what she'd imagined the other side of the world would look like. Ruined for humans, unable to support life in the way any mortal would recognize. But far away. Just as far as the dark woods where she'd planted her flag.

"I suppose this building is ancient, empty all these eons since the Numina left us. How incredible that the lights still glow—that the building still stands. It should have fallen ages ago."

Slowly, she stepped around the portal, peering into the ruddy gloom. It made her heart flutter faster, her breath come shorter, but she'd already broken her fear. Conquered it. She could look into this wretched realm and face it, just as she had the other.

It was, after all, so far away.

It could not hurt her.

Her view shifted as she moved about the sphere, leaving Oliver behind to study the portal from that side. But Hanne—she had to see everything about this strange place. There, in what looked to be the center of the octagonal space, stood two great thrones. Also bone, but bleached to the color of chalk.

One throne was occupied. The other, waiting.

Hanne stepped closer, trying to see who—what—lounged there. It was huge, that much she could tell from this angle. White. Winged.

Hanne blinked.

Beyond the rip, the air shimmered, shuddered, tore in two.

The occupant of the throne stood before the rip, gazing back at her with deep, bloodred eyes. Flesh like white alabaster, lined with veiny sigils. Its wings rose behind it, white-membraned.

It smiled at her, showing teeth. Row after row of yellowing, razor-sharp teeth.

Hanne screeched and leaped back, her heart a hummingbird's wing. That face, that *beast*.

Daghath Mal, the rancor king.

This wasn't a portal to a fallen land. This was a portal into the Malice, straight to the rancor king's throne. This was the portal Rune had jumped through to save his beloved Nightrender, when he'd forsaken his duties as the king of Caberwill—and his wife.

On the far side of the portal, the rancor king lifted one hand toward her. Hooked claws scraped the rip.

Hanne screamed and stumbled backward. Her vision grayed, tunneled, and the only thing she could see was that face—those claws.

At her scream, everyone came running: first, Oliver, who dashed around the edge of the portal; then Nadine and Lieutenant Crosswind; and, finally, Mae, clutching an instrument of some sort.

"Hanne!" Nadine's worried face filled her vision. "What is it? What did you see?"

Beyond Nadine, Hanne looked up into the red sphere, but from this angle, all she could see was the high ceiling beyond. There was no sign of the pale monster.

"Did you see it?" Hanne whispered. She couldn't remember falling, but she was crumpled onto the ground, her gown crushed beneath her. Her rear and elbow ached where she'd struck a rock. She couldn't stop staring at the portal.

Nadine looked over her shoulder, then shook her head. "I'm sorry. I don't."

Oliver helped Hanne back to her feet, while Lieutenant Crosswind removed his jacket and offered it to Hanne. "Your Majesty," the lieutenant said. "Perhaps you'd like to rest in our barracks."

Hanne swallowed hard as she found her balance, letting Nadine and Mae take her by the elbows. "Yes. I need to sit."

Slowly, they took her out of the malsite, beyond the yellow line. The barracks were rustic, still under construction, but they had four wooden walls and a roof, and inside, she could avoid the windows. She could avoid looking out at the malsite.

Her heart still raced. Her thoughts were ribbons of fog. She tried not to blink, because every time she did, she saw that face. She could almost feel the claws scraping down her throat and chest.

Nadine pressed a damp cloth against Hanne's forehead. Hanne hated being treated as though she were sick, but the cool cloth did feel good against her flushed skin.

"It was the rancor king," she said, once the heat had retreated. She clutched the glass of water someone had given her. "The red portal—it leads into the Malice. Into the rancor king's own castle. I saw him. Face-to-face."

Nadine looked petrified. She could barely speak. "How wretched."

"It must have been terrifying," Mae said, gentle. "But the portals are one-way. He couldn't get to you. We don't even know that he could see you."

He *had* seen her. Of that, Hanne was certain.

"Mae." Still trembling, Hanne turned to the scientist. "The malice here. Will it work?"

Mae consulted her notes, then stretched to look outside one of the windows. "Yes," she said after a moment. "Yes, Your Majesty. You'll have your malice machines—and you'll have them before your deadline. I promise."

Hanne nodded slowly, letting her gaze drop toward the glass of water in her hands. Tuluna had given her this command. Tuluna had said it was the only way to give the Malstop time to reset. They had been explicit about what Hanne needed to do in order to begin to bring the peace she had promised.

But burning worlds, the idea of those hours while the Malstop was gone. The chaos that would flood from the Malice. The bodies that would rot in the battlefields. And that beast—Daghath Mal—would be free to lay waste to Salvation.

Unless Hanne was there to stop him.

She would have to face him herself, she knew, with her shard, her crown, and an army at her back.

"I am the Dawnbreaker Queen," Hanne whispered. "I will confront the darkness. I will be radiant—and anything that does not thrive in the light will burn."

20.

NIGHTRENDER

"I want to kill something."

On the other side of the table, Draft looked up and raised an eyebrow. "Are the books being mean to you, Lady Nightrender?"

"I would never harm a *book*. I simply grow weary of them." Nightrender dragged her fingers through her hair.

"It's nearly dawn, isn't it?" Draft asked. "Perhaps it will cheer you to learn that we are having sweet rolls for breakfast today."

"I would not mind a sweet roll." Nightrender didn't need to eat much, but even she could not resist twists of warm bread with a rime of crystalized honey on top.

Draft grinned, and Nightrender was—once again—reminded of how glad she was that she had asked for the young woman to work as her assistant. In the last few days, they had been through dozens of volumes and papers on the Shattering (as understood by mortals), the Numina (again, as far as mortals were aware), and the unsettling beliefs regarding Nightrender's creation. (There'd been a sect of people who'd insisted she'd been *born*. Like a *human*. Out of someone's *body*. "But what of this alleged mother?" Draft had asked, horrified. "Didn't anyone think of those wings? That poor woman.")

Nightrender wasn't sure what she'd expected to find, as far as the weapon went. An ancient prophecy? Some kind of riddle? A journal entry from some long-dead priest, describing a mysterious artifact that must have been a Relic? But she hadn't seen anything like that, not even in the oldest of texts.

Either the mortal-authored books did not hold the answer—or the answer been burned away four hundred years ago. It seemed entirely possible that, once again, humans were the architects of their own destruction.

Draft rubbed her eyes. "What if we don't find anything?"

"The Numina foresaw a crisis of this magnitude," Nightrender said softly. "They intended for me to use the weapon. The answer to its location exists. If not here, then perhaps in the great libraries of Embria or Ivasland."

"Will you go?"

"If I must." She hoped that wasn't necessary. The temptation to fly into the Malice to rescue her soul shard might prove too much. And should the draining come upon her again—as it had many times already—she did not want more strangers to see her in that state. It was enough that Draft had noticed Nightrender removing herself to the back of the collection room.

"I want the answers to be here," Draft muttered. "I want to be the one to find them." She looked shy. "I— I don't want you to regret what you did for me."

"There is no librarian more thorough, Draft, no assistant more devoted. And that is what I will tell the grand priest, should he inquire."

Draft's cheeks were bright red. "Thank you." She stood and stretched. "I'm not used to sitting still for so long. I'll return shortly."

Despite what Draft might believe, Nightrender did understand the bodily functions that ruled mortals.

When Draft reappeared a few minutes later, her eyes were lit with news. "You'll never guess what I just heard. Queen Johanne has returned."

"I didn't realize she had gone anywhere." That was less exciting than Draft's expression had indicated. "You find the movement of royals to be compelling washroom chatter."

"Everyone does."

Perhaps this was why the Numina had not made it necessary for Nightrender to relieve herself several times a day. "I would think everyone would get the business done with as quickly as possible."

Draft dropped into her seat and leaned forward. "Listen: the queen and her most trusted ladies left in carriages yesterday morning."

A prickle of unease worked up Nightrender's neck.

"No one knows exactly where they went, but it couldn't have been very far if they're back already. I've been thinking what towns are close enough for her to visit like that. Small Mountain, but that's gone now. Though perhaps she went to look at the ruins."

"Perhaps," Nightrender agreed, though if she'd gone as some sort of memorial, she would have made a public display of it.

"I'm going to find out," Draft announced. "One of my friends knows a maid who cleans the queen's chambers. Certainly *you* must want to know what Her Majesty is doing."

Nightrender went still. She wasn't like royals who traded secrets as currency. She didn't manipulate people into owing her favors. She simply requested their help. And then requested again. And then again, because they usually hedged or avoided the first few times.

But she did need to know what Queen Johanne was doing—why she'd left Brink, how she intended to rescue Rune, and whether she had any plans that might get in Nightrender's way.

"Yes," Nightrender said. "But I want you to understand that I have no wish to compel you to tell me anything, nor do I wish for you to take any action that might bring you harm."

Draft blinked a few times, but then nodded. "I appreciate that." She leaned forward again. "From what's going around, the queen had a fright while she was away. One of the girls in the washroom said that Her Majesty's ladies-in-waiting passed her earlier and they were all saying how they would need to be *very* careful when they discussed *the journey* or *what she saw.*"

"Interesting." Queen Johanne was many things, but easily frightened was not one of them.

"She is Embrian." Draft took a book off the unread pile. "And it shows in the way she treats her servants. Still, she is the queen, so I hope she's all right. But you prefer King Rune, don't you?" Draft tilted her head. "Everyone says you and he are close."

Close. Yes. In the back of her mind, in a faraway sense, she could feel him even now. She could follow the tether that bound their souls together all the way to the Malice. And if she focused, she could feel his heart pounding, an echo of her own. His soul—a literal shard of her own.

Close. That was a word for it.

"As much as I can be with a mortal," Nightrender said at last. "All of you will one day die, but I will exist until my purpose is fulfilled; it is in my best interests to maintain some distance, when such a thing is possible."

A sad look passed across Draft's face. "That doesn't sound like an easy way to live. How will you know when your purpose is fulfilled?"

"When the darkness no longer poses a threat to Salvation, when the Dark

Shard no longer has a foothold on the laic plane, and when mortals no longer need me to defend them: only then will I reach the natural conclusion to my duty here."

"What will happen after?" Draft asked. "Will you die?"

Nightrender went quiet; she hadn't thought of it like that before. Death. Perhaps there was no reward for fulfilling the purpose for which she'd been made. "I'm unsure," she said after a moment. "But unless the Rupture can be closed and the planes mended, there will always be a need for a protector."

Fortunately, voices sounded in the hall before Draft could ask more unsettling questions. Wheels squeaked, and the scent of coffee drifted into the room.

"Sweet rolls!" Draft bounced up and hurried to meet the meal cart.

Just then, a spark shot through Nightrender. Rune was about to use the feather.

Slowly, she stood and moved to the back of the collection room, where she could stand out of sight behind the bookcases.

"Is she all right?" asked the meal girl.

"Sometimes she needs privacy," Draft whispered back. "Don't pry."

A weak smile pulled at Nightrender's mouth. Draft was a tireless protector.

Her smile faded as the prickling in the back of her head grew. It wasn't too bad—not yet—but she could feel Rune's anticipation. Something was about to happen. At least this time she was prepared for it. Usually, it was sudden, a great draining of her energy, as if he were somehow channeling her power.

Once, after it had happened, she'd heard his voice: "*Thank you.*" As though he were talking to her.

She'd also...felt something. The heat of breath on her throat. A gentle, ghostly finger trailing up her spine. It had been such a faint caress, such an intimate sensation. Perhaps it had been her imagination.

She thought about it often. No one had ever touched her in that way, nor had she ever desired it. But with Rune, she did. She wanted more.

She shouldn't, though. And if Rune was going to think of someone in his private moments, he should not think of her.

Suddenly, she heard his voice again. Somewhere inside the Malice, Rune's heart was pounding as he spoke with someone else—someone she could not hear.

"If those rancor catch us," Rune was saying, *"we're dead."*

A thousand alarms blared in Nightrender's mind. Rune was on the cusp of doing something brave and reckless, she knew. But for what reason?

"It's only three. We just need to be faster."

Three rancor. She'd seen him kill rancor in Daghath Mal's throne room, but then he'd been armed. Healthy. Ready for battle. Not trapped in the Malice for days upon days.

These rancor might kill him. Perhaps Daghath Mal would prevent that, as part of the truce, but Nightrender could not count on it—especially as his army arrived and made their agreement less and less useful.

Nightrender staggered, clutching her heart. She needed to get to him. She needed to go *now.*

She stormed from out behind the bookcases and grabbed her baldric and sword.

Draft leaped to her feet, a half-eaten sweet roll dangling from her fingers. "Lady Nightrender? What's wrong?"

"I must go." Nightrender flared her wings. She would have to fly faster than she ever had before.

"You said you couldn't—"

"Find my weapon, Draft." Nightrender tore into the hall, out into the library's central room, and pushed off the ground. She flew straight up, crashing through the skylight in an explosion of glass. Shards showered into the library, flashing in the morning light as they hit shelves and books and sprayed across the floor.

But Nightrender didn't see it. She was up, wings shedding glass as she shot through the sky—to the Soul Gate, and to Rune.

21.

RUNE

Thoman would provide the distraction, it was decided.

"Once you've drawn them away, run." Rune jerked his head. "As fast as you can. Don't stop for anything. We're both making it out."

"I'm not missing this chance," Thoman said. "Don't worry about me."

Rune almost insisted that he wasn't worried. But before the words came out, he realized they weren't true. Thoman was a good man. Not perfect. How could anyone be? But he'd been willing to put aside their differences, their ranks, their experiences—everything, so they could help each other.

"You be careful, too," Thoman added. "There could be other rancor we didn't see. Or the lock might not work anymore. Or—"

"We'll make it." A rasp caught Rune's voice. "We both will."

With a firm nod, Thoman grabbed the sling they'd fashioned with fabric cut from Rune's jacket. He already had a pocketful of rocks. And after flashing a brave smile, he vanished into the scraggly brush.

Rune waited, scanning the guard tower for movement. A rancor passed in front of a window, jerking, stuttering. Two more joined it, training their eyes on the gate.

Were they always guarding it? Or had Daghath Mal sent them here in case Rune tried to leave? Or in case the Nightrender returned?

He touched the feather to his mouth, careful not to cut himself. "I'm going to see you soon. I promise," he breathed, then slipped it back into his boot.

A scream sliced through the gloom.

And in the tower, three rancor straightened—listening.

The scream went on, an eerie, inhuman sound, and then two of the rancor threw themselves out of the tower, mushroom-gray flesh gleaming.

Leaving one behind.

Rune could see it from here. The beast was glaring toward where the others were moving in search of Thoman.

The long scream cut off. Then there was the *crack* of a stone hitting a rockface at high speed—meant to send the rancor in the wrong direction.

Still, the third rancor didn't move.

Burn it. But then, one was better than three. As long as Rune could get to the plinth that housed the gate lock, that was what mattered.

One deep breath. Then he was off, sprinting toward the plinth. He tried to keep his footfalls quiet, but rocks and pebbles crunched under his boots. Dry grass hissed in his wake. Even with the noise Thoman was causing, Rune was loud.

Hairs suddenly prickled on the back of his neck. The prey-like awareness he'd developed here sharpened. And a long, low growl reached him.

Rune abandoned stealth. He dashed for the pedestal at full speed. His heart turned to thunder in his ears.

Weight slammed into him, sending him sprawling forward.

He caught himself at the last second, turned, brought the rancor bone around to hit the creature with a *thwack*. But the rancor hardly reacted. It merely bent and ripped the bone out of Rune's hands, then snapped it in half as it screeched: "He's here!"

Its voice was a nightmare, like an avalanche tumbling toward him. Just looking at a rancor—Rune shook his head to clear it. He needed to move. To act. If he was caught now, so close to escape, the rancor king would surely drag him back to the castle where he'd be trapped forever. He'd be searched, the feather would be taken, and that would lead to his inevitable corruption. What would *that* do to the Nightrender?

Just as panic started to seize him, he remembered: *the feather.* It was still in his boot.

Rune drew the feather. Power crackled up his fingers, his arm, and into his whole body. And before he could truly think about it, he thrust the feather deep into the rancor's gut. So sharp was the tip that he hardly felt it slip into flesh. Hot energy rushed out, searing into the rancor.

Rune's breath caught in his chest.

His grip went numb.

For a moment, he saw nothing but white-blue light, heard nothing but the fire roaring through him. Then, gradually, he became aware of a separate roaring: the rancor keening.

It disengaged and threw itself backward. Rune staggered to his feet, brandishing the feather as a dagger. A sulfuric stink emanated from the rancor's wound, while black blood poured down its body, hissing when it hit the ground.

"King!" the rancor screamed. "King!" It was calling for Daghath Mal.

Rune lunged again. He sliced the black-glass feather across the beast's throat—then spun away as blood sprayed. Droplets burned Rune through his armor in seconds. Acidic gore covered his hand, but light pulsed through him, healing him.

The rancor stopped screaming and dropped to the ground. Motionless. Dead. He'd killed it.

A shout pierced the fog of his victory.

Thoman. He should have been here by now. But the sounds of rocks sliding, rancor shouting, and brush snapping made it clear that he was still alive.

With a faint, frustrated growl, Rune ran for the tower. When he reached it, he touched the Nightrender's feather to a vein of wood running through the stone. Nothing happened.

"Come on," he whispered, flicking the feather like flint against tinder. "Please. I need you."

Rune had never been one for prayer—the Numina had abandoned this world long ago, leaving the Nightrender to fight their battles while they retired to the Bright Land—so when he whispered, *"Please,"* it was for the one he knew would help. If she could.

Pale blue fire bloomed from the feather in a hot rush. Rune leaped backward just in time to avoid getting burned to death. And there it was: a perfect distraction to take the rancor off Thoman.

Rune lifted his voice over the rush of flame devouring the rancor outpost. "Let's go!"

The blaze roared, heat billowing. Though the sun was up (somewhere), the light from the fire made his vision strange. He moved away, cupping one hand over the side of his face to shield his eyes.

No Thoman. Nothing.

Rune glanced again at the plinth. The portcullis. The promise of freedom through that tunnel. There were no rancor near him. He could go.

But he would never forgive himself for leaving Thoman behind.

"Burn it." Rune started for the sounds of shouts, scuffling—where he hoped he'd find Thoman.

Just then, Thoman crashed through the underbrush. He was torn and bloody, but whole. A rancor lumbered after him, and just as it leaped for him, Thoman ducked and rolled out of the way.

Rune lunged for the beast, the feather tight in his grip. He jabbed the feather into the rancor's side, then dodged as the creature spun and set its yellow eyes on Rune.

"Soul shard," it hissed, mouth gaping open to reveal twin rows of teeth and a forked tongue. "Your death will destroy her."

"You won't kill me," Rune said. "Your king needs me."

The rancor laughed, and it was the sound of mountains crumbling. "Does he?"

Rune caught only an edge of movement before Thoman barreled into the rancor, heaving it off-balance and into the fire. Flame caught immediately, blackening it; an unearthly howl rose above the roar of fire.

"Where's the third one?" Rune asked. "Did you kill it?"

Thoman shook his head. "It disappeared!"

"Burn everything. *Run!*" Rune darted for the plinth, Thoman two steps behind him.

The distance was not far. But in the way of nightmares, Rune felt as though he moved in slow motion. His limbs were heavy. His vision tunneled. A piercing noise rang in his ears. Every footfall sounded far away.

But finally, he and Thoman stood before the plinth. The black bars of the portcullis waited mere steps from here. Beyond them, the Malstop rose—an impassable wall of shimmering energy.

This was it. Escape was imminent.

"Hurry," Thoman urged. "The key. Now."

Behind them, there was a great flap of wings, like thunder breaking again and again.

Stomach twisting, heart racing, Rune looked over his shoulder. And there he saw it: alabaster white flesh streaked with bloodred sigils.

Daghath Mal had arrived.

22.

NIGHTRENDER

She was falling.

Rushing filled her head: the pound of heartbeats, the roar of blood, the howl of wind past her ears. Air keened as it cut against the razor edges of her feathers. Though she gasped for breath, her lungs were blocks of ice as she dropped from the sky. Faster, faster, the light flowing away from her as the pulling intensified.

She kicked and clawed for height, straining her wings. But then she was spinning, tumbling head over heels, unable to tell up from down. Light streamed away from her in bright banners.

And then it stopped.

Relief filled her as she flared her wings, catching air just moments before she would have hit the trees. Strength poured back into her, and at last she was up. Back in the sky. Flying.

This was the second time since leaving the castle that she'd nearly fallen out of the sky, with so much of her power streaming toward the Malice. Whatever was happening to Rune—he was drawing her energy through the feather too much, too fast.

She *had* to get to him.

The Malstop was close. Through her tunneled vision, it was a beacon, showing her the way to her soul shard.

Nightrender careened through the air, screaming toward the Soul Gate. She couldn't fly fast enough. Her wings were leaden with exhaustion. Even her sword weighed her down.

But she kept flying, faster and faster, cutting through the sky.

Another pull. Another drop. Nightrender spiraled downward.

She spread out her wings, straining to slow her descent, but she hadn't gained enough height before. She was too close to the ground. She tucked her wings against her body as she hit trees first, their branches sharp and unforgiving, snapping as she crashed down, breaking through the canopy at alarming speed.

She slammed into the ground with a crash and shower of twigs and leaves. Dirt plumed around her as she rolled onto her hands and knees, panting as she pushed herself up.

Then she began to run. Pine boughs whipped against her face and throat, catching strands of her hair and shredding against the sharp edges of her feathers. She hardly felt it.

Forward.

One step after another.

The trail of energy was clear to follow, present even as her vision blurred and dimmed around the edges. She pushed herself, unable to stop, unable to resist the compulsion to help her soul shard.

Burn everything—

Rune's voice rose up in the back of her mind, filled with horror. In a flash, she saw what he saw: a giant, white rancor.

Daghath Mal.

23.

RUNE

Rune didn't wait. He thrust the feather into the recess.

Light bloomed from within the plinth, white and hot. Ahead of him, metal screeched. Around him, the din was incredible: the rumbling gate, the burning building, the humming Malstop, and the thunder of the rancor king's wings. Behind him, the rancor king slammed into the ground, making the earth shake.

Rune staggered, still gripping the feather as he braced himself against the plinth. "Go!" he shouted to Thoman. "Run now!"

The moment the heavy portcullis lurched off the ground, they sprinted toward the gaping hole in the mountain—a vast, dark tunnel pierced only by the distant glow of the Malstop.

"No! Where did you get that feather?" Daghath Mal flickered in the corners of Rune's vision as he pursued.

Ahead, Thoman had already ducked under the portcullis. He urged Rune faster from the other side. "Come on! You're almost here!"

The gate wasn't yet high enough for Rune to run beneath. And somehow, perhaps because he hadn't left the feather in the lock, the portcullis was no longer rising.

It was closing.

Fast.

Rune threw himself to the ground and rolled beneath the heavy black bars. Rocks dug into his spine. Something sharp cut his head. But he was through.

Except— Except his right leg felt strange. And then—

Talons dug into his ankle, squeezing hard enough that claws pierced through his boots to the skin. Warmth bloomed as blood soaked the leather.

The rancor king grasped Rune's leg on the other side of the gate. And the beast had it positioned underneath one of the bars: a metal spike lowered straight toward Rune's thigh.

On the other side of the portcullis, Daghath Mal grinned, his mouth peeling so far back that Rune could see bloodred gums. "Got you."

Panic flared inside Rune, even as Thoman moved to help—grasping the bars as though he could prevent them from lowering. Desperately, Rune thrust the feather directly into Daghath Mal's face.

It cut deep.

The rancor king roared backward, growling, spitting blood. And, most pertinently, he let go of Rune's leg.

Thoman grabbed Rune by the shoulders. They moved as one, with Rune shifting his leg clear of the bars just in time. The spike grazed the side of his thigh, slicing through his armor, before hitting the red dirt. Then, as Daghath Mal recovered, Rune was pulling his leg the rest of the way through—out of the rancor king's reach.

Daghath Mal lunged for the gate, his clawed hands squeezing the metal so hard that it bent and shrieked. Black blood ran down his face, pouring from the gash in his cheek.

"We have to run." Thoman heaved Rune to his feet. "Before he rips open the bars."

That was not a possibility Rune had considered before. But given the fury on the rancor king's bloodied face, the beast intended to try. "I will tear you into pieces," he growled. "And I will feed your remains to my army."

"Do your worst." Rune flicked the gore off the feather—straight into Daghath Mal's eyes—and started running.

He had never run so hard in his life. His legs pumped, his lungs burned with the hot, ammoniac air of the Malice. The tunnel was so long, so dark, but in the distance, the searing glow of the Malstop beckoned him. Its hum echoed throughout the tunnel, reverberating deep into Rune's bones.

And then he could hear the grinding of gears, the clatter of iron. The gate on the far side was lifting, rising just high enough that Rune and Thoman could pass through.

"Faster!" Rune shouted. "We're almost there!"

A pair of ghostly figures appeared on the other side of the Malstop, barely visible behind the bright shimmer. Rune pushed himself, willing the ground to fold beneath him, to carry him as though on a wave. Why, *why* could he not fly?

The two figures pried their fingers into the Malstop and split it open, creating a narrow pass.

"Go!" Thoman shoved Rune forward, between the ghosts.

Rune fell through the Malstop, elbow then shoulder hitting the ground as he rolled. By the time he scrambled to his feet, Thoman was through and the ghosts—whose bodies rippled in time with the pulsing hum—were running their translucent hands down the seam in the Malstop. The barrier was solid once more.

The iron portcullis rumbled closed, clanging to the ground with a deafening bang.

A faint, delirious laugh escaped Rune.

He was out. Free. His head still spun as he staggered into Thoman and embraced him.

The Ivaslander threw an arm around him. "I can't believe it. We did it."

They leaned on each other for a moment, both gasping, both wiping at the sweat pouring down their faces as they looked up at the blue sky, as they breathed in the clean, untainted air.

"I'd forgotten," Thoman rasped. "I'd forgotten how beautiful it is."

Mountains. Forests. Plains. Rune had to agree: Salvation was *so* beautiful.

"I didn't imagine this day would ever come." Thoman glanced away, but not fast enough to hide the tears shimmering in his eyes. "How can I thank you?"

"There's no need to thank me. You helped me just as much." Rune took a long breath, letting the clean air fill his lungs. His heart rate was finally slowing, his peripheral vision returning. Every part of his body hurt, especially his leg, but he was going to live. "The Malice would have killed me if you hadn't taught me how to survive it."

"We helped each other, then." Thoman sighed. "Still. You could have left while I was distracting the rancor. You didn't have to wait. You chose to help me. I won't forget it."

"What kind of man would I be if I left you to die?" Rune shook his head. "Besides, we've been through so much together. I'd say you're my friend."

"Or a brother," Thoman said with a laugh. "I never had a little brother. But if I had, I'd want him to be like you."

Rune's heart squeezed, but not in a painful way. Not in a missing-Opi kind of way. Instead, he wanted this to be true. Thoman was a good man, smart and funny, honest and caring. He was, truthfully, a lot like Opi.

No one could replace Opi. That was impossible. But this friendship—this brotherliness—could fit in the hole he'd been carrying since Opi's death.

"I'm honored you would say that," Rune rasped. "Truly."

He blinked, clearing his vision, and looked up at the words stretched across the top of the stone:

ΛFTER TΉE SΉΛTTERINÇ: WΛR.
BEFORE TΉE MENDINÇ: PEΛCE.

"What do you think that means?" he asked.

Thoman shook his head. "I suppose it's talking about *the* Shattering, when the planes broke apart."

"But the Mending? I've never heard of that."

"No? In my time, there were prophecies of the planes being mended again. But most people didn't actually believe it. How do you *fix* the world?"

"I don't know. I—" Dust stirred under a sudden gust of wind, under a wide shadow that rippled across the white flagstones. Wings.

Rune looked up; his breath caught at the sight. Great feathered wings stretched black against the blue, blue sky.

The Nightrender slammed into the ground, her sword drawn. Her hair was a windblown mess; she wore a feral expression as she marched toward the gate, wings spread wide. Fury spun off her in dark waves, like heat shimmers.

She was glorious. Fierce. A little frightening, with battle burning through her veins.

And she had come for him.

"Nightrender," he breathed.

All at once, she stopped. She stared at him. The anger evaporated from her eyes. Her wings lowered. And her sword—her precious sword—clattered to the ground.

With a breath as fine as spun silk, she whispered, "Rune."

24.

NIGHTRENDER

Rune stood before her, dressed still in the uniform he'd worn to war. His hair was shaggier, and there were cuts across his face and neck and hands. He wore no sword, but in his fist he clutched a feather—*her* feather—as though it were everything to him.

And he was alive.

So alive.

When their eyes met, his were filled with recognition, warmth, and—most of all—the look of awe he always watched her with. His mouth moved in the shape of her name: *Medella*.

Frisson swept through her as she dropped to her knees, all the breath flying out of her. Rune was *alive*. And Daghath Mal was still trapped in his cage.

She had not failed. Not yet.

As she sank the rest of the way to the ground, sagging with a heavy and aching relief, Rune closed the distance between them in half a dozen long strides. Then he knelt before her, and his hand lifted, pausing only a breath away from her cheek. She could feel the heat radiating off his skin, but uncertainty filled his eyes.

"You're here." His voice shook.

"You are my soul shard." Nightrender took in more details of his condition: the shredded clothes, the dark hollows under his eyes, the dullness of his dehydrated skin. The Malice had been hard on him, but he could recover from these injuries. Others—invisible wounds—would take a lifetime. "I will always come for you," she said softly. "I will always find you. I will always save you. If I can."

Rune's hand trembled beside her face; the tips of his fingers brushed her temple. "How did you know I needed you?"

"I heard you," she whispered.

Then all his indecision seemed to vanish, because his fingers slid into her hair, and when he gazed down at her—those brown eyes so warm and gentle and understanding—it was with a look of such intense longing that Nightrender could hardly stand to see it.

Slowly, he drew her closer until her forehead touched his collarbone and her cheek pressed against his chest. Warmth skimmed across her back as he wrapped his arms around her shoulders, and he rested his chin on the crown of her head.

"I heard you," she whispered again. And now she heard the pounding of his heart.

Never before had she been held this way, *touched* this way. The sense of being comforted, of being protected, was such a foreign thing. So caught up in her own feelings, she was slow to realize that Rune was speaking into her hair, his words fast and muffled.

"—Warmth, and I felt as though you were helping, keeping the darkness from taking over. And you were. You saved me in there, over and over. Did you know? Did you know?" His fingers curled, nails pressing against her scalp and spine.

"Nightrender." The hollow voice came from beside the gate.

She pulled away from Rune, telling herself not to pay attention to the way his hands lingered on her shoulders, her wrists. That the maintainers and a stranger by the gate had seen her on the ground like that—the shame made her flush. But she forced her face neutral as she fetched and sheathed her sword, then strode toward them with all the dignity she could summon.

The stranger was a gray-looking man, with the ragged remains of an old Dawnbreaker uniform. His skin sagged over his skull, worse by the second.

"This is Thoman," Rune said. "I— Thoman, are you all right?"

Thoman's voice hissed, like air seeping through a crack. "I'm not sure. Nightrender, I'm honored—" The man doubled over and coughed, red dust spraying out of him. "I can't—"

Oh.

Nightrender's heart wrenched as she helped the man sit on the ground. "Dawnbreaker," she said softly.

He looked up. Color drained from his eyes.

"Your long night is over. It is time to seek brighter lands." They were the words she spoke to all dying Dawnbreakers.

Thoman's mouth twitched into something between a smile and a grimace. "Thank—" He looked at Rune, who was kneeling beside him. "Brother. Never thought I'd see blue sky again. . . ."

All at once, the beat of his heart stopped and the light faded from his eyes. Skin and muscle and sinew crumbled, as though he'd died a very long time ago.

Nightrender laid him down on the ground just as the ligaments went to dust and scattered in the breeze.

"What?" Rune's face was pale as he turned to Nightrender. "What happened?"

It was Known who answered. "He was dead, King Rune. Only dark magic held him together, and when he left the Malice, it fell away."

"No." Rune shook his head. "That's not right. He just— He was—" Rune shook his head again. "No."

Nightrender laid a hand on his shoulder. "You gave him something he would never have had in the Malice: peace, at the end."

Rune's expression remained horrified as his gaze dropped to the bones of his friend. "He deserved better."

Sorrow stabbed Nightrender's heart. Rune had lost so many people—his brother, father, mother, all his guards—and here was yet another.

Unknown stepped forward. "I will take Thoman away from here."

Rune shoved his fingers into his hair. "What are you going to do with him?"

"He will rest with the other Dawnbreakers whose remains were never claimed."

"I claim him," Rune said. "He's my friend. He should come home with me."

Unknown wavered. "Is that wise?"

"Of course. I—" Rune swayed on his feet. There was something wrong with his right leg, Nightrender realized suddenly. His trousers were covered in blood, completely saturated.

"You're not well," Nightrender said. "Your wounds—"

Rune staggered, then dropped to his knees beside Thoman's bones. Tears streaked down his face, slicing through the grime. His voice was soft, weak from blood loss and exhaustion. "He's my friend."

Just as Rune slumped over, Nightrender knelt and caught him. "Take Thoman's remains somewhere safe," she said to Unknown. "Rune may claim them later, but for now, my Dawnbreaker deserves rest."

Unknown nodded.

Nightrender lifted Rune off the ground, holding his unconscious body against hers. He wasn't a small man, but she held him with ease now that her power was stable. "He needs healing," she said to Known.

The maintainer—the *Numen*, she couldn't forget—guided Nightrender into their tower, up the stairs, and into the infirmary. Together, she and Known brought Rune into the washroom, where they deposited him on a chair and wiped the worst of the grime off his face and hands—even though one still clutched her feather tightly.

"Rune." She gave him a small shake. "Wake up."

His eyes fluttered.

"We need to wash you before your injuries can be treated," she said.

Known added, "You will need to be undressed for it."

"I have nothing to hide," Rune murmured. "My leg . . ."

"We will take care of you." Nightrender found the shears and sliced away the remains of his uniform. More cuts and bruises marred his skin, but none so bad as the gash across his right thigh, and the claw marks below it. Rancor marks. Daghath Mal's marks.

Known scowled. "You will need to purify those to ensure the rancor king does not gain a hold over King Rune. I can smell the corruption forming."

"I know." Nightrender set her jaw as she cut her palm and drizzled her own blood into the wounds. Immediately, the flesh sizzled, and Rune's whole leg jerked, but he was—mostly—unconscious again.

They washed him. Dried him. Treated every injury. And finally dressed him in soft white clothes. Then Nightrender took him to a bed near the window, where she drew a fine wool blanket over him.

Known cleared their throat, yanking Nightrender's attention away from her soul shard. "Have you made progress finding the weapon?"

The weapon. Of course. "Not yet." Nightrender faced Known. All this time, they'd hidden their numinous nature from her. Unknown, too. This anger toward them was a sour feeling in her stomach, but she couldn't shake it. Instead, she spoke around it. "I will return to Brink with all haste and resume my search. If I cannot find it there, I will travel to the other kingdoms. Perhaps now that King Rune has returned, he can help."

"If you cannot find it?"

"I *will* find it." Had they always doubted her?

"Then do not delay. The Malstop won't last much longer."

"If you knew anything about the weapon—its location, for example—I would retrieve it and fly into the Malice immediately to use it." Nightrender's jaw muscles ached. "I am not delaying for my own personal amusement. I don't know where it is. Mortals don't know where it is. This weapon the Numina hid from me may be gone."

"It is not gone," Known said quietly. "Merely lost."

"The distinction hardly matters if there are no clues that lead me to my prize."

"Truly, I wish I could offer more guidance." The Numen gazed at her for a long moment. Their form rippled. "I can feel the Malstop shuddering. My partner is doing everything they can to hold it. I must join them." Then they were gone—out the door.

Nightrender scowled after them.

She had to move past this bitterness, she knew. It wasn't like her. Numina or not, Known and Unknown had helped her as long as she'd existed. And they were *here*, while all the others had gone. That counted for a lot.

Nightrender let out a long breath, then sat on the bed beside Rune. His eyes moved on the other side of his lids; he was dreaming.

"I am sorry about Thoman," she murmured.

Rune groaned in his sleep, turning his head back and forth. But when Nightrender pressed her palm against his warm cheek, he sighed and stilled.

"The rancor king has lost his leverage against me," she murmured. "I could enter the Malice now. I could kill his rancor." Perhaps she should. It would buy her more time to find the weapon. It would once again ease the pressure on the Malstop.

But Daghath Mal would expect her now that Rune was free. He would be waiting—and she was not ready to fight *him* yet.

She needed the weapon.

Rune would help. He would muster whatever was left of the Caberwilline army and turn them into Dawnbreakers. Because he *would* do that now, she was certain. He had experienced the Malice and he would not subject his people to that nightmare if he had the power to stop it.

"You're a good man." Slowly, she leaned over him and brushed a soft kiss against his forehead. But that was all. She would not—could not—force him to choose between his desire for her and his duty to his wife and unborn child. That was his duty to his kingdom, his honor.

Her own feelings—well, they did not matter.

25.

RUNE

When he awakened, the Nightrender sat beside him, her body bowed over his, her forehead resting on his shoulder, her wings tented above them.

At once, he became keenly aware of all the points of contact, from the weight on his shoulder, to the slight pressure of her palm against his chest—just over his heart. One of her wings lay across his leg. She had never touched him like this before. Not so long. Not so intimately.

It didn't mean anything, of course. It couldn't. She was simply relieved he was safe, not corrupted by the Malice. Still, he allowed himself a moment to enjoy this, to bask in the feeling of her attention, and listen to nothing but the susurrus of feathers as they breathed in time together.

Gently, her fingers curled over his heart. "I know you're awake."

"I didn't want you to move." He turned his face into the dark curtain of her hair. She smelled like lightning. Like battle. Like wind. "I missed you." The words were soft—so quiet only she could have heard him.

"I hated leaving you there." The hand over his heart tightened, and the blankets muffled her words. "But I could not think of another way to make him spare your life."

Rune combed his fingers through her hair, tucking strands behind her ear only for them to fall again. "It's all right. We did what was necessary."

She lifted herself and leaned on one arm. Dim light shone around her, bathing her face in shadows.

Beautiful. The way her mouth curved, her head tilted, and her eyes held a thousand secrets—he couldn't look anywhere else.

"You're my soul shard. I should have been more careful." When she touched his face, he stopped breathing. "I shouldn't have hidden that from you."

"I told you before: I already knew." He cupped his hand over hers, threading their fingers together. "I've felt it my whole life."

A faint smile turned up one corner of her lips.

Dear Numina—known *and* unknown—but he couldn't stop noticing her lips. That brief kiss they'd shared in the Malice—it haunted him. He wanted to do it again. Right now.

He started to lift himself onto his elbow, but pain crackled through his body and he dropped back to the bed with a groan.

The Nightrender sat up straight. "You sustained many injuries while in the Malice. Tell me how you feel."

"I feel like someone tried to saw my leg off." Suddenly, he recalled the circumstances of that injury: the portcullis, Daghath Mal, and running through the tunnel with Thoman.

Thoman.

Cold horror seized him as he remembered the way his friend had fallen apart in front of his eyes. The ghostly figure had said they were going to take his remains away.

Guilt chased the horror. He'd been thinking of kissing the Nightrender when he should have been mourning Thoman, asking after Caberwill, and wondering about Hanne. The Nightrender had already told him what a soul shard was and was not, and *regardless*, he'd already made other commitments.

He hated himself for it—for marrying someone he could never love, and for loving someone who could never love him. Not like he wanted.

He pulled in a heavy, shuddering breath, and forced away the pain of Thoman's loss, his guilt, and his longing. He pushed everything deep down, where he could deal with it later. When he was alone. When he didn't have immediate concerns to see to.

"I was supposed to tell you..." He tried not to look directly at her again. He had to clear his head. "I needed to tell you that the rancor king plans to take down the Malstop."

The Nightrender lifted an eyebrow.

"I don't know how," he admitted. "It was just—the way he said it. He seemed certain it would happen."

"The maintainers are diligent in their duties. Though he may succeed in causing another flicker, the maintainers will raise the barrier again."

The tightness in Rune's jaw eased. "Good. I just— I needed to tell you."

"I understand."

"How is Caberwill? Do I still have a kingdom?"

The Nightrender nodded. "You should return quickly if you want that to remain true. Queen Johanne faces great opposition."

He could name a hundred people who would oppose Hanne's rule, including a significant number of the Crown Council. But most immediately, it seemed likely Rupert Flight and Charity Wintersoft were causing problems. How severe those problems were only depended on how much time they'd had to work against him. "How long was I in the Malice?"

"Two weeks."

"Two weeks," he echoed. "It felt longer." He glanced toward the window, where he could just see a sliver of the Malstop. "But Hanne has held the throne?"

"At the time that I left: yes. She even demanded that I fly into the Malice to rescue you. She—" The Nightrender stood and shook out her wings. "She seems to greatly desire your return."

Another burst of guilt crashed through him. Hanne had been working on his behalf.

"What made you come? Did you do as she asked?" Rune sat up, ignoring the pain that came with every movement.

"No. I refused." The Nightrender's jaw tightened as she turned away from him. "Until I could not resist the compulsion any longer."

A *compulsion.*

That was why she'd come for him. And why she'd been so wild with rage when she landed at the Soul Gate.

The Nightrender looked over her shoulder, a cautiously light note in her voice. "Your queen offered an army in exchange for my going in to rescue you. I believe she would have delivered."

"What?" Hanne was going around offering *his* army to people? And the Nightrender declined? "I thought you loved armies."

"I do." She poured a glass of water and handed it to him. "But an army alone will no longer suffice. I need a weapon."

"A different weapon than your enormous obsidian sword?" Beloved was already the most powerful weapon he'd ever seen.

"Yes."

"And did Hanne help you with that?"

The Nightrender frowned. "No. I was forced to make other friends."

That didn't sound like her. But it seemed good.

"Much has happened in your absence." Briefly, she told him of the unlocked memory, the weapon, and her quest to find it. "It will destroy the rancor king."

"I thought you couldn't kill him. The law of conquest, right?"

"The weapon does not kill. It *unmakes*. You cannot become something that no longer exists."

"I see." At least, he thought he understood. He'd been an average student at best; some things were beyond him. But if the Nightrender believed it was the only way, he would do anything in his power to help her. "Though why was that memory locked? And what are these maintainers? How do they have any control over your memories? Doesn't that feel invasive?"

She glanced downward.

Abruptly, Rune remembered that Daghath Mal had also had access to her mind. And he'd used that connection to spy on her, to taunt her, to coerce her.

It was unfair. Cruel. Before the Red Dawn, she'd been treated with reverence, yes, but also as a weapon against the dark. Not a person. And after... even less a person. And with that very darkness seeing into her most personal thoughts. Now these *maintainers*, opening and closing the doors of her mind.

They had no right.

But he would not burden her with that now; it was clear she didn't want to talk about it.

"So why," he asked, "would the Numina build such a powerful Relic only to hide it from you?"

The Nightrender's shoulders lowered, tension falling out of her. "Those are all fair questions. Some I can answer. Others—it isn't my place."

Rune drained the water glass and put it on the nightstand.

"The maintainers are immortal, and have served this world since the Shattering, when the Rupture belched out the first rancor and the Numina drew blades against the darkness."

Shivers of unease swept through Rune. If the maintainers had been here since the Shattering—before the Malstop—then they were even older than the Nightrender. Legends whispered of other planes, moving in and out of alignment with this one.

The maintainers could be anything. From anywhere.

Still, if the Nightrender trusted them, then he would, too. "And they say this weapon will unmake Daghath Mal?" he asked.

"They believe it is the best chance for Salvation." She sat beside him, keeping several hand-widths of space between them. "If I cannot find it, I could try again to drive Daghath Mal back through the Rupture."

"That seems like a good plan...."

"No. His name is now known in Salvation."

"And rancor kings are summoned by name," Rune said, nodding. "Eventually, you'd be right back here in this position."

With fewer memories to guide her. Assuming anyone bothered to summon her.

"Indeed." Her voice turned rough. "The other option would be to embrace the law of conquest—and to immediately throw myself into the Rupture. It would be near impossible for anyone to summon me from the Dark Shard. Only you know my name."

She would become the rancor king in Daghath Mal's place? Imprison herself in the Dark Shard for eternity?

"No." Shadows pressed at the edges of Rune's vision as he grasped for her hands and squeezed. "No, you can't."

Her expression tightened, halfway between grief and fear. "I swore to protect Salvation. I would do anything—"

"And I would go with you." He met her gaze, silently begging her to see how serious he was. "I would follow you anywhere. Even into the Dark Shard."

Horror filled her eyes, and for several seconds, she stared at him, as though waiting for him to recant. When he didn't, she said, "Then we must find the weapon. It is the only way to be sure he never returns."

Woodenly, Rune nodded. "We'll find it. I swear to you."

"All right." She glanced downward. "You're squeezing my hands very tightly."

He released her immediately, drawing his hands back to his lap. "Sorry. But I meant it. While I was in the Malice, you saved me over and over. Your—" He straightened and glanced around. "The feather. Where did it go?"

The Nightrender motioned toward the nightstand. "In there. I had a difficult time prying it from your grip."

He twisted and took the long feather from the drawer. It was unbroken. Clean. Gently, he traced a finger up the spine and pressed it to his heart.

The Nightrender gave a small shiver, her eyes locked on the feather.

"Do you want it back?" He hesitated, then offered it to her. "I don't know if you can use it again."

She shook her head. "It has served its purpose."

"To get me out of the Malice?"

"Yes. I am the key. A single strand of my hair is all that is needed to open the gate."

"But a feather for me?"

"A weapon, as well as a key." Her eyes searched his. "And a link to me. You were able to channel my powers. Heal yourself. Stave off the corruption. I didn't know what was happening at first. But I understand now."

Rune turned the feather over and over, letting the light catch on the smooth barbs. It was beauty and danger all at once.

She was quiet a moment. "If you wish to keep it, you may. If not, I will burn it."

"Yes." He touched the blade of the feather to his heart. "I want to keep it." One day, if the world survived this Incursion, the Nightrender would go back to her tower, leaving him with nothing but memories of their time together. Of these feelings that ruled him. Of how much he wanted her. And, perhaps, a feather.

"Then it is yours."

He nodded. "I'm sorry. About before. When you asked for an army and it wasn't given. I should have listened when you tried to tell me how bad it would be. I should have fought harder for you, to have men join you in the Malice. I thought I knew, but I didn't truly understand what was at stake—not until now. I should have sent armies with you the moment I became king. I should never have denied you."

She smiled—pale and sad, but filled with understanding. "All that matters is what you do now."

For someone who (until recently, anyway) remembered everything, she was remarkably quick to let go of the past.

Rune tucked the feather into a pocket, then heaved himself up. His right leg twinged, but it no longer hurt like before. "We should go. We need to find your weapon." He held out a hand for her.

She took it, pulled herself up, and stood directly in front of him. "I think you will like my new friends. They all enjoy books."

Rune grinned. "How do we get home? Do the maintainers have horses somewhere?"

The Nightrender shook her head. "That would take too long. We will fly." "But I can't."

"I know." Her mouth pressed into a line. "I will carry you."

He hesitated. "With your hands?"

"No. I will carry you in my teeth, by the scruff of your neck."

He blinked and studied her serious expression. "You're joking."

"Yes."

His shoulders relaxed as he let out a faint breath of amusement. "Well, it was very funny."

"Thank you. Even though you didn't laugh."

A short, surprised chuckle burst out of him. "You won't drop me, will you?"

"I won't," she said. "But if anything happens, I'll catch you."

26.

HANNE

Hanne had barely set foot in the observatory when Mae delivered the good news. The machines would be ready by the end of the day.

"Metalsmiths worked around the clock to finish the bulbs, but they've all been cast. They only need to cool before they're installed." Mae wore a proud smile. "The filters were challenging to build, but that's taken care of. The only thing left to do, once the final assembly is complete, is deliver the machines."

"And we have a plan for that?" Hanne asked.

"Yes, of course." Mae waved Hanne over to a large table in the center of the main workroom. A map lay across it, with colored Xs marking intervals along kings' roads. "Delivery is, of course, an immense challenge, especially with the devices needing to release their loads simultaneously. I've taken the liberty of fitting them with timers, which will detonate small explosives and expel the malice in a single direction. But there are several other complicating factors."

"Such as?" Hanne gazed down at the map, at all the towers around the Malstop that would need to be climbed and evacuated.

"First of all, *where* the malice comes from could determine how long it will last in the containment bulbs. The malice in the portal site isn't quite as potent as that of the ever-burning forest, which may allow the bulbs to hold it for a little while longer."

"Isn't that good?" Hanne asked. "That will give riders longer to deliver their devices."

"It may be," Mae allowed, "but what if it isn't enough time? Should we look for other malsites to fill the devices? Sites closer to the towers?"

"They would have to be bipermeable malsites."

Mae nodded. "And those are not as common, especially since we don't know which ones the Nightrender destroyed already. The ever-burning forest near Boone has been cleansed, for example. Which is a shame, because it was relatively close to the Malstop and we know roughly how concentrated the malices was there. We could have made the calculations to time the deliveries to this tower, and this one too." She pointed to a pair of guard towers on the southeast side of the Malstop.

Hanne had never thought she would be annoyed that a malsite had been cleansed, but here she was, annoyed. If the Nightrender wanted to cleanse malsites so much, why couldn't she have started with the gravity voids? Those weren't useful to anyone.

"I see." Hanne crossed her arms. "Do we have any viable malsites, besides the portal site?"

"Potentially here." Mae pointed to a small circle on the northwestern tip of Ivasland, not very far from the border it shared with Embria. "This is a ghost town. There's a moat around it now, with a series of water mills keeping the water moving."

"Does the water prevent the dead from crossing?" Hanne asked.

"Who knows. It may be that the dead can't leave the malsite, and the fact that they stay within the moat is because the moat is outside the pellicle. Regardless, it's a challenge to get into, and the ghosts are rumored to be violent. So it would be dangerous to collect malice there."

"And we don't know how potent the malice is," Hanne said. "Unless that's been studied sometime recently?"

Mae shook her head. "No, Queen Abagail was the first to allow actual study of malice and malsites. She believed that if we were burdened with so many malsites, on top of poor climate, we should at least try to understand them."

"The three kingdoms lived around the malsites for four hundred years," Hanne said. "Studying them led only to the position we're in now—this alliance against Ivasland, the scattered army, the—" The livestock army and the siege on Solspire. But she didn't want to talk about those things right now. Mae didn't need to know *everything*. "We do need that type of study now, of course. But we're in a different place than we were even one year ago."

A flash of annoyance crossed Mae's face, but she smoothed it away quickly. "Ivasland was burdened with more malsites than Embria or Caberwill. They demolished so many of our industries, made it more difficult to farm the land...." She shook her head.

There were no maps (outside of Ivasland) that indicated that one kingdom had any more malsites than another. If such a thing was true—well, perhaps Ivasland had done something to draw more malice toward it. Malice merely flirted with time; perhaps, in the self-attracting way that malice did, it pulled itself toward a future where people were building machines to move it around.

A knot of unease twisted inside Hanne's chest, but she forced herself to breathe around it. She was doing this for the world. Yes, it would be terrible in the short term, but it was cauterizing a wound to stop the bleeding. It was pushing the arrowhead through the flesh in order to safely remove it. It was amputating a limb to prevent the infection from spreading to the heart.

It was necessary.

Horrible.

But necessary.

"So you think we might be able to use the ghost town to fill the devices going here"—she pointed to the guard tower nearest—"and perhaps here?" She slid her finger across the paper.

"Yes, I think it's worth trying, but there isn't much time. The moment the first devices are finished, we'll have to send them to the ghost town. Perhaps we'll get lucky and someone will discover that a portal lets out near there." Mae shook her head. "I wish we had more time to test and adjust our plans, though. I don't like just pushing forward."

"It must be the equinox." Tuluna had been clear on that. "What about some of these other towers?" She pointed to a handful in Embria and Caberwill.

"Ah, yes. These two"—Mae indicated a pair in Caberwill—"we can fill using the portal malsite. I believe we can use it for this one, too." She pointed to one slightly farther out. "To make that one, we'll need fresh riders stationed at each of these Xs, to carry the device along at top speed. I can coordinate with your guard captain, perhaps, to assign his best riders on his swiftest steeds. They'll simply pass it along to the next rider until the last one takes it to the tower."

"Will the machine stand being jostled like that?" It wouldn't do if the mal-device detonated before it was time.

"Every machine must be taken at top speed in order to reach their destinations before they burst," Mae said. "The best I can do is ensure they're carefully packed, to minimize vibrations."

"Hmm." Hanne was beginning to see what a logistical nightmare this was. But Tuluna had never said it would be easy to follow their word, to bring peace to the world. Tuluna had always maintained that it would be difficult and take true dedication. "And what of these towers? How will we get the devices there?"

"This is possibly my least favorite delivery," Mae said.

Given that nothing had sounded particularly straightforward so far, Hanne's chest tightened again.

"There is a portal that lets out here, and here." Mae pointed just north of a tower in Caberwill, and then one in Embria. "We'll send riders—with their packages—through the portals and they should be able to reach the towers in time."

"Well, that doesn't sound too bad. Using the portals sounds quite clever. Why don't you like this plan?"

Mae pressed her lips into a line. "I'm nervous about taking contained malice through a portal."

"What do you think might happen?"

"Perhaps nothing." Mae shrugged. "Perhaps a lot of things. Malice is unpredictable. The fact that the mal-device that detonated there created portals is a huge boon to Caberwill, but what of the one in Silver Sun? It gave the mine teeth and ate people."

To say nothing of whatever had happened in Small Mountain; no one had survived to talk about it.

"It's that unknown that makes me nervous," Mae went on. "Who's to say the malice won't adhere to itself and trap the rider inside the portal, so that he is stuck in a sort of . . . between place? If it's a place at all? Perhaps it's nothingness. Or cold. Or . . ." She shrugged again. "I don't know what it's like going through the portals, not having gone through one myself. And I haven't had the opportunity to interview anyone who has. But imagine stepping into one—and being caught like that for the rest of time. Assuming you even exist in time anymore."

A shiver ran through Hanne, and for a moment, she felt as though she was back in that time slip, staring out at the yellow ribbons as they barely moved in the breeze, staring at the wall of sunlight when night had long since fallen for her.

Trust me, Tuluna whispered. **Trust me.**

I do. Hanne had always trusted Tuluna. They had never led her astray.

"I suppose it could swallow the person carrying the mal-device, if it broke the containment bulb and the malice combined. Or turn the rider inside out. Or a thousand other things." Mae spread her hands wide. "Or it might do nothing at all, if the malice being carried is the same malice from the portal site. I don't think I'd want to try it with malice from a different malsite—at least not without a lot more information."

None of this was all that comforting to Hanne. "All right, with those risks in mind, what is our contingency plan if our rider is swallowed or trapped? Do we have enough materials for extra machines?"

Mae hesitated. "We have enough materials for two extra machines."

And there were three that might get sucked into some kind of in-between void, not to mention the two that might get vibrated into detonation, and of course the handful that might not arrive on schedule because of petty annoyances like time and space.

"Very well." Hanne crossed her arms. "What about the malice bonded with the titanium in the containment bulbs? Will those go through the portals without adverse effects?"

Mae nodded. "From what I've been able to determine, yes. While we were visiting the portal site, I had a small sample of the alloy made and sent through. They appear to have arrived on the other ends intact, and there were no visible signs of stress or corrosion on the metal. So I don't think we risk losing any machines that go through empty."

"And the malice from other sites filling these machines? Should we anticipate any negative reactions from a bulb—made with the portal site malice—being filled with malice from, for example, ghost town malice?" She was starting to sound paranoid even to herself now, but she had made a pledge to Tuluna. Nothing could go wrong. Nothing.

Mae looked uncertain. "I think it will be fine."

"You think."

Mae shrugged.

Hanne was beginning to feel deeply uncomfortable with all the non-chalant shrugging happening during this conversation.

"I simply can't say." Mae motioned toward her assistants working in other rooms of the observatory. "We needed more time to experiment and test hypotheses, but you have a firm deadline you say cannot be delayed, which means there are unknowns as we move into the final stages of this project."

"If the deadline were flexible at all," Hanne said, "I would give you the time you want. But it isn't. What I find difficult to believe is that in all your experiments in Ivasland, you never asked these kinds of questions. I thought this would be work that you'd done months ago."

"Given that we only started bonding malice to titanium when you came to us—doing these experiments months ago would have been quite impossible." Mae, infuriatingly, shrugged again.

Hanne pressed her hands on Mae's shoulders. "Stop doing that."

"Stop doing what?" Mae shrugged, even though Hanne tried to push her shoulders down.

"Stop shrugging!"

Mae did it again.

"Are you *trying* to annoy me?" Hanne's voice went higher.

Mae laughed in that adorable way she did. It was almost—*almost*—enough to make Hanne forget she was irritated.

"This isn't supposed to be a joke, Mae." But the corners of Hanne's mouth were pulling up, completely against her will.

"I'm aware." The malicist grinned. "But you've asked for the impossible. I'm delivering it. And for better or worse, we're going to discover a lot of interesting things very soon. Isn't that thrilling?"

Hanne finally allowed herself a real smile. "I suppose so. But I do need it to go well. I hope the delivery and detonation of the devices will be quite boring."

"It'll never be boring to me." Mae bounced on her toes. "I'm most eager to measure the wave of malice—its speed, the intensity, the distribution of malsites...."

"And it doesn't bother you that we're taking the entire Malstop down? On purpose?"

Mae shook her head. "It's going to go back up, as you said. It always does. Plus, the opportunity to study a planned flicker—that's not something any malicist has ever had before. We'll learn so much. And perhaps we'll be able to predict flickers in the future, to better protect people."

That was a fine plan. The more Hanne thought about it, the more she knew she'd been right to bring Mae here. Even Mae seemed to agree: Mae was grinning at her again.

Hanne found herself grinning back.

All at once, Mae leaned forward and kissed Hanne. It was sweet, filled with laughter—and then a deeper longing as Hanne kissed her back.

The way Mae held her, touching her face and shoulders and waist...it shifted something immeasurably huge inside of Hanne—a weight: a terrible loneliness she'd so successfully learned to live around that she'd forgotten it was there.

How can you be lonely? Have I not always been here for you?

That was true. But Tuluna was a being from another plane, a guardian, a mentor, a figure Hanne *worshipped*. Not someone Hanne wanted to kiss.

"Hanne," Mae whispered against her ear.

A shiver traced up Hanne's spine. No one had ever said her name like that before. "Later," Hanne said softly, "you're going to come to my rooms."

Mae drew back a fraction; her nose pressed against Hanne's. "Oh?"

Hanne tilted her face forward and kissed Mae again. "I'll have a change of clothes sent for you. So no one suspects."

"And your ladies? Won't they care?"

"Why should they?"

"I suppose they shouldn't." Mae pulled back and smiled, excitement sparkling in her eyes. "All right. Tonight, then. Whatever shall we do—" Mae tilted her head and stared over Hanne's shoulder. "What is that?"

Hanne scowled, but she wasn't going to fall for it. If Mae didn't want to visit her tonight she could have just said.

But then, some of the other workers were emerging from the other room, their eyes wide and curious as they faced the western window—the same place Mae was looking.

Hanne followed Mae's eyes, looking through the floor-to-ceiling windows, searching for whatever had caught everyone's attention.

At first, she saw nothing. Just silvered clouds drifting over the tops of mountains, and the pale Malstop in the distance. Then she spotted the dark shape growing. Black wings, bigger than any bird's, beat quickly through the sky.

The Nightrender. It had to be.

But there was something strange, like she was carrying a large, heavy object on her back. As the Nightrender drew closer, Hanne could make out legs. Arms.

The Nightrender was carrying a *person*.

166

"What is happening?" Mae breathed. "Who—"

Certainty settled itself into Hanne's chest. She knew. Of course she did. There was only one person the Nightrender would deign to *carry* through the sky like that.

"It's Rune," Hanne said. "She has King Rune."

Her position here was saved.

Hanne wasted no time. She'd left the observatory within minutes, and now she was in her dressing room, Lea twisting her hair into elaborate braids and Maris applying cosmetics to her face while Cecelia chose a dress befitting of a queen receiving her king.

"I will, of course, visit his rooms tonight." Mae would simply have to wait until after Hanne was finished with him; surely the malicist would understand that Hanne's duty to the kingdom came first.

Your feelings for her are a distraction.

Perhaps. But Hanne had never asked anything for herself—not in all the time she'd been following Tuluna's guidance. Surely she deserved this.

This is a critical time. We cannot afford for you to let your guard down.

I'm not. But her protest went unanswered. Tuluna always knew Hanne's deepest truths.

Her gaze cut to Sabine, who was, as she usually was, sitting by the window with her knitting. "Ask some of the chattier maids to draw a bath for me before I go. Ensure his rooms are arranged neatly—whatever we need to do in order to get word back to the Crown Council that we are passionately in love and there are sure to be a dozen heirs."

"Of course, Your Majesty." Sabine turned her knitting. "I will also spread word through my network. They will make certain that everyone is talking about it."

"I like your straightforward approach," Hanne said, because Nadine had told her that a critique got better results if a compliment came first, "but let's also make sure the information is spread naturally, without too much of our interference."

Just then, Nadine walked into the dressing room, a folded note in her hands. "I've just received word of the king's movements. The Nightrender took him to the temple, and he will be arriving in Honor's Keep within a half hour. Lady Shadowhand believes he is speaking with the grand priest."

That made sense. Everyone knew that Rune and Dayle Larksong were good friends.

"Surely he intends to see his wife next?" Hanne didn't like the message it sent that Rune would see anyone else first, but if she had to come second, at least it was to someone as respectable as the grand priest. That the old man was their ally (of sorts) on the Crown Council didn't hurt.

"I will do my best to ensure you are the first person he sees when he reaches the royal wing," Nadine said. "But I think you may do well to call the Crown Council to session in, say, an hour from now. They need to see that he is ready to work for the kingdom, that he is alive, fit, and dedicated to victory over Ivasland. Make sure he's on your side when it comes to the Solspire siege. Oh! And we should ensure that he sees his sisters."

"Good," Hanne said. "Arrange it all with Rune's— Wait, who takes care of Rune's schedule? Where are his guards? Doesn't he have advisers? Valets?"

Nadine bit her lip. "His people went into the portal with him. If they're not here, they're dead."

These Caberwilline kings went through men very quickly indeed. "Have Captain Oliver find someone trustworthy to reinstate Rune's personal protection."

"At once." Nadine vanished through the door again.

Lea tied off the braid. Maris finished powdering Hanne's cheeks. As quickly as possible, Hanne was dressed in a silk gown, and when she gazed into the mirror, she saw red. Red coronet, red lips, red gown. There were several shades and depths of red in the gown, from blood to ruby to rose. It invited someone to look a little longer, as did the figure-flattering cut. Her obsidian shard hung from her throat, a deadly reminder of her power.

"Dawnbreaker Queen," Maris whispered. "How the people will talk."

"Good," Hanne said once again. "Now it's time, isn't it? Take me to my king."

27.

RUNE

Flying had been a lot more terrifying than Rune had anticipated. The wind. The dizzying height. The bruises where the Nightrender's grip had remained firm the entire duration of the flight.

But true to her word, she hadn't let go of him once. Her hold had never slipped, never weakened, and every time Rune had felt the agonizing nothing beneath him, she had told him to look up—toward the mountains, across the woods, all the way to the northern plains. It had been the third most terrifying experience of his life (after facing Daghath Mal, and then facing Daghath Mal again), but it had also offered the unique opportunity to see his kingdom—his world—from a spectacular height.

From the sky, Caberwill looked so small. So fragile. This beautiful slice of Salvation could crumble apart the next time the Malstop fell. Too easily he could imagine his kingdom collapsing into the molten blood of the earth.

But now that Rune was on solid ground again, taking one of the secret pathways from the temple to the royal wing of Honor's Keep, he felt... off-balance. It seemed wrong that he should struggle to stay upright *now*, since he was a creature of the land, after all, but flying had been so...so...Well, Rune desperately wanted to do it again—and he didn't. Too wonderful. Too frightening. It was hard to know how to feel about it.

And now he was home.

He'd wanted to dive immediately into helping the Nightrender find her weapon, but Grand Priest Larksong had urged him to tend to the kingdom—and Hanne.

So here he was. Tending to the kingdom. Tending to Hanne.

When the passage let out at the sunroom, he pushed open the hidden door and slipped inside. It was empty, lit by cloud-diffused afternoon light, but for a moment, he could see echoes of his family here: his sisters, still small children, playing by the windows; his brother, a young man, studying the law with their father; and his mother, dutifully training Rune in swordplay in the background, so that he could better protect his older brother.

The vision evaporated when he noticed the large rug had been replaced. It was a similar design—the Caberwilline crest with a dragon claw clutching a crown—but this was newer, the line edges sharper. There were no thin patches from Rune's family walking the same paths for years upon years.

It was a new rug because the old one had been discarded. Because his mother had died on it. And it hadn't come clean.

He closed his eyes, swallowing back a desperate cry.

The Malice had taken so much from him. His friends. His family. Perhaps even his future.

Daghath Mal was the thief of all thieves.

Voices sounded in the hall, shattering his building grief and anger. He pushed them aside for now. He needed to be a king. A brother. A husband.

Woodenly, he stepped into the hall just as Hanne, her ladies, and her guards were exiting the queen's chambers.

Rune froze, half expecting to see his mother emerging from her rooms after. But no. Grace Highcrown was dead. Which meant...

"You're living in my mother's chambers?" The words were out before Rune could stop them.

The bustle of activity paused. One by one, ladies looked up.

"Rune!" Hanne pushed forward, her arms open to him. Red silk fluttered around her, making Rune lurch backward.

Red sky. Red dirt. Red air. He wished he could banish the color from the kingdom.

"My love." Hanne stopped before him, her tone all welcome and worry. "What's wrong?"

He shouldn't have such a strong reaction, but he couldn't help it. Every time he looked at her, he saw the Malice. He saw Daghath Mal's red sigils knifed onto his alabaster body.

Rune set his jaw. "Nothing. I'm— It's disorienting to be home."

Sympathy filled Hanne's face. "I understand exactly what that's like, returning to the real world. After I escaped the malsite, nothing felt quite real—not for a long time."

Rune's shoulders dropped a little. Strangely, Hanne was probably one of the few people in this world who might understand.

"It will get better," she was saying. "You will get used to the duality of your new life, the before and after."

Perhaps, but— "You've moved into my mother's chambers."

Hanne tilted her head. "And you've moved into your father's chambers. Rune, you're the king of Caberwill, and I'm your queen." She took a step toward him, then, after a moment, touched his arm. "There's so much we need to discuss. I never gave up hope."

Rune rubbed his temples. "I should meet with the Crown Council. I should hold court and let the people see that I've returned. And my sisters—I must visit them."

"Of course." A smile curved the edges of Hanne's mouth. "I've already arranged all of that for you. Now let's get you changed out of... What are you wearing?"

Rune tugged at the collar of the white shirt. "You said you've already arranged for the Crown Council to convene?"

Hanne nodded and stepped aside, giving him space to walk past her. "Yes. And you're probably hungry. I've taken the liberty of sending for refreshments. Later, you and I can dine in your chambers. Alone." She flashed a suggestive look.

Rune's throat tightened as he strode down the hall. He knew, of course, that *alone time* was part of his duty to the kingdom—and to Hanne—and he'd be a liar if he claimed that didn't interest him *some*. But his heart pulled in another direction.

"I wish you looked a little more excited about that," Hanne muttered.

"Sorry." And he meant it. She deserved more than he could give her. "But I've only just returned. There's already so much to do. And now..." He stopped in front of the king's chambers. His chambers.

Perhaps Hanne had been right to move him here. He was the king of Caberwill: he needed to behave like it. This was no time for humility, or for showing public grief. No, he needed to prove to the people that he could be strong enough to carry them through these challenges.

If only he felt capable of carrying anyone, let alone himself.

A guard in Caberwilline livery opened the door. Rune stepped through.

The rooms looked more or less the same as they had the last time he'd seen them, decorated in the strong, subtle style that Caberwill's kings preferred. Bloodwood wainscoting, solid wood furniture with strong lines, and paintings of mountains and battles. Busts of dead kings stood watch atop a long sideboard, while swords, maces, and other large weapons rested in display cases.

Of Rune's own belongings, his books had been moved over, stuffed into the narrow shelves that had previously held King Opus's personal treasures. Rune also found his journals, his own blankets, and a handful of other odds and ends he recognized from his old rooms. The clothes in the wardrobes, too, were his.

It didn't feel like his space, though. It felt as though he were an imposter, an intruder. These rooms would always be his father's rooms, in the way the crown prince's rooms had always felt like his brother's.

Rune sank into a chair in the bedroom.

Hanne appeared in the doorway, still in red. "Rune?"

"Tell me what's happened since I've been gone."

Hanne sat across from him. "Well, a lot. But the most important thing you should know is that I've taken care of everything. This alliance is paramount to me."

"That's good." He gathered his strength. It was time to put his crown back on, metaphorically speaking. "I've heard that you have faced a great deal of pressure. What's happened? And what have you done about it?"

"Well." Hanne pressed her mouth together. "Rupert and Charity tried to have me deposed. Because you weren't here."

Rune went cold. "But—"

"They were convinced—or wanted to be convinced—that you were dead. They were going to elevate one of your sisters."

His poor sisters. They deserved better than this. "Let me guess: Charity was going to make herself regent?"

"Indeed. But I insisted that you were alive, that you would come back." She smiled. "And here you are."

She wasn't telling him something. There was no possibility that either of those councilors would simply back off because *Hanne* said to. "What else did you do?"

She closed her eyes and sighed. "Don't be mad."

This wasn't good.

"I told them I'm pregnant."

Rune went absolutely still. His mind stopped working for a moment, too busy struggling to put those words in order. Then he rasped, "Are you?"

Hanne laughed. Actually *laughed*. "No. Not as far as I'm aware. But I had to say something, and I knew they wouldn't challenge me—for a few more months, anyway—if they believed I was carrying your heir. It was the only way."

Rune wanted to sit down, but he was already sitting down. "All right. Is there anything else I need to know about that?"

She flashed a smile of pure, manufactured innocence. "Yes. If anyone asks, we've been *passionately* in love since you came to Embria."

"I see." Rune was in a war between embarrassment and awe; it was no small thing for someone in Hanne's position to admit to such activities before the wedding—even if that admission was a fabrication.

"It was the only way to persuade them. The men might not have known how it works, but the women had questions as to how I could know so quickly, considering the wedding date. I had to tell them something."

Embarrassment won.

Rune would simply have to throw himself back into the Malice.

"We will have to make an actual effort, though." Hanne leaned forward, her voice low and urgent. "Your return has bought us more time, and I can tragically lose this fictional child if needed, but we must be cautious."

Certainly there would be people who didn't care if Rune's Embrian bride lost a child, but many would grieve yet another blow to the line of succession. And, on a more practical note, it would make the Highcrown line appear weak. That was not acceptable. "No."

Hanne's tone was gentle and firm at the same time. "Rune, as I said, I will do anything to ensure that our alliance prevails. We will be victorious, conquering not just Ivasland, but the Malice and the rancor king as well."

Rune looked up. "You know about the rancor king?"

"Yes." Hanne closed her eyes, a strange expression passing over her face. "I know all about Daghath Mal."

At the sound of Daghath Mal's name, Rune tensed. This was what the

Nightrender had feared, wasn't it? And why simply sending the rancor king back to the Dark Shard was not enough. His name was already out. Too many people knew it.

If they couldn't find the weapon, Rune had no doubt the Nightrender would choose the law of conquest: she would kill the rancor king, become the rancor king, and step into the Dark Shard.

And Rune—the only one who knew her name—would willingly follow.

But his kingdom...

Now that he was back, doubt crept in. He had responsibilities here. Family. They had to find that weapon. They *had* to.

Hanne folded her hands, then refolded them. "Rune." Strange, but he'd never seen her look nervous before. Was it real? Or an act? "How did you escape from the Malice? Did you— You must have had a key?"

Something made Rune hesitate. The look in her eye, more testing than curious? Her tone?

He felt certain the feather should remain a secret. "I don't know," he said after a beat. Because she *would* believe that he'd simply stumbled into freedom. He nodded at the big shard of obsidian that hung from her neck. "I heard what you did with that."

She touched the smooth facet. "My only regret is that I could not save your mother." Her hand dropped back to her lap. "You said you heard. Then you did not receive the letter I sent to camp before the mal-device detonated."

"The letter never reached me. I wish it had. It would have been a kinder way to learn of my mother's death."

Hanne swallowed. "How did you learn?"

"The rancor king told me. He told me how terrible it was, how violent. He told me that she suffered in the end. Is— Is that true?"

There was a war behind Hanne's eyes—truth versus comfort. He could see her weighing the benefits of both before she simply nodded.

It meant something—something good, he hoped—that she'd chosen truth.

"How do you think the rancor king knew what happened to Queen Grace?" Hanne murmured. "Can he see through lesser rancor's eyes?"

"It would not surprise me. He has done similar before."

Hanne frowned. "What do you mean?"

Rune shook his head, wishing he hadn't said anything. That was the Nightrender's secret to share or not share. Not his. "Nothing. I just... assume he can, based on what I saw in the Malice. The way rancor called to him. The way he seemed to control them. It was like they could hear him speaking."

"How revolting." Hanne's throat worked. "You know, I hate to say anything positive about Ivasland. Nothing good comes from there."

Normally, Rune would have agreed. Thoman, though... He'd been good.

"But sometimes I think Abagail had the right idea: studying malice, trying to understand it."

"How could you say that? Queen Abagail's decision has destroyed countless lives."

"But don't you think the ends can justify the means?" Urgency filled her words. "For example, if we were able to predict Malstop flickers—"

"You can't predict something inherently unpredictable."

"Or if we could take care of the malsites ourselves. Without the Nightrender's help."

Rune was already shaking his head. "Malice must be destroyed, cleansed from this plane. Only she can do what is needed."

"But she didn't. Not four hundred years ago."

"She was prevented from doing so," Rune corrected. "People—our ancestors—forced her back to sleep before she was able to finish her work."

"Because she killed people. Kings. Queens. Like us."

"Not like us." Rune looked at Hanne, revealing what he had learned from the Nightrender. "Rulers who forsook the Winterfast Accords. Rulers who called forth the rancor king."

"That's impossible."

"It isn't. They did it on a winter solstice, a day of power." In his mind, he could still see the book he and the Nightrender had looked at in the temple library, the notes scratched in the margins. "Each house burned prisoners in sacrifice. They spoke his name, not knowing the other kings spoke it, too. They drew Daghath Mal out of the Dark Shard—into our world."

Hanne's face was white, marked only by the red on her mouth and the kohl on her eyelids. "Why?"

"Because of the three-kingdoms war." Why else? It was always about the war. "They wanted to win. He promised them peace. His peace."

Her breath was shallow. "I see." She combed her fingers through her hair. "They were fools. We are better than they were, and we will make better decisions. It is *not* a violation of the Winterfast Accords merely to study—"

Rune shook his head. "No, I'm not better than anyone. And I know this: malice is the substance of evil. It is chaos, the bane of reality. No one who works with it comes away from it unaffected."

She tensed, her shoulders lifting, her eyes hardening. "Would you say that if Ivasland had used the mal-devices as a tool to *move* malice—like that time slip—away from inhabited places? Or perhaps thrown it into the sea?"

Rune imagined malice-polluted waters, the monstrosities fishermen might dredge up from the depths.

"Or," she went on, "they might have created a designated space for it. Or thrown it back into *the* Malice. Imagine if they had used the machines for something good. If we tried—"

"But they didn't use their machines to make life better for people. They used the malice as weapons."

Hanne pressed her lips together. "Many things have a terrible duality. Take steel: it can become a shield, meant to protect, or it can become a sword, meant to kill. Should our ancestors have shunned steel?"

"Metal and malice are nothing alike. One comes from our own earth. It is natural. Neutral. And the other—it is meant for only one purpose, and that is to corrupt. Our ancestors knew the difference when they created the Winterfast Accords." Rune shook his head, half in disbelief that he had to explain this to her. "We mortals should never touch malice, never let it tempt us. It cannot be used for good. And anyone who thinks otherwise is lying to themselves—as you saw firsthand in Ivasland. No doubt Queen Abagail believed she was doing the right thing."

Hanne's voice came out breathy, as if she were desperate and confused—two emotions she rarely displayed, and never together. "Do you think it's possible that *he* spoke to her? That *he* told her to make those devices?"

"It wouldn't be proper to speculate. Mankind has the capacity to make terrible choices all on our own. We can't blame him for every wrong in the world." Still, he couldn't forget what had happened to the Nightrender. He spoke slowly. "It is possible, though...for the rancor king to form a connection with someone, for him to be a dark voice whispering into their mind. I suppose..."

Hanne lurched to her feet and started for the door. "I— I need to go. You should prepare for the council meeting. I'll find you later."

Without another word, she was gone.

How strange.

Her ladies would take care of her. And she would take care of herself. She always did. But he couldn't deny she had seemed frightened, so as he heaved himself up to prepare for the council meeting, he made space for her on his list of worries. Whatever was going on with her—he would find out.

28.

HANNE

Who are you? Hanne thought. *Tell me who you are.*

You shouldn't listen to him. Annoyance roughened the voice's tone. (Hanne could no longer think of them as Tuluna. Not until she knew for sure.) **He was trapped in the Malice for so long. Do you think he escaped unscathed? He must be corrupted. He is trying to turn you against me.**

But how could Rune have known Hanne heard a voice? He couldn't. What he'd said—a dark whisper in someone's mind—hadn't been about *her*. He'd been talking about Daghath Mal's communication with his minions.

Sweat dampened her face, neck, and chest.

She was nearly to her rooms; she walked faster, eager to lock herself inside and think in private.

How can you give credit to his words?

And why are you so desperate for me to ignore him?

The voice went quiet. The space in the back of her mind where they always spoke felt...dimmer.

Behind Hanne, footfalls grew louder. Closer.

Captain Oliver and her ladies hurried to keep up. She could hear their whispers, their questions about why she'd come storming out of the king's chambers. Had there been a fight? Was the king angry with her? Was he displeased about the way she'd handled the council in his absence? Or had *he* done something wrong?

The speculation grew more intense, more detailed, until Hanne stopped and spun around. "Leave me. Go. Go *somewhere*. I don't care where. Just leave me alone."

"Your Majesty?" Cecelia tilted her head. "Please, let us assist you."

"I just need to walk and think."

"But the council—"

"I'll be there. I don't need any of you hovering over me in the meantime." Hanne started to march off again, but then she had another thought. "Send

Nadine to the sunroom. Oliver, watch the door. The rest of you—" Hanne waved them away.

Before anyone could ask further questions, Hanne lurched into the sunroom—the same room Queen Grace had died in, that Rune had emerged from not a quarter hour ago—and slammed the door after her.

"Who are you?" she asked.

There was a stirring in the back of Hanne's mind. Attention. *The voice's* attention. She'd noticed it before, but the sensation had always brought comfort. Now she couldn't ignore the suspicion that rose along with it.

I am who I've always been. Your friend. Your guide.

"Why do you really want the Malstop to come down?"

Are you doubting our work? Do you think *he* knows more about the nature of malice than I?

Hanne was doubting everything now.

Everything.

Nadine arrived shortly, closing the door behind her. "Hanne?" Her voice trembled. "They said you were upset."

Upset. That was one word for it.

Hanne faced her cousin, keeping her voice low and urgent. "Be honest with me. Don't tell me what you think I want to hear. Don't be supportive. Just *honest.*"

Nadine's eyes widened. "Very well."

She spit the questions out all at once. If she didn't, she'd never be able to ask. "Am I doing the right thing? With the mal-devices? That is, is it possible for malice to be used for good?"

Just like that, Nadine's face went blank. It was the same mask she hid behind when they played Mora's Gambit, the only expression of hers that Hanne had never learned to read.

"Well?"

If Nadine said no—if she agreed with Rune . . .

"Did King Rune say something?" Nadine asked. "Does he know?"

Hanne shook her head. "We spoke of the machines in general, but I don't think there's any way he could know about the observatory project."

Unless . . . He'd said Daghath Mal told him about his mother. Could the king from beneath have said something about the mal-devices as well? No. No, Rune didn't know. If he had, he would have confronted her about it. He was not a subtle man.

Perhaps he's learning. From you. From his time in the Malice. He's different than he used to be, isn't he?

Hanne squeezed her eyes shut. *Was* Rune different? She'd spoken with him for no more than a quarter hour. But he'd seemed...himself. Opinionated, driven, and easy to embarrass.

"What's this about?" Nadine's tone was cautious. Gentle. And she wasn't answering the question.

"You've expressed uncertainty about the observatory project before. Do you still feel that way? Do you believe that it's too dangerous to harness malice? Are we crossing a cosmic line?"

The blank expression returned. "I'm hardly a philosopher or moral authority."

"I asked you," Hanne said softly, "because I trust you most of all. I want your guidance."

I thought you trusted me most of all. The voice sounded hurt.

"That means everything," Nadine said. "Really. But there is a great deal of pressure in that trust."

Hanne firmed her mouth into a line. Nadine had never said a word about the pressure before. Had she been hiding it all this time?

Nadine looked out the window, her face lit with the warm glow of afternoon. "The Winterfast Accords were established for a reason: malice is poison. Only the Nightrender can touch it. Destroy it."

A pit opened up in Hanne's stomach. "But what if she's only trying to keep us from harnessing its power? What if she doesn't want us to become more powerful than her?"

Nadine's tone was grim. "Why are you asking these things?"

I want to know if the voice in my head is Tuluna...or someone else.

The voice was silent.

"When the Malstop comes down," Hanne said, "many people will die. The Malstop will return, of course, stronger than before, and we will go to war with the rancor king. But is it worth it?"

Say yes, Hanne wished. *Say yes.*

Yes, whispered the voice.

"I, too, want peace for Salvation," Nadine said cautiously. "If this is the way, then I am with you. Always. Even if I don't understand it."

Everything inside Hanne's head was spinning. It was so hard to think.

Tuluna had always been a friend to Hanne. They always told her what she needed to hear—even if it wasn't what she wanted. She hadn't *wanted* to marry someone just so she could murder him, but it was the only path to peace. And she didn't *want* to take down the Malstop, even for a moment, but peace *demanded* sacrifice.

Rune had said Daghath Mal offered the kings and queens of old peace. His peace. At a terrible price.

She couldn't talk around the truth. Not anymore. Not to Nadine.

Don't.

She had to.

Please. Hanne.

Cold determination settled over Hanne. The voice could scold her. Lecture her. Guilt her. But it couldn't stop her. "Nadine," Hanne said, "for years, Tuluna has guided my steps."

Her cousin gave a nod. "Of course. You have always been their most faithful—"

"No, I mean, I have heard their voice. In my head."

Nadine turned away from the windows; shadows darkened her face. "You hear a voice."

"I'm not lying."

"I know you're not." Nadine's throat worked as she studied Hanne's expression. "But how is that possible? They're in the Bright Land."

Discomfort twisted in Hanne's stomach. She'd just assumed she was special. Chosen.

Nadine moved to a chair and carefully lowered herself into it. She wore that expression again—the unreadable one. "When did this happen?"

"It started when I returned from—" Darkness. Trees. A green light. Hanne pushed past her fractured memories of that night. "When my parents took me away. When I changed. When I returned, there was Tuluna." Her words kept catching, like her mouth knew she wasn't supposed to talk about it, like it knew she'd been holding all of this inside her for nine years for a very good reason. No one would trust her if they knew she heard a voice.

Not even Nadine.

"I shouldn't have told you," Hanne whispered.

She has been critical of our work since you arrived in Brink. This will not help.

"I'm glad you did." Nadine remained sitting, her face lowered and her hands clasped tight. Her knuckles were white. "It explains so much. It explains this idea of using it for our own gain—"

"No, for the world," Hanne insisted. "I wanted to help the world."

Nadine nodded. "I know. But this voice... Is it really Tuluna?"

"That's what I don't know." The words came out thin. Pathetic. Hanne shoved her fingers into her hair; her nails dug into her scalp. "They told me they were *tenacious*. And I was alone. Scared. I thought—"

Hanne's vision was blurry, liquid, as though she'd been crying. When she wiped her face, her fingers came away wet.

"Oh, Hanne." Nadine stood and took her by the shoulders. "What is happening?"

"Just tell me the truth." Hanne's world tipped side to side. She stayed upright only because Nadine held her. "Yes or no: Are you Tuluna?"

Nadine gasped, as though suddenly realizing Hanne's voice—potentially their patron Numen—was present right now. But she didn't speak.

And neither did the voice.

"Are you Tuluna? Or"—Hanne put words to her deepest fear—"are you Daghath Mal?"

They offered no reply, but she could still feel their attention.

Panic kicked in Hanne's chest. The voice had never lied to her. Never. So if they would not answer this one question... there was only one conclusion to draw.

"I've made a terrible mistake." A shiver seized her full body. She no longer knew which plans had been hers, and which had belonged to the voice.

To *him*.

"Nadine, I need to halt the observatory project. I need to stop Mae and the others. The Malstop—"

On the far side of the room, a dark figure appeared from nowhere. It was difficult to see through the tears, but it seemed as though he carried something—a large sack, perhaps?

"Who—" But Hanne's reaction was too slow.

Hands clamped around her wrists, roughly yanking her arms behind her back. Metal bit into her skin just as she tried to fight. And when she opened her mouth to yell for Captain Oliver, a strip of cloth slipped in, muffling her voice.

"Oli—" Nadine's words were cut off, too, as another person gagged her.

How many were there? Where had they come from? Oliver was supposed to be watching the door, so how had these men gotten into the sunroom?

Even as the questions swirled through Hanne's mind, a burlap sack fell over her head and everything went dark.

29.

RUNE

If the Crown Council was happy to see him, it was only because he wasn't Hanne.

There were exceptions, however: Dayle Larksong smiled when Rune entered the chamber, and his sisters leaped out of their chairs, escaped their governesses, and threw their arms around him.

"Rune!" Sanctuary squeezed him.

"You're back." Unity's face was buried against his ribs, so her words were muffled, but he caught them well enough.

Rune awkwardly hugged them back. When was the last time they'd offered this kind of affection to him? Not in years. They'd been close with Queen Grace, but now ... Now they were all orphans.

Rune hugged his sisters tighter. "I missed you," he rasped. "I'm sorry I was gone."

Unity looked up at him. She didn't say anything, but the uncertainty was clear in her eyes—gray, like their mother's.

"Some of them said you were dead." Sanctuary pulled Rune lower so she could whisper in his ear. "They wanted you to be dead. Duchess Wintersoft and Earl Flight. Hanne is removing them from the council."

Dear Numina, known and unknown. Hanne had been making changes to the Crown Council? It wasn't anything Rune hadn't advocated for before, but Hanne was playing with fire here. Rupert and Charity were bad enough when they worked against one another. When they were on the same side ...

"Thank you." As their governesses hurried toward them, Rune gave his sisters another squeeze each. "That's helpful to know." Then the older women drew the princesses back to the other side of the room, to the little writing desks placed there. "What's this?" he asked.

"Hanne"—Sanctuary winced—"*Queen Johanne*, I mean, told us to observe council meetings. She said we should learn, whether or not either of us ever rule."

"She's right." Perhaps it had been politically useful for Hanne to insist the princesses join the council meetings, but it had also been practical. Right now, Sanctuary was the heir, with Unity just behind.

"Your Majesty," Grand General Emberwish said, "it's so good to see you alive and well. After the ambush, I admit, I feared the worst. Now that you've returned, I'll recall the troops searching for you."

"Word of your return has already spread," said Swan Brightvale, the merchant chancellor. "I've heard that several of the noble houses are planning celebrations in your honor. My Brink merchants are preparing to work through the night to make these celebrations memorable, many of them public. If you'd like to attend any of them, please let me know."

Rune nodded as graciously as he could. "My priority is the kingdom."

"Of course," Chancellor Brightvale said. "Obviously. But it might do the kingdom good to see you."

"I'll think about it." This was a little uncomfortable. The council had never expressed much support of him—next to none, in fact—so their politeness was unsettling.

Rune let his gaze roam over the chamber. There were more guards than usual—mostly near his sisters—and the secretaries all looked tired. But aside from Hanne, who was clearly taking her time getting here, there was only one person missing.

"Where is Charity?" he asked.

"I believe she had an errand to run." Grand Physician Asheater gazed at Rune. "And I would like to see you at your earliest convenience. You may be the king of Caberwill, but you're still my patient, and I want to make sure you're healthy."

"Of course. But first . . ." Rune faced the door just as a soft knock sounded. Though he hadn't known the Nightrender meant to join this meeting, he wasn't surprised to see her stride into the council chambers. He'd felt her nearness like heat.

Everyone else tensed, their shoulders stiffening. Some rose from their seats, while others checked for weapons. The princesses' guards stepped in front of them. The Nightrender's jaw tightened, but that was the only indication that their reaction bothered her.

"Welcome, Lady Nightrender." Rune smiled at her and offered a chair next to him. "Please, join us."

"Thank you." She moved to the chair but didn't sit, instead nodding toward Dayle Larksong. "The grand priest informed me of this meeting. I would like to hear King Rune's account of his time in the Malice. Pretend I'm not here."

Rune released a faint snort. No one—no matter whether they loved her or hated her—could ignore the Nightrender.

When she finally sat in the offered chair, the entire room went silent. Everyone watched her. At first, Rune assumed it was because they'd never seen her sitting before. Then he realized what he'd done: he'd given her the queen's chair.

Typically, the queen sat across from the king, but someone had moved the chair since that side of the room was crowded with extra secretaries, security, and the princesses. It hadn't even occurred to Rune that he might be making yet another blunder.

If Hanne actually showed up, she'd be furious.

It was too late to change anything, so Rune forced himself to face the council and give his account of going through the portal sphere, the battle in the throne room, and his imprisonment in the bone castle. Finally, he described his trek across the Malice before escaping through the Soul Gate.

And losing Thoman.

The only things he didn't tell them were the Nightrender's secrets: their connection, Daghath Mal's presence in her mind, and the feather.

The Nightrender spoke softly, but everyone heard. "Salvation is in the most danger I have ever seen."

Grand Priest Larksong's eyes were haunted as he gripped the tiny bottle of crushed obsidian he wore. "And this rancor king—he intends to take Salvation by destroying the Malstop?"

"Can he do that?" Stella tilted her head. "I know sometimes it appears weaker, but even when it flickers, it always comes back."

"That's true," Noir said. "And if the rancor king has been here for four hundred years, why not assume there won't be another four hundred years before he acts against us? We can't live in fear."

"He already has acted against you." The Nightrender stood, letting her gaze travel across the council room. "Recall Queen Grace. That rancor was *sent*."

People gasped. Sanctuary and Unity made small noises of despair. And the chamber went heavy with fear. Rune closed his eyes, breathing through the reminder of his mother's death.

The Nightrender's tone softened as she addressed Sanctuary and Unity. "Your Highnesses, my condolences." Then she looked at Rune. "And you as well."

He forced a nod. "You're right. The rancor king has already moved on Caberwill, perhaps in more ways than we know, and with more help than we understand." He hadn't forgotten the bag of rancor-summoning materials the Nightrender had found weeks ago.

"Dawnbreakers are needed," the Nightrender said. "Warriors who will fight rancor at my side."

"The entire army of Caberwill won't be enough," Tide said, "and by all accounts the army of Embria no longer exists. As far as Ivasland—they have a standing army, albeit a small one, but they'll be busy trying to quell the riots in Athelney."

"Then it will have to be more than armies," the Nightrender said. "It will have to be nobles and commoners alike, everyone who can fight. Ivasland's machines of war will be needed, as well as every Caberwilline blacksmith and every Embrian tactician."

"That will stop a rancor king?" Noir leaned her elbows on the table.

"No. It will allow the Malstop to stabilize through the purging of rancor," the Nightrender said. "I will stop the rancor king. Unfortunately, the Rupture will remain. It will continue admitting rancor to this world until the Dark Shard passes out of alignment with the laic plane."

"Surely there must be a way to close the Rupture for good," Lelia said.

"Evil has always existed in this world," the Nightrender said. "Even before the Shattering, it was here."

"Why should we trust you?" Rupert asked. "You are responsible for the Red Dawn. And since your return, we've lost both king and queen."

Her stare was withering. "I cannot imagine an information chancellor without judgment is very useful."

Rupert opened his mouth to speak, but Rune didn't give him a chance. He stood and motioned toward the door. "Rupert Flight, you are dismissed."

Silence. Questioning glances. Someone cleared her throat.

Then Rupert asked, "From this meeting?"

"From this council." Rune's heart was pounding, but he squared his shoulders and steadied his voice. "The end of the council period is approaching. As I'm sure you must anticipate, I will be replacing you for the next term. You might as well leave now."

The man's face gave nothing away, but at last he nodded and left the room. His assistants (and spies) went with him.

"That was bold," Swan muttered. "He will retaliate."

Rune turned to the grand general. "Have Flight and his people monitored."

"Of course, Your Majesty." Tide nodded at one of his men nearby, and the man quickly went out the door.

"Now." Rune addressed the council—what was left of it—once again. "We will assist the Nightrender. We will give her men to fight, but we will also have a great need for tradesmen of every skill. I will guarantee you whatever resources you require. The council will not vote on this matter: I am making a unilateral decision as king."

Uncomfortable quiet settled on the room. This was, Rune realized, a risk. They might declare him unfit due to his time in the Malice.

Dayle pushed to his feet. "For the record, Your Majesty, I would have voted with you."

"As would I." Tide stood, too.

Then, one by one, the rest of the council rose and bowed. His sisters, the secretaries, and everyone else—aside from the Nightrender—genuflected.

Rune's heart felt huge—too huge for the cage of his ribs. But somehow, he thanked them for their faith in him. Somehow, he gave specific orders to specific members. And somehow, he arranged for dinner with his sisters, new personal guards for himself, and a full report of everything that had happened in the last two weeks.

When he was finished, he stepped away from the table and found the Nightrender waiting by the door, watching him with a faint, nearly undetectable smile. "Tell me what you'll do now," she said as they left the council chamber together.

Rune sighed. He needed to find Hanne. It seemed impossible that she would miss an opportunity to reestablish herself as queen in front of the council. And he needed to find a way to fix his blunder of having the Nightrender sit in the queen's chair—a gaffe she didn't seem to realize he'd made. Either way, it was embarrassing. For a lot of reasons.

But first . . .

"The weapon." He'd promised he would do everything in his power to help her, and he meant it.

30.
NIGHTRENDER

The collection room went silent as Nightrender and Rune entered. Everything had been cleaned since she'd gone storming out, and she'd already made her apologies to Draft and the other librarians. But even though they were aware the king had returned to Caberwill, they clearly hadn't expected him to turn up *here*.

Still, everyone stood and bowed, until Rune said, "Please, sit. I don't mean to interrupt. I just wanted to see what progress you've made. The Nightrender has told me how diligently everyone has been working."

He wore an easy smile, one she knew was a mask. But it cut the tension from the room, allowing the librarians to introduce themselves one by one. Within minutes, they were all discussing the best books they'd read, including Rune.

He was a good man. A kind man. Gentle and vulnerable, but capable of standing against the unforgiving night of the Dark Shard. And the way he'd kissed her back in the throne room— The way he'd held her outside the Soul Gate—

She was not *meant* for wanting someone.

She shook her head. This was not the time for examining emotions. For her, that time was never. Instead, she picked up a new stack of notes her assistants had made.

On the third page down, there was a sketch of a winged figure. It looked a little like her, if she squinted the right way. Rail thin, wings outstretched. The artist had given her only a single leg.

She held up the paper. "Tell me which one of you drew this."

The librarians looked at one another. Rune tilted his head.

"And tell me why," Nightrender added. It was concerning that any of her assistants were drawing her—and drawing her so poorly. If they were going to add their, ah, artwork to the pile of very important notes, they could at least practice first.

"I saw it in a few different books," Draft said. "I thought it was interesting. It sort of looks like you."

Nightrender frowned. "This isn't your original composition, then."

"No!" Draft sat back, blushing furiously. "Did you think—? I'm really a much better artist than that. Here." Draft pulled a slim volume from a shelf, one with the Nightrender's sigil embossed onto the cover, stamped with carefully preserved foil. "This is why I copied it." She flipped through the pages until she found the one she wanted.

The sketch was smaller than Nightrender expected, taking up only the lower left quarter of the page. As for the accompanying text, it simply read: *A weapon, meant for destroying.*

Her hopes fell. She had thought—just for an instant—that a mention of *a* weapon would be *the* weapon. But it had just been about her. The woman-shaped weapon.

She had always thought of herself that way, true. But it was difficult to see this evidence that mortals also viewed her as nothing more than a blade to slice through darkness.

Rune was staring at the copy Draft had made, his frown thoughtful. "Draft," he asked, "have you ever been to the Nightrender's tower?"

"No."

"Tell me what you're thinking," Nightrender said to Rune.

"I've seen this before." Rune traced his forefinger along the drawing in the book. "Strange."

"You have?" Draft's whole face flushed. "I mean, you have, Your Majesty?"

"Everyone has always assumed this was you." A light filled Rune's eyes—hope. "But what if it isn't?"

Nightrender drew back, indignant. "Tell me who else you think it would be. Tell me if you know other winged warriors."

Rune laughed. "Come with me. I need to show you something."

"It's dark in here," Draft commented as they wound their way up the narrow stairs to Nightrender's quarters. The poor girl looked miserable. "And dirty. Does anyone clean in here?"

Nightrender had no trouble seeing through the gloom, but she lit a spark of numinous fire, letting it burn on her fingertip. Immediately, the cobwebs and layers of dust were even more obvious. "No."

Draft made a noise of deep discomfort, the kind only a person who prided herself on spotlessness could produce.

At the top of the stairs, Rune pushed open the door to Nightrender's room, and Nightrender let the light fade away. He went straight to the summoning shrine.

Though it was a Relic, created by the Numina themselves, it didn't look like anything special. To the casual observer, it was only a large stone that rose as high as Rune's waist. .

"Your room is tidy," Draft said proudly, as if that was Nightrender's doing.

Nightrender followed Rune to the shrine, watching as he traced his fingers across the stone. "Tell me what you're thinking," she said.

"Look at this." Rune scooted to one side. "What do you see?"

Still uncertain, Nightrender knelt in front of the shrine to view it as Rune did. "It is the same drawing from that book." She considered what that meant. "The stone must be difficult to draw on, so I can forgive the fact that it looks nothing like me...."

"Except I don't think this is you," Rune reminded her. "Tell me, do you remember what it looked like before? Early on."

He gave her a faint, hopeful smile, as though to apologize for asking her to search through her fracturing memory. But the maintainers *had* slowed the erosion, and perhaps there was something left....

No.

It was gone.

She must have seen the shrine a thousand times, though the shrine wasn't typically stored in "her" bedroom. Even if she hadn't paid much attention to it—and why should she?—even a glance should have been perfectly preserved. But there was nothing. Not a moment she could recall.

Except.

There *was* something, just the briefest flash from long ago, when she'd walked past. The context was lost, but that moment was clear: new tapestries decorated the castle walls, and servants had been filling a washtub with buckets; the castle had no running water yet. And there, on a dais in the corner, the summoning shrine had stood proudly in a circle of lit candles, with coins, meticulously cleaned raven feathers, and other assorted offerings scattered around it. The drawing scratched onto the stone—it was the same as it was now.

The memory flashed out, snatched away from her just as quickly as she'd seen it. She rocked back on her heels, her breath coming in short stutters.

"Lady Nightrender?" Draft asked. "Are you all right?"

Rune touched her shoulder, steadying her. "I'm sorry," he whispered. "I shouldn't have asked."

"It's fine. I'm fine." Nightrender sucked in a breath. The memory was gone, but she *remembered* remembering. She remembered that she was about to say—"The marking was the same before. It hasn't been worn by time."

He nodded. "That's what I thought." Worry filled his eyes. His hand remained on her shoulder, but he didn't seem to notice.

"What does that mean?" Draft pressed.

"It means"—Rune stood and stepped away from the shrine—"that if I'm right, then you have helped save not only Caberwill, but all of Salvation." He turned to Nightrender. "Those could be your wings. And that line might be one of your legs."

"It might be both of my legs pressed together," she countered. "See how the wings aren't truly shaped like wings, just arcs."

"If it's you, where are your arms?"

"By the wings. Pressed to my legs. I don't know. I'm not an artist." She frowned. "Just tell me what you think it is."

Rune faced her, and his smile returned. "I think it's the weapon. Perhaps not an exact representation, but—doesn't it look like a sword to you?"

"Yes!" Draft cried. "I see it!"

There was only one sword Nightrender had ever cared about: Beloved, Defender of Souls, and it was strapped to her back right now. "I have a sword I wouldn't like to carry another in its place."

But she could see it, too, now. And there was no time to waste. The shrine was a Relic; it needed her living touch—her divine energy—to open.

She pressed her palm to the carving and released a pulse of numinous power.

Light erupted through the room, blue-white and blinding. The mortals shouted and covered their eyes, but Nightrender watched as the stone split vertically along the drawing, revealing a small shelf.

As the light faded, Draft asked, "Is it in there?"

Rune laughed. "Who would have thought the most powerful weapon the Numina ever made would be right here in Caberwill?"

Nightrender didn't share in their giddiness. She reached into the hollow and withdrew part of a hilt. It was only the pommel and grip, no cross guard, no blade.

The light faded and the shrine closed.

"Is it—" Rune stepped closer. "Is it broken?"

"Incomplete. The other pieces are likely in the Ivasland and Embrian shrines."

"Oh." Disappointment colored Rune's tone. "And it's small. A dagger, not a sword."

Nightrender gazed at the partial hilt in her hand. He was right: it lacked a good reach. She would have to get close to Daghath Mal to use it. But still, she had the first piece. She knew where the other two were likely to be. All she had to do was get them, put the dagger together, and lead these mortal armies into what promised to be a terrible and bloody battle.

Just then, the subtlest sound of stone scraping stone reached her.

"Brace yourselves!" Nightrender thrust the hilt into an inner pocket as the world lurched.

The floor rocked. Nightrender gripped Rune's shoulder, holding him upright as the tower swayed; Draft held on to her forearm. In the deepest part of the castle, Nightrender could hear cracking and splintering. She had experienced earthquakes before, even those devastating enough to level small towns. But this one—it just kept going. The rumbling, the shaking, the shouts—

"How long can this last?" Draft screamed. "The other one wasn't nearly this long."

The minutes grew longer, like being trapped in a time slip. The fear in the tower room became not *when* the earthquake would end, but *if*.

Then a terrible shriek rent the air. Dissonant and howling. Down in the city, screams crescendoed into uncontrolled terror. And dread coursed through Nightrender's veins.

She drew Beloved and stepped in front of her companions just as two huge beasts hit the balcony rail hard enough to send chunks of masonry falling into the city.

Winged rancor.

31.

RUNE

The rancor were enormous, as big as those he'd faced in the Malice, with barrel chests and bat-like wings. The beasts swung around to face the Nightrender.

A terrible polyphonic roar shattered the glass in the balcony door.

Rune glanced at Draft. "Run. Sound an alarm. Gather all the guards and have them outfitted with obsidian."

He didn't need to tell her twice. In spite of the swaying tower and the roar of the earthquake, Draft dived into the stairwell as Rune drew his sword.

The Nightrender was already upon the rancor, Beloved whipping through the air as she fought.

"Bring them inside!" Rune shouted above the rumble and chaos.

Without missing a beat, the Nightrender swept around and drew the rancor into the room, preventing them from flying away to recover or attack anyone else.

Rune swung, muscles straining as his blade bit into grayed mushroom flesh. Then, as he yanked his sword free of the creature, he staggered back on the unsteady floor.

Everything was moving: the rancor, the tower, the whole burning earth. The Nightrender, too, became a blur of motion in the corner of his eyes. Ripples of numinous power flickered around her, shooting down the length of Beloved.

Rune parried a swipe of sharp claws, and when the Nightrender drew that rancor's attention away, he thrust the tip of his sword through the membrane of the creature's wing. It tore open like a sheet, weeping streams of tarry black blood.

It took everything in him not to recoil, but to attack again. The Nightrender fought, and so would he.

One rancor surged toward the Nightrender, its claws ripping at her armor. In the same moment—while the Nightrender was busy defending herself—the other leaped onto Rune, pinning him against the floor. Blood oozed from its damaged wing and dripped onto the stone beside Rune, then, as the thing shifted, onto his cheek.

Rune smelled the acrid stench of burning an instant before blinding pain swept through him. Claws slammed into his chest. Bone cracked—one of his ribs.

Through the shock of agony in his face and chest, he thrust his sword into the creature's throat. It was a lucky blow, cutting right through an artery. Viscous blood spewed from the wound, shooting across the floor in an angry burst until the pressure waned with death.

Rune turned away from it, forcing himself not to wipe the blood across his face and expose more skin to the burning. Instead, he joined the Nightrender as she battled the second rancor. He sliced into its nearest wing, distracting it with the pain while the Nightrender thrust Beloved up and into its skull. White-blue light surged up the black sword and burst through the beast's body. The Nightrender spun and fanned her wings out wide, shielding herself and Rune just as the rancor exploded, its melted parts striking the walls and ceiling with loud slaps.

Rune quickly exited through the broken door, and narrowly avoided the large rancor-equivalent of a spleen that dropped from the ceiling and splatted on the floor.

His chest burned—partly because of his cracked rib, but more because he was beginning to experience hope. They'd found the weapon—part of it, at least. Once she had the rest of it, she would be able to destroy Daghath Mal, and Rune would never have to live in a world without her.

"Tell me why you're staring at me like that."

Before Rune could form a response, the Nightrender pricked her thumb on the tip of her sword, then smeared the scarlet bead of her blood across Rune's cheek—just where the rancor's blood had burned him. Immediately, the wound cooled and the pain faded, and when he touched his face, his skin felt whole and healthy.

"How did you do that?"

"My blood neutralizes rancor blood. We are opposites." She tilted her head. "Guards are coming up the stairs. Others move through the castle. And—"

Rune saw it, too.

It was dark, but the city below was bright with burning lamps and torches. Screams still sounded through the streets, even though—at some point during the fight—the earthquake had ended. (Not that Rune could pinpoint at what moment, but he was grateful nonetheless. It was hard enough to battle evil even when the ground stayed put.) But it wasn't the darkness or the fires or the distant glow of the Malstop that had drawn the Nightrender's attention.

Seven pale shapes threw themselves from the sky toward Brink, letting out terrible roars as the first one crashed into a building. Stone burst open like melons. People ran, but dirt and debris plumed through the air, even as huge chunks of rock collapsed inward.

Rune's heart wrenched as he thought about the people trapped in there. *His* people, likely preparing a celebration for his return. "Nightrender—"

Her wings flared wide as she turned toward the city. "I will end this."

Just as she started to fly, Rune caught her wrist. "Take me with you."

She didn't ask questions. She simply wrapped one arm around him, crushing their sides together, and leaped into the air. His cracked rib flared with pain, making spots of black appear in his vision, but he forced himself to breathe through it as the Nightrender carried both of them off the balcony and toward the city.

This flight was different from before, with his side pressed to hers. They remained more or less vertical as she carried him across the castle wall and into the city, where the seven winged rancor were rampaging through streets and buildings.

People flooded the streets, all running in different directions—some choosing the switchbacks that would take them down the mountain, while others went for the castle, where guards were emerging on horseback, armed with swords and arrows and maces.

"I must put you somewhere," the Nightrender said. "I will fight them in the air."

Rune pointed to a house where a rancor had just landed on the steep roof and was ripping through the shingles with its great claws. As the Nightrender swept toward it, Rune looked up for one last scan of their surroundings. He caught sight of fire bursting through the darkness, rancor carrying his citizens into the sky, and blood—blood everywhere.

The moment his feet touched the rooftop, the Nightrender was off into the sky again, flapping her wings high as she went after the rancor that had carried someone away. Then she was lost in the darkness, visible only as lightning strikes when power rippled around her.

Rune dropped through the hole in the roof, landing with a jarring pain in his chest, and drew his sword. The attic was dark, but a faint glow shone through another hole alongside the door, where the rancor had burst through.

Rune followed, his sword at the ready as he descended the stairs, careful of the gaps and missing boards.

The hall below was in shambles, with torn curtains and broken glass everywhere. Rune followed the rancor's path of destruction down another stair, and there, in the grand hall, he found the beast stepping on the shredded-open body of a man. On the far side of the room, a woman and three children scrambled away from the creature. She was trying to usher them out the nearby door, but already the rancor was starting to block the way.

Rune didn't wait. He didn't think. He surged forward, his sword arcing through the air. He cut the edge of the nearest wing and ducked as the rancor spun to swipe.

One of the children screamed, and the rancor turned again, lunging for the child.

"No!" He plunged his sword into the beast's side, then dived away from the spurt of blood. As the rancor roared, Rune shouted, "Run!"

Across the room, footsteps pounded on the floor, but by now the rancor was thoroughly engaged by Rune, who danced across the floor with his sword shining in the dim light. Everything was chaos, reeking of acidic blood and sweat.

The rancor hurled itself at Rune, who ducked around a thick wooden beam. It splintered as the beast crashed into the column; dirt and debris rained from the second floor, thick and choking. Rune blinked through a haze of tears and dust, sucking in a breath around his aching rib, and slammed his sword into the rancor's left flank.

The beast let out a furious roar and lunged again, but in these close quarters, Rune was faster; the rancor's size was as much a disadvantage as it was a danger.

For long minutes, Rune ducked and parried and attacked. Then, breath heaving, black tendrils coiling at the edge of his vision, he cast his sword into the rancor's gut, then drew away.

Rancor didn't seem to feel pain like mortals, but even they needed their blood and intestines all in the correct spaces. Add that to the shredded wings, the various other injuries Rune had inflicted—this beast was fighting back on pure malice and adrenaline.

The stench of burning flooded Rune's nose. Blood smeared across the floor. It dripped from the steel of his sword, which was growing more corroded with every strike. It wouldn't last much longer; he needed to end this fight.

A bone-rattling roar shook the house. Rune, who'd been catching what remained of his breath behind the broken column, could feel the hot, stinking bellow of the rancor rustle past his hair, sting across the cuts on his face. With a wild cry of his own, Rune spun away from the column and drove his sword up and into the rancor's mouth and brain.

Teeth clamped around steel, as though to stop the blade from penetrating farther, but it was too late. The rancor reached for Rune, claws plucking faintly at his clothing, but the beast fell to the floor in a pool of its own blood, next to the man it had killed before.

Grimly, Rune pulled the sword from the rancor. The tip fell off, right where the creature had bitten into the already-weakened steel. Even so, Rune used the stub to saw off the creature's head, keeping his obsidian jewelry near the tough flesh to help soften it.

When the rancor was in two separate pieces, Rune sheathed what was left of his sword and found a corner where he could vomit. Only when his stomach was empty did he realize that it didn't matter where he got sick. The floor was ruined anyway. The whole house.

He staggered outside to find the military pushing through the streets, rounding up civilians and herding them into safe places: well-guarded noble houses, stable yards, and other defendable spaces with enough room for hundreds of people.

"King Rune?" A soldier hurried up to him, her face twisted with worry. "Where's your guard?"

Rune shook his head. "I don't have one. I was with the Nightrender before. Is she—"

The soldier pointed upward, where the Nightrender flew around a trio of rancor, her whole body engulfed in numinous light. Energy illuminated her sword, jumping through the air and into rancor, keeping them corralled, even as they struggled to fight back.

But she was unstoppable now, the Nightrender. She was glory, all fire and purpose.

She'd been so fettered before, constrained by that link between her and Daghath Mal. But now she was unrestrained. Now he was witnessing the true splendor of her power, and it was clear that she had been meticulously crafted for this. She was *everything*, a goddess in her own right . . . and he was just some mortal who shouldn't even be king.

"This is the last of the rancor she's killing now." The soldier's voice was filled with just as much awe as Rune felt.

Rune nodded. "What's your name? I'm looking for new personal guards."

"Rose, Sire. Rose Emberwish."

"Are you related to the grand general?"

"He's my great-uncle. I don't think he'd allow me to become a personal guard for royalty. Too dangerous. They say that, without fail, every single one of your guards has died."

"That's true," Rune admitted. "If you don't want the job—"

"I do!" She clamped her mouth shut. Then: "I mean, I do want it, Your Majesty. I'd like to be the first one to live, though!"

"I'd like that, too. But you deserve to know there's likely to be more death. We're going to war against these beasts."

"My answer hasn't changed, Your Majesty." A smile tugged at the corner of her mouth. Then she turned as the Nightrender landed behind them, flicking melted rancor parts from her wings and sword. "Lady Nightrender."

The Nightrender nodded at Rose. "I saw your efforts in getting everyone to safety. You did very well."

Rose bowed a little.

"Rune." The Nightrender touched the pocket where she'd placed the hilt taken from the summoning shrine. "I believe this is what they were after. I believe they can sense it, like a beacon."

"So the stone was shielding it?" Rune guessed.

She nodded. "I will take it somewhere safe, somewhere rancor cannot go. Then I will retrieve the others."

Rune nodded. He wanted to say something else, to thank her for defending his city so valiantly, to ask to go with her—wherever she was going—but he had duties here. So he just kept her gaze for a moment, yearning for all that they were never meant to have, and watched as she flew away—north.

He turned back to the castle. There was so much to do. He needed to check on his sisters, meet with the council, ensure that supplies were distributed to everyone. . . . And—of course—he needed to see to Hanne.

32.

HANNE

It was impossible to tell where she was being taken.

Hanne had tried to count steps and seconds. In spite of the gag in her mouth and the sack over her head, she'd attempted to make note of the turns they took as her captors carried her and Nadine through tight spaces, but the truth was that she didn't know Honor's Keep very well. The castle was old, filled with hidden passageways, which must have been how her abductors had sneaked into the sunroom.

By the time they'd thrown her—and Nadine—into a carriage, her sense of direction had evaporated.

Then the earthquake struck—and everything was chaos. There'd been shouting and pulling, men barking orders. Something about a rancor attack, something about people dying, something about fires. Wood cracked as rocks crashed nearby, sending up clouds of debris that clogged Hanne's nose and throat, even through the heavy fabric over her head. The rumble had been all around her, overwhelming. She had the sense of the mountain ready to eat her.

Thank all the Numina, the earthquake was over, which gave Hanne a hysterical sort of relief. Her abduction was simply an abduction once more.

She just . . . had to figure out what to do now.

She knew they were being taken away from Brink.

Did you do this? Hanne asked the voice. *Did you command these people to take us?*

It was quiet, though. It heard her—of that Hanne was certain—but the sense of being ignored was palpable, as though it had simply crossed its arms and turned away.

This was a nightmare. Even breathing required so much effort: she was inhaling her exhales, now with extra dust from the earthquake. The gag only made things worse. And though it was totally dark under the bag, she swore she could see gray tendrils reaching across her vision. Perhaps she would faint from lack of oxygen. The dull thud of her heartbeat seemed slower. Sluggish.

On the bench next to her, Nadine was crying, her gasps and sniffs audible even through the coverings.

Rage surged through Hanne. How *dare* anyone make her cousin cry.

Did you do this? Hanne asked again.

No answer.

Hanne's hands were crushed behind her back, and she couldn't speak out loud. Still, she pressed her shoulder to Nadine's and fought to make a noise that was more or less an approximation of *Are you all right?*

"Mmm."

"Shut it," barked one of the men.

As a queen, Hanne was not accustomed to taking orders. But it seemed entirely possible her captors would hurt Nadine in order to get what they wanted, so Hanne just bit harder into the gag.

This mysterious voice had used her—and now it was discarding her.

Darkness rose up in her mind. **This wasn't me. This was you. All you. What enemies have you made?**

Rupert. Charity. Someone else from the Crown Council. The rebels in Solcast. Ivasland—though Ivasland was more inclined to assassination.

I would not do this to you. Firstly, it doesn't benefit me to have you taken.

But it could. Somehow.

Secondly, I care for you.

That wasn't possible. *You had a rancor chase me into the malsite. You coerced me into working on that machine. You sent a rancor to murder my mother-in-law.* Sweat and tears coated Hanne's face; the bag was thick with her breath. *You started all of this—tricking me into marrying my enemy. You are not capable of caring for anyone.*

She was making a lot of assumptions about the voice, she understood that. It had not said what it was. But she could not shake the fear that she knew *exactly* who'd been speaking to her all these years.

I want only to escape this prison. You know how that feels.

A prison.

The Malstop.

It *was* him. Daghath Mal. The king from beneath.

In her head.

Blood roared through her ears, drowning out all other sound even as she sensed movement beneath her. The carriage took off through the tunnel, Hanne and Nadine inside.

And back in the castle, high in the observatory tower, Mae and her workers were finishing the mal-devices, ready to fill them with malice and detonate them around the Malstop.

And there was nothing Hanne could do to stop it.

Hanne's head ached—around her eyes and sinuses, and at the back of her jaw where she kept biting the gag—but at least she could breathe through her nose now; unfortunately, the inside of the sack was saturated with tears and snot.

"Mmm mmm?" Whatever Nadine wanted to say was lost under her own gag.

"Mm," Hanne replied, because she had to say something.

She wished she could give Nadine confidence that they would escape. She wished she could apologize that Nadine had been caught up in this.

Finally, the carriage rolled to a stop, and the door screeched open. Hanne couldn't see anything beyond the sack over her head, but the air on her hands felt cool, and bugs buzzed somewhere in the distance. Night had fallen.

"Come along." At the man's rough words, Nadine moved away from Hanne. She heard the thump of Nadine's feet hitting packed dirt, her cousin's grunt as their abductors yanked her away. Then Hanne was next; they dragged her out of the carriage and that was when she smelled it.

Even through the stuffiness of the bag, the ammonia odor of malice filled Hanne's nose. It went straight to her head, rolling through her.

Do not be frightened.

The captor shoved Hanne forward, forcing her to walk. Unable to see, she stumbled, but wasn't permitted to fall. The man grabbed the back of her sack and yanked her upright—choking her in the process.

Hanne gagged until the pressure against her windpipe eased.

For a moment, she considered stopping right there. She would refuse to move.

But the tip of a blade pressed against her still-bound hands, cold and sharp, and she stepped forward. Hands fell on her shoulders—one man standing to either side of her, preventing her from straying.

Her captor directed her this way and that, ordering her in seemingly random directions. But Hanne felt it, the gravity of malice. She knew it, recognized it. The *wrongness* rolled off the spheres of malice, making her stomach turn over in revulsion.

They'd brought her to the malsite, the portals.

"Mm!" Hanne protested, but the gag smothered all her words. She couldn't fight, couldn't run. She couldn't even cry out before her enemies sent her somewhere far away: one of the dark lands, perhaps, fallen to malice eons ago. Or the Malice itself, that throne room where she'd seen Daghath Mal's face.

Ahead, Nadine let out a sharp yelp of surprise—which was abruptly cut off.

Hanne tried to call out for her cousin, even around the gag, but before anything else happened, someone shoved her forward and everything went cold.

And white.

White nothingness pierced through the weave of the sack, glaring into Hanne's eyes. She gasped, but nothing filled her lungs. Her chest burned with the need to breathe. Pressure filled her head until it seemed her eyes might burst out of her skull.

This was it.

She was going to die. She might come out on the bottom of the ocean, or perhaps on the edge of a cloud. The other side of the world, or straight into the rancor king's grasp. They could have shoved her into any portal. She could be going anywhere.

Heat flared and air rushed into her lungs as Hanne fell out the other side.

A horn sounded—two long blasts—and somewhere nearby, Nadine was screaming, sobbing.

Hanne scrambled for her cousin, but the shackles bit into her wrists and hands grasped her shoulders.

Which meant someone had come with them, or someone had been on the other side to claim them.

So perhaps they weren't in Daghath Mal's castle?

She couldn't smell the malice anymore, just acrid smoke and some sort of cloying sweetness, like rot. Death.

Hanne went still, listening as hard as she could. Beyond the sound of Nadine weeping, the wind rushing through trees, and the plaintive buzz of crickets, there was another noise: a low rushing, rhythmic like a chant.

Voices.

Before she could sort out what they were saying, someone ripped the sack off her head, taking strands of hair along with it.

Light burned her eyes, making them tear up again, but she could just see the rip in reality where the portal let out, and a copse surrounding it. Her guard—a burly man in plain clothes—yanked her to her feet.

As she turned, she caught sight of lit torches in the city, and masses of people moving together like schools of fish, and a crumbled tower illuminated by small fires.

As the chanting resolved into words—"Hang Jo-hanne! Hang Jo-hanne!"—Hanne finally recognized the besieged city of Solcast, and the burning palace of Solspire.

The captors hadn't sent her to the dark lands, or the Malice, or anywhere else.

They'd taken her home.

33.

NIGHTRENDER

It was not a peaceful flight.

Nightrender flew north as quickly as her wings would take her, but the rancor were always in pursuit. Some dived into towns and villages below, tormenting her with the destruction they caused. She could smell the blood of innocents soaking into the earth. And she could hear the cries for help as people noticed her flying overhead.

She couldn't stand their suffering: when she could, she descended, killing rancor after rancor before taking once more to the sky, carrying the first third of the weapon to Winterfast Island.

So she flew, she fought, and she flew again.

At last, Nightrender reached the edge of Salvation. Waves crashed against the high cliffs of northern Caberwill, the spray stretching all the way to the top, where the fishing villages perched quietly in the pre-dawn glow.

Already, some of the fisherfolk were descending the stairs carved into the cliffs, empty nets in their belts, poles over their shoulders, and lunches clutched tightly in their free hands. Others—the sea guards—followed after; harpoons, machetes, and other weapons waited in the fishing boats below.

At least not *everyone* had forgotten the dangers that lurked.

Then Nightrender was over the water, crossing the narrow channel between Salvation and Winterfast.

It was a remarkable island. Only those Nightrender had invited could reach it, for it was a numinous sanctuary, and the only place she could hide the hilt without worry.

Before her, the tower rose up. It was difficult to look at in this condition. It had been only four hundred years, but weather and sea spray had had their way with it, and without people there to maintain its splendor, her home was falling apart.

Nightrender alighted on the balcony of her chamber on the top floor. This was where she had slept for centuries at a time. It hadn't changed since the last time she'd been here, aside from the snow that had blown in through the balcony door. None of it had melted—Winterfast never got above freezing—so it was just scattered across the bed and wardrobes and floor like dust, white and shimmery.

Her boots crunched the snow as she strode through the room, gazing around at the place she spent so much time, but little seeing.

She took the stairs down to the library, where so many of the books had fallen to time. Others, she realized as she walked fully into the room, had been destroyed.

Not even the books in her own home had been spared after the Red Dawn.

But as she moved deeper into the library, she realized that not *all* the books had been ruined. Some had been here for thousands of years, protected by locked, leaded-glass doors.

Like the Soul Gate, and like the island itself, these displays were accessible only to her—or a key she provided. These books would have been useful to her while she'd been hunting for the weapon with Draft. But she'd forgotten about them until now.

Mortals hadn't destroyed them—but they'd destroyed her memory of them.

Nightrender gritted her teeth and stared hard at the surviving tomes, branding the covers and spines and titles into her mind.

"You can tell me anything you want to remember," Rune had said after they'd fought the rancor in the malsite, *"and I'll remember it for you. I will not forget. I will never forget anything you tell me, I swear it."*

Perhaps she could tell him about this library. The books here. He still had the feather—a key. That would let him enter this place.

At last, she came upon a display case with an illuminated manuscript page sealed inside. It was beautiful, with art all around the border. But what caught her eye was the symbol—the figure everyone had mistaken for her.

The dagger had been drawn in the center of the page, with the writing flowing around it like a stream parting for a stone. But whatever the page said, Nightrender could not quite read it.

Strange. She'd never before encountered something she could not read, a language she could not speak.

Unless . . . she'd forgotten how to read this.

She touched her temple, but of course she couldn't feel the missing memories or carved-out knowledge. It was simply gone.

Still, this page seemed to relate to the weapon, so she placed the hilt inside the drawer beneath the glass, then closed it.

The corner of the paper flickered, illuminated. A shimmer ran down the length of the page, and for an instant, a handful of words became words that she could read. She caught *light*, *First World*, and *Shattering*, but then it was gone. The page was unreadable once more.

Nightrender waited, opening and closing the drawer—just in case—but the lettering never changed again. And finally, with no reason to linger here—no *real* reason, beyond the peaceful solitude—she climbed back upstairs and launched herself off the balcony.

Her duty to humanity could not wait.

34.

HANNE

The city was silent.

Hanne had often seen Solcast in a quiet state: the reverent hush of crowds as the Fortuin family rolled through in their coaches, or the held-breath anticipation as Rune Highcrown and his retinue arrived. But this—this was different.

This was a deathly quiet, the kind that came from swallowing back screams. This was all eyes on her, a small figure striding toward the siege-shattered palace on the hill. Her brilliant red dress fluttered about her legs, the shredded lengths of silk catching and releasing from her ankles. A guard held a sword at the small of her back, forcing her forward one step at a time.

Hanne wished she could turn around to look at Nadine, who was following behind her, but she'd tried it once and the guards had not approved. So she focused on her destination—the palace—rather than the thousands of people who lined the street.

But the people continued to catch her eye.

A thin man held a child on his hip. Both bore shadows beneath their eyes. Both stared at her with absolute hatred.

An old woman drew invisible shapes in the air—the names of Numina, perhaps, those of justice and vengeance, silently calling on them to punish Hanne for all she'd done.

And a girl no older than Hanne spit on the road, right where Hanne would walk.

These were the people of Embria. Her people.

These were the people who wanted her dead.

Because of Daghath Mal.

Why must you blame me? His voice curled in the back of her mind, so familiar.

Hanne glanced east, toward the Malstop. From this vantage point, she could see only the top of the dome, a brilliant blue-white crescent against the black sky.

It was still there, she told herself. There was still time to stop the observatory project, if only she could get her hands on a dove and a piece of paper.

You should be thinking about how to free yourself and destroy the enemies who did this to you. That is what a true daughter of tenacity would do.

Perhaps he was right, but everywhere she looked now, she saw signs of hunger and hatred, poverty and neglect. Had Solcast always been like this? Or were these people from other towns, come here to join the riots?

Had *Embria* always been like this?

Hanne's feet ached as she continued up the street, the glares of her people as good as bruising her. At last, the grim procession reached a raised platform just before the ruined palace gates.

No, not just a platform. Gallows. The rope was waiting.

"Up," her guard commanded.

Hanne climbed up the shallow stairs, and Nadine came after.

A man was already standing at the top, a portly fellow with a number of silver pins on his collar. Most prominent was a circle with rays coming out of it. "I'm Gerald Stephens, magistrate of Silver Sun, and I am honored to have the opportunity of this address. Tonight, after all, is historic. Tonight, the Fortuin family falls."

A wild cheer rose up, a mountain's roar compared to the silence of before. The shock of it traveled through Hanne, burning her ears. She wanted to run, but the crowd had closed in, blocking every avenue of escape. Alone, Hanne might have braved the swords and torches, but Nadine wouldn't have made it.

"As you all know, the mine at Silver Sun was recently devastated by a terrible machine, designed and built and planted by Ivasland. We were prepared to punish the Ivaslander who'd dressed as one of our honorable miners—but then he said something more shocking than any of us could have dreamed: an *Embrian* had helped finish the machine. An *Embrian* was complicit in these illegal, immoral acts. It is one thing to see Ivasland breaking the Winterfast Accords. Of course they would. But an Embrian? We are above that, aren't we?"

"Yes!" the crowd shouted. "We're above that!"

"Immoral Ivasland!"

"Defend the Winterfast Accords!"

The shouts went on for several minutes, until at last the magistrate raised his hand and everyone went quiet. "Yes, yes," he said, "we expect that terrible behavior from Ivasland. And we may not be shocked to learn that one or two Embrians may fall sway to that way of thinking—those who have no love for this kingdom, no respect for Tuluna. So imagine the shock it was to learn that Johanne Fortuin, our own crown princess, took part in this betrayal of everything we believe in. And the Nightrender confirmed it!"

A round of jeers and boos rose up. Someone threw a dirty stocking toward the platform, but it fell short.

"Crown Princess Johanne, who went and married our enemy for the sake of an alliance Embria didn't need. Crown Princess Johanne, who eagerly donned the crown of Caberwill. She has always loved everyone else more than Embria."

Hanne tried to shout around her gag, to protest this vicious slander against her good name, but her voice was lost beneath the rage that poured through the square.

"Princess Johanne betrayed this kingdom!" shouted the magistrate. "Her efforts led to the deaths of hardworking Embrians, men and women just trying to make better lives for their families!"

Another roar. More stockings and undergarments flew at her.

"The Fortuins have betrayed us from the beginning!" someone shouted. "They've stepped on us for generations!"

"The Fortuins are bad for Embria!"

"Hear! Hear!" another cried. "Hang Jo-hanne! Hang Queen Kat!"

The chant rose up again, as before, but louder, surrounding her with fury.

The noise was *incredible*, everyone calling for her death. A bubble of panic formed in her chest. She'd known, of course, what they wanted to do to her. She'd read the coded communication her mother had sent, asking for help. But now that she was here, surrounded by people who all wanted to *kill her*, this whole rebellion was suddenly *real*.

And—as she looked up at the rope—it seemed very likely that someone might follow through on the demands to have her hanged.

The crowd quieted as Magistrate Stephens started talking again: something about her parents, something about generations of abuse and how Embria could endure no more of it. Apparently it wasn't enough for them to punish her for the mal-device; now they wanted to punish her for what her parents and grandparents had done. That wasn't fair at all.

But instead of hanging her then and there, the guard prodded her again—off the gallows and back onto the street, through crowds of people intent on throwing insults, rotten fruit, and stones.

After several minutes, they pushed through the crush and Hanne looked up to realize where she'd arrived: Solspire, the great palace of Embria. Her home.

She'd seen it while walking up the avenue, with its destroyed tower. But up close, just from the courtyard, the damage was so much worse than she'd expected.

The metal and wood double doors had been thrown off their hinges, beaten down with a battering ram until there was little left but splinters. The front hall, which had been grand and filled with golden statues, was thoroughly looted. Hundreds of people were sitting or standing along the walls, mostly huddled near the large fireplaces where kettles and cookpots hung over the flames. They were all squatting in *her* home.

As they moved farther in, the devastation to Solspire only became more evident: marble floors cracked, tapestries shredded and burned, rooms completely stripped of all useful and valuable objects. Hanne had been gone mere weeks, but walking through this terrorized building, she had the sense that she'd been absent far longer. Years. Centuries.

Hanne forced herself to take steady, even strides, even though every step took her closer to the place where they would hold her.

The dungeon. She knew.

She had spent more time there than she would ever admit to anyone—not as a prisoner, of course, but as a princess interrogating her enemies. She'd learned to be hard there, learned to read faces for lies, and learned to *tell* lies. Promises like "Yes, of course you'll be shown leniency if you just tell me the truth" were swiftly swept aside. The dungeon was also where she'd learned to hurt people, to ignore their cries of pain, to keep cutting until *she* knew they couldn't take any more.

That, too, had been a lesson: understanding that people could endure more than they believed.

Now she was being taken there to learn a new kind of lesson.

I've already been beaten and tortured, starved and neglected, trapped in a malsite, and left to fend for myself. They won't do anything new to me.

That was what she told herself, anyway.

But deep down, she knew it would have been better if they'd just hanged her. At least it would have been over quickly.

One shuffling step at a time, she made her way down the slick stone stairs, the spiral drilling deeper into the earth. The air grew colder and damper with every step. All the cell doors were wooden, but there were bars over windows, and smaller hatches where food and waste buckets could be slid through. Nearly all of these doors had faces pressed against the openings now. Nadine gave a quick, indrawn breath at seeing them. It took Hanne a moment longer to realize why so many looked familiar.

She knew them.

These were the faces of Embrian nobility. The lord and lady of Runnisburg. The high lady of Felin. And the two lords of Shady River.

Everyone looked haggard, their faces thin and pale, their skin spotted with pimples. They looked *hungry*.

Hanne held her head high as she strode past her people, then marched deeper into the dungeon. They went on and on until they finally reached the very bottom. The air was frigid down here, and the floor slick with water on uneven stone. They walked all the way to the very last cell, and only then did one of their guards produce a ring of keys and unlock the door.

"Go on." Another guard shoved Hanne forward.

She grunted and raised her shackled hands slightly, even though the movement hurt her shoulders. Mercifully, the metal clicked and the pressure fell away from her wrists. Nadine's cuffs came off next, and then both girls were shoved into the cell. The door slammed shut behind them, followed by the sound of footfalls retreating.

Quickly, Hanne pulled off the gag and tossed it.

The cell was shaped like a pie slice—a quarter circle with small bite taken out of the center where a ventilation shaft ran from the top to the bottom of the dungeon. Warm air was supposed to be forced down the shaft to keep prisoners from taking a chill, but any heat was lost in the upper cells well before it reached the lowest levels.

Nadine kept her voice soft. "This is the dungeon? It's worse than I thought it would be." She turned a knob, which rotated a chemical light. It was behind a mesh of bars, though, preventing Hanne from breaking the glass to use as a weapon.

"Well, it's a dungeon. It's not supposed to be good." Hanne raised her fingers to touch the obsidian shard at her throat, but it had been taken earlier, along with all her other obsidian pieces. Nadine's, too. Abducted, thrown in prison, and *robbed* by an angry mob of killers who thought they were more qualified to run the kingdom. "The upper cells are slightly better. There's sometimes running water."

"Isn't that a faucet?" Nadine nodded to a spout along the ventilation shaft. "And a drain?" She motioned to the small grate at the bottom.

"Technically, yes. But there's only a certain amount of water permitted for prisoners. Unless our captors are kind, most of the water will get used up before it reaches us."

Their captors were not kind. Neither of them had to say it.

"These bottom cells are where we always kept the worst prisoners. The traitors. Those who violated others. The ones that killed."

"But—"

But Nadine didn't fit any of those descriptions, Hanne knew. It seemed very clear—to Hanne, at least—that Nadine was only here because she had been unfortunate enough to be talking with Hanne at the time of the abduction.

And to the ones who'd taken her, Hanne was a traitor. To them, she had betrayed Embria. She was responsible for the deaths of everyone who'd died in Silver Sun. And the entire army, perhaps—although she hadn't been the one to slaughter the livestock and cook it.

"You're here because of me," Hanne said softly. "I'm sorry."

She hated to admit such a thing, but she'd done a lot of soul-searching in the last few hours. By now, she could admit that this was—to some extent—her fault.

But mostly it was Daghath Mal's fault.

She'd been a child when he'd entered her mind, afraid and alone, uncertain what had just happened to her. She'd needed someone, and he'd been there: comforting, protecting, giving her everything she didn't know she'd needed.

But now everything was a question. Her whole life. Her plans.

Her peace.

She'd wanted *so* badly to bring peace to Salvation, to unite all three kingdoms under her sword. Her flag.

It had been a lie, though.

It wasn't a lie, Daghath Mal murmured. **I have never lied to you.**

You are the master of lies, a prince of deception.

I promised you would be queen, and aren't you? Sooner than you anticipated. I promised you would be *my* queen, and that is also true.

It was, she had to admit. She was his pet queen, the queen who would destroy the world for him.

And with no kingdoms but my own, how could there be war? Perhaps it wouldn't be the type of peace you hoped for... but *you* would have been safe. I would have protected you from the world.

No one else in her life had ever made that promise, not even Nadine. But knowing what he was now, Hanne could never go back.

You may change your mind, he said. **And I will welcome you when you do.**

Hanne shook her head, forcing herself into the present—to see whether Nadine had acknowledged her apology. She hadn't.

"A queen should never apologize to her subjects."

Hanne stiffened. The voice sounded as though it belonged to her mother.

Now Nadine looked up, and her round eyes met Hanne's. Nerves tightened in Hanne's chest as she approached the central shaft.

Through a small grate, she could see another dim chamber on the opposite side of the shaft. And though she was silhouetted, backlit with a small supply of light tubes, Hanne had no difficulty seeing directly into the hard blue of her mother's eyes—a mirror of her own.

"This *is* your fault," Queen Katarina said. "I told you to send help."

Hanne stiffened, but forced her expression to stay neutral. "You lost the kingdom to a peasant revolt. I'd say we both bear some responsibility."

"The army was *eaten*." Katarina's voice slid into a dangerous range. "Again: your fault."

"Hardly."

Katarina lifted her chin and turned away. "You've ruined us."

Of course Queen Kat was incapable of admitting responsibility. Hanne sighed and tried to peer beyond the back of Katarina's head. "Father, are you there, too?"

"Hello, dear." King Markus Fortuin's voice came from the dim.

There were two other cells on this floor. Hanne tried to look into them, but if those cells were occupied, she couldn't tell. "Is anyone else down here?"

"Not on this floor," Katarina said, "or the one above us. I believe Nadine's parents are somewhere up there. I've heard them talking a few times. Those cowards—they tried to surrender. To *peasants*."

So any conversation Hanne wanted to have with her parents could potentially be overheard. It was a trick Hanne had used with prisoners before. Partners would be given cells on the same floor, forcing them to speak through the vents; they wouldn't always know that Hanne—or one of her spies—was listening.

That Stephens man could be doing the same thing right now.

Hanne retreated to the nearest bed and sat on the hard stone. There were a few blankets, if such tattered things could be called blankets, and a pillow filled with straw.

Hanne looked across to Nadine, who had perched glumly on her own bed.

"What do we do?" Nadine asked quietly. "How long do you think they'll keep us here?"

Hanne gathered her blankets and pillow and took them across the space to sit with Nadine. Resolutely, she folded a pair of blankets into a sort of cushion for them to sit on, then pulled the other blankets around their shoulders so that they could share body heat.

Nadine leaned her head on Hanne's shoulder and sighed. Slowly, her shivers stopped.

"I don't know what to do yet," Hanne admitted. "I need to think. I need to find out—"

You should ask them, Daghath Mal whispered. **Ask them what they did to you.**

The problem with thinking was that someone was always listening.

"Were you serious before?" Nadine's voice was barely above a whisper. "Back in Honor's Keep, about Tuluna? Or..."

"Yes." Hanne closed her eyes and took a deep breath. Then she pulled a blanket over their heads to muffle her voice. "It's the truth."

Careful.

"I fully believed it to be Tuluna the Tenacious. This voice guided me. Helped me. Made me stronger. I believed I was their chosen."

Beneath the blanket, Hanne couldn't see Nadine's expression, only feel the shortness of her breath.

Hanne forced herself to say the words. "But it's not Tuluna. I was wrong. It's Daghath Mal. It's the rancor king. And even though I believed I was doing what was right, I think I've been on the wrong side. I think I'm the villain."

35.

RUNE

By the next morning, it was clear that Hanne was not actually in Honor's Keep.

"Where is she?" Rune stood inside the queen's parlor, this space that used to belong to his mother, and gazed around at all the changes that had been made since her passing. The curtains were red now, with golden trim; a game of Mora's Gambit was set up on the round table near the wall, the expensive pieces all in their little boxes; and a tapestry with the Fortuin crest hung on the far wall beside the balcony door.

But there was no Hanne.

Three ladies-in-waiting stood in a row. Rune knew their names—Cecelia, Lea, and Maris—but he wasn't sure which one was which. Also present was Lady Sabine, one of Hanne's longtime advisers, who seemed to always be knitting, and Captain Oliver.

No Hanne. No Nadine.

"Well?" Rune crossed his arms over his chest. Behind him, Rose—now dressed in the livery of the king's personal guard—moved around the room, looking behind mirrors and inside cupboards, as though the queen might be hiding.

"We aren't sure." Captain Oliver shifted his weight. "Her Majesty and Lady Nadine went into the sunroom to speak—"

"This is after the queen left my rooms last night?"

Captain Oliver nodded. "Her Majesty and Lady Nadine were speaking quite animatedly. I didn't listen to their conversation, of course, but I could hear their voices through the door. Then, after a while, everything was quiet. I knocked to check on them, but it isn't unusual for Her Majesty to ignore those." He said it in the way that indicated he'd been on the wrong end of those knocks in the past. "Only when the earthquake struck did I go inside. And the room was empty. I have no idea how she could have left without my knowing."

Rune closed his eyes. He hated telling Embrians, even ones who lived here now, but— "The sunroom has a secret passage."

All three ladies-in-waiting glanced at one another. "A secret passage," (possibly) Cecelia said. She turned to Lady Sabine. "Did you know about it?"

Rune had half a second to wonder why an old Embrian woman would have known about any secret passage, but no one from Embria was *just* what they seemed. Of course Hanne had brought her own spy.

"If I had known about the passage, do you think I would have permitted her to go into that room?" Lady Sabine's eyes snapped to Rune's. "Where does the passage lead?"

"It branches off in several directions. One of those directions leads into the tunnel through the mountain. South. Out of the city." Rune clenched his jaw. "Captain, I'll have my people search the entire network of passages. If she's still in the city, we'll find her."

"And if she's no longer in the city?" Lady Sabine asked.

"We will pursue her in whatever direction she has gone." Or, potentially, whatever direction she had been taken. He couldn't see Hanne leaving of her own volition right now—not when he'd just returned. Unless there was something else going on, something that would take her away from Brink without leaving word with anyone, even her ladies, guard, or spy mistress.

And that seemed rather far-fetched, unless all these people were lying to him right now.

Well. They were Embrian. They lived in complex layers of deceit. So perhaps they were lying.

He would have to employ his own spies to find out what they knew.

"I would like to join your men in searching the passages," Captain Oliver said.

Definitely not. "My people know the passageways well. I assure you, if there is any trace of Queen Johanne, they will find her."

With that, he turned and left the queen's chambers.

Rose stepped up alongside him. "I can recruit people to search the passages if you wish. And guard the sunroom entrance, now that, ah, others, know about it."

"Yes, thank you." Rune's head was aching. He needed a spy of his own, but he'd dismissed Rupert yesterday without a replacement. "Do I have a secretary yet? A valet? Is there anyone assigned to help me? Or am I supposed to organize all these things myself?"

"I will find out, Sire."

The king's office was Rune's next stop. He'd been there many times as a prince—and crown prince—but never as king. And given that this was the location of his father's murder only weeks ago, he didn't particularly want to go there now. Still, a king has certain responsibilities. They couldn't be put aside for emotions.

Guards stood at attention as Rune approached.

"Your Majesty." The nearest one gave a small, respectful bow.

Rune nodded in return and opened the heavy wooden door.

The blood had been cleaned from the walls and floor some time ago, but even so, Rune's eyes went straight to the dings on the desk that hadn't been there before, the tiny nicks in the wood paneling on the walls. By all accounts, right now, just in the doorway, he was standing where someone had died. A guard. And there, to the right of the desk, was the place King Opus Highcrown III had been discovered in the middle of the night, slain in his own office by an Ivaslander assassin.

That hot rage flared up in Rune again, the same uncontrollable feeling that had sent him riding south with the army not even a day after his coronation. He would have removed Ivasland from the map if he'd been able.

"Sire?" Uncertainty entered Rose's voice.

The rage retreated. Rune sucked in a breath and stepped inside, over the place his father had died, and took a seat at the king's desk. The room looked different from this angle. Smaller, somehow, as though the impressive parts were all for those sitting on the guest side.

"You look good there," Rose said from the doorway.

With a frown, Rune touched the desktop, smoothing his fingers over the polished bloodwood. "Please have Draft"—he realized abruptly he didn't know Draft's surname—"from the library brought here."

"Right away." Rose let the door swing shut as she stepped away. Her voice was muffled as she addressed the guards outside: "Don't leave your station. Don't let anyone in without asking His Majesty first. I'll return soon."

Then her footsteps retreated down the hall, and Rune was alone.

He closed his eyes, letting his palms run across the smooth surface of the desk, feeling the sturdiness of the chair beneath him.

It didn't fit him. The desk. The chair. Any of it. This space belonged to his father.

He took in a long breath.

It belonged to him now. He didn't have to like it. He didn't have to feel ready for it. But he did have to acknowledge it.

"This is my office now," he whispered. "My desk. My chair."

He opened his eyes and, jaw tight with that feeling of intruding, began to open drawers and look through them. Writing tools. Paper. A bit of poetry scrawled in Unity's tidy handwriting, dated three years ago.

A journal.

The blue ribbon marked roughly three-quarters of the way in. There was no lock on the leather cover, but Rune couldn't bring himself to open it. Not yet. Not when the pain of his father's death was so raw.

Rune pushed himself up, filled with the urgent need to go back to the sunroom where his mother had died. And then perhaps, just to torment himself more, he'd stand in the hall where his brother had died. Because why not, at this point? He was already hurting. Why not pick the wound open a little wider?

Fortunately, someone knocked on the door.

"Enter."

When the door opened, it was Draft on the other side.

"Come in." Rune tried to calm his speeding heart. He shouldn't have thought about his parents so much. Definitely not his brother. He should have simply sat down and gotten to work.

Draft closed the door behind her, but didn't move from that area, as though she, too, knew exactly what had happened in this room. Well, she'd been a maid.

Rune wondered if she'd been tasked to clean the mess.

"I wanted to ask how you were doing," Rune said. "After the battle yesterday, I meant to check on you."

"You're a king," Draft said. "You're very busy. And you got what you needed, right? The weapon piece?"

"She has it. She'll go after the other pieces, too."

"That's good."

"I'm glad to see you're unharmed," Rune went on.

"That's not why I came to talk to you," Draft said. "I mean, I came because you sent for me, but I also came because I told the Nightrender that I would listen for her."

Rune frowned. It didn't seem like the Nightrender to ask for people to spy.

"I don't know if I should be telling you this," Draft went on, "seeing as how the queen is your wife. But I know she's missing. And I know that you need her back."

Rune's breath caught. "How do you know she's missing?"

Draft tilted her head. "I said I was listening, Your Majesty."

Rune motioned for her to continue.

"Some of my friends are maids in the queen's chambers. That's how I knew that Queen Johanne was missing. And that's how I know that Prudence Shadowhand and Victoria Stareyes are the queen's nominations for the council next period. But they'll both work for her, not you."

"That's what your maid friends said?"

"Lady Shadowhand was in the queen's chambers late last night. My friend thinks Lady Sabine and others were asking her to find out what they could about the queen's whereabouts."

Before they had admitted to Rune that Hanne was missing. And if Prudence Shadowhand hadn't come straight to Rune to inform him that his *wife* was missing, it could only be because Sabine had asked her not to tell him. To wait.

But why?

"They're hiding something." Rune sat, finally motioning for Draft to sit, too. "I need to find out what it is."

Draft lowered herself into the seat Rune used to occupy when he'd come to get scolded by his father. "I can help. Please."

Rune wasn't in a position to turn down help.

But spying on a queen, or even the queen's household, could cause serious problems for someone like Draft. "Are you sure?" he asked. "Have you truly thought about what it means to pick a side like this?"

"The Nightrender chose you." Draft leaned forward, her expression earnest. "She cares for you. And if she does, then so do I."

"I appreciate your assistance," Rune said. "And I will accept it. Of course."

"I won't let you down."

"Thank you." He wished there was a way to say it that truly conveyed how much it meant to him that anyone would find him worthy of putting their life at risk for him, but it wouldn't be very kingly, so he settled for a faint, uncomfortable smile.

Once they'd agreed on meeting times and who could be trusted to pass on information, Rune bid her a good day, and she left.

But he wasn't alone for long. Rose had been waiting outside, and there was a line of nobles, chancellors, and other important figures who needed to see him.

It was time for him to be king.

36.

HANNE

There was no telling time down here, but two small meals of hard bread and moldy cheese had come, so Hanne estimated it had been at least a full day. Perhaps two. Her stomach felt dreadfully hollow, and her throat parched. Her thoughts were becoming bits of fluff, floating away when she tried to catch them.

But in all that time, however much time it had been, Nadine had not spoken another word to her.

After Hanne's confession, Nadine had stood and crossed to the opposite end of the cell—which wasn't very far, but as far away as she could get. And there she had sat for hours, getting up only to claim her half of the food, or to use her bucket.

It had been hard enough for Hanne to admit the truth to herself—that it wasn't Tuluna in her mind—but saying those words to Nadine . . . It had nearly choked her.

Hanne swallowed a dry knot lodged in her throat. For so long, she'd believed this voice in her head to be a friend, a mentor. And because of that faith, the monster who'd masqueraded as Tuluna the Tenacious knew all her deepest fears, her darkest secrets, her most hidden desires.

I would have known whether or not you told me anything, he said. **I can see what you see. I can feel what you feel. And I can know what you know.**

A shudder ran through Hanne.

The cell is dark, he murmured. **The light needs to be turned, but you feel too weak to lift your hand and do it. You're hoping Nadine will.**

Hanne reached for the nearest light and gave the glass several sharp turns to mix the chemicals once again. The glow expanded across the cell, and inside Hanne's head, Daghath Mal gave a low, amused chuckle.

It's cold, too. You lost feeling in your toes some time ago, so you keep wiggling them—but it hurts.

"Stop," she breathed. "You don't have to prove anything."

And you're worried that if Nadine has stopped loving you, no one else ever will. You fear you're not the kind of person anyone but her *could* love, which is why you didn't mind marrying Rune, and why you never pursued Mae, even though you want to. You fear that you are unlovable. And now that Nadine isn't speaking...

"Stop!" Hanne's voice scraped her dry throat as she surged to her feet. Lightheadedness gripped her, stealing her vision for a heartbeat. But then it returned, and she could see that Nadine had finally looked up from her clasped hands.

"Stop what?" Nadine asked quietly. "Stop thinking about what you told me? Stop worrying about you?"

Hanne couldn't make herself speak.

"I can't just forget that you told me those things," Nadine went on. "Or that you *didn't* tell me for so long."

Hanne opened her mouth to respond, but the words wouldn't come out.

Nadine glanced at the vent shaft, and with a deep breath, she crossed the cell back to Hanne's side. "You said it happened after you returned from— You know. But what happened while you were away?"

Hanne closed her eyes, forcing her shoulders to drop again now that Nadine was near. "I can't remember all the details of that"—she bit her lip—"excursion, but there are flashes. They're painful. Nightmarish. I think there were times I was close to death."

Muscles flexed around Nadine's jaw, but she knew when to speak, and when to let Hanne figure out what she needed to say.

"I know that I looked different after," Hanne went on. "Prettier." Hanne looked at Nadine from the corner of her eye, but the confirmation didn't come. Her cousin had never commented on that; she was too kind and polite. "And I behaved differently. We both know that. But all this time, I haven't been able to remember what actually happened there. I think— I think I didn't *want* to remember. But now I wish I'd been braver. I wish I'd asked my parents what they'd done to me."

And this was her chance.

Hanne surged toward the ventilation shaft. "What did you do?"

On the opposite side, there was no response. Hanne banged on the vent again.

"What did you do to me? Years ago. When I was a child. When you took me away."

"You wouldn't have made it." The voice on the far side belonged to her father. King Markus Fortuin walked closer to the vent, and finally Hanne could see the shadowy shape of him through the grating. "When you were young, you were so sensitive. So gentle. You took after my mother's side of the family, the Holt side, and no matter how we tried, we could not forge you into a Fortuin."

Hanne glanced back at Nadine, who'd come a few paces closer to the shaft herself. Her expression was lost in the shadows.

But Hanne knew what she was thinking. Her own memories of her childhood were murky at best, like another lifetime. It was only after she'd been taken away that her memories became crisper—more real.

She'd also seen portraits of herself from her childhood, which had all been hidden away as she'd grown into a young woman. The face in those early paintings wasn't the face she saw in the mirror now, and not only because she was older. No, the child before she'd been taken had been tall for her age, gangly, with mouse-brown hair that hung in limp strings around her face. She'd had the most awkward, uncomfortable smile, which showed all her crooked teeth.

She hadn't been an *ugly* child, but this Hanne, the one in the present, couldn't look at those portraits without her lip twitching in disgust. She preferred the way she looked now, with her curling blond hair, heart-shaped face, and straight white teeth. She wasn't tall anymore, but petite, and that didn't bother her; her diminutive height caused people to underestimate her.

I did that.

It was true, too, that she had been a shy child, one who couldn't stand up for herself, whose voice was small and whispery, who'd hidden when she was supposed to join her mother in the throne room. She had never told anyone what to do, never gave orders to servants, never asked for anything.

Such passivity was unbecoming of a crown princess, Katarina had often told her. She would need to be stronger, or she would not survive in Embrian court.

I saved you, Daghath Mal said. **I made you strong.**

"Tell me, Father," Hanne breathed. "Tell me what you did."

Markus had the good grace to wince, to appear ashamed of his actions. "There was a legend about a place of power, where people had gone to cure ailments or receive blessings. We thought perhaps we could help you—give you a chance to find your own footing for your future as queen."

"That's enough, Markus." Katarina appeared on the other side of the shaft. "What we did, we did for her. If she doesn't appreciate that anymore, then she will never be the queen we wanted her to be. She will always be that weak little girl, the one who cried anytime a bird flew into a window, the one who didn't understand that some of us were born to rule and others were born to serve."

But darkness bloomed in the back of Hanne's mind, a repressed memory bursting back to the fore of her thoughts.

Watch, said Daghath Mal. **I will show you what they will not.**

Ice coated yellow ribbons. Bells jangled nearby, dark and warning.

Hanne's parents had led her here, each of them holding one of her hands as they guided her away from the guards who'd been left at the road. Hanne had paused to look at a tall rock, gray and pitted, with scratches covering one face. It almost looked like a person—a person with wings.

Her parents dragged her forward, toward a larger stone—an altar.

"What is this place?" She was old enough to be cautious, but not experienced enough to understand that this was not a normal rite of passage, that most parents didn't bring their children into the winter woods for . . . whatever this was. Perhaps it was something meant only for royals. There seemed to be a lot of that.

She'd known about the yellow ribbons, of course, and the bells. She'd known they meant danger. But she trusted her parents.

"This is going to help you be strong," Katarina had said. "Smart."

Hanne, by that point, knew that she was neither of those things—not strong or smart—but that both were required of her if she were going to be queen one day.

She'd worn red then, too. The finest spun wool, dyed crimson with hemlock and chokecherries. Even with the cold pressing around her, she'd felt warm in her layered dress, the sleeves long and snug, the hood that pulled up over her ears.

Still holding on to her parents' hands, Hanne had approached the altar with growing trepidation. A peculiar smell permeated the air, like the stink of sour milk mixed with a full chamber pot. Hanne wrinkled her nose, but the odor only grew stronger. The altar was so much bigger than it had looked from a distance. Had it grown? Now it seemed it was almost twice her height.

"What is it?" Hanne couldn't help but stare at the sharp lines carved into the stone, like writing, but it wasn't in any language she'd ever heard of. (There was only one language now, but there were legends of other languages in the past, from when people had come from fallen continents.) "What does this say?"

"I don't know," Markus said. "It's probably nothing."

"You'll have to climb up." Katarina wore gold, a striking star against the swath of white snow and the dark trees. Obsidian hung from her neck and wrists and fingers, heavy and black. "All the way up to the very top."

"What if I can't?" Hanne's voice had trembled with cold and fear. She didn't have any obsidian, not even a speck.

"Then you won't be worthy to be queen."

Hanne's breath caught. "Did you have to do this, too?" The words were white puffs on the still air.

"No. I was born strong and smart. I was born with Tuluna's tenacity. You, my little dove . . . You will have to take that tenacity another way."

Hanne bristled at the dove comment. She wasn't a bird. She wasn't a messenger. But she wasn't fit to be queen, either, that much was clear, and until then—well, perhaps she wasn't much better than a dove.

"All right. What do I do once I'm up there?"

Her parents glanced at each other. Then her mother said, "You will know. It will be obvious."

Her father, who'd always been gentler, knelt to give Hanne a kiss on the forehead. "We'll be here waiting for you when you finish."

Hanne still didn't understand what she was supposed to finish, but she didn't want to disappoint her mother, who expected so much from her, or her father, who always seemed worried about her. She needed to prove that she could do this—whatever it was. So she made a circuit around the altar until she found a handhold, and then she began to climb.

Immediately, she slipped and fell, her mittened fingers sliding on the snow and ice that had gathered there. She tried again, this time making sure to wipe away the snow and dig her fingertips into the ice, testing before she pulled herself up. She didn't fall again.

At last, she heaved her arms and chest up over the lip of the stone, then threw her left leg over—and finally rolled onto the top. She gasped for breath; she let the cool air sting her throat for a few minutes, waiting for her heart to stop pounding.

"I'm up," she called.

No reply.

"Mother?" Hanne peered over the edge of the stone, scanning below for her parents. "Father?" It was dark, but she should have been able to see them against the bright snow.

They were gone. They'd left her.

They hadn't even waited to make sure she made it up.

And the ground seemed farther away than it should have. A wave of dizziness swept over Hanne, and she pulled herself back onto the top of the stone, looking around for whatever she was supposed to do, now that she was up here.

Her mother had said it should be obvious.

Hanne's fingers were numb from the cold and the climb up, but she brushed snow off the stone and looked around. She found more of that strange writing, visible mostly because of the way ice filled the marks and gleamed darkly in the starlight.

But that was all. Nothing was obvious. There was no clear task, no instructions that she could read.

"Mother?" Hanne leaned over the edge again. Somehow, impossibly, the ground seemed farther away than ever. "Father? Are you there?"

No. She knew they weren't. They'd abandoned her.

Had they left her here to die?

She knew she shouldn't, because she would get into trouble, but that was when Hanne began to cry. The tears gathered and froze in the corners of her eyes, stinging when she blinked through the rime. Fresh tears trickled down her cheeks. Her face hurt with the freezing,

Why had they left her? Because she was too weak? Not smart enough? Not clever enough, bold enough, or anything else enough. She just wasn't *enough*.

A quiet sob escaped her. She couldn't get down, but she couldn't stay up here, either. Though there'd been starlight just moments before, now silver clouds raced across the sky, spitting snow.

The stink of cat piss rose up, cutting through the numbness of her frozen nose. And somehow, impossibly, the stone was higher—all the way up to the trees now.

"Help." Hanne shivered, pulling her hood lower over her head. "Somebody?"

She was so cold. Inside her mittens, her fingers felt like icicles. She tucked her hands into her armpits, wiping her face with her sleeve every few minutes. Surely her parents would come back for her. They needed her, didn't they?

So deep in her own tears and panic, Hanne didn't notice the lights at first, the green glow that came from the etchings in the stone. But gradually, the light intensified, shining up around her. And the light was *hot*.

Snow and ice melted beneath her. Water soaked into her dress, making it heavy, weighing her down, but it didn't matter. She was warm. She wasn't going to freeze to death. She would survive this.

A loud *crack* sounded beneath her. The stone?

Heart pounding, Hanne squinted through the bright lights. And at once, she realized the etchings didn't make words in some long-dead language. They made teeth. Two rows of sharp teeth that were widening, separating, opening—

Hanne fell.

Into the stone she descended. Into the dark. Alone.

The memory stopped there. Hanne staggered back, heart racing.

"Hanne?" Nadine's hands steadied her. "What happened? Are you all right? You just—faded for a moment."

A moment? For Hanne, it had been hours. Every excruciating second of her time at that altar was etched into her mind, hardening into scars. There were other things, too, that Daghath Mal hadn't fully shown her, but she knew enough. She remembered enough now, on her own.

The claws cutting into her face.

The heating and breaking and re-forming of her bones.

The infusion of green light into her veins.

There'd been so much screaming, sobbing, begging for mercy that would not come. It had been excruciating, a thousand years of torture, but she didn't need to experience all that again—not those moments. They had been terrible and violent, and now they were closer to her consciousness than ever before. But Daghath Mal knew the worst had been the beginning. The worst had been her parents holding her hands, her parents lying to her, her parents leaving her there.

They truly had abandoned her in a strange place, where nothing made sense, where reality shifted on a whim.

"You took me to a malsite." Hanne pressed her fingers into the grate. "You left me there, defenseless, to be brutally reforged into the daughter you'd wanted all along."

Markus said, "No—"

"You did. I remember. But you didn't know what would happen to me. I could have died. I *should* have."

"We knew you would endure," said Katarina, "if you were worthy."

"I was a *child*."

"You were a Fortuin. We were never worried about you."

Hanne held her ground, thanks only to years of training. She could not show weakness or emotion. "You should have been worried. You should have asked yourselves what you were doing, breaking the Winterfast Accords, using the power of a malsite like that. And you have the nerve to hate Ivasland for their machine!

"But even worse, you gave the rancor king a window into our world. A foothold. A weapon."

"What do you mean?" Markus asked. "How—"

"After you left me in the malsite, I thought I was alone. I wasn't. The stone where you were set to sacrifice me was not an altar after all, but a pathway to darkness. It swallowed me whole. It would have killed me, but I told the darkness that I was a princess, that I would be queen one day, and that I was meant to endure this."

Water dripped nearby, but that was the only sound.

"I told it that my parents had sent me there, that I needed to be stronger to be a queen like you wanted, and it asked me if I wanted that as well. I was a child, so I wanted nothing more than to please you. I said yes, I would do anything to make you love me.

"So the darkness remade me into the perfect crown princess, the one you'd always wanted, and for a while, I thought it had worked. But it didn't. You never *loved* me; you were simply less disgusted by me."

"That's not true," Markus argued. "I always loved you."

Hanne laughed, letting them hear her disbelief, her disgust. "No. The only one who ever loved me—before *and* after—was Nadine. But you—Mother, Father—you never bothered to ask what had happened to me. When you found me in the snow a week later, completely changed, you accepted the new me, never questioning what I had survived. You never wondered if—when I'd been ripped open and remade—something else had been placed inside of me. A tether. A connection. A bond with the thing that shaped me."

"The rancor king," Nadine murmured.

"Yes." Hanne turned away from the ventilation shaft and her parents peering at her from the other side. She wanted nothing more to do with them. She was done with her mother's impossible demands, done with her father's passive complicity. They could die in the dark for all she cared. "The king from beneath saw an opportunity to effect change in this world. He used my voice, my hands. And now, the final Incursion will come for us, all because my mother and father wanted a more perfect daughter.

"This is how the world ends," Hanne whispered as the light dimmed. "Through one act of petty selfishness after another."

37.

NIGHTRENDER

She told herself she needed to check on him, to make sure he was unharmed after the rancor attack, but the truth was, she just wanted to see him.

It was very late—or very early, depending on one's perspective. He was probably sleeping. He *should* be sleeping. Still, Nightrender found herself alighting on Rune's balcony, listening to the susurrus of sheets and blankets twisting as he tossed and turned in his bed.

Then, a whisper, both in her mind and in the castle: *How do I do this?*

He had the feather.

I don't know how anyone ever believes they're ready to rule.

Nightrender stepped closer to the balcony door, but stopped herself before she reached it.

I wish you were here with me.

Her chest twisted with wanting; she denied herself no longer. Nightrender stepped inside the dark parlor and waited while—in the other room—Rune's breath hitched and his heartbeat raced. He rolled out of bed and grabbed a weapon, moving quietly.

When the shape of him appeared in the doorway, though, and he saw her outline against the window, his shoulders dropped and he placed his sword on a shelf. "I was just thinking about you."

His hair was mussed, and he wore only a long nightshirt and loose trousers. In the dim light, everything about him was perfect. Inviting. Warm.

One day, perhaps not too long from now, she would forget him. Rune in battle. Rune kissing her. And Rune like this: gentle and unguarded, looking at her the way he always did—like he couldn't believe she was real.

A flare of longing lit within her, chased swiftly by guilt. He had taken an oath. She had (mostly) witnessed it. For the good of Salvation, and his own sense of honor, Rune needed to protect that oath—and the heir that had been promised.

It had never bothered her before, that her soul shards married other people for love or politics. It shouldn't have bothered her this time.

But it did.

She hated that she couldn't have him, and hated more that one day her memory of him would be stolen, cut away like those of her previous soul shards. Nothing would remain, not even this desperate ache for him.

A choppy breath escaped her.

"Nightrender?" He stepped closer. "Medella?"

She could barely form the words. "I had to see you."

"Is something wrong?" Another step closer.

"I—" She shook her head and turned toward the door again. "I shouldn't have come. Forgive me."

"No, wait." Rune crossed the room in several long strides. As she reached for the door, his hand closed on hers. A faint spark passed between them, like static. "Don't go. Tell me what's wrong." His other hand touched her spine, directly below her sheathed sword. Shivers raced across her skin; feathers rustled as the sensation of his palm on her back rippled all the way to the tips of her wings.

Another memory. Another moment to be torn away from her when she wasn't expecting it.

Another sensation she wouldn't even know she should miss.

"I must go to Ivasland." Her whisper came out rough. "My duty . . ."

"I know. But sit for a moment. Here." He guided her to a small chaise, thick with deep blue cushions, the Highcrown crest stitched with silver thread.

Slowly, Nightrender unbuckled her sheath and placed Beloved on a small end table. Then, she sat where Rune had directed, carefully adjusting her wings while he went to the sideboard and poured two glasses of water. When he returned, he handed one to her. She drank it all at once.

"More?" He offered the second glass.

She drank it, too. Then he brought the whole pitcher, which she quickly drained.

He set the glasses and pitcher aside, then sat next to her, turned to face her. "I can see you're upset. Tell me why."

Where should she start? The world was falling apart and she was expected to save it . . . but *she* was falling apart and there was no one to save her. The midnight sky of her memory was darkening.

Her eyes felt heavy, too full. She blinked to clear her swimming vision, but the blurring persisted.

Was her sight failing her, too?

Callused fingertips brushed across her face. "You're crying."

Nightrender blinked again, but it didn't help. "I drank too much water. I'm overflowing."

"That's— Medella, that's not how it works. Haven't you ever cried before?"

A huge, choking sob came out of her. "I don't remember. I can't—"

A dam broke within her. The enormity of her loss rose up, overwhelming every other thought, every other feeling. This grief for lifetimes she could no longer remember—the grief for everything she was going to lose.

Even this moment with Rune—with his arms wrapped tight around her shoulders, his face pressed into her hair, his heart pounding against her cheek—would be taken, seared away by the cut made four hundred years ago.

Nothing stayed.

"I don't want to forget." She squeezed her eyes shut, as if that could trap the tears inside, but her face was slick with them. Hot. Her head throbbed with pressure. "There's a library in my tower. At Winterfast. Most of it's destroyed, but"—her breath came harsh and ragged—"there's enough that I could have taken Draft there to look. And the others. And you. But I forgot about it. My own home."

Rune squeezed her tighter.

"The Incursion must be stopped. My memory is the least important problem, but it's causing us such—"

"That's ridiculous." Rune's hands slid to her shoulders as he pulled back and met her eyes. "They are important. *You* are important."

"I am the weapon," she rasped. "The warrior. I cannot be broken."

"You're also a woman." Rune's fingertips dug into her upper arms. "And you are more than your ability to fight rancor."

"I was built to—"

"That doesn't mean you're not a *person*. You try to hide your emotions, but they are real. You're allowed to feel them." Rune released her shoulders and cupped her face instead; his palms were cool against her flushed skin. "You think I don't understand, but all my life, I've been told the same as you: Don't feel so much. Be strong. Hard. Ready to fight as needed. My parents didn't want me to grieve for my brother—and I was given no time to grieve for them when they were taken, either. I had to be present for the kingdom. So I do understand, at least a little."

"It's not the same."

"It's not," he agreed. "But that doesn't change the fact that you are a person with feelings."

Another sob racked her, the deluge of tears hot and drowning. Rune held her close while she surrendered to the torrent of grief. How could she go on like this?

She pressed her face into Rune's shoulder, gasping, struggling to swallow back the sadness. But it was all escaping, everything she'd kept locked inside, and it was dragging her along with it. An undertow of heartbreak.

"It's all right," Rune murmured against her ear. "I've got you."

And he did. His arms tightened around her, steadying until her shaking subsided. Her face cooled. Her eyes weren't so heavy. Only when they breathed in time with each other did he relax his embrace.

"Thank you," she whispered into his shirt, now damp with the ocean she'd released. Gently, his fingers smoothed down her hair and the back of her neck. It felt good. Calming.

"Do you feel better now?"

"Yes. And no. All my problems remain. But I don't feel *as* wretched."

"Crying can be like that." He gave a faint chuckle.

Nightrender didn't move for several long moments, not until she'd recovered some of her composure. "I am still afraid," she admitted softly, "to become less. Salvation relies on me. And as much as I want an end to my endless battle—I don't want it like this."

"Perhaps the maintainers could help you?"

The Numina. There was another tangle of emotions, but she didn't have the energy for it. "The maintainers already slowed the loss. Perhaps, with more time, they could find a way to stop it entirely, but..."

"Time is not something you have." Rune sighed.

"I will end this Incursion. Go back to Winterfast. Sleeping there preserves my mind, as well as my body." She closed her eyes. "Until then, I am making new memories every moment." Like now. A memory of being held. Protected. Cared for. "And I will hold on to each precious one for as long as I can."

Warmth touched the top of her head: he kissed her there. "We will have the weapon," he said. "Soon. I will help you in every way. And when the dagger is complete, when the armies of Salvation have joined you at the Soul Gate, when you've destroyed the rancor king—then you'll go back to Winterfast. And the greatest scholars, priests, and alchemists in Salvation will devise a way to seal the cut in your mind. You will lose nothing else."

She gave a small nod. She could see her future: waking up in Winterfast hundreds of years from now, pain flashing through her at the heartbreak of separation. At knowing Rune was dead.

But it would be this moment she'd recall first.

When he pledged to help her.

And she believed him.

38.

RUNE

"Someone's coming," the Nightrender whispered.

Rune went still, his hand pausing midway down the length of her wind-blown hair. "How long before they get here?"

She twisted, turning her face against his shoulder once more. "Two minutes."

"If they won't be here for two whole minutes, how do you know they're coming *here?*"

She lifted one shoulder in a halfhearted shrug. "It's Draft. She smells like too much coffee."

So the maid-turned-librarian-turned-spy had been up all night. A visit this early could only mean she'd learned something—and it was urgent. "I suppose I should get dressed before she arrives."

The Nightrender didn't move.

"Or we'll both be very quiet and hope she goes away." He rather liked that plan, the two of them stealing an hour or two before she had to leave for Ivasland.

When she'd come in earlier, he'd thought he was dreaming. But she'd looked wrecked. Anguished. All this time, she'd been so burning *stoic* about losing her memories. He wished she'd talked about it more before now. Or that he'd asked.

He should have asked.

"No." Slowly, the Nightrender pushed herself up. She looked resigned. "Neither of us is capable of ignoring duties."

He wished he could. Not just this one, but all of them. At least for a little while.

Rune stood, cringing at the pain in his rib. And his leg. And all his other injuries yet to finish healing. "You're right. I should hear what Draft has to report."

The Nightrender paused mid-reach for her sword. "Draft is spying for you."

"She volunteered her services."

"Regarding..."

"Hanne. Nadine. They're missing. It's possible they were taken. But knowing Hanne, it's also possible she and Nadine went somewhere on their own without telling anyone."

If he hadn't just witnessed the Nightrender break down crying, he probably would have missed it—the way her expression shifted into sadness at the mention of Hanne's name. It lasted only an instant, and he couldn't be sure what it meant.

"I'll get dressed," he said. "Will you get the door?"

Her expression hardened. "I will."

Rune hurried into the bedroom, throwing on a black-and-gray uniform and combing his fingers through his hair. When he emerged once again, the Nightrender was just admitting Draft into the parlor.

"Your Majesty." Draft offered a quick curtsey. "I'm sorry for the hour."

"It's all right. What have you learned? Has Hanne been found?"

"Unfortunately no," Draft said. "However, my friends have reported that the queen's ladies speak of the observatory constantly. Lady Lea has gone there three times since Queen Johanne's disappearance. They're all very worried about where she is, but determined to finish this 'observatory project' for her, as they call it."

Rune stilled. The observatory? A project? "The observatory hasn't been used in decades." He took his sword off the shelf where he'd laid it earlier. "What do you know about this project?"

"Nothing for sure, but my friends think the queen is spying on the people of Brink, having her enemies watched."

That certainly sounded like something Hanne would do. "Let's visit the observatory. We'll get the truth of it." Rune headed out the door, the Nightrender, Draft, and Rose—who'd been standing guard in the hall—falling into step with him. In this early hour, the halls were near empty.

"I hope you and your colleagues are using caution," the Nightrender said to Draft. "Collecting information on queens is always a dangerous task, no matter the queen, no matter how liked or disliked she is."

"We are. Everyone understands how sensitive this is. None of my friends have ties to Lord Flight or Lady Shadowhand."

"What about Lady Sabine?" Rune asked. "She's Hanne's personal spy mistress."

Draft shook her head. "She's Embrian, and obviously working for Her Majesty."

Finally, they reached the observatory tower.

"I'll go first." The Nightrender drew her sword and began to climb the stairs.

Rune took a light globe and followed. The middle path of the stairs was scuffed, dust moved aside from people walking up and down. It lent credit to the idea that Hanne and her ladies had been spending an inordinate amount of time here.

"I smell malice," the Nightrender announced.

Now that she mentioned it, the scent touched the back of Rune's throat as well, ammoniac and rotting, a vile mix of sweetness and death. It made his nose and throat burn, and for a moment, he had to grip the wall and breathe through the redness curling around the corners of his vision.

"Your Majesty?" Rose's voice came from behind him.

Rune blinked, clearing his vision, and started up again. "I'm fine, Rose."

"Yes, Sire."

Rune clenched his jaw, keeping his gaze straight ahead.

At the top of the stairs, they filed into a large room with glass windows that extended from floor to ceiling. Tables, crates, and other articles of furniture littered the space. Rune nodded to Rose to check the other rooms. She moved forward, her dagger unsheathed.

"I don't hear anyone," the Nightrender murmured. "A few bugs crawling in the walls, but nothing else."

Someone—assuming they survived the Incursion—was going to have to deal with the bug problem the Nightrender kept pointing out.

Rose emerged from the lower room. "An unmade bed, piles of dirty clothes, and a wash area. Someone was living here, but not for long. A few weeks at most."

"Queen Johanne told the Crown Council that she was pregnant, but perhaps she . . ." Draft shot Rune a guilty look. "I shouldn't suggest it."

Perhaps Hanne had been keeping a man up here, Draft meant. Someone who looked enough like Rune. And now that Rune was back, Hanne's ladies had cleared the stranger out of the tower before he could be discovered.

"It's true," Rune said slowly, "that Hanne was being less than honest with the council about her condition, but what happened *here* had nothing to do with that. The stink of malice is overwhelming. This is something else."

The Nightrender looked up, those dark eyes seeing straight into his soul. "She lied to the council. And to me."

Hanne had lied to the Nightrender about being pregnant, too? Perhaps she'd thought that would induce the Nightrender to rescue him from the Malice.

Well, he could demand answers from Hanne once he found her. And this place was certainly a clue to what had become of her. "Before she disappeared, she was asking what I thought about malice—if I believed it could be used for good. That must have been related to this project."

"You think Queen Johanne and Lady Nadine left Honor's Keep to complete it?" Draft asked.

"Perhaps they were *taken* because of it," Rose said. "And we must consider the possibility that Her Majesty's abductors are in control of this project now. I'd like to conduct a full search of the castle, temple, and city, in case it's been moved to a different location."

"Use cats and hounds," the Nightrender said. "They will be sensitive to the odor of malice."

Rune gave a quick nod, granting permission. "Have the queen's chambers monitored as well. Abduction or not, it's possible that Hanne's own people finished the observatory project. Watch Ladies Shadowhand and Stareyes, too; they're loyal to Hanne."

"Of course," Rose said. "I'll look into all of it."

Already exhausted by the day—even before dawn—Rune approached the nearest window and stared out at his kingdom. There was a panoramic view of Caberwill from up here, and a clear line of sight to the Malstop in the distance. It shone bright against the black sky.

Movement in the glass made him shift his focus from the view outside to the dark reflection. The Nightrender stood behind him, her wings stretched wide. From this angle, it looked as though Rune himself had wings, black and huge.

He stood, transfixed by the image until she shifted away. "I must go immediately to Ivasland."

To get the second piece of the weapon. Right. To stave off whatever additional devastation Hanne had brought them.

As the Nightrender moved toward the smaller, central stair that led to the roof, Rune motioned for Draft and Rose to wait. Then he followed the Nightrender onto the roof.

It was chilly up here, with wind whipping around them, but Rune hardly noticed as he caught sight of the sky above. He stood, head dropped back, and drank in the familiar night, the galaxy a spiral of illumination, a spinning vortex. He'd seen the sky over Salvation a thousand times before, of course, all his life, but after the endless red of the Malice, how could he ever take such a sight for granted again?

"It's beautiful. I know." The Nightrender stood at his side, wings outstretched to buffer the wind. "I always look, too. Every time."

"Has it changed much?" Rune had seen sky maps from a thousand years ago. They were missing major stars, or had those stars in different positions. They'd also included stars that weren't in the sky anymore.

"It is different than it used to be. The sky is in motion, just as we are." She glanced at him, the shape of her silhouetted by starlight and limned with silver. The wind shifted. Feathers rustled, and a ribbon of dark hair blew into her face. "I meant to thank you," she whispered. "For earlier."

"If anyone asks, I'll tell them you were overflowing from too much water."

A faint smile turned up the corner of her mouth. "I needed you. You were there for me. I am grateful." She stepped away. "Use the feather if you need to speak to me."

Use the feather? But before he could ask, she was soaring high into the sky, a dark shape against the brilliant spiral above.

Then, as the cold started to creep through his clothes, he bent and drew the feather from his boot. It gleamed in the starlight, rainbow shades hidden in its blackness.

I heard you, she'd told him at the Soul Gate.

And right before she'd come into the parlor, he'd said he wished she was there with him.

He let out a low, nervous laugh, suddenly unable to recall if he'd said anything embarrassing while holding the feather.

"You're probably going to wish I didn't know you could hear me through this." He touched the flat of the feather to his mouth, smiled, and then slipped it back into his boot.

As he turned to the stairs again, his smile fell away. It was time to confront Hanne's ladies and find out what they knew about this observatory project—and Hanne's schemes.

"Are you sure this is wise, Your Majesty?" Rose asked.

Rune and Rose stood outside the queen's chambers, waiting for someone to answer the door. "Second-guessing myself will do no good," Rune said. Besides, they'd already knocked.

There was a scuffling inside, a few muttered orders Rune couldn't quite make out, and finally, one of Hanne's ladies-in-waiting opened the door. A petite brunette, her eyes wide with surprise.

"Your Majesty! It's barely dawn!" She snapped her mouth closed. It didn't matter what time the king called upon someone.

"Good morning, Lady"—he made a quick guess about which one she was—"Cecelia."

She offered a quick curtsey, then stepped aside to allow him entrance. "Has there been any news about Hanne?"

Rune motioned for Rose to stay in the hall before he followed Lady Cecelia into the parlor, where Lea and Maris curtsied from either side of a game of Mora's Gambit, and Lady Sabine was making a show of pushing herself up from her chair by the window—an act, if he'd ever seen one. Still, he motioned for her to remain sitting, and she did, taking up her knitting once more.

It was clear they'd all been talking before this, and there'd been a hasty effort to look casual now that he was here.

"Let me be up-front," Rune said. "I have not yet discovered Queen Johanne's location, but I believe you already know where she is. It's in your best interest—and hers—for you to tell me everything immediately."

Lea gave a faint gasp, but no one else said a word.

Rune held his ground, maintaining a faintly annoyed expression as he looked from lady to lady.

Cecelia shifted her weight, betraying nerves. And on the far side of the room, Lady Sabine had, apparently, finished doing some personal math. She abandoned her knitting and came toward Rune. "We believe Rupert Flight and Charity Wintersoft are behind Her Majesty's disappearance."

Well, that wasn't wholly a surprise, but abducting a queen was a serious offense. Would they really risk it? Her observatory project must have been a direct threat to them. "Go on," he said.

Lady Sabine's eyes narrowed. "As you know, the former councilors attempted a legal coup while you were gone. Queen Johanne put a stop to it. However, both Duchess Wintersoft and Earl Flight are"—she smiled, with teeth—"persistent. I believe they saw another opportunity to do harm to Hanne."

"By taking her? What do they have to gain by removing her now that I've returned?" The plan to put a princess on the throne only stood a chance during Rune's absence. Unless, perhaps, they meant to assassinate him?

"The plot was likely in place well before your return, Sire," Lady Sabine said. "After all, she was taken only hours after you reached Honor's Keep."

Rune nodded slowly. That made a plot to murder him less likely, but not *un*likely. Considering his return had interrupted their coup and he'd immediately dismissed them from the Crown Council . . . They would both have to be watched.

"And where is she?" Rune put his hands behind his back, forcing his shoulders straight. He wasn't the intimidating presence that his father had been, but he was tall and broad, and he used that to his advantage now.

"Embria. As for where exactly, I don't know. My"—Lady Sabine's lips thinned into a line for a moment—"connections have gone quiet."

A chill worked through Rune.

"The whole of Embrian peasantry has turned against Hanne," Lea volunteered. "And the entire Fortuin family."

Rune had caught up on the council minutes, which had listed all of those problems: Silver Sun (which he'd known about before), a mob marching on Solcast, something about livestock.

"They were calling for her head," Maris said. "The peasants have been trying to murder Hanne for weeks. And now they'll get their chance."

One of the ladies-in-waiting made a small, pitiful sound of despair.

The possibility that Hanne was dead struck Rune harder than he'd thought it might. He didn't love her. He didn't even trust her. But he couldn't help but care about her.

"The rebels will not show her any mercy," Sabine confirmed darkly. "It's not the Embrian way. No, Your Majesty, they'll destroy her. Mob justice is no justice at all."

"I need her alive." Not just for himself, but for Salvation. If Embria had made similar decisions to Caberwill, then only a few people knew the location of the summoning shrine: it was either Hanne or her parents, and Hanne—for all her many faults—had something resembling a conscience.

It seemed Rune's original suspicions had been wrong: this didn't have anything to do with the observatory project. *That* was a problem for tomorrow. Because if Hanne wasn't dead already, she would be soon.

Rune turned and started out of the room.

"Your Majesty?" Lea asked.

He paused, his hand on the door. "You're all confined to your quarters. Meals will be delivered to you. Guards will be stationed outside."

"What about Hanne?" Lea asked.

He clenched his jaw. "I'll get her back."

Within the hour, Rune had penned a note to the Embrian rebels and sent it via dove. Echo, his secretary, had run up to the aviary to take it, and while he waited for her to return, he bent over his (father's) desk and rested his forehead on the cool wood.

"I've got men ready to arrest Flight and Wintersoft at your command, Sire." Rose stood in the doorway, ready to warn him if anyone approached.

"Good. The moment we have enough evidence, I want them sent to the dungeon." He blew out a breath. "To think they would be so brazen as to abduct a queen. And to work with Embrian rebels."

"Do you think they'll see reason? The Embrians, I mean."

"Perhaps." His voice was muffled against the desktop. He turned his head.

"But what is reason? They've been mistreated for so long, and now they learn that their own rulers not only broke the Winterfast Accords, but indirectly killed their own people in one of the most terrible ways imaginable. Add that to the other atrocities...the inequality..."

Rose frowned. "So you don't think this will work?"

"I think I must attempt the diplomatic way first. I reminded them about the alliance, about the Incursion. I implored them to think of Salvation. I begged them to give me back my queen and take their fight to the Soul Gate."

"If we knew who was leading the rebellion there, we might have some ability to anticipate their receptiveness. But the reports are too conflicted."

He pushed himself up straight again. The prospect of success seemed very grim indeed. Embria, embroiled in its own burgeoning civil war, could not be relied upon to send warriors into the Malice. And Ivasland, if the limited information was correct, had ceased all productivity; workers were on strike, while scholars wrote mountains of invective against the crown, and the army—what there was, anyway—had fractured into different factions.

Rune sighed and glanced at the feather, which rested on the edge of his desk, dark and gleaming. He touched the smooth barbs, careful of the sharp edge. "I hope you're having better luck than I am."

39.

NIGHTRENDER

Ivasland was not how Nightrender remembered.

For one thing, there were stars in all the windows, made from light rods. For another, the fields and villages were quiet, the university empty, and the streets of Athelney were packed with people chanting at the royal residence.

"Ivasland needs answers!" they called as one.

"Medicine not malice!" another group shouted.

Some held signs, but most carried light rods that had been lashed to one another in the shape of stars, just like the windows. The lights shone ominously from above, even during the day.

"No more malice machines!"

What a nice change. Not everyone was willing to destroy the world for their wars.

But even as she thought that, she spotted a smaller group of counterprotestors, chanting things like "Ivasland ingenuity!" and calling for victory over their enemies at any cost.

"Who do the Winterfast Accords benefit?" a young woman called.

"Them!"

"Who do the Winterfast Accords oppress?" she asked.

"Us!"

The protests wove through every street of Althelney, all focused on the royal household. The guards who usually organized people into groups before they visited the king and queen were absent. Either they'd joined one of the movements or they'd been overwhelmed by the immense crowds. It seemed like all of Ivasland was here; the noise of their anger was incredible, even from high up.

There was no time to wait for the protestors to disperse on their own, so Nightrender descended, dropping from the sky without ceremony into the courtyard in front of the royal residence. Immediately, people began to scatter.

"Run!"

"The Nightrender!"

"She's come to punish us for breaking the Winterfast Accords!"

Nightrender flicked dirt off her wings and tucked them behind her, gazing around at the people fleeing. It cut her, still, to see them running, not bothering to hide their terror. But she pulled herself tall and strode toward the royal residence. And when the people realized she wasn't there to murder them indiscriminately, they watched her with fascination.

"She's here for the queen!" someone declared, and the idea rippled through the crowd. "*We* didn't break the Winterfast Accords. Queen Abagail did."

"Should we stop her?"

"And protect the queen? No. She made her choice."

Nightrender reached the double doors, shut tight and bolted on the other side. She grasped both handles and yanked the doors off their hinges, wood and metal screaming as she flung them out of her way. The crack of the doors against the ground caused new shouts and screams, and as she entered the building, none followed her inside. They huddled by the broken doors, watching.

Though it was past noon and cloud-filtered sunlight fell across the city, the interior of the residence was dark. Nightrender's eyes adjusted immediately to the gloom, so she had no trouble spotting the queen of Ivasland emerging from a doorway.

Queen Abagail Athelney cut a smaller figure than Nightrender, wearing a blue tunic and trousers, with a small gold pin at her breast. She held herself straight and proud, though, and her hair was meticulously brushed and braided. Shadows beneath her eyes spoke of sleepless nights.

"Lady Nightrender." Though Queen Abagail's voice was strong, her gaze kept darting behind Nightrender—to the crowd of people watching just outside the door. "How generous of you to tear yourself away from the Highcrowns to visit me."

"You've been so busy with your malice machine. And I've been busy cleaning up your mess."

Queen Abagail's jaw flexed. "So you've come to kill me?"

Faint gasps came from the doorway.

"No," Nightrender said. "I require access to your summoning shrine."

"I don't see why you need it. You're already here."

"That does not concern you. But for the sake of Salvation—and your people—lead me to it now."

"My people." Queen Abagail's lip curled as she turned away from the doorway and her subjects crowded there. She stared at the empty thrones.

Nightrender narrowed her eyes. There were neither guards, nor a secretary, nor anyone else. Even the rest of the building was quiet. No shuffling of maids. No clerks sifting through papers. Not even a priest.

It was only the queen here.

No king.

Nightrender gentled her tone. "I need the shrine. Take me to it, and I'll leave you to your responsibilities here."

Queen Abagail glanced over her shoulder. "Protect me, and I'll take you to the shrine."

"I am not your bodyguard," Nightrender said. "You must answer to your people, as all monarchs eventually do."

"Everything I did was for the greater good of Ivasland." Queen Abagail's voice trembled. "Caberwill and Embria have had their boots on our throats for decades. We cannot afford water. My people are starving. And I thought—" She dragged in a long, shuddering breath. "I thought if our enemies understood our true might, we could shake them off."

"You breached the Winterfast Accords."

"It was for my people," Queen Abagail insisted. "Everything was for them."

"She had the malicists killed!" someone yelled from the door. "Everyone knows now."

A handful of agreements rose up, but no one crossed the threshold. Perhaps they were still waiting to see whether Nightrender would do their work for them.

Nightrender sighed and turned her attention back on the queen. "I am here for the shrine, not to hurt you. As for your people—you must make the argument that you are yet worthy of the crown. I cannot do that for you. Though"—Nightrender turned toward the doorway—"I would caution you against harming her. Violence only feeds malice. And the Incursion is already upon us."

"We *should* be better than her," a young woman said. "She may be willing to help malice gain a foothold in Ivasland, but I'm not."

"Nor am I," a man agreed.

"She has so much to answer for," someone else said. "Her actions cannot go unpunished."

"A trial," the first woman suggested. "And a vote—to see if she remains or if someone else takes the throne."

Queen Abagail's face was ashen. "What you've already done to Baldric—"

"Was exactly what he deserved!" someone farther back cried. They hefted a makeshift star. "He ordered the military to move against us."

Nightrender held up a hand as she looked between the queen and her angry subjects. "I did not come here to provide mediation. Work this out later." She made her voice hard, raising it so all would hear. "The Malstop is buckling under the pressure from within. I must end this Incursion with haste. Help me. Or, if you won't, stop delaying me."

From the doorway, several people looked back—toward the Malstop, where it shone against the afternoon sky.

"It looks strong to me," a man said.

"The Malstop has held for hundreds of years," someone else agreed. "It will continue to hold."

Nightrender's jaw clenched. "Queen Abagail, the shri—"

But before she could make her final appeal, a faint buzzing zipped through Nightrender's bones; a wave of sickness rolled through her stomach.

The sky went fully dark.

Nightrender moved toward the door. The protestors moved backward. Slowly, they lowered their chemical stars and looked up.

"What's happening?" someone asked. "I feel sick."

Nightrender's breath came short as she stepped outside to get a better look, to scan the sky for the sun. But an unnatural twilight gripped the land, causing bugs to sing and bats to swarm.

"Something's not right." Queen Abagail, apparently forgetting about her fear of being murdered, came to stand by the door next to Nightrender. "It's only afternoon."

"It's the Incursion," Nightrender whispered. "Lead me to the shrine before it's too late."

It was already too late. Beyond the crowds of protestors with their lowered lights, beyond the battered buildings, beyond the sparse woods and lazy hills—a sickly green bloomed over the sky.

The light shot straight into the center of Salvation, slamming into the Malstop with an explosive force strong enough to powder a mountain.

Seconds later, a terrible cacophony—like metal twisting, like stars screaming, like earth cracking—hit the city. People clutched their heads, trying to protect their ears, but the noise was too great. They doubled over, crying for help as a rumble shot through the earth, shaking buildings and throwing people off their feet. The crowd wailed, while Queen Abagail gripped the doorframe, her knuckles turning white against the deep brown of the wood.

Nightrender stood tall, her balance better than most, and kept her gaze on the green light consuming the Malstop with increasing horror. She knew what the green light was. She had seen it too many times, battled it every awakening.

It was malice. It coated the Malstop like oil.

"What is that?" Queen Abagail pressed her hands to her chest. "What is happening?"

There was no need for Nightrender to answer. The queen was asking only because that was what mortals did when something was too horrible to be true.

Slowly, agonizingly, the green light faded, leaving behind nothing but darkness.

The world quieted—a held breath. The birds stilled, the bugs hushed. Unnatural night blanketed Salvation. Even the light rods went out; Athelney was dark and quiet.

"Where is it?" someone whispered.

"Where is what?"

It was hard to see what wasn't there.

"The Malstop." Nightrender's voice rang across the courtyard. "It's gone."

40.

HANNE

Dark laughter rumbled through the back of her head.

What? Hanne made her thoughts into acid, as though she could burn him away. *What are you so pleased about?*

Across the cell, Nadine paused where she was turning the lights. "Can you feel that? It's like— Like a static." She rubbed her arms. "Something is different."

She was right. The air felt sharp. A bitter taste stuck to Hanne's tongue.

Hanne stood, the dirty silk of her dress dragging on the floor where it had torn. "What do you thi—"

An image bloomed in her mind.

She was standing on the parapets of a tall castle, bone crunching beneath her feet. All around her, the air was red, deep and bloody. Clouds skittered across the sky, and where they parted, Hanne could see that the redness went on forever. There was no end to it.

It looked like the Dark Shard—but in the distance, there were towers. *Human*-made towers.

They were faint, wrong from this angle, but Hanne had seen the guard towers her whole life. She had studied them more carefully over the last few weeks, once she had been given orders to send the mal-devices there and destroy the Malstop.

She should be panicking, she knew, but her hearts—plural?—beat steady rhythms in her chest, and her breathing remained even. Her mouth, too, pulled into a wide smile—wider than should have been possible.

Only when the clawed hand passed in front of her vision did Hanne realize that she wasn't seeing out of her eyes. Bone-white flesh, yellowed claws, and the hint of immense bat wings in the periphery of her vision: she was seeing through *his* eyes.

How?

But more important was what he looked at: he stared across the Malice, toward the very edges where there should have been a white-blue barrier. Now there was nothing, only red sky pressing outward. Soon, he would be able to go there. He would be able to leave his prison.

Soon.

The vision faded.

Hanne came back to herself, her head pounding. "The observatory project. It worked."

"What?" Nadine touched Hanne's arm.

"The Malstop is gone."

Nadine paled, horror drawing open her mouth. "No. How long have we been here? The equinox—"

"Is now. Today." Hanne swayed on her feet as darkness crawled across her vision. "But armies were supposed to be in place. We were supposed to kill rancor. The Malstop was supposed to come back."

But none of that was happening. Nothing was going how she'd meant for it to go.

First the night, Daghath Mal whispered. **And then, as the substance of my world presses into yours, I will be free.**

Nausea roiled in Hanne's stomach as she sank to the bench and buried her face in her hands. "I'm sorry," she rasped. "I'm so sorry."

She had doomed the word.

Thank you, my beautiful queen. I couldn't have done it without you.

41.
NIGHTRENDER

While the protestors were still discussing whether or not the Malstop would return, Nightrender grabbed Queen Abagail by the arm and dragged her into the receiving room. "I need the summoning shrine," Nightrender hissed. "I need it immediately."

Queen Abagail yanked her arm away from Nightrender. "How dare you touch me." She was trembling, her eyes wide with fear. "What did you do to the Malstop?"

"I did nothing. I was here with you. That was *malice*."

"When will it come back?" Queen Abagail's voice was small. "When it flickered before, it was gone only a moment."

Nightrender glanced through the broken doorway again. The sky was still dark. The Malstop had not returned. Nor had the sun. "I don't know." The maintainers usually brought back the Malstop as quickly as they could. They were probably in their towers right now. "The summoning shrine. Your kingdom depends on it."

Queen Abagail's eyes were wild, but the threat to her kingdom reached her. "Fine. This way."

Nightrender followed the queen deeper into the royal residence, up a set of stairs, and into a large room at the back of the building. Crates lined the walls, while sheets covered large pieces of furniture. Dust coated everything.

Another storage room.

But the shrine was there, the shape of it obvious beneath a gray sheet. When Nightrender picked her way through the mess on the floor—her wings tucked tightly in to avoid destroying objects in her path—she could detect smears in the dust, shoe prints, and even the dried-up residue where someone had sneezed. They'd lifted the sheet to look at the shrine, then let it fall back into the dust.

"You were going to summon me." Nightrender glanced over her shoulder, toward the doorway where Queen Abagail stood uncertainly.

"No." She shifted her weight. "Baldric talked about it once. He thought we should call on you to destroy the malsites, but I persuaded him to try it my way first."

"The machines."

Queen Abagail nodded. "I'd reminded him about the Red Dawn, and the punishment for summoning you when there wasn't an Incursion. He'd thought the malsites would have been enough to warrant your coming here. But neither of us could argue away the Red Dawn. Neither of us could take the risk."

Nightrender slipped the sheet off the shrine, revealing the same pitted stone as in Caberwill, the same figure on the front.

She didn't open it yet. Instead, she surveyed the room for exits, but aside from the door she'd come through, there was only a small window. Not big enough for her to slip through, unless she wanted to take the whole wall with her.

"King Rune will send his army to the Soul Gate." Nightrender stood straight and gave the young queen a pointed look. "With the Malstop down, rancor will spill across the lands. You will need to be ready to fight. Be ready to defend your people. Take them into any safe locations you have."

Queen Abagail shook her head. "There isn't—"

"Ivasland has always been able to protect its people from Incursions. Do not be the first to fail."

A look of defiance hardened Queen Abagail's face. "I would love nothing more than to protect—"

"Then do it. South of Athelney, you will find a series of caverns. The network is vast, and once was filled with stores of food, water, and weapons. The walls, floors, and ceiling are filled with tiny shards of obsidian."

The queen drew a sharp breath. "Ivasland has been sitting on obsidian this whole time?"

"Yes. It is your greatest secret, this place, and even during the most difficult of times, your predecessors never mined it, as it is the safest place for Ivaslanders to go during an Incursion. The obsidian in the ground will not immunize you against rancor, should they attack directly, but it will prevent malice from affecting you the way it will anywhere else."

A beat of silence. Then, "All right. I'll send people there. And King Rune—he's going to the Soul Gate?"

Nightrender nodded.

"I'll have to regain control of my army."

"Anyone who can fight will be needed," Nightrender said. "Without the Malstop to shield Salvation, this will be a battle like no other."

"You think the Malstop will be down that long?"

"It's possible."

"It's difficult to think about fighting alongside Caberwillines and Embrians," Queen Abagail was saying. "How can I ask my people to do that? They're already so angry..."

"I cannot tell you how to be a queen the people love. You must discover that on your own."

"But you must know something. You've seen so many rulers."

A knot tightened in Nightrender's chest; she forced herself to speak around it. "Centuries ago, all three kingdoms put aside their differences to train Dawnbreakers, to send them into battle together. When an Incursion was imminent, there was only one war that mattered. That is what you—and your people—must remember." Nightrender turned back to the shrine. "You should go. This will be unpleasant."

Queen Abagail frowned, but left. Nightrender gave her a few minutes, listening as the queen presented herself to the protestors outside, announced that she was working with the Nightrender to help all of Salvation—and Ivasland in particular—and asking them to remain calm and gather their belongings.

When the expected resistance sounded, when Abagail Athelney called for order, Nightrender placed her hands on the summoning shrine. She released a pulse of power and, as before, the shrine opened to reveal darkness. Nightrender reached inside, grasping until her fingers closed on a curve of wrought metal. The cross guard.

She tucked it into her pocket, then rushed from the room, wings giving her lift as she flew through the door.

The rancor were close. She could feel the disruptions they caused in the air, smell the vile odor of their malice.

Nightrender wheeled around a corner, her wings slicing into the wood. At the far end of the hall, a door stood half open. She ran for it, threw the door the rest of the way open, and drew her sword.

A swing, almost before she realized what she was doing, and Beloved sliced across the palid mushroom flesh of a rancor.

The beast shrieked, raking its claws toward Nightrender. She spun away, wings fanning. Blood spurted from its flesh where her feathers cut. Then it was down.

Another crouched in the shadows, its eyes narrowed and teeth dripping with gore. It lurched for her, claws out, jaw wide.

Light flashed through the room as Nightrender swung Beloved in a wide arc. The blade cut through the beast's throat. Black blood spilled across the floor, sizzling where it ate through the rug.

"What are you after?" another rancor cried. "What are you doing?"

Nightrender killed that one, too.

But the trio hadn't come alone. As she pushed outside, slinging the balcony door wide, she spotted three more winged rancor. They shot down from the sky, shrieking as they slammed straight into the crowd of Ivaslanders.

Screams sounded across the courtyard. Then, the clash of metal as people turned the weapons they'd intended for Queen Abagail on the rancor.

Nightrender burst from the royal residence and drove her blade into the first rancor she saw. Before it could fight back, her numinous power flooded into it. She moved onto the next one.

And the next.

And the next.

Blood—rancor and human—slicked the ground by the time she'd killed all the beasts. People were sobbing, while others moved bodies away.

"This won't be the last," Nightrender announced, her voice carrying over the false night. "More will come."

"What do we do?" That was a man whose arm was being bandaged. "When will the Malstop return?"

"I wish I could tell you." Nightrender raised her eyes to the eerie darkness in the north. It had been nearly an hour since the Malstop fell; what could be keeping the maintainers? "I understand that you are in the middle of an uprising. However, leadership is required in this moment. Queen Abagail has agreed to help me end this Incursion. If you want to fight for your home—for your future—I encourage you to join her."

Queen Abagail stepped forward. "I've heard your protests. And changes *will* be made. But first, we must fight." She turned to Nightrender. "Those who are willing will meet you at the Soul Gate. Our machines, our tactics, our warriors: they will be yours to command, Lady Nightrender."

"Good." Grimly, Nightrender flicked the rancor blood off her sword and sheathed it. Then she lifted into the air, wings pumping through the darkness as she flew toward Winterfast to hide the cross guard.

And though she glanced toward the center of Salvation more than once, the Malstop remained dark.

42.

RUNE

Rune couldn't get over how dark it was. Morning had come and gone, but the sun failed to rise.

The Malstop was missing. Down. Destroyed. That was the only thing anyone was talking about. Already reports were piling onto his desk. Chancellors, nobles, and generals had been in and out of his office all morning, asking what to do, demanding supplies and rescues, and giving him the latest news from doves crashing into the aviary.

It was like this everywhere. People were terrified. Malsites had erupted out of the ground like blisters. Others had exploded into the sky, forming pockets of deep green gas or *changing* the wildlife somehow. One report described a cross between a hawk and wasp. Another said a dragon had formed out of trees and bears and fire. In the north, lakes were burning. And other missives declared the entirety of the Deepway Woods was gone—completely erased from the map of Caberwill.

There were a thousand unverified claims, but they all seemed possible to Rune. He'd traversed the Malice. He'd seen what could happen there.

Now it would happen here. At home.

He pushed away from his desk and the mountains of papers. It was afternoon, but the window was dark. He peered out anyway, hoping to see the edge of the Malstop that should have been visible from here.

It wasn't.

He could feel its absence, half see the negative image of where it used to be. And when his eyes unfocused, he could see the redness of the Malice blooming outward.

"Sire?" The office door opened and Rose stepped in. "Another group of refugees has come to Brink. They're from Cliffside."

"Give them whatever we can spare." Burn everything. How dare his parents and grandparents leave the kingdom so unprepared for an attack of this magnitude? The truth had been in front of them for years, and they had ignored it.

Now it was on him.

Rune sighed. "Rose, send someone to fetch my sisters."

While Rose stepped into the hall to wave down one of the patrolling guards, Rune pulled a sheet of paper from his desk, dipped his quill pen in ink, and began to write. By the time he'd finished, Sanctuary and Unity were lurking in his doorway, both of them looking uncertain.

"Come in," Rune said. "Sit down." He wiped off his pen and capped the ink.

Both girls sat straight-backed with their hands folded in their laps. "Are we in trouble?" Sanctuary asked.

"No." Rune slid the paper across the desk to them. "You're not in trouble at all, but I wanted to talk to you about something important."

They both waited.

"I don't know what's going to happen in the future. I don't know why the Malstop fell, or when it will return." That was a slight fib—he had a pretty good idea Hanne's observatory project had something to do with it—but he didn't want to frighten his sisters more than necessary. "But no matter what happens, the kingdom will always need someone sitting on the throne, someone guiding the people.

"None of us were ever supposed to be the reigning monarch. Neither of you. Not me. But we are now in a position where we have to look out for one another. I may be on the throne today, but Hanne was right that both of you need to be trained: educated in government and law in case you're ever called to serve the people of Caberwill, as I was."

"I don't want to be queen over Unity," Sanctuary said. "I don't care that I'm older. I think she'd be better."

Unity shook her head. "People listen to Sanctuary. No one listens to me."

"You're both right," he said. "And that's why, if something ever happens to me—"

Unity's eyes went round, welling with tears.

"If," Rune repeated, "something happens, then you will both be queens. Sister queens."

They glanced at each other. "What does that mean?" Sanctuary asked.

"Sanctuary, people listen to you. You have an authoritative way of speaking. You're commanding. And you're tall, like Father, and getting taller every day. People respond well to a stature like yours."

"She's always getting new dresses," Unity observed.

Rune bit back a smile. "And Unity, you're clever and thoughtful, and you've always cared deeply about what is fair or unfair. That empathy would serve you well as a queen.

"The two of you together would be a powerful team. You would lead the kingdom well, I think, if you put your minds to it. But you would do it as sisters—as equals." Rune tapped the paper he'd just written. "That's what this outlines. It's an agreement between the three of us, that if one of you is elevated to queen, the other is as well—and you'd do it without a regent."

"You don't think we'd need one?" Unity's eyebrows knitted together. "Duchess Charity always said either of us would be a good queen, but we'd need guidance."

"You'd have the Crown Council for that," Rune said. "Just listening to them argue their opinions will help you make informed decisions together."

The sisters looked at each other again, communicating in some invisible way.

"This may never even happen," Rune said. "I don't plan to die, after all."

Unity looked down at the paper, reading. "And when Hanne comes back, you'll have an heir of your own."

Rune cringed, but he didn't argue.

"So this is just in case," Unity said, "so the kingdom is never without a leader."

"Yes." It was easier, for now, to agree. His future with Hanne was an unknown, complicated by the alliance, the question of whether it was even needed now. . . .

That was his burden, not theirs, so he looked at his sisters in turn and asked, "Will you sign?"

"Do we have a choice?" Sanctuary asked.

He nodded.

"If we don't sign," Unity said, "and something happens to Rune, one of us will be queen regardless. Probably you, first, unless you abdicate, and then it's just me on my own."

Sanctuary swallowed. "And we wouldn't have anything official saying we don't need a regent."

Unity nodded. "This makes both of us have to do a job we don't want, but it protects us, too."

"Then I'll sign it," Sanctuary said. "If you will."

"I will." Unity took the pen, but paused before her other hand closed over the ink. "We should have witnesses. Otherwise people might not believe us—*if* we ever need to use this."

Rune went to the door and cracked it open. "Rose, are any councilors out there? Any nobles?"

"Echo has a message that just arrived at the aviary. The grand priest and grand physician are also here, as well as the education chancellor."

"Send them all in."

Within minutes, it was done. Rune, Sanctuary, and Unity signed the agreement, followed by the witnesses.

"Now," Rune said, addressing the newcomers, "I know you all came here for a reason, and this was not it. What do you need?"

"I came to offer the temple obsidian for the fight against the Malice," Dayle said. "All the ancient artifacts and weapons. Spears, pendants, bracers—anything that will help drive back the darkness."

Rune nodded deeply. "Thank you. Everything will make a difference right now."

Stella was next. "I need approval assigning medical students to assist physicians at the Soul Gate."

"Granted." Rune signed the paper she'd brought. "And Lelia?"

"Food for the orphanages. No matter what happens, no matter where the army is now, many children will soon lose their parents."

"Of course. Thank you for thinking of them."

The councilors left, and Rune turned to Echo. "Rose said you had a message from the aviary?"

She pulled a strip of curled paper off her desk and offered it to Rune.

The mark on the outside signaled urgency, for the king's eyes only. Rune snapped the seal, found a magnifying glass, and scanned the text. His stomach dropped. "Thank you, Echo."

With a bow, the secretary stepped out of the room.

"What is it?" Unity asked. "Can I see?"

Well, there was a chance she might be co-queen one day. Rune handed her the glass and paper.

"Is this from a spy?" Sanctuary was leaning over the message along with her sister. "One of our spies?"

Rune nodded.

Queen Johanne is in rebel custody. Trial. Guilty. Execution pending.

"She's to be executed?" Sanctuary scowled at the note. "By her own people?"

"Yes." Rune returned to the dark window. Lights dotted the city below, both candles and globes. He checked his watch again; the sun should be lowering toward the horizon now, and the entire city should be awash in golden light.

Burn this darkness. And burn Hanne for getting abducted when she was the only one who might know where the final summoning shrine was hidden.

Rune needed a solution. What would his father have done in this situation?

Well, he would have used the army.

But Rune's army was needed at the Soul Gate.

He spun and marched to the door. "Rose, ready my guard. We're going to Embria."

Unity lurched up. "What if you don't come back?"

Rune nodded to the agreement still resting on his desk, the ink barely dry. "Then you'll rule in my stead. But I will come back."

They didn't ask him to promise. They knew he couldn't.

Rune hadn't seen the portal site since it had settled. His last memories of this place were wild, chaotic, with his soldiers getting caught in giant spheres of malice that transported them far away. He remembered the mayhem as he looked through the darkness and saw *her*: the Nightrender fighting an army of rancor.

Now there were fresh yellow ribbons, bells clinking gently in the wind.

The ammonia odor of malice was strong, but it smelled like this everywhere since the Malstop collapsed.

Rune dismounted. Rose and the other three guards followed, leading their horses to the rough guard station.

A soldier—a lieutenant, judging by the insignia on his jacket—strode out, a light rod in one hand. "State your name and business."

"Rose Emberwish. On a mission for the king." Rose produced the papers she'd shown to men at various checkpoints along the way. None of them had even noticed Rune there with her, dressed in the same uniform his royal guards wore. "A *covert* mission, Lieutenant"—she looked at his jacket—"Crosswind."

The lieutenant glanced at the credentials, Rune's signature at the bottom, and nodded. "Very well. Where are you looking to go? I can help you find the right portal."

"Solspire," Rose said. "As close to the palace as possible."

"Popular destination." Crosswind handed the papers back to her and motioned for them to follow. "Keep a tight hand on your horses if you're going to bring them. Most don't like crossing the yellow line, let alone going through one of the portals. I've seen some unhappy mounts lately."

Rune fell into the middle of the line of guards as they stepped into the malsite. They stepped between the drifting spheres, Rune taking in the destinations of each one. A forest. A room. A snowy landscape. They were all dark, save the locations lit by torches, candles, globes. Wait—on the far side of the malsite, there was a brighter portal, like daylight.

"What do you mean Solspire is popular?" Rose asked, drawing Rune's attention back. "Did someone else go there recently?"

"I can't tell you any names." The lieutenant glanced back at Rose. "I shouldn't have said anything."

It was confirmation enough. Not many people had unfettered access to the portal site. The queen. The council. Former councilors whose access hadn't yet been revoked.

They continued winding around the portals until finally Lieutenant Crosswind stopped in front of one that showed a dark clearing.

"That destination is guarded," Crosswind said. "Embrian rebels patrol the breach at all hours." He eyed their horses, packs, and dark uniforms. "Be quick. They sound a single horn blast every hour, and two blasts when some-one comes through the portal."

"How do you know that?" Rose kept one hand on her horse's flank, patting him occasionally, as she gazed into the portal. "You can't hear anything on the other side."

"Good thing. I don't want to imagine the noise of all these places." Cross-wind shook his head. "Our initial scouts sent reports and warnings. A full list of destinations was being complied for the crown, but—" The lieutenant glanced to where the Malstop should have been.

"Thank you, Lieutenant." Rose motioned to Rune and the others. "Everyone mount up."

Rune hauled himself onto his horse, then reached down to pet the dark, sweaty neck as the poor thing danced, trying desperately to avoid the drifting portals. None were dangerously close, but the reek of malice was strong, bur-rowing into his nose and sinuses, all the way into the back of his throat.

"Let's go." Rose kicked her horse, and though it refused to step into the portal at first, she dug in her heels, gave a sharp cry, and in they went. The next horse was equally unhappy about being asked to venture into a bubble of malice, but Rose and her mount were visible on the other side now, so the next went, then the next.

Just as Rune was ready to go in, Lieutenant Crosswind looked at him and asked, "Aren't you—"

Rune kicked his mount and they leaped into the dark sphere.

As before when he'd taken a malice portal, everything went cold and white. He existed and didn't exist all at once, and he felt as though all the tiny pieces that made up his whole self were flying across Salvation—like the distance was being squashed and stretched beneath him.

He emerged from the breach of light, his skin tingling and the odor of malice filling his head. His ears popped.

The moment the last guard came through, a horn blared nearby. Once. Twice.

A third time.

That must signal uninvited guests.

"Go!" Rune kicked his horse into motion again, aiming for the lit city. His escort followed, streaming after him. There was the twang of bowstrings, shouted orders, but Rune and his guards were all in black, their horses dark, and they'd hidden their light rods inside pockets and packs.

Only the sound of hooves gave them away, but they simply kept running, pounding forward. Finally they reached the wall that surrounded the city.

There, all but one of the guards dismounted; he took the horses and led them away from the city, while Rune, Rose, and the other two pulled on gray cloaks to blend into the stone.

Under normal circumstances, the wall would have been carefully patrolled, with guards peering down into the darkness. But the rebels were largely not looking for invaders, so Rune and his guards slipped along the outer wall, and when they reached the city gates—thrown open and flooded with people rushing in and out—they simply joined the crowd.

In their black uniforms and gray cloaks, they stood out among the brightly dressed Embrians, but in spite of the street globes and light rods, the avenues were dark. Cold. Rune shivered, even under the wool of his uniform and cloak. Without the sun's heat, the air was far cooler than it should have been.

And it was only the first full day without the Malstop.

They hurried through the crowd, Rune in the lead now. It had been just a few months since his first journey here, but the city was entirely different. Where statues of the Fortuin family once stood, now there were piles of rubble. But not every monument had been razed; many had been painted over, chipped away at, or vandalized in more creative ways.

As they pushed closer to the palace, which rose high on a hill, they passed by the mansions where Embrian nobles lived. Several had small armies surrounding them, guarding the residents inside, but most had broken windows and messages painted along the outer walls: *Burn the nobility* and *House of rancor* and worse.

Finally, they reached Solspire grounds. The palace looked nothing like it had before, with its clean towers shining in the light. No, entire walls had been knocked in; its facade was crumbing with what seemed to be hammer strikes; and the outer gate had been beaten in with a battering ram.

Half a dozen armed men stood atop the steps leading into the palace grounds.

"What do you think, Sire?" Rose asked as their group moved toward the side of the road, deeper into the shadows.

Rune frowned as he pulled his hood lower. There didn't appear to be an obvious way around the rebel guards, and he wasn't familiar enough with Solspire to know secret passages in and out of the building. He would have to announce himself and hope for an audience with their leader.

"At least they're unlikely to have me killed," Rune muttered.

"As for the rest of us . . . " Rose said.

But just as Rune started forward, cries rose up throughout the city.

"Burn me," Rose muttered. "What now?"

But Rune knew. Even as people stopped what they were doing and looked up into the dark sky, Rune felt the tug on his soul, the heat and harmony between them, and the taste of her name on his tongue.

Medella.

With a thunderous clap of pitch-black wings, the Nightrender landed directly before the gate.

Her hair was snarled, her armor again ragged. But as she pulled herself straight and lifted her chin, she was still the most beautiful person in existence.

Without needing to search, the Nightrender glanced over her shoulder, met Rune's gaze, and smiled. Just a flash. But it struck him like a bolt of lightning.

She turned back to the guards, who'd all drawn their weapons.

"Nightrender," one said. "What are you doing here?"

Her voice rang through the dark city, strong and demanding. "I have come to end the Incursion. I will speak with the acting ruler immediately. And my Dawnbreaker, the king of Caberwill, will join me."

43.

Nightrender

The gate to Solspire opened, the great palace of Embria revealed in all its ruinous glory. In decades past, it must have been a terrifying and beautiful sight to behold, but now, during the uprising and Incursion, it appeared haunted, its walls smeared with soot, gallows raised in the front gardens, and blood slung across its marble walls.

As Rune came to stand beside her, she could feel him shudder at the sight. His guards, too, seemed disturbed.

"Tell me who is in command," Nightrender said to the Embrians.

"Magistrate Stephens, Lady Nightrender." The man's knuckles were white around his sword; he was no soldier, but a farmer playing dress-up.

"Take us to him," Rune commanded.

With haste, the Embrian rebels guided Nightrender, Rune, and his guards up the wide drive, through the courtyards, and toward the shattered facade of the main building. One of the ancient oak doors hung open; the other had been rammed off its hinges and lay in pieces across the great hall.

"You could have flown into the palace." Rune's voice was quiet enough that only she could have heard it.

She cast him a sideways glance. "Unless you've been hiding wings all this time, *you* could not have flown in."

Surprise flashed across his face. Then a smile. A tight nod. "Thank you." His arm brushed against hers as they entered the palace, stepping over the remains of the door. "The Malstop is gone."

"Indeed." Nightrender had flown past the Malice on her way here, skimming the places where the two realities struggled against one another. The air had been turbulent, hot and stinking, with tendrils of red sky slithering even further into this long night of Salvation. "The spread of that world into this will take some time. The substance of the Dark Shard does not evenly mix with the laic plane. But every moment without the Malstop brings Salvation closer to an endless night."

"How long does it usually take the maintainers to raise it again?"

Nightrender pressed her mouth into a line. "Never this long."

"Could they be in trouble? Can we help them?"

"Perhaps. But obtaining the final piece of the weapon is my first objective. The maintainers are aware of this. If they need my help—I will be there soon." She swallowed a knot of uncertainty. "But an army to ensure their towers are secure would not go amiss. I'm unclear on the maintainers' ability to defend themselves."

"I've already sent troops."

Heat filled her heart. He'd sworn to help—and she'd believed him—but knowing it was done was such a relief.

She would have pressed him for more information, but they turned into a large drawing room where Magistrate Stephens sat at an ornate desk, piled high with papers and other clutter. At one corner sat a huge chunk of obsidian—a shard of Black Reign.

"Magistrate," said one of the rebels, "the Nightrender and King Rune Highcrown."

The magistrate looked older than when she'd last seen him at Silver Sun, worn from his campaign against the Embrian royalty. Slowly, he rose from his chair, but he did not bow. "How may I help you?"

Nightrender turned to Rune and nodded for him to speak. If he was here, rather than at Honor's Keep or with his army, then something was wrong. Something *else.*

Rune straightened his shoulders. "Queen Johanne. I know you took her. And I know you plan to execute her. I cannot allow that to happen."

Then Rune had come here for the summoning shrine, too.

The magistrate gave a heavy sigh. "I see. You wish to interfere with this revolution. And you've brought the Nightrender to intimidate me. But the Fortuin family has committed thousands of crimes against the Embrian people. Now they must answer to us."

"I am not King Rune's enforcer," Nightrender said. "I do not interfere with mortal politics. But I do need to speak with Queen Johanne."

"Didn't you interfere by announcing her involvement with the mal-device?" Magistrate Stephens shook his head. "I suppose it doesn't matter.

The attack on Silver Sun was only the latest atrocity brought by the Fortuin family. We've spent centuries under their oppressive rule, and we won't stand for it any longer."

Rune was nodding. "You're having a revolution. I understand. And normally, I wouldn't try to stop you. But there is only one fight that matters anymore, only one battle we must win, only one tyrant we must throw off: the rancor king has brought down the Malstop."

The magistrate went pale. "What is a rancor king?"

"Unkillable," Nightrender said softly.

"He was summoned before the Red Dawn." Rune's mouth tightened. "And without the Malstop caging him, Salvation will be his if we don't act. Your rebellion won't matter, because any survivors will be under *his* rule. You would trade one brutal monarch for another."

The magistrate's gaze flickered to Nightrender. When she gave a small nod, he said, "I didn't summon the rancor king. This isn't my fight."

"No one alive today summoned him," Rune pointed out. "But it is your fight. It is all our fight. It isn't fair, but if you intend to rule Embria—if you believe you will do a better job than those who came before you—then you must begin by addressing the greatest threat to your people.

"I know what you must think of me," Rune continued. "You see a foreign king and assume I want Embria for myself. But I am here to tell you that this is not an invasion by another kingdom. The Dark Shard is spilling into Salvation. If you thought what happened in your mine was terrible, just wait. It can get worse. It *will*. Unless we stop it."

"I understand you," Magistrate Stephens said. "But the Malstop will return. And the darkness will be pushed back. . . ." His eyes drifted to Nightrender. "Right? It's always happened that way before. Hasn't it?"

"Only because the leaders of the time did what was needed," she said.

Rune nodded. "After the Red Dawn, our ancestors refused to acknowledge the threat of Incursions, passing on the problem to their decedents. This grim inheritance has now fallen to us, but *I* will not ignore the call to fight for Salvation. Not again." He let out a long breath. "All my life, I have resented the generations that came before me, those who saw the need to act, but did not; those who heard the cries for help, but did nothing. I told myself that I would be better than my predecessors, that I would break the cycle they began. And so, when the Nightrender takes what she came here for, I will march on the Malice."

The magistrate nodded slowly. "Perhaps Embria can be of service to Salvation. But what does this have to do with Johanne Fortuin? Surely she is not needed in this fight."

"All are needed," Nightrender insisted. "She has information critical to the assault against the rancor king. We cannot risk that knowledge being lost."

"I see." The magistrate was thinking. Weighing.

Rune pushed again. "We need only speak with Queen Johanne once. But I would ask that you reconsider execution. Our violence feeds malice. Decide her fate after."

Magistrate Stephens stared down at his overflowing desk—the papers, the pens, the large shard of obsidian. Finally, he nodded. "I will grant one audience with my prisoner. As for a stay of execution—I will consider it." His eyes cut to Rune. "I, too, wish to be better than those who came before me."

While Rune and the magistrate spoke on the most urgent details, Nightrender stretched her senses to hear what was happening throughout the palace. A number of people discussed the fallen Malstop, while others ran the news of Nightrender and Rune's arrival. Would they join the fight at the Soul Gate? Still others passed on warnings of new malsites: time anomalies, molten graveyards, and chimeras stalking the outskirts of the city.

"I'll take you to her now." Magistrate Stephens stepped around the desk, shook Rune's hand, and then led them out the door. Dozens of people shifted through the halls, moving out of the way as Nightrender and Rune followed together, Rune's guards trailing.

"You're a bold king," Nightrender murmured. "Coming here. Asking for all this. I'm grateful to have you with me."

"I refuse to fail you again." Rune's gaze held steady on hers. "You are the Sword of the Numina, and I am yours."

Another rush of heat. A moment of thunderous heartbeats.

Then they descended into the dungeon, where every step echoed, walls dripped with moisture and mold, and the air left a sharp, bitter taste on the back of her tongue.

"How far down?" Rune asked.

"The Fortuin family is at the bottom," Magistrate Stephens said. "As well as Nadine Holt."

"Tyrants, they are," said a man who'd followed them down—one of the magistrate's guards. "Only place for them is the prison they built."

Rune's voice was soft, meant only for Nightrender. "I hope I never make Caberwill hate me so much."

With her wings shielding them from view, Nightrender bumped the back of Rune's hand with hers. "You could never."

An instant later, he'd threaded their fingers together and squeezed.

How incredible, Nightrender thought. *How significant a simple touch.*

But she pulled away before she was ready. He was not hers. Not in that way.

The air grew colder and damper as they reached another landing and a set of doors. People glared out from barred windows. "Let us free!" one cried. "I can pay you!"

"No one is going free," the magistrate declared. "You're lucky to be alive."

Finally, they reached the bottom of the dungeon. Four doors awaited them. The first was empty. The second held a man and a woman.

"Release us!" Queen Katarina looked as Queen Johanne would in twenty years: severe and sharp, regal even in captivity. Here was someone who'd never doubted her authority or her birthright. "Release us and we'll discuss your terms."

The magistrate and his men walked past.

"Prince Rune." Queen Katarina's tone shifted, somewhat more placating. "*King* Rune. Surely you cannot ignore this."

Rune shook his head. "Forgive me, but I'm sure you recall our alliance forbids Caberwill from interfering with Embria's internal workings. Your imprisonment isn't due to an Ivasland invasion, so—"

"Treaties can be reinterpreted," Queen Katarina insisted.

"Perhaps. But I must treat with the one in charge. That does not appear to be you."

"You will regret this," she hissed. "If you think what Ivasland did to your brother and father was terrible, see what I will do to your little sisters. My servants in your castle—"

All three of Rune's guards stepped forward, but the king did not move at all. Quietly, he said, "I will not forget that threat." Fury threaded his tone; his fists were tight. But whatever else he wanted to say, he resisted. Instead, he turned his back on the imprisoned queen. "Let's go."

Nightrender went with him. "She cannot reach your sisters," Nightrender said softly. "Not from here."

"Either way, I will have their guards doubled." Rune glanced at her, his expression hard. "I can't lose anyone else. I *won't.*"

"I understand." Nightrender halted as they reached the final cell, where blue eyes peered out of the shadow.

"Hello, Hanne," Rune said.

Nightrender stepped forward. "Queen Johanne, tell me where your summoning shrine is. Please."

The young woman frowned. "I don't know what you mean."

"If you won't tell her what she wants to know," Magistrate Stephen said, "then we're done here. The Nightrender's personal request to see you is the only reason we've come." He started to turn away, ushering his men back up the stairs.

"Wait!" Queen Johanne shifted behind the door. "What shrine? I'm just not sure what you mean. It's cold and I'm hungry. And my cousin and I were abducted! Imprisoned! Give me a moment to *think.*"

Nightrender crossed her arms. "The Malstop has fallen, likely due to your actions. I have no moments to give. Tell me where the shrine is located."

The dungeon was quiet, save the drip of water, the shuffle of feet, the rush of breathing.

"I want to help," Queen Johanne said at last. "But I can't. Because I just don't know what that is."

44.

HANNE

"What do you mean you *don't know what that is?*" Rune came toward the door, scowling. "It's the shrine you use to summon the Nightrender! All three kingdoms have one."

"Not us." Hanne stared out through the window, begging him to see the truth in her eyes. Beyond him, the magistrate looked ready to lose the key to her cell. She needed to get out of this cold, damp dungeon—and find a way to excise Daghath Mal from her mind. "Please, ask me something else. Let me help some other way."

"There is nothing else," Rune said. "I'm sorry, Hanne. If you don't know where it is, we need to go. The Soul Gate—"

A curious sense welled up inside Hanne—but not *her* curiosity. *His.* The rancor king's.

"Don't." Hanne swallowed a lump in her throat. "Don't tell me anything you're doing."

Dark laughter filled the back of her mind. **Mind what risks you take. If the Nightrender learns of my presence, you will surely not last the hour. That magistrate will be the least of your troubles.**

Hanne shuddered. "My goal has always been peace. Please believe that it was all in service to Salvation."

Rune let out a long sigh. "It doesn't matter anymore, Hanne. We just need the shrine. Embria *did* have one. Before. If you don't know where it is—"

"That must be it." Hanne gripped the bars, pulling herself closer to the window as an old, half-buried memory unlocked in her mind. "My ancestors. When I was young, my governess told me that the first royal Fortuins tried to destroy the shrine after the Red Dawn."

The Nightrender scoffed. "Mortals cannot destroy my shrines."

"No? So they hid it." Hanne didn't bother to disguise the urgency in her voice. If she didn't get out of here, the rebels would kill her—and Nadine.

Perhaps Hanne deserved it, but Nadine didn't. "But the knowledge of *where* was never passed on. I don't even know what it would look like."

Rune gave a frustrated grunt. "It's a large stone, about waist-height." He held up a hand to demonstrate. "It has a marking on one side, like—"

"A winged figure?" Hanne glanced at the Nightrender. "You?"

"Certainly you saw the shrine in Honor's Keep," the Nightrender said. "The Embrian one is identical."

A chill swept through Hanne. The darkness. The altar. The green light.

The stone she'd passed on the way there.

"No," she murmured. "No, it couldn't be." But it could be. Her ancestors must have sent it away after the Red Dawn so that it could never be used. Hanne kept her voice soft. "I think I've seen it. A long time ago. But you won't like where it is."

"Tell me." The Nightrender offered no space for refusal.

Hanne locked eyes with the Nightrender. "I'll *take* you there."

"Out of the question." The magistrate stepped forward. "She doesn't leave. She's my prisoner."

But Hanne focused on the Nightrender. She was the real power here; the men would obey their champion. "I've seen it. I can show you exactly where it is."

Something had been done to her there. Something dark. Something she hadn't asked for, or understood.

But she was beginning to.

"She's lying," said Magistrate Stephens. "She'll say anything to escape justice."

"She's telling the truth." Nadine squeezed up to the door beside Hanne. "Please, listen. This isn't a ploy. If Hanne says she can help, she will."

"Let me take you there," Hanne urged. "And Nadine. She must come, too."

Nadine put her arm around Hanne's shoulders and squeezed.

"We will remain prisoners. We will be in the Nightrender's custody. Surely no one could argue that she is anything but qualified to hold us."

Rune looked at the Nightrender, one eyebrow lifted.

The way he looks at her for permission . . .

She had bigger problems.

When she glanced at the vent between cells, she could just see her mother's eyes glaring back at her. She'd heard what Queen Kat had said to Rune earlier, the way she'd threatened Sanctuary and Unity, the callousness in her tone. She wanted power above all else. She didn't care whom she hurt. Not even children were granted mercy.

Not even her own daughter.

Hanne returned to the door. "Neither of us need to know what you're doing, Lady Nightrender. Neither of us will interfere, beyond leading you to the malsite where your shrine was hidden."

"And what about after?" Magistrate Stephens crossed his arms. "Embria deserves justice."

"You have my parents. I am *their* daughter. I am what they made me."

And what Daghath Mal had made her.

"Allow me this moment to remake myself," Hanne whispered. "Please. I will do everything in my power to help the Nightrender and save Salvation. Should I survive, I will return to Embria. I will be your prisoner once more."

"Hanne, no." Nadine took her arm and squeezed. "You can't agree to that."

"I proposed it," Hanne said. "And he's not wrong that the world must be protected from me."

Nadine bit her lip, but after a moment, she nodded. "I'm with you."

Hanne wanted to say that Nadine should not receive the same punishment— *she* was a good person and deserved freedom—but the Nightrender spoke up.

"Queen Johanne's assistance would be beneficial. Without her, it is possible that none of you will survive. So it seems you have nothing to lose."

Hope stirred in Hanne's heart. She had the Nightrender. Now everyone else needed to fall in line.

I imagine she'd kill you if she found out about me.

Hanne clenched her jaw.

She could not allow you to live. I see everything you see. I know everything you know. What a risk.

It didn't matter what Daghath Mal said now. Hanne had persuaded the Nightrender to take her—not just out of this cell and away from the angry rebels who wanted her dead, but to the only place Hanne might undo what had been done to her.

"Very well." The magistrate was pale as he addressed the Nightrender. "Take her. And if there's still a world left after this, I want her back."

"There will be a world after this," the Nightrender said softly. "That was never in question. The risk is the world becoming a place you cannot survive."

Within the hour, they left the palace and rode east as fast as their horses could carry them, the Nightrender flying ahead. The endless night stretched in all directions, unbroken save the bobbing chemical lights as the caravan careened down the road.

Hanne had not expected the darkness, but as she glared out the window of her prison wagon, she understood that this was only the first wave. Soon, that pulsing redness in the center of Salvation—no longer held back by the Malstop—would spread across the map.

Then, Daghath Mal would come and true darkness would fall.

Millennia ago, after the Shattering, Salvation had been where humanity made its last stand against the Dark Shard. If Salvation fell, there would be nowhere else to go.

She wished the horses could move faster. She wished she had wings so that she could fly to the malsite and rip this nightmare out of her mind.

Do you know what to do?

She would figure it out.

What makes you think it's possible?

If it could be done, it could be undone.

Will you sit on the altar and hope I go away?

She would sit on the altar and *force* him away.

You have no idea the sorrow those thoughts bring me.

"Do you think Sabine got your message yet?" Nadine picked at the cuff of her sleeve. "How long does it take a dove to reach Brink?"

"Can a dove survive all the way to Brink anymore? That's the question we should be asking." Hanne dropped her gaze to her ink-smudged hands. She'd been trembling when Rune had given her the pen, nearly incapable of producing the micro-code her ladies could decipher. Then, because Rune had insisted on reading the note, she'd had to rewrite it in plain script.

The message had been brief, instructing Sabine and Hanne's ladies to cooperate with the grand general, find Mae and the others from the observatory project, and order them to find a way to repair the Malstop. Move malice. Do *something* to mitigate the damage. Because this had all been a terrible mistake.

Rune, too, had written several notes, including one to his grand general, another to Queen Abagail of Ivasland, and more to the Crown Council. Then he'd addressed Magistrate Stephens and several of the high-ranked rebels; Hanne hadn't been able to hear what he'd said, but she'd witnessed from a distance and realized this: Rune was becoming a leader people wanted to follow. They were beginning to love him the way they had never loved her.

And Hanne—she had betrayed everyone she'd ever cared about. She had lived her life as a puppet, unaware of her own strings. Never special. Never chosen. Only . . . convenient.

That's not true. I have always cared for you.

In the wagon, Hanne twisted to see out the window. They were nearly to the turnoff. "Rune!" she called.

A moment later, Rune rode up beside the wagon, holding a light globe aloft. "Are you feeling better?"

Hanne glanced at the empty food wrappers, the water sacks, and the pile of blankets. "Yes." Then, because Nadine was giving her a *look*: "Thank you."

He nodded. "The Nightrender sensed a malsite. She's gone ahead to clear it while we move past—"

"No!" Hanne lurched to her knees. "That's the one. That's where we need to go."

Rune's eyebrows raised. "Good. Then she can get the shrine and—"

"I need to go there." Hanne threw the blanket from her shoulders and struggled for the door. It was locked from the outside. "Rune, I have to go there."

"Why?"

"Because I—" She couldn't say it. "Please. Please, take me there. Don't let her destroy it yet."

Rune shook his head. "I'm sorry, Hanne. Getting the shrine is our priority. You've already slowed us down by refusing to just *say* where it is. And I understand. You wanted to get out of that dungeon. But you can't delay us anymore."

He wasn't *listening* to her. He didn't understand.

So Hanne did the only thing she could think to do: she reached through the bars, snatched the keyring off his belt, and brought it to the door as quickly as possible.

The lock was on the outside, so she had to choose a key, try to fit it, and move on to the next. It was not a fast process. And before she'd made it through three keys, Rune had called a halt and was off his horse, trying to pry the keys from Hanne's fist.

"Let it go." He pulled at her fingers. "I don't want to hurt you."

Hanne gritted her teeth and fought for the next key—without losing her grip on the whole ring.

He will never forgive you for this.

While Hanne struggled with the keys, Nadine reached for the window and grabbed Rune's jacket, throwing him off-balance just long enough for Hanne to get the fourth key into the lock. It fit.

"Hanne, you have to stop!" Rune lunged for her again.

"Break my fingers if you want," she grunted, struggling to turn the key as other men—the guards assigned to her—rushed to the wagon. "But I cannot stop."

The tumblers clicked. Nadine grabbed at Rune again. And Hanne threw open the door just as the guards arrived. She scrambled, throwing elbows as she jumped to the ground and squeezed between the men trying to subdue her.

But the darkness was on her side: with so many bodies blocking chemical illumination, the men could not see her to capture her again. She was out of the press before they realized. Then she climbed onto Rune's horse, urging it to run before she'd even finished mounting.

"Hanne, wait!" Rune and the guards moved to intercept her, but they were too slow. Hanne was racing away, glancing back just long enough to find Nadine still in the wagon. Her cousin nodded.

Hanne thundered into the frigid night.

But this night was not natural; there was no ambient light from stars or the moon—just absolute darkness. As she rode away from the caravan's glow, the horse shied and twisted to return to safety.

Frantically, she dug through Rune's saddlebag until her fingers closed around a metal rod. After a hurried shake, a beam of light shot out and the horse—though not quite comforted—resumed moving in the direction Hanne wanted to go.

Voices and hoofbeats crescendoed behind her; the light would certainly make it easier for them to follow, but it didn't matter if they caught up eventually—only that she reached the malsite first.

"Go," she whispered to the horse. "Run."

Hooves pounded on the ground. Wind stung her eyes. Evergreen boughs slapped her arms and legs.

"Faster!" She bent low. Red silk trailed in shredded ribbons behind her.

Through trees, around brush, over rocks: Hanne retraced the path her parents had taken her on as a child. The stink of malice filled the air, strong enough to make her eyes water.

The dark was disorienting, and she hadn't been here in so long. What if she was going the wrong direction?

But soon, she heard bells. Strips of yellow flashed at the edge of the light's range. And a terrible polyphonic growl—horrifying and far too familiar.

Rancor.

Hanne clutched the light rod and urged her stolen horse faster. She was almost there. But the horse heaved loud, panicked breaths. Cold sweat dampened its neck and flanks as Hanne wrestled for control. But the horse, unwilling to run toward the invasive predator, started to turn—to carry Hanne away from danger.

"No!" Hanne jerked at the reins.

Do not separate us.

Static gripped Hanne's mind. She slipped, her hand loosening on the light. The horse whinnied and reared, and Hanne fell.

You were meant to be mine!

Her shoulder and head hit the ground, pain a hot knife. Then, with Hanne's ankle trapped in the stirrup, the horse took off, dragging her behind.

She cried out at the assault of rocks, plants, and a sharp pain in her leg. Something snapped. Red flared in her vision. Blood roared in her ears.

Then everything stopped.

She was in the bone castle again. Ruddy light pulsed around her. And

Daghath Mal gazed up at the Rupture—which had swollen to five times its former size. Rancor sacs oozed out from several points, dropping to the floor with disgusting *splats*.

Why are you so eager to abandon me now?

A wall dilated, revealing the red world outside. Daghath Mal flew onto the roof of a tower, his great wings pumping the heavy air. Then he gazed down at his terrible domain, all jagged rocks, skeletal brush, and strange, shimmering pockets of air.

You could have ruled all of Salvation from my side. Together, we could have created a final peace between the three kingdoms.

The view before her was a nightmare, with sludgy rivers of blood and rocks that opened round, anguished eyes. Trees with teeth lunged onto a small, bald animal, but before the creature was swallowed, it turned its giant, bloodshot gaze against them—and stretched up, its mouth expanding so that it devoured the entire copse at once. Then it was small again, with sap running down its face.

This was not the peace Hanne had tried to build.

It is a different kind of peace than you imagined. The kingdoms will dissolve. But the forever war will end. Only the struggle for survival will continue—and that will sustain me. The chaos. The greed.

Below, several rancor emerged from the castle, moving toward the two immense towers on either side of the Soul Gate.

You've disappointed me, my little queen. But perhaps you're simply having a fit. You're so young. Of course you're angry now. But we can make amends. We can both have what we want. Tell me, how would you like to be the queen who saved Salvation? The queen who held back the beast? The queen who brought peace?

A chill swept through Hanne. That was exactly what she wanted.

Oh, how they would love you, he breathed into her mind. **They would praise your name, revere every word you spoke. You would be more than their queen: you would be their savior.**

Hanne could imagine it now, the grateful thanks when they kissed her hands, the monuments built in her image, the annual celebrations of her great victory over darkness. She could envision herself wearing the finest silks and wools, dyed with brilliant colors, and, of course, wearing the obsidian crown, its spikes pointed toward the sky as everyone around her lowered their foreheads to the ground.

She could half hear their cries of gratitude, the songs in her honor, and the hushed way people would say, "It's the obsidian queen!" as her carriage slipped through villages and towns—and the cheers following in her wake.

Yes, she could imagine a world in which she was the savior of Salvation, a queen universally adored for one courageous act: putting an end to this darkness.

With that warm image in her mind, she found she could speak. Think, rather. *But why? How would peace—my peace—benefit you?*

I would still get mine. Later.

A chill stole through her.

Daghath Mal's words came gently. Like before, when she'd thought he was Tuluna. **The world would bow first to you, the beautiful queen who drove back the darkness. And then, after seventy years, Salvation's elderly queen would die peacefully in her sleep. The world would mourn the greatest loss of the generation.**

She didn't like thinking about her death, but peacefully in her sleep sounded all right. *After I die, my daughter will become queen. Then my granddaughter after her.*

No. Daghath Mal's wings spread wide around him. **The good queen held back the darkness with her every breath, but when she dies, the Malstop will fall. Your peace will become mine. I will be the king who conquers.**

But...

You will be dead. You will never have to see my peace. Only yours. He swept his gaze across the red wasteland. **I think my peace will be so much sweeter after decades of yours.**

Seventy years of her peace.

I know you don't understand why I make this offer, why I would delay my own reign to allow yours. I know you don't see its benefit to me. But hear this: I care for you.

You're a rancor. You can't care for anyone.

That's not true. His words were fierce—hurt, almost. **From the moment**

we met, I have always looked to your happiness. You wanted to be strong and clever and beautiful, and so you are all those things and more. And then you wanted power and influence and fear, and so you gained all that. And finally you wanted to be queen of all of Salvation and here I am, offering it to you. Take it. Say yes.

Saying yes would be so easy. She could have the life she'd always wanted. But then what?

If she wouldn't be around to see the suffering, to experience any of it herself, what did it matter to her?

But Hanne's peace couldn't be *real* with the threat of Daghath Mal looming in the future. It would be a false peace, a lie.

I am a liar, Hanne reminded herself.

But she did not lie to herself. If she wanted to be a queen, a *true* queen, then she could not sacrifice future generations for her own happiness.

It was difficult to think about them—people who didn't yet exist—as needing and wanting something from her, and her being obliged to provide for them. But wasn't this the very thing Rune was always talking about? How his parents and grandparents and great-grandparents had all pushed past the problem of Incursions, never taking the actions necessary to protect their descendants?

If Hanne wanted to be better than them—if she wanted to remake herself—there was only one answer she could give.

No.

Please, my chosen. Anguish filled his words. **Hanne.**

I said no.

Truly, I am sorry to hear that.

Light splintered around her as the rancor king sent her away—back to the dark forest, where the horse was running and she had fallen to the ground. She wasn't being dragged anymore, but her head and shoulder roared with pain. The agony in her ankle was near blinding. And even as she registered that she still held the light rod and could move the beam, a winged creature came hurtling down toward her, its form shifting and stuttering.

The rancor was taller than the others she'd seen, with an orange tint to its pallid gray flesh. Nose holes dripped with viscous brown fluid. Slowly, its mouth pulled back into a horrible smile. "Puppet princess." Its growling voice was an assault on her ears. "No longer under his protection."

Hanne struggled to move away, but the creature lunged and she was too slow. Claws slashed at her chest—but didn't connect.

Instead, the Nightrender's black sword pierced it through the eye; blue-white light grew inside its head.

As the glow intensified, the Nightrender flung the beast away. Around the edges of wide-spread wings, Hanne could just see the rancor explode in a rush of light. Gore and slime and tarry black blood flew across the forest, hitting trees and brush with wet, sizzling slaps.

A numinous light surrounded the Nightrender, shimmering around her body, her wings, and even her sword as she flicked rancor viscera off the blade. Her motion was graceful, natural in a way no mortal could ever achieve. *This* was the champion of three kingdoms.

"Nightrender." Hanne's voice was raspy, desperate.

The Nightrender turned. Shadows concealed her expression, but her stance was all danger. "Queen Johanne. Tell me what you are doing here."

Hanne tried to look around, to see how close she was to the malsite. But the truth was, it didn't matter how close she'd gotten. She couldn't get there on her own. Not with these injuries. Not with rancor hunting her.

So she choked back her pride, gasping out the words through the fog of pain. "I need your help. The altar. Please."

The Nightrender didn't move.

It seemed only the truth would move the Nightrender. Hanne had damaged the world too deeply for anyone to trust her. To help her without question.

Hanne closed her eyes. If the Nightrender killed her for this—well, at least she would be free. "It's Daghath Mal. He's a voice in my head. And this is where it started."

A gasp. A flutter of wings. And the hiss of the Nightrender's sword cutting through the air: that was all Hanne heard before darkness took her.

45.

NIGHTRENDER

Nightrender's blade sliced clean through the rancor's neck. Gummy black blood spilled, hitting the ground with a hiss. And then it was down, its vile body thumping against the rocks. Dead as quickly as it had arrived.

Distantly, the sound of voices wove through the darkness: Rune, his guards, and those sent along to mind Queen Johanne.

The queen who, by her own admission, provided eyes and ears for Daghath Mal. And hands, it seemed. The mal-devices, the destruction of the Malstop: he'd directed her all along.

So what had changed? Why did she want free of him now?

Or was this another of Daghath Mal's tricks?

Nightrender was still contemplating the queen when Rune and his company arrived, all their weapons drawn as they spread around the malsite, keeping to the safe side of the yellow line. Swords gleamed in dozens of chemical lights.

"The rancor are gone," Nightrender said. "For now." She hadn't yet opened the shrine, nor had she finished destroying the malsite. She'd been focused on killing the *fourteen* rancor that had been waiting to ambush her.

Nightrender had dispatched them quickly enough, though the number had seemed high for a forgotten malsite in the middle of the woods. But now that Nightrender knew Daghath Mal had been aware she would come here—and indeed that Queen Johanne had *told* Nightrender to come here—the number made more sense.

Daghath Mal's minions had been waiting for her.

A wagon door screeched. Footsteps pounded on the ground. An instant later, Lady Nadine had crossed the oil-slick shimmer of the pellicle and dropped beside the queen. "Hanne!" She touched her cousin's face and hands. "What happened? What did you do?" She turned round eyes up at Nightrender, accusing. "Did you hurt her?"

Nightrender sheathed her sword. "I did not touch her."

Boots crunched the brittle grass in a familiar cadence. Rune paused beside Nightrender, his elbow brushing hers. "What happened?" He knelt beside Queen Johanne and touched her throat. "She's alive. But there's a lot of blood."

It was true. Blood oozed from several wounds. "She lost control of her horse and was dragged a ways before I could cut the stirrup." Nightrender bent and moved the queen's golden hair aside. "She needs medical care. The head wounds first. And her ankle."

Rune glanced around the space and—when he spotted the man he was looking for—called for the medic. "Quickly!"

"Why didn't you help her?" Lady Nadine bared her teeth at Nightrender. "You were just standing here. Were you going to watch her die?"

"I knew you would arrive soon." Nightrender rose. "And I was trying to decide if she intentionally led us into an ambush."

"What?" Rune looked between them. "How could she possibly do that?"

Lady Nadine's face went white. "She didn't. She just wanted to help. And look, isn't that the thing you wanted?" She pointed toward the summoning shrine, half buried in the muck. "She was telling the truth."

Nightrender narrowed her eyes, weighing the urgency and attempted deflection. "You know her secret."

Somehow, the young lady paled even more. "I—"

Just then, the medic reached them. He went right to work, identifying the queen's injuries and pulling bandages and ointments from his bag. "We'll need to move her back to the wagon before I can properly—"

"We can't take her away from here," Lady Nadine said. "Not yet. Not until..." She looked at the altar, a large, flat-topped stone with rancorous sigils carved into it.

"My lady, she needs immediate care. And this place"—he gestured around the malsite—"is not clean."

"Stop her bleeding," Nightrender said. "Then return across the yellow line."

Rune was clearly confused, but when the medic checked with him, he nodded in confirmation. With a deep frown, the man finished his work and left.

Nightrender knelt, keeping her voice low. "The queen is possessed by Daghath Mal."

"What?" Rune was incredulous.

Nightrender continued. "I believe she has been doing his bidding—"

"*She didn't know!*" Lady Nadine leaned forward, whispering earnestly. "She believed she was hearing Tuluna the Tenacious. It was only after the observatory project that she realized it was something else!"

Nightrender glanced at Rune, the way his expression revealed that he, too, was remembering the climb into the observatory tower, the stink of malice, and the questions about what Queen Johanne had been doing there. "Tell me of the observatory project," Nightrender said.

Misery filled Lady Nadine's voice. "Mal-devices. One for each of the guard towers around the Malstop. To take down the barrier."

"*What?*" Rune's face was ashen. "I— What? Why?"

Fury coiled in Nightrender. The explosion she'd witnessed, the strands of malice slithering across the Malstop—all Queen Johanne.

"It was supposed to come back right away," Lady Nadine sobbed. "Stronger. And we were supposed to have armies stationed everywhere to fight back any rancor that slipped through." She was weeping now, tears streaming down her cheeks. "She believed it was the only way. She believed Tuluna wanted her to do that."

"Hanne brought down the Malstop because the rancor king told her to." Rune shook his head. "But she was caught in that malsite. In the Deepway Woods. And sent to Ivasland—"

"To work on the mal-devices." Lady Nadine wiped her face, but her tears didn't stop. "To meet the people who would help destroy the Malstop. He was using her all along. But the moment she realized, she wanted to stop. She intended to tell Mae and the others to halt the observatory project. But it was too late. We were taken."

Muscles ticked in Rune's jaw. "Who would ever think—"

"*Tuluna* told her to do it." Lady Nadine clutched Queen Johanne's hands and looked at Nightrender. "Please. She believed this was the only place to sever the connection. It was done here. It could be undone here. That's why she insisted on coming. She thought if you knew— She thought you would—"

Kill her. Because of the Red Dawn. Nightrender's reputation would be forever tarnished by her own unspeakable act—by her own unwanted connection to Daghath Mal.

It seemed entirely possible that he'd targeted a vulnerable human *because* he'd been able to do it to Nightrender first.

A sobering thought. One she could not ignore.

Nightrender stood. "Take her to the altar. I will do my best to free her."

"Thank you," Lady Nadine rasped. "Thank you."

"I make no promises. I've never done this before." Nightrender turned to Rune as he gently lifted Queen Johanne into his arms. She was still unconscious, but the bleeding had stopped.

Carefully, he took her to the altar and laid her atop its carved surface, letting Lady Nadine adjust her cousin's hair and shredded dress before fully releasing her. Then they both stepped back.

"What now?" Lady Nadine asked.

"Return to your people. Decide what you want to tell them about this." Before Lady Nadine could protest, Nightrender added, "I am certain the rancor king does not wish to be cut off from her. This malsite appears to be a conduit to him. So, I would advise taking cover."

Lady Nadine cupped Queen Johanne's face for a moment, then retreated beyond the yellow line.

Nightrender turned to Rune. His face was twisted with confusion. Frustration. "Tell me what you're thinking," she said.

"Does *everybody* have a monster riding along with them?" He gave a short, mirthless laugh. "Am I the only one who doesn't?"

"Perhaps." Her wings blocked them from view of his company, so she stretched out her fingers, brushing his knuckles with hers. "It must be difficult to consider all the private moments of yours he witnessed through others."

"I wasn't thinking about that. Well, I am *now*." Rune's gaze flickered to his wife. "No, I— I was thinking that I should have seen it. I'm your soul shard and her . . . you know. But both of you were suffering and I didn't notice. I'm sorry."

"You cannot expect to notice something that was intentionally hidden from you." Nightrender hesitated. "I do not know her reasons for hiding it, but *I* didn't want you—or anyone else—to think me weak. Vulnerable. You already knew about my memory. I couldn't confess to something else I didn't yet understand."

By the wagon, Lady Nadine was addressing the others. "Queen Johanne has taken ill. But she knew the Nightrender could cure her with numinous magic. That's why she's here."

"No pressure," Rune murmured. "Should I go?"

"You should stay. You're the only one I know who's ever cut a connection with Daghath Mal."

"That was because of what I am to you. I don't know how to unbind Hanne."

"You don't have to. Just"—she caught his eyes—"stay with me. Until it's done."

He inhaled a shaking breath. Touched the tips of her fingers. And nodded. "I will."

Then, setting her jaw, she shook out her wings and faced the altar. She closed her eyes. When she opened them, her vision shifted. In the same way she could see the oil-slick barrier of malsites, she now saw a dark nimbus surrounding Queen Johanne. A thorny cord spun away from her—toward the Malice.

"What are you going to do?"

Nightrender drew her sword.

"Wait—"

Numinous light shimmered down the black blade as she swung, slicing through the line. Queen Johanne shouted as it spiraled away. Her eyes flew open. But Nightrender wasn't finished.

"Hold her down," she ordered.

Rune grasped Queen Johanne by the shoulders and leaned, pinning her while Nightrender touched Beloved to the queen's heart, where the stump of the cord still protruded, struggling to grow back—to reconnect with the other end. But power pulsed through the sword and into the girl, lighting sparks around, burning off the shadowy halo.

The queen convulsed atop the altar, staring up with wide, terrified eyes. Her mouth dropped open, though she didn't scream again.

"It's all right," Rune said over and over. "She's helping you."

Nightrender poured more light into Queen Johanne until, at last, the final wisps of darkness were burned away. Then she lowered her sword and stepped back, allowing Rune to tend to his queen.

"Take her to safety. I will finish here."

When Rune lifted Queen Johanne off the altar and carried her beyond the yellow line, Nightrender, Sword of the Numina, Hammer of the Gods, did what she had been built for: she drove Beloved deep into the base of the altar, flooding the sigil-marked stone with divine energy until beams of holy light shot out in all directions, slicing through the darkness. She cut the malsite into ribbons, shredding the pellicle with razor-sharp light. And she purified the ground, cauterizing the deep-rooted infection, ensuring that it could never grow back.

Salvation was still dark with unnatural night when she finished, but *this* malsite was gone. Even the mortals seemed to sense it. Though the bells chimed and the yellow ribbons remained, the air had shifted. The stink of malice was gone, leaving only what blew in.

Nightrender sheathed her sword and stood in front of the summoning shrine. It was the last one. It held the final piece of the weapon.

Rune stepped up beside her.

"You should go before I open it." Nightrender's arm brushed his. "Rancor will come."

He nodded. "They're probably on the way here already."

Nightrender gazed down at the half-buried shrine. The figure on the front—the dagger—was still visible, even after centuries of weather rushing across its face. "You should send someone back here. To take the shrine."

"It's Embria's."

"Put it somewhere safe, where someone will use it in the future." Nightrender shifted her weight away from Rune. She needed to get used to this, being without him. He'd never been hers. "Go. I'll retrieve the weapon and put an end to Daghath Mal. You have my feather if you need to communicate with me."

Rune was watching her, uncertainty in his eyes. "Meet me at the Soul Gate before you face Daghath Mal. I'll have your army."

When he was gone, Nightrender opened the shrine, took the final weapon shard, and drew her sword.

As Nightrender approached Winterfast Island, sunlight warmed her skin. What a relief to fly away from the darkness, to leave it so far behind that she could hardly see that part of the sky.

No one else could escape, though.

That thought weighed her down. All those people, everyone she was meant to protect—trapped in that unwavering night, knowing that even if they did manage to get away from the black sky for a few days, it would catch up. There was nowhere they could go that was safe.

It was with those heavy thoughts that Nightrender swept around Winterfast Tower, landed on the balcony, and entered her home.

As she walked by the bed, still rotting and stained with age, she considered how one day, she would go back to sleep here, and she would awaken to find the whole world different again.

Don't think about that now, she ordered herself. Worry about anything beyond this moment was a luxury she could not afford.

Resolute, she descended to the library.

The glass case with the page of the illuminated manuscript was still there. As before, she could not quite read it. The letters looked like those she was familiar with, but they were all arranged in odd orders, like someone practicing their hand from a copybook.

But the figure in the middle, the sketch of the weapon . . .

Nightrender pulled open the drawer beneath the glass case. There, on a fold of velvet, waited the first two pieces: the hilt and the cross guard. Now she produced the blade. It was blacker than night, with two edges and a sharply tapered point. The material was smooth, but it did not shine or reflect light in the way obsidian did. It was completely matte, even more than onyx, as though it absorbed every spark of light that touched it.

Carefully, Nightrender placed the blade on the velvet between the hilt and cross guard. A chill worked through her at the sight of these three pieces together.

This weapon, she understood, was a last resort. That was the reason that the dagger had been broken into pieces, kept safe in the only Relics people were unlikely to lose. And that was the reason that all knowledge of it had been locked deep within Nightrender's mind, so that even she could not access it without numinous assistance, under the most dire of circumstances.

To kill a rancor king was to become a rancor king.

Such a beast had to be destroyed utterly, every piece of him stripped apart, all the way down to the very atoms. And one could not stop with just his body. No, his soul—or whatever twisted, corrupted thing he now possessed—had to follow.

The tower was tomb-silent around her, as still as if the rest of the world no longer existed. Yet, as Nightrender lifted the hilt and the cross guard, the sensation of being watched washed over her.

She glanced around the library, half certain she would find someone lurking in the shadows, but there was no one else in the room. Just her. And the weapon, of course.

With a thunderous boom, the hilt and cross guard snapped together, a dark light shimmering around the two pieces. Now sealed, it was impossible to tell where they had been split.

The echo of their joining sounded through the tower, rattling through to the bones of the world. Only when it faded did Nightrender lift the blade, mindful of its edges. She braced herself, feet apart and wings extended, and held the tang to the opening.

Snap. The tang slid deep into the hilt. The blast that followed rocked the tower, making Nightrender drop the dagger onto the velvet cushion as she stumbled backward a few steps. The noise reverberated, its tremors pulsing in all directions. Above, through the layers of stone and sky, even the stars shuddered as the weapon was completed.

Silence, again.

A terrible sense of dread filled Nightrender as she steadied herself, shook out her wings, and folded them back. She sucked in a long breath. And then released it.

It was time to see this dagger, this weapon so terrible that its creators had hoped it would never be used, a Relic of such devastating power that even she—the immortal Nightrender charged with protecting humanity—was not meant to know about it.

She approached the glass case and the open drawer beneath it. At first, Nightrender saw nothing but a dagger-shaped hole in the velvet—no weapon at all. But as she looked more closely, she could perceive the slight dimple in the cushion, a gentle pressure where the dagger rested atop it.

The dagger was so black that no part of it reflected light. Instead, it seemed to absorb illumination. The more she looked at it, the deeper it pulled her. The sight of it was unsettling, as though she were looking at nothing—the absence of light, the very essence of darkness itself. And she could not make herself look away.

Quickly, Nightrender slammed the drawer shut.

She blinked and focused her gaze on bookcases, on marble floor tiles, on the display case itself. Her breath was ragged, and her hands—her hands were *trembling*.

"Dear Numina," she whispered around her pounding heart. "What a horror you have wrought."

She wished, for a moment, that she were still ignorant of this thing, that it did not exist, that her makers had not conceived of such a calamitous weapon. That she would need to use this . . .

First, she would find something to contain it. She needed more than a sheath; she needed a way to cover the hilt as well, for she could not bear to look at any part of it longer than necessary.

The top drawer—where she'd been keeping the pieces—held only the velvet and the weapon, but there was another drawer beneath it, one without a handle.

She pressed the face. It popped open to reveal a shallow and narrow space containing an obsidian-lined envelope, just the right size to accommodate the length of the blade and the width of the cross guard. Nightrender placed it on top of the glass case, trying to work up the nerve to look at the weapon again—to touch it again, now that it was complete—and that was when she noticed the manuscript page. Something had changed.

The writing looked the same as it had before. The image of the dagger was still present. No, the only thing that had changed was her ability to read it.

LIGHT EATER

Nightrender gazed at the dagger's name for a long time, letting the sound of it slide through her mind until it fell off her tongue and she whispered, "Light Eater," into the empty library.

The display case rumbled beneath her hands.

Nightrender read on, her heart filling with dread as her eyes moved down the paper.

Most of this was not a surprise. It was largely what she'd put together with Draft, Rune, and the others: Light Eater was for only direst catastrophic emergencies, when all other options had been exhausted. The blade would end any kind of creature it was used against, including rancor kings and other monstrosities from the Dark Shard—and beasts from every other plane as well.

Once there was a single world, the First World. It was chaotic, unruly, but whole. Then, the Shattering broke it apart.

Light Eater is a tiny, forgotten fragment of that event. It can temporarily exist inside other planes, and has been forged into the direst of weapons.

This dagger absorbs matter. It is unknown what lies beyond the dark horizon of its blade, what becomes of Light Eater's victims. Most theorize they are scattered inside this absolute darkness forever, as shattered as the First World. This, it is accepted, is the only possible fate, stretched out and streaming into nothingness....

This. This was how it destroyed: by ripping apart its victims, down to the smallest, most basic parts, and sending everything to a pocket plane where they drifted for eternity.

Death seemed kinder.

But she closed her eyes and thought about what Daghath Mal had done in this world, the chaos he'd caused, the destruction he'd wrought. She thought about how he had stolen away into her mind—and Queen Johanne's—using them to influence the world. And she thought, more pressingly, about what he would do in the future.

The countless deaths he would inflict. The terror of malice spreading across the world. She would not flinch away from using this dagger on him, if need be.

Jaw tight, she bent over the page again to finish reading.

What followed were instructions: how to carry Light Eater (the obsidian envelope she'd already found), how to look at it (not directly, if possible), and how to dismantle it and store it away when its job was finished.

And then came the warnings.

Line after line cautioned against holding the dagger for too long, against looking deep into its darkness, and—imperatively—against allowing the blade to touch anything the wielder did not want to destroy. One scratch was all it took for Light Eater to feast.

But it was the final warning that sent Nightrender recoiling, her gasp hissing through the quiet library.

She reread the final passage, just to be sure she had understood correctly. But the writing was clear.

No wonder the weapon had been hidden from her, the knowledge of it unlocked only during a time of powerful need. Certainly, Light Eater would destroy Daghath Mal. It would send him away, freeing this world from his influence, saving countless lives from the nightmare he was unfolding across the land.

But there was a cost. The knowledge of this price had been hard won, a tragedy for the Numina who'd spent their final hours shaping this pocket plane into a weapon.

The one who wielded the weapon was not immune to its effects. The dagger would take its victim—and the bearer as well.

If Nightrender used Light Eater to destroy Daghath Mal, then she, too, would be destroyed.

46.

HANNE

She awakened to the noise of catapults. The squeak of ropes on wood, the men yelling, the *ka-chunk* of tension released. Then, slowly, she registered the voices, soft and feminine. Familiar.

"I thought she was supposed to be here already." That was one of Hanne's ladies. Maris.

"She was." Nadine's voice came from close to Hanne. "I don't know where she could be."

"How long can we hold out without her?" Cecelia asked.

"Not much longer. The medical tents are overflowing. When I took my shift this morning, it was—" Lea drew a long breath. "I've never seen such suffering."

"The supply lines are struggling as well." Maris sighed. "So many people are needed to protect them from rancor attacks...."

They were all quiet for a moment.

"Does it bother you that we contributed to this?" Maris asked.

After a beat, everyone offered a soft "Yes."

Lea's voice was tight. "I hope she gets here soon. We need her."

The Nightrender. They were talking about the Nightrender. But she'd been in the malsite looking for the shrine. Had she gotten it? And—

Memory stabbed through Hanne's head: breaking out of the wagon, stealing Rune's horse, begging the Nightrender for help.

She must have made a noise, because the women all went quiet and Hanne could feel them *looking* at her.

"Hanne?" Nadine's cool palm touched Hanne's forehead, then cheeks. "Her fever's down," she said to the others.

With a faint groan, Hanne forced open her eyes, but everything was too sharp and bright. She squinted and turned away from the light globes.

There was a general flurry: water pouring into a glass, pillows being pressed behind her, and globes disappearing into baskets. After a few dizzying moments, Hanne realized she was inside a small tent. Nadine, all her ladies, and Sabine were there.

And Mae.

The malicist was on the far side of the tent, standing over a small table littered with papers and pencils and bits of some kind of machine. She glanced over at Hanne and smiled faintly. "Glad you're alive."

Quickly, Hanne wiped the sleep out of her eyes and finger-combed her hair.

"Here, drink this." Nadine pressed the glass to Hanne's lips. She sipped. The water was cold going down, trickling like ice all the way into her stomach. Nadine set the glass aside. "You've been unconscious for a long time. Do you remember what happened? Are you . . . alone?"

Hanne reached for anything after the Nightrender standing over her, that dark sword drawn, but there was nothing.

Until she blinked.

A memory flashed: the altar, Rune, and Malstop-blue light crackling into her.

The shock of it passed quickly, but a deep, unsettled feeling spread throughout her. Something was . . . missing. It was quiet inside her head, with only the echo of her own thoughts in the place where Daghath Mal had been for nearly a decade.

For a horrifying moment, Hanne was so deeply, unfathomably lonely.

She knew she shouldn't be—Daghath Mal had been a parasite, an invader, a spy—but for years, he'd been there with her, guiding her, making her feel special.

She wasn't special after all.

"Hanne?" Nadine's voice was soft as she sat beside Hanne. "Did it work? What the Nightrender did?"

Haltingly, Hanne jerked her head in something resembling a nod. Every muscle in her body hurt, but the stiffness was only the result of sleeping on a hard cot. She should be in a lot more pain. She'd been bleeding, hadn't she? And her ankle had been caught in the stirrup. . . . But where there'd been sharp, overwhelming agony, now there was only a distant, dull ache.

Nadine offered another drink of water. Hanne accepted. And at last, she could clear her throat enough to speak. "It worked."

Nadine visibly relaxed. "Thank all the known and unknown Numina."

Hanne wasn't ready to think about Numina for a while. Perhaps not for a long while. "Where are we? When did you all get here?" She'd sent for them, but...

"We're at the Soul Gate—the entrance to the Malice." Nadine ran her fingers through her hair. "Obviously it's not the only entrance anymore, since the Malstop is still gone. But it's the best place to bring an army."

"Three armies," Sabine corrected, not looking up from her knitting. "In addition to his own men, your Rune persuaded the rebels in Solcast to fight with him. And Queen Abagail is here, too."

Across the tent, Mae shuddered. "She knows I'm here, but King Rune accepted my request for asylum. At least temporarily."

But the Malstop was *still* gone. Hanne forced herself to think. Then she could act. "So the armies have engaged. What progress has been made?"

Maris glanced down. "Not much. The Ivaslanders brought huge machines that fire obsidian shards into the Soul Gate, but no one has been able to get there yet. Rune says we must reach the towers, though."

"Why?"

"Something about the Malstop. But they're seething with rancor and other"—Maris wrinkled her nose—"things. Yesterday, I saw blood pouring down one of the walls. Then a whole swarm of flies came out and—"

"That's enough." Sabine set down her knitting. "We should let Her Majesty rest."

"I've *been* resting. I'm ready to do something." Hanne pushed herself off the cot, swayed, and sat back down. The dizziness abated. "Where's Rune? I should speak with him."

"He's at the front," Nadine said.

Right. Because Caberwilline monarchs loved to risk their lives by personally leading their armies, even though they had perfectly good generals to do that.

"I'll send a messenger to let him know you're awake. And that you want to see him." Lea stepped out of the tent.

Hanne stood again, this time with Nadine's help, and limped toward the table where Mae worked. "What's all this?"

"I'm trying to figure out how to make a new Malstop." Mae glanced up, her eyes meeting Hanne's for only an instant. "Your note said we should work for King Rune and the grand general, and what they want is a Malstop."

Hanne inspected the blueprints, but she didn't understand what kind of machine Mae could be building. "Is it possible?"

"I think so." Mae shuffled through the sketches. "We know that malsites have their own barriers—pellicles—due to the self-attracting properties of malice. But here, there's an unlimited amount pouring out of the Rupture, so it doesn't get contained the same way. It's just pushing and pushing. However, I hypothesize that a super-condensed field of malice would act as a pellicle. It's not ideal, because it is still malice, but it could hold for a little while." She sighed. "I've made a small-scale version work, but we need something immense."

"To think that is even possible." Hanne shook her head. It seemed so many things were possible—even for people without dark voices in their heads.

Mae lowered her voice. "I was worried when you were taken."

"You were?" Well, of course she'd been worried. Every malicist in the observatory project had been at risk of exposure. They were *still* at risk.

Because of Hanne.

Well, because of Abagail first. But then because of Hanne.

"Of course. We're friends." Mae's gaze dropped to Hanne's lips. "Aren't we?"

Hanne's mouth twitched with a faint, surprised smile. "Of course," she echoed.

"Your Majesty." Lea moved toward a large trunk. "If you're going to see the king, you need to get dressed."

Abruptly, Hanne realized her most significant layer was her dressing gown, and that the air really was quite cold. But what her ladies removed from the trunk wasn't exactly winter formal, either. "Is that armor?"

"King Rune doesn't leave the front." Lea held up the dark leather jerkin. It had a good cut, at least, and would be flattering to Hanne's figure. (Which was not the point of armor. Of course.) There was also a filigreed design down the breast and sleeves, made with delicate gold thread.

The rest of what Lea said caught up with Hanne a moment later. "He won't leave the front even for me? But I'm the queen."

All the ladies looked to Nadine, who straightened her shoulders to bear the responsibility of delivering unwelcome news. "Technically— Well, Embria is under new leadership. The nobility has pledged loyalty to Magistrate Stephens. Those who refused are in the dungeon."

Hanne hated every word of this.

"The magistrate has popular support," Nadine went on. "As well as the recognition of King Rune and Queen Abagail."

White flared around the corners of Hanne's vision, and for a moment, she swayed with new dizziness. "Rune recognized Stephens. As ruler of Embria?"

All the ladies nodded somberly.

"He needed the rebel army," Sabine said. "Since yours was no longer available."

"I see." But if Stephens was ruler, what did that mean for her? "I'm still queen of Caberwill, aren't I?"

There was another awkward pause. This time, it was Sabine who answered. "Technically, yes, but . . . the alliance stipulates that the king wed an heir to Embria, and as your parents lost the kingdom . . ."

Nadine nodded. "So technically—"

Hanne was really growing to hate that word.

"You're King Rune's consort, without any real power of your own." Nadine licked her lips. "It's not yet clear if you're even still married."

"What?" Of course she was still married. That didn't go away just because someone had stolen her kingdom. Did it? "How can my marital status be unclear? It was consummated."

"I believe there's a clause regarding a mutual agreement to *stay* married, should the alliance come under question. Either party can annul the marriage if the treaty conditions aren't met."

That sounded vaguely familiar, but Hanne hadn't questioned that part very much. Considering she'd intended the marriage to be short-term, anyway.

Nadine shrugged helplessly. "There's been no discussion about it, what with you being unconscious, and Rune having other things on his mind."

"Like waiting at the front for the Nightrender," Lea muttered.

That sounded like Rune. "I'll just have to make sure he understands that we're still married." Without him, she would surely fall into Magistrate

Stephens's hands—and right back into the dungeon with her parents. Then the rest of what Lea had implied caught up with her. "Wait, where is the Nightrender?"

"No one knows," Maris said. "But people are dying without her."

Outside, the screech and thunk of another catapult sounded. A man screamed.

When she was presentable and ready to remind Rune of all the reasons he'd married her, Captain Oliver escorted Hanne through the support lines: hundreds of blacksmiths, cooks, medics, and messengers, all working to keep humanity in this fight.

In a field, dozens of young men were practicing with clubs, hammers, and spears. Their faces were too far for Hanne to see clearly, but it was obvious they were terrified. These were farmers and cobblers who'd been given the most basic of weapons—the only kind they might be able to wield—to fight the fiercest of predators in all of Salvation.

They were going to die.

As they moved down a once-white road that wove through the mountains, toward a pair of immense towers, Hanne forced herself to look up—to where the Malstop should have been.

The sky was a wall of *red*. Like a gaping wound, blood-tinted gas spilled over the mountains, running down the slopes, and crashed into the regular world with pure violence. The space where the two realities met was filled with lightning, whirlwinds, and shimmery patches that didn't quite match what was happening around them.

It appeared to stop some distance away from the two towers and iron portcullis, but evidence of its expansion was everywhere: supply carts floated in gravitational anomalies, spiked barricades were flattened against the red dirt, and unidentifiable bits of metal lodged into the ground.

Screech. Thunk. A catapult fired a glittering black load toward the Soul Gate. Small shards of obsidian blanketed the path leading through the portcullis.

"Where exactly is the front?" Hanne asked softly.

"Beyond the mix." Captain Oliver pointed toward the swirling mess of clashing realities. "Just remember to breathe normally when we go in."

As they approached the mix—as he'd called it—they dismounted and sent the horses back with a groom.

"They don't like going through," the captain explained.

Of course they didn't. No one in their right mind wanted to go *into* the Malice—the now-expanded Malice.

Even so, Hanne stepped through, staggering under the reek of ammonia and decay. The stench of the Dark Shard flooded through her, sticking in her lungs and coating her eyelashes. She forced herself to breathe, even as the pressure changed, her ears popped, and there seemed a moment that she fell—only to stagger out on the other side of the mix.

"It gets easier." Captain Oliver offered his arm.

Hanne accepted, steadying herself, then scanned the area until she spotted a wide tent, its flaps held open by metal spikes. Rune stood by the entrance, speaking with military men. All the kingdoms were represented—plenty of somber grays and blacks for Caberwill, dull linen for Ivasland, and random colors for Embria's rebel army, which didn't have a proper uniform.

All the men wore obsidian. The ground surrounding the tent, too, was littered with shards of black glass, most of it embedded in the red dirt where it wasn't likely to stab someone in the foot.

Rune glanced out the opening—like he'd been watching for her—and when their eyes met, he excused himself from the others.

Hanne stepped away from Captain Oliver, meeting Rune halfway. He looked her over, concern in his eyes. "You're awake."

Hanne nodded.

"And he's..."

"Gone," Hanne confirmed. "He's gone."

Rune nodded, shoulders sagging in relief. "Stephens wanted me to send you back to Solspire, once he heard about your great wagon escape."

Hanne looked over Rune's shoulder just in time to see Magistrate Stephens watching her from inside the tent, suspicion clear on his face. The man wore her pendant, the shard of the obsidian crown.

Burn him. That was *her* obsidian.

She would have to get it back. Later.

For now, she returned her attention to Rune. "His men would have killed me before you'd finished saying goodbye."

"I know." Rune pressed his mouth into a line. "That's why I refused."

She wasn't sure why it was always a surprise, this repeated realization that Rune was a decent person. Had their positions been reversed, she would have forced the shrine's location from him, then abandoned him to the dungeon, assuming he deserved it for being weak.

But he had a strength of his own, didn't he? It was different from hers—more like Nadine's. But where Nadine was loyal solely to Hanne, Rune was loyal to humanity. No matter the cost.

Hanne let her eyes drift over the Soul Gate. From this side of the mix, she could more clearly see the immense towers; these were not the bent fingers of the guard towers she'd seen all her life, but high monuments spun up from the mountainside. They rose into the deep red sky, seemingly endless.

Below the towers, the iron portcullis that once barred the tunnel was ripped out and twisted. The white of the path was warped and buckled, entire stones either missing or floating in midair.

"Where are the rancor?" Hanne asked.

"In the towers. On the other side of the tunnel. Attacking the edges of our encampment and disrupting supply lines at all hours." He paused as another load of crushed obsidian flew, crashing to release a cloud of sparkling black dust. "We're holding them back."

"Until the Nightrender arrives."

Rune glanced at the tunnel entrance, grief passing over his expression. "Yes."

"There are people who don't think she'll come." As in, most people.

"She will."

"She's not usually late, is she?" Hanne wasn't sure *exactly* how long it had been since she'd run into the malsite, but it had been *days* at least. "And where did she go? I thought she wanted the shrine."

Rune hesitated. Then, softly, he said, "She was looking for a weapon. Something that could destroy him."

Him. Daghath Mal.

"And that involved the shrine." Hanne let her eyes wander back toward the tunnel—imagining she could see Daghath Mal somewhere far beyond. Again, that unwanted loneliness washed through her. She hated him. She did. But it was hard to let go of what she'd thought she had. "Then why isn't the Nightrender here using it? Why the delay when lives are at stake?"

"I don't know. But she will come." He said it with such conviction that Hanne couldn't help but believe him . . . and she couldn't ignore the longing in his voice.

"Rune, we should discuss our alliance. Our marriage." It was pointless for him to be pining after the Nightrender, wasn't it? Wouldn't she just go back to her tower after this? (If there was an *after this*. And if the Nightrender actually bothered to come here and help out.)

It was clear, just by the way he tilted his head, his eyebrows drawn in and a frown turning down the corners of his mouth, that he'd been thinking about this, too. And he knew, certainly, that all he had to do was say the word and their marriage would dissolve. He could be free of Hanne, the person he didn't love, the person who'd brought about the worst Incursion of all time.

He'd been weighing his options, and he clearly hadn't come to a decision yet.

"We should," he said after a moment. "But first, we must fight."

As he spoke, a shadow fell across Hanne's eyes. She looked up, squinting against the hot red light. And there, black against the burning sky, she saw wings.

The Nightrender had arrived.

47.

RUNE

A thousand emotions hit Rune as the Nightrender landed beside him, tucked back her wings, and pushed a tangle of windblown hair off her face. His heart lifted at the sight of her deadly grace, at the heat her nearness ignited within him.

In this whole burning world, she was the one person he most wanted to see.

"You're here." He didn't bother to hide his grin.

She gave a small, single nod. "After I left Winterfast, I decided to clear away some of the more dangerous malsites."

"Really?" He motioned around at the encampment, the dark towers, and the ever-expanding Malice. "Is this not more urgent? And I got your army. I know how you like armies."

A fleeting smile pulled at one corner of her mouth. "Of course. Thank you." Her expression darkened. "One of those malsites turned people inside out. Another trapped them in a loom."

"A loom?" Hanne—Rune had almost forgotten Hanne was there—narrowed her eyes. "That doesn't make sense. Do you mean a loop? A time loop?"

"I mean a loom." The Nightrender turned her gaze on Hanne. "The malsite formed in a textile district."

"Oh."

Rune had only a limited idea of how looms worked, but he did understand that the machines held threads at very high tension, then forcefully compressed them.

He didn't pursue that line of thought any more.

The Nightrender looked at him again. "I will address your people, then engage the rancor king. I believe he still resides in his castle."

"He can't leave the Malice," Hanne said. "He's trapped inside this red."

But at the rate it was spreading, Daghath Mal would have access to the entire continent in mere months. They had to stop this now, while it was still possible.

"In the meantime," the Nightrender went on, "your men should focus on the towers. I believe Daghath Mal will recall some of his rancor to protect him, which should afford you more opportunity to rid the towers of their presence. When you are successful, the Malstop should return. I cannot say what will happen with this space"—she motioned to encompass all the redness that had spread outside the original boundary—"but perhaps the more clever among you can find a way to move this substance of the Dark Shard into its cage once more."

Hanne pressed her mouth into a line. "I'll make sure of it."

The Nightrender studied Hanne for a moment, her eyes going in and out of focus until she blinked, nodded, and offered Hanne a faint, forced smile. "I'm glad to see that you're now free of his influence. I had not thought to look earlier. That connection was not something I thought possible."

"I suppose I should thank you," Hanne said.

"It isn't necessary."

"Very well."

Rune cleared his throat.

"But of course," Hanne went on, "I am grateful. I didn't have a plan on my own. I was just...hoping." She lifted her chin. "And you? You got what you needed?"

"I was successful."

Rune motioned toward a black leather envelope secured to her belt. "Is that it? Can I see it?"

The Nightrender stiffened as her hand slipped over the package, as though to hide it. "No. No one should see this."

He suppressed a shiver. If it made her uncomfortable—it must truly be devastating. "All right."

"Now," the Nightrender said, "I will address the people." Without waiting for either of them to respond, she took off again, hovering above the bluff as soldiers gathered around her. The noise of the war machines stopped, the roar of voices went quiet, and even the wind seemed to die.

"She does know how to command attention," Hanne muttered.

"That almost sounded admiring." Rune looked at her askance. "Don't you hate her?"

She gave a one-shouldered shrug. "I admire all my rivals. Otherwise they wouldn't be worthy of such a position."

Hanne was different than she'd been before. Less certain. More human. But still very much the princess he'd married. He stuffed the problem of their marriage back down. He didn't want to think about what would happen to her if he annulled the agreement—or what would happen to him if he didn't.

By then, the crowd had finished gathering, and above, the Nightrender began to speak.

"Welcome, Dawnbreakers. As were my warriors of old, you have been called to this most difficult of tasks. You are the defenders of Salvation.

"You already know what insurmountable odds we face. I do not have to tell you what is at stake." Her gaze swept across the crowd; when her eyes met Rune's, he shivered with the memories of all the people he'd loved. "But know this: your deeds will be written in history. Those who are lost need not be forgotten."

The men didn't speak—this was not a moment for cheering—but many brought their fists to their hearts, nodding.

"In our first offense, your priority must be the towers—the key to the Malstop lies within. When the Malstop rises, go through the gate. Slaughter as many rancor as you can. And when you are finished, return to the towers. There, you will find help."

She paused, looking over the men. Before, she'd made a practice to know all her Dawnbreakers by name, she'd told him once. Most of those faces and names were gone by now, but Rune was certain she was doing her best to commit these faces, at least, to memory.

Behind her, the red world boiled, dark and deadly. In the distance, a gray smudge streaked across the sky—a winged rancor—then disappeared behind a mountain peak.

The Nightrender kept her focus on the army, but power flickered around her fists. "I know it seems hopeless. The Malice will always be here. But remember: some battles are fought solely for the sake of resisting. Of enduring. Of surviving."

Then she flew through the mix and out the other side. The military and support there needed to see her, too. To be heartened by her presence.

"It's about time she got here." Queen Abagail walked up beside Rune. "What took her so long?"

"She was clearing malsites."

"Why?" Magistrate Stephens, too, had come to stand with them. "We've been dying without her."

"I know. But she's here now. And we need to prepare for our part."

"The towers." Stephens turned toward the immense structures, considering. "If we're to make our assault on them today, I will ready the hunters and miners."

"I believe the majority of obsidian incendiaries are ready. I'll ensure they're distributed throughout the ranks." Queen Abagail turned her eyes on Hanne, who'd remained standing beside Rune. "And what about the . . . project your friend is working on?"

Ah. Mae. The malicist from Ivasland.

Rune had caught up on that aspect of Hanne's life—the abduction of a foreign operative, the observatory, the planned destruction of the Malstop. Mae was another complication, another question for the future, but for now she was working for him, developing a temporary pellicle. Furious as he was at her for her part in Small Mountain, Silver Sun, and the Malstop crisis, he was not in a position to turn down her assistance. If anyone had the knowledge to fix this, it was Mae.

He answered for Hanne. "I'm told there's significant progress. But now that the Nightrender is here, we should focus on our original plans, rather than contingencies."

"She'll finish it," Hanne said. "And then she'll find a way to move all this malice back in there where it belongs." She jabbed her finger at the Soul Gate.

"My people will do it first." Abagail lifted her chin.

"All efforts in moving malice will be appreciated," Rune said. "We're not in a contest. Now let's go over the map again."

The map was a crude drawing of the Malice, one Rune had made when they'd arrived, based on his wandering alone, as well as everything Thoman had told him about the area. The war committee had looked at it before, but as the wait for the Nightrender grew longer, they'd had to focus on the more immediate problems, such as not dying by rancor attack and ensuring that everyone was rotated out of the Malice before they began to suffer corruption. Only Rune had the feather, and he couldn't use it on everyone.

"Very well." Stephens motioned at Hanne. "But I insist she not be part of our talks."

"Hear this—" Hanne started, but Rune interrupted.

"I agree with him." Rune waved for Captain Oliver to come take charge of the queen. "In the interest of peace."

Hanne's jaw clenched, but after a moment she nodded and marched toward the edge of the bluff, glaring at the Soul Gate as though she could see Daghath Mal from here. Captain Oliver followed after her.

"All right," Rune said, "let's—"

Wingbeats sounded. The Nightrender landed beside him, clearing her throat. "I will face the rancor king shortly," she said. "But first, I would like to speak with you. If you can spare a moment."

Rune would spare a thousand moments for her, if that was what she needed. "Of course."

A few minutes later, he'd excused himself from Abagail and Stephens, then cleared his tent and drew the flap closed so that they were alone in the cramped space. Only a handful of chemical lights remained lit, casting the Nightrender in a cool glow, soft against the hard angles of her face. Deep shadows lined her eyes as she regarded him.

He poured a glass of water for her. "Your speech was good. Everyone was very encouraged."

"Perhaps." She drained the water.

"Was there something you needed to talk about?" Not that Rune was complaining. He wanted all the time in the world with her. But she'd spent valuable days clearing malsites that could be dealt with later; something was wrong.

The Nightrender blinked. "I only wanted to see you before I go."

Warmth built in Rune's chest. "I'm glad."

"And I wanted to make a request." There was a hitch in her voice. "You can say no." For a moment, she looked nervous. It was such an unusual expression on her—he almost didn't catch it.

Rune took her glass and put it aside. "I don't plan to deny you anything ever again. If it helps to know that." They were standing so close that he could feel the heat of her body, hear the rustle of her wings, see the shimmer of uncertainty in her eyes.

But she nodded, and softly she whispered, "I would like for you to kiss me again."

He glanced first at her lips. He couldn't help it. For weeks, he'd thought about that kiss, hating himself. That wasn't what being her soul shard meant. And for weeks, he'd replayed those few seconds, the look in her eyes when he'd pulled away, the way she'd thanked him.

He'd understood it would never happen again.

But here she was. Asking. Well, stating a request.

The Nightrender swallowed and looked away. "Forgive me. I should not have—"

He cupped her face. Took a step closer. And he kissed her.

Her faint gasp whispered across his lips, but an instant later, she was kissing him back.

Rune groaned with acute relief, letting his fingers slide into her hair, draw down the back of her neck, over her collarbone. Her skin was warm, smooth, perfect. Down her shoulders, arms, wrists: he memorized the shape of her, the ridges of her muscles. And when he traced down the backs of her hands, he found her fingers splayed wide.

He drew back. "Is this—"

Her eyes were wide. Dark. Filled with urgency. "I don't know what to do with my hands."

A low, amused breath escaped him as he brushed a strand of hair behind her ear and kissed her. "Anything you want." Another kiss, deeper this time. "Tell me what you want."

"I want—" She closed her eyes and swallowed. "Say my name. I want to hear you say my name."

Rune pulled her close, grazing the shell of her ear with his mouth. "Medella."

She shivered against him. "Again."

"Medella." He kissed her neck.

There was a sharp pressure against his ribs: her fingers digging into him. Then, so carefully he ached for more, she copied him: first, she held his face, kissing him before she combed her fingers through his hair and down his neck, shoulders, and arms. Sparks trailed after her, snapping blue and white everywhere she touched.

"I'm sorry." She lifted her hands between them, gaze on the halo of lightning. "I hope I didn't hurt you."

He gave a rough laugh, and moments later, they were kissing again; her teeth scraped his lips, his hands found her hips, and their bodies pressed close together. It felt so good, so satisfying; he wanted more.

Slowly, though, she pulled back, letting her hands fall to her sides, her wings fan, and her gaze linger on him. "I must go now." Her voice was low, a little husky. "I don't want to."

He didn't want her to go, either. He wanted forget this whole burning world and simply be with her. Forever.

"You need to let me go," she whispered.

His hand was still tight against her hips, he realized. Reluctantly, he released her. "After this, I want to kiss you again. Every day. For the rest of my life."

"Rune—"

"I know, but pretend with me. Pretend we can have that. If you want it, too."

She drew a shaking breath, watching him with round, dark eyes. "I do want that."

A wave of joy crashed through him, so bright and intense he could hardly focus. All this time he'd thought she didn't—couldn't possibly—feel this way about him. But she did.

And after this, instead of what they both wanted, she would return to Winterfast, where she would sleep for centuries with whatever was left of her memories.

He wished he hadn't wasted so much time. Alliance be burned—he should have obeyed his heart.

"I must go."

"I know." Rune kissed her again, just once more before she left. "I love you," he whispered against her lips. "I always have."

When they parted, her eyes shimmered. A tear slipped down her cheek, taking the path he'd traced earlier. She looked at him, long and steady, and then went to the tent flap, where light cut through the opening. She pushed it open, looked over her shoulder, and said, "This is what I was built for."

Then, with a rustle of wings, she was gone.

For several minutes, Rune just stood there, reliving every touch, every caress, every perfect kiss. He had to find a way to help her, a bandage for her memories. The maintainers, perhaps, could help—if he rescued them from the rancor. And then, her soul shard in the future—*his* soul reincarnated—would find her. Perhaps then she could be happy.

It wouldn't be with him, at least not like he wanted *now*, but for her...

Rune bent to touch the feather, but the tent flap whipped open and Hanne came inside, her expression incredulous.

"What just happened?"

A crushing guilt descended on him as he struggled to explain. "I'm not sorry it happened, but I am sorry I wasn't more considerate of you—"

"She was crying." Hanne raised her eyebrows. "What did you do?"

"Sometimes she drinks too much water—"

Hanne was shaking her head. "She was barely holding herself together. So if something happened between you—"

"We kissed."

Hanne stared at him as though he were the biggest fool in the world. "She didn't kiss you because she just now realized she wanted to. She's obviously wanted that for a long time."

"Really?" That was wonderful news. But again, so much wasted time.

"She was saying goodbye."

Every emotion inside Rune plummeted. "What do you mean?"

Hanne blew out a long breath. "I can't believe I have to explain this to you. I'll use little words: she decided to act on her feelings because she knows she's not coming back. Whatever weapon she got—it's either not going to work, or it'll work too well and destroy her, too."

"The law of conquest?" To kill a rancor king meant becoming a rancor king. Could destroying one have a similar consequence? Or was it the weapon? She'd said he shouldn't see it.

He should have asked a lot more questions.

"Honestly," Hanne went on, "do you think the *Nightrender* would have delayed going into battle for so long if she thought she was coming back? She cleared malsites before coming here. Why? Because she didn't want to stick us with the worst of them after she's gone. She gave that speech about how to proceed after the Malstop is restored and the worst of the Malice has been contained. Why would she need to say any of that ahead of time if she planned to return?"

Rune's whole body felt numb. This was why the weapon had been hidden for so long. This was why it was a last resort.

He'd known their *after this* was only pretend. But going back to Winterfast? Him finding a way to save her memories? That was supposed to be real.

She had said goodbye, and he hadn't realized.

A wave of numbness crashed through him. His voice sounded hollow. "I have to stop her."

"What are you going to do?" Hanne asked. "Are you going to run after her? Even if you could catch up, how would you stop the *Sword of the Numina* from fighting rancor? The world is counting on her."

"I don't know. But there has to be another way." The Nightrender—Medella—had already lost so much of who she was. She shouldn't have to lose her whole self, too.

And Rune... Well, he'd lost most of his family, his friends—he wouldn't lose her. Not like this.

Hanne was watching him, her expression torn between sympathy and fear. "I might have a way. You won't like it."

"Tell me."

"Before the Nightrender excised him, Daghath Mal made me an offer. I would rule as queen for seventy years—until I died. He would wait until then to resume his conquest."

The words spun through Rune. All he could think about was the Nightrender flying to her death—no, her *destruction*. How long would it take? Would he feel it? His soul was part of hers, so perhaps. "I don't see how that helps us."

"I will accept his offer," Hanne said. "I'll be his puppet again. And that will give you and the Nightrender seventy more years to figure out another way to stop him."

But the Nightrender's memories. She needed Winterfast.

"Why would he do that?" Rune shook his head, struggling to think clearly. "You already said no, I assume. So why would his offer still be good after you rejected him?"

Hanne's jaw trembled. "Because he loves me."

"That's impossible." Rune had *met* the rancor king. Daghath Mal was incapable of love. "He's more likely to kill you than let you be queen."

"It's the only plan I have." Hanne bit her lip. There was a darkness behind her eyes, a cold terror at the idea of facing Daghath Mal. But she was determined. Hanne always was. "So," she said sharply, "do you want to stop the Nightrender from sacrificing herself?"

He didn't need to think beyond the one word: "Yes."

48.

HANNE

They didn't wait. Within minutes, Hanne, Rune, and their guards were racing through the Soul Gate—deeper into the Malice, heading straight for Daghath Mal.

Armed with swords, obsidian-tipped spears, and anything else they could carry on horseback, the group charged through the tunnel. Rune hadn't told anyone what he was doing, and Hanne wasn't in the habit of giving people information they didn't need. But even so, she'd imagined the arguments and justified them to imaginary people (who, strangely, wore Abagail's and Stephens's faces):

They needed the Nightrender. In the future, not just right now.

Hanne would be a fair queen. She'd learned a lot from Rune, the mistakes of both their parents, and the fact that Embria *and* Ivasland had suffered rebellions of the people. Plus, she would have Nadine. Nadine would never let her do anything too egregious. Again.

And if Daghath Mal denied her—well, she had a plan for that, too.

The thunder of hooves on red dirt echoed. In the faint light, Hanne could see barrels of kindlewater, rigged to explode to clear the tunnel for the army. But there were no rancor here—not living ones, anyway.

They passed body after body. Broken rancor littered the path. And as they entered into the Malice proper, the devastation to the rancor became clear:

Black blood stained the ground, collecting into puddles and hissing where ruddy sunlight hit it. Bits of rancor dripped off rocks, brush, and a strange stone tower. The entire area reeked of sulfur and ozone.

"Dear Numina," muttered one of Rune's guards—Rose was her name. "How many do you think there are?"

"Dozens." Rune's voice was hard. "She killed dozens of them."

"She left only a quarter hour ago." That was a different guard.

"We need to hurry." Rune didn't say it, but his meaning was clear: the

Nightrender had only bothered to kill all these rancor because she wouldn't be able to do it later.

Hanne urged her horse forward, down the slope, and through the high brush. The red air was overwhelming, the pressure of it too much on her skin. But as they rode, she put that aside. Soon, she would face Daghath Mal. She would look at him directly, not with an image in her mind, or through a portal. No, she would be in the same space as him.

And she would say yes.

She would be his queen.

She would gain everything she'd wanted at the expense of her own soul.

But if, as Rune had wondered, Daghath Mal no longer wanted to treat, then Hanne would resort to the last option available, the only other action she could take to make up for all the damage she'd caused:

The law of conquest.

49.

NIGHTRENDER

Saying goodbye had been harder than she'd expected; every step out of that tent had felt like torture; every wingbeat into the Malice ripped her heart from her chest. She'd hardly been able to look at him, in the end, lest he see the truth in her eyes.

She wasn't coming back.

There was no *after this* for them. Nothing to make work.

There was only her fight. Light Eater. And then... nothing.

She wondered if it would hurt.

Don't think about that, she told herself. *Just do the work.*

She couldn't imagine it *wouldn't* hurt.

Slowly, Nightrender stalked her way through the wild, red land of the Malice by foot, rather than wing, seeking rancor that lurked in skeletal forests and bloody rivers. Some were armed with crude weapons, but most fought with their claws and teeth—and died by her sword.

Already she'd killed four hundred and fifty-seven. Decapitated. Burned. Gutted.

Viscid blood oozed down Beloved's blade. She flicked it off; the ground where it hit began to sizzle. On her body, her armor tingled, stitching itself back together where a rancor had swiped her leg. Another spot had scratched and worn when she'd fallen against sharp rocks; now it, too, repaired itself, strengthening ahead of the next battle.

Her final battle.

She could delay it no longer. After killing what she could in the wasteland, it was time to put an end to Daghath Mal.

Low, thorny scrub crunched under her boots as she strode up to a ridge. From there, she had a clear view of the bone castle. It was different from before. Taller, with new traps set to spring on the unwary: false floors, pillars of fire, and trip-lines to activate dozens of spikes. Sludge dripped from the narrow windows set into square towers, filling a slow-moving moat. For an instant, rotten-green eyes lifted above the surface—but the creature vanished.

What was *that*?

Nightrender flexed her fingers around Beloved, letting numinous energy skitter across the honed edge. Then, with a mighty pump of her wings, she jumped from the ridge and flew toward the moat.

The beast leaped at her. It was huge, bug-shaped, with bulbous eyes, a segmented body, and teeth as long as her forearm. Sludge streamed after it as it snapped at her.

She dodged, whipping her sword around to slice open the soggy yellow flesh. Brown fluid poured out, making it howl and fall beneath the surface. To hide from her. Escape.

But Nightrender was faster. She speared its central segment, heaving the entire thing onto land, where she had a greater advantage.

It rolled, screeching and clicking—just as two additional pairs of legs erupted from its front and back segments. The whole creature ripped apart in a mess of blood, tendons, and stringy wet pops.

It was two creatures now.

With bile burning up her throat, Nightrender sliced across one monster's face, blinding it. The second reared and slashed at her with long claws, but it was too slow. She snapped her wings wide, feathers cutting deep.

Brown liquid splashed across the red dirt.

The beast fell to its side, raising its claws as Nightrender approached. But there was nothing it could do now. She drove her sword into it, released a pulse of purifying power, and flicked its corpse away, where thick brush would contain most of its debris.

The first one was up again, though, sniffing the air with its wide nose holes. It shambled toward her, mouth gaping. Venom shone on the tips of two fangs.

But it was slow, awkward, and already injured. Nightrender killed it quickly, a deep thrust into its brain. Slowly, it deflated, leaving behind a wrinkled sack of flesh and venom.

"Impressive." Daghath Mal stood on the castle side of the moat. "Do you know what that was?"

Nightrender said nothing.

"Most of what you find here is native to this plane—altered by the power of my home. That, however"—he waved a taloned hand at the bug-beasts' remains—"was something my soldiers brought through. A gift for me, now that the way is large enough to let such things pass."

Then she was doubly glad she had killed it.

"I did not come here to converse with you," Nightrender said.

"Of course not." Daghath Mal sighed as though put out. "You've come to send me back to the Dark Shard."

"Yes," she said. "This is not your world." She resisted the urge to touch Light Eater's envelope. She was not ready for it. Not yet.

"It will be my world. Soon, I will conquer this continent. The waters surrounding. The lands beyond." He tilted his head, a show of thoughtfulness. "My princess believes the other lands are covered in darkness. Perhaps that is true. But they will become mine, too. In time."

He was very patient.

But so was she.

"On the subject of my princess," Daghath Mal said, his tone darkening. "You took her from me. You turned her against me." A low growl emanated from the rancor king's throat. "She was *mine.*"

"She was never yours." Nightrender flew across the moat. Her sword was still drawn, still dripping, but she didn't attack. Not until she cleared the castle. Not until she could finish Daghath Mal with Light Eater. "You trapped her. Tricked her. Exploited her. You meant to corrupt her the same way you sought to corrupt me."

"No." Daghath Mal's deep voice rumbled across the Malice. "Not the same."

Nightrender stepped toward him.

"I used her. Yes. The way any parent uses their child to shape the future."

"You are not her parent."

"She was *mine,*" Daghath Mal seethed. "Those mortals who birthed her abandoned her in every way that mattered. But I never did. And you took her from me. *Cut* her. Do you know how much it hurt?"

"She asked me to do it." Nightrender's words were a needle, deliberately

321

driven into an open wound of emotion. "She *begged* me to set her free. She rejected you."

Rage flashed across the beast's face. A low growl rolled out from him like faraway thunder.

"You didn't need her anymore." One step forward. Two. Nightrender drove her words deeper. "She'd already done as you commanded, tearing down the bars of this prison. You got what you wanted. So you can end this act, this little game of pretend you've been playing. As if you could love anyone but yourself."

"You don't know *anything* about it!" Fury strained his voice as his wings rose and his fists curled—and all around him, the world started to move: a wave of dark sludge splashed from the moat, scorching the ground where it hit; the castle wall split open, revealing a dark interior, filled with hundreds—perhaps thousands—of rancor.

In the center of that immense chamber: the Rupture.

It was huge, swollen and oozing with sacs of newly arrived rancor. Without the Malstop, the flood of rancor would drown Salvation in darkness. No mortal army would be able to repel the sheer numbers.

As long as Daghath Mal was here to call them.

She could feel the chill of Light Eater, even through its obsidian envelope and her armor.

Not yet, she thought. *Clear the castle. Then—*

She didn't finish that thought. Grimly, she lifted her sword and plunged herself into the red-lit castle.

Rancor rushed at her, claws out, their jaws unhinging as they surrounded her.

But she was ready: she spread her wings wide, cutting through their pallid flesh; her sword arced through the bloody gloom, slicing through skin and muscle and tendons—even bones. The beasts screamed, struggling to attack even as internal organs sloughed from their emaciated bellies.

More came for her. The stink of ammonia and rot and acrid blood was overwhelming, but Nightrender never let up. One after another, she killed her enemies. Their screams only made her stronger.

Clear the castle. With hundreds of rancor skittering at her, reaching, grasping, it seemed an insurmountable task. But she was the Nightrender, the Sword of the Numina, the champion of the three kingdoms.

And she was at her full power.

Beloved arced around, carving through her enemies. Rancor fell before her like chaff, bodies piling high.

A *crack* sounded above the fray: on the far side of the chamber, a wall broke open. Bones and mortar gaped for a long moment—then a slab of wall crashed to the floor, crushing rancor beneath it.

Nightrender bared her teeth in a wild grin. She thrust Beloved into a rancor's skull. Bright white-blue light flickered around her, a nimbus of holy energy. Sparks flew out, catching on other beasts, burning holes through them.

But another rumble came from the ground.

Nightrender took to the air just as a gap opened in the floor: the dark maw of a fissure. Dozens of corpses plunged into the yawning blackness; if they hit the bottom—if there *was* a bottom—Nightrender couldn't tell.

Her wings pumped, carrying her higher.

Rancor crawled up the walls to reach her, screaming obscenities, stretching their claws for her. She cut them down one after another, then snapped Beloved so that guts and bile slipped off the blade.

She couldn't tell how many she'd killed—so many rancor both dead and living had fallen into the fissure or been crushed by the crumbling castle. Some had even fled through the Rupture, limbs contorting as they vanished.

Claws wrapped around her ankle, jerking her downward. Nightrender hissed, her wings beating as she twisted to chop the creature's arm clean off. The rancor—and its arm—disappeared down the hole.

Nightrender flew away from the fissure and dropped to the ground. Beloved flashed, obsidian shining in the darkness. Power flowed through her hands and wings, down the length of her sword, crackling all around her. And sprays of blood darkened the air, those fine droplets stinging her lungs with every inhale.

Another volley of rancor hurtled at her, but there were fewer now, and they had to trample their lifeless brethren to reach her. When she killed them, the remaining creatures fled—either through the Rupture or into another part of the castle.

She let them go.

It was time to face Daghath Mal. It was time to use Light Eater.

Bodies, chunks of bone walls, and the Rupture: they dominated the chamber. There was no sign of the rancor king.

"Daghath Mal!" she shouted. The Rupture swallowed her voice. "Come out and fight me!"

Just then, a section of the wall began to close. He was leaving—likely assuming her next task was to send him back to the Dark Shard. And in that case, he didn't want to be too close to the Rupture.

If only she believed that would be enough.

No, the only answer—the *only* chance for humanity, if she was going to keep losing memories like this—was to ensure Daghath Mal no longer existed.

Nightrender leaped into the air and kicked through the opening just before it vanished. A hall waited beyond, red-lit and empty. Still, she could sense his presence nearby—a blot of deeper corruption in this malice-filled wasteland.

She stalked through the hall after him. Then, as the rumble of the walls became a roar, she sped into a sprint—but it was too late. The bone walls rearranged themselves until the broken-off ends of femurs and humeri pointed inward: directly at her.

And with a heavy, grinding noise, the walls began to close in.

A bone shard speared her left wing, sending sharp pain tearing through her.

Nightrender jerked back, but now she was too close to the other side, where more bones knifed out.

Quickly. Too quickly. The hall was closing, making the air stuffy and hard to breathe as the remains of Dawnbreakers past moved to impale her.

Gritting her teeth, Nightrender twisted sideways and brought Beloved up and around, shaving the bone spikes down to stubs. Then, before she had no more room to maneuver, she gathered numinous power into her fist and punched a hole through the wall. Mortar and splinters of bone exploded into the space beyond.

The throne room.

She peeled the hole wider and dived through, tucking her wings close against her body.

"That was disrespectful."

The rancor king's voice echoed through the chamber as Nightrender got to her feet and gauged her surroundings. Thrones, ruby lights, and pockets of darkness. Across the way, the rift from the portal malsite shone; she hadn't destroyed that one, though she probably should have. No other rancor were here—not yet, anyhow—so it was just Nightrender and Daghath Mal.

She flexed her hand. Blood reddened her knuckles. Her wing hurt, too, but she might be able to fly short distances.

"You know what I think?" Daghath Mal watched her, those terrible eyes taking note of every weakness, every vulnerability. "I think you enjoy the fight. You may tell yourself that all you want is an end, but you were *made* for this. And it shows."

"Then you should be terrified of me."

Daghath Mal's mouth peeled back into a too-wide grin. "It's your mortal friends who should fear you. Look at this castle. How many Dawnbreakers died here? Hundreds of thousands. Yet you continue to bring new armies to my doorstep, sacrificing them for your fight. Even now, near your Soul Gate, my servants are moving against your mortal resistance. Now that the full force has arrived, there's no more reason to wait."

Nightrender tried not to think about the thousands of men and women she'd spoken to just hours ago, their frightened faces, the brave show they'd put on because she was there. How many had died already?

She had to end this—to end *him.*

Beloved whipped around, numinous fire glittering along its length. But Daghath Mal's form blurred.

Then.

White-hot pain. Her injured wing crunched. Bones snapped and feathers broke off.

Nightrender screamed and lashed out, her good wing flaring, her sword whistling through the murky red air. But agony roared through her, darkening her vision. She caught only a grainy hint of Daghath Mal's talons wrapped around her wing, blood pouring from his feather-shredded palms.

"What were you doing at the summoning shrines?" He squeezed and twisted. Pops and cracks shot through, excruciating. "Why were my rancor drawn there?"

With a shrieking gasp, Nightrender wrenched herself away, but the damage to her wing was done. Every movement was torment. Every twitch. Every breath of air. The pain was overwhelming. Consuming.

Broken feathers littered the floor, smeared with blood.

"You must have been doing *something*," Daghath Mal said, advancing on her again. "Are there other Nightrenders? Were you summoning help?"

She clenched her jaw. In one torturous movement, she lunged forward and thrust her sword deep into his gut.

Lightning spiked across the chamber, cutting through the rancor king's body, shattering the throne. The thunder and echo rang through her head, distracting her—for a moment—from the incapacitating pain in her wing.

She drew back her sword.

In his abdomen, a burning hole gaped, smoking as char expanded outward. The injury should have been devastating, but his face merely twisted with fury as he attacked her, ash and slime flying after him.

She lifted Beloved and blocked, cleaving off two of his talons. Acidic blood sprayed out; Nightrender staggered away.

Claws scraped her injured wing—another rancor. She spun and killed it, but there was another behind it. And another.

Half a dozen poured in from a dark hall. Nightrender slew them, heaving her sword through the air, flexing her good wing out. Streaks of numinous lightning blasted across the chamber. Bone walls cascaded down, throwing plumes of dust and ash high into the red sky. Blood and gore burned through her armor; she could feel the fabric buzzing against her skin, struggling to repair itself. Still, the stabbing agony of her left wing threatened to consume her.

This was it. If she didn't act now, there would be no other chance. Rancor would continue flooding through the Rupture, as long as Daghath Mal was here to draw them.

There was only one way to stop this. Only one hope for humanity.

The moment hit her, a tide of grief for a life that could never be hers. She was a creature of battle, a weapon, not meant to want anything more.

She would do what was needed. For Salvation. For her soul shard.

She turned back to Daghath Mal, slipping her hand into the black envelope at her waist. The dagger's grip was cold, but it hummed in her hand, hungry.

"What is that?" Daghath Mal laughed, spewing clouds of green and yellow fumes through the air. Malice. He was breathing pure malice.

Nightrender dived toward him, Beloved in her right hand, Light Eater in her left. Battle hummed through her body as she slashed, missed, ducked a sweep of his wing—only to be thrown back by his other wing bashing her head.

Black vines curled around her vision as she climbed to her feet, but she struck out. All she had to do was cut him—

Light Eater wasn't in her hand.

She'd kept her grip on Beloved, but the dagger was nowhere to be found.

No. Such a weapon could not fall into Daghath Mal's hands. If he used it on anyone but her—if he used it on *Rune*—

Daghath Mal flickered toward a pile of bones. "This little thing? It is enticing...."

Light Eater sat among the bones, a void against the bleached white and brittle yellow. Almost thoughtfully, Daghath Mal bent to pick it up.

Nightrender lunged for it, pushing past all the pain and fear as she dived the last few steps. Her chest scraped the ground. She reached. Her fingers closed around the hilt. And she turned, straight onto her broken wing. The sharp pain sliced through her, but all her focus was on lifting Light Eater.

The tip of the blade scraped Daghath Mal's alabaster skin.

He lurched backward, shock written across his face. But he didn't seem worried. Not yet.

Dizzy, gasping, Nightrender struggled to her feet. In her grip, Light Eater buzzed, an audible hum that made her ears ring. "My purpose"—she fought for breath—"is fulfilled."

"What?" Daghath Mal twisted to see the cut, a clean black slice across his skin. He scratched at it, as though it itched.

"No!" A human voice.

Rune's voice.

She staggered away from Daghath Mal to see beyond the ruined castle walls. Rune—with Queen Johanne and a small contingent of guards—was riding toward her.

"What did you do?" Queen Johanne leaped off her horse, running. "If you'd just waited two minutes! I had a plan!"

"Ha— Hanne?" Daghath Mal turned, a strange sort of hope on his face. "You came." He lifted one arm toward the young queen as though she might save him, but it was too late.

It looked like fuzz at first. Dust motes. Then, starting with his outstretched arm, a thin stream of particles flew into Light Eater. He screamed, but it didn't last; his chest unspun, then his face and throat. More and more of him spiraled away, descending into darkness so complete no light could touch it.

Finally, he was gone.

Bittersweet satisfaction filled Nightrender. She'd done it. She'd beaten him.

She'd saved Salvation from Daghath Mal. The rest...they would have to do themselves.

"Wait!" Rune ran for her, boots pounding against the bone floor. "Nightrender, please!"

She staggered toward him, but already her body felt unstable, not quite *solid* anymore.

"I had a plan!" Queen Johanne turned on Nightrender. "I was going to buy us time! Seventy years—"

"It wouldn't have mattered." Her voice, too, had a sudden hollow quality to it. "This was the only way. No loose ends. No—"

Her legs gave out. Her knees hit the ground. Every piece of her body hurt beyond anything she'd ever experienced. And now she was coming apart.

50.

RUNE

He was too late.

He'd known it the moment they'd arrived at the broken castle, the ground shaking and the sky ripping open.

Still he'd hoped. He couldn't *not* hope.

So he'd run faster than he'd ever run before. He'd screamed her name. He'd begged her to hear him—to wait.

But he was too late.

In her hand, she clutched a slash of darkness, a hole in the world, a pocket of nothingness.

The weapon.

"Rune." The Nightrender gripped the hilt, her knuckles taut against her gloves. Her expression twisted with pain as she reached for him.

"No!" He lunged for her, leaving everything else behind. His heart thundered in his ears. Blood rushed through his head. His boots hit the ground, too heavy, too slow.

Five steps away.

Four.

Three.

The dagger slipped from her hand.

Two.

Her eyes went wide. Frightened.

One.

Her cry of pain cut through the roar in his head.

Rune threw himself over her, as if there were any chance of stopping what was already happening.

Her wings—her beautiful, deadly wings—shimmered, falling into nothing right before his eyes.

"No!" His fingers scraped through her remaining feathers, but they, too, were going. Fire burned through him, panic, terror, and the terrible familiarity of losing another person he loved. "Please, no."

The Nightrender's eyes met his. And though her mouth made the shape of words, no sound came out.

The edges of his vision went gray. Tears blurred what was left.

"Please, don't go." He touched her face, her hair, her chest. "I need you."

But as light peeled out of her, flickering toward the black dagger, the truth was so clear: Rune had never been able to save anyone. Not his brother from the assassin, nor Hanne from the malsite, nor John and the other guards from the rancor king, and not Thoman—his most unlikely of friends—from the cruelty of time. He hadn't even been *present* when his father and mother had died.

That Rune couldn't save the Nightrender—the one he would have pledged his entire life to serve, if she would have had him—should not have come as a surprise.

He would have given anything to help her, though. Anything. Everything. The whole world.

His own life.

The ache grew, widening, intensifying, and something hot and golden *pulled* out of him.

It was agony, like being ripped apart, like he himself were falling into the dagger with her. Slowly—everything felt slow—Rune dropped the rest of the way onto the Nightrender. His temple hit her shoulder. His arm found her waist.

Then everything disappeared.

An immense pulse of energy rushed past him.

Outside—through a window (where had the window come from?)—a wave of white-blue streaked across the red-and-black sky. A roar, a cheer, a rallying cry: they all rose up. Siege weapons fired, kindlewater erupted into flames, and then, so low he almost couldn't hear it, a deep hum resonated, vibrating his bones, settling in his chest.

Rune closed his eyes.

Opened them.

The window was still there. And beyond it, a wall of energy crackled.

But a vast hollowness stretched inside him, so he closed his eyes again and tried not to think about this unspeakable break in his soul.

"The Malstop is back."

Hanne was sitting beside him, staring out the window. Dark hollows hung beneath her eyes—evidence of her own exhaustion—but she seemed, overall, in one piece.

A bolt of pain shot through him. The Nightrender. Her falling apart. Falling into the dagger.

"Without Daghath Mal, the rancor army fractured." Hanne's tone was somber, but steady. "Some of them melted into puddles. Others flew back into the Rupture. And the rest—our armies were able to overcome. We took back these towers—obviously—and rushed you and other wounded in. A short time after that, the Malstop returned."

"I felt it." Rune turned back to the window to stare at the light. His neck ached. Everything ached. "How long has it been?"

"Just a couple of days." She shifted her weight. "But we do have days again."

Rune nodded.

"You're in a private room, at least for now. Most of the injured are being treated on other floors, but there's still a lot of fighting. Some rancor were trapped outside the Malstop, so we have to be careful of those still. And there are a lot of new malsites. Early reports are estimating up to ten times as many as we had before. I suppose it would be more, but..."

But the Nightrender had spent days destroying the worst of them before she'd gone into the Malice.

He clutched at his heart, but nothing stopped the pain.

"Athelney is gone," Hanne said. "The university. The square. Even the royal residence. It's just—"

"Gone," Rune murmured.

Had they really accomplished anything? It seemed the world was worse off than before.

Some battles are fought solely for the sake of resisting. Of enduring. Of surviving.

Hanne nodded. "I've been thinking about what I did. And what I couldn't do before—when we tried to reach her...."

Rune dragged in a shaking breath, reliving the feel of her wings disintegrating under his hands, her final, soundless words. His heart cracked wider. It had broken so many times now. How much more could it take?

"I'm annulling our marriage, Rune," Hanne said. "Neither of us wants to be married to the other. And politically, I'm poison for you. Embria is in Magistrate Stephens's hands now, and everyone there would like to see me dead. And likely everyone in Ivasland, as well. If you're going to have a productive relationship with either kingdom, having me at your side will only make things more difficult."

Rune could only nod. She had a valid point. "You won't challenge Magistrate Stephens for the crown?"

She pressed her mouth in a line. "If I were to challenge him, it would be after he discovered exactly how difficult it is to rule an entire kingdom. The choices that must be made. The compromises. The lines that get crossed." She nodded to herself. "The people will become disillusioned with him, too, no matter what sort of government he decides to set up."

"He's not a bad man," Rune said.

"He's not a good one, either."

Rune wasn't sure he was in a position to judge such things anymore. "So now that we're not married, what will you do? Before you reclaim your kingdom, then conquer Ivasland and probably mine as well."

She snorted. "I don't want to fight with you. Or Abagail, even though I hope she falls into a ditch and breaks both legs."

Considering what Queen Abagail had done to Rune's family, he wasn't above that hope, either. But he wasn't about to say it out loud and start a war.

"My immediate desire is for some kind of treaty that will protect me, my ladies, and the malicists. They were following my orders." She licked her lips. "We can never make this right. The harm we caused, the pain we brought—we can't fix it. But there is damage we can try to undo. The malsites will need to be cleared somehow, and now that—" Hanne's jaw tensed and she shook her head. "My people are the most knowledgeable when it comes to moving malice. I'll consent to all the oversight you see fit."

"I can try." But not right now. Currently, the only thing Rune could focus on was breathing around the boulder inside his chest.

"Thank you." Hanne started to stand, but changed her mind and leaned toward him instead. "Everyone else has been waiting to speak with you. If you need to fall asleep again, because of your injuries, do it quickly."

From the corner of his eye, Rune could just see Grand General Emberwish, Magistrate Stephens, and Queen Abagail lurking in the doorway. There seemed to be a crowd of others behind them—other generals and military figures come to make reports.

Though he didn't want to see anyone, clearly there was work to be done. The three kingdoms needed leadership, and all the leaders were here. Together. Not fighting one another. For the first time.

But later, when night fell and all he could see was the Malstop through his window, he would think about her again. Mourn her. Grieve the moments they'd never had.

He started to sit up, but before he could pull himself together, the room went dark and the door closed. A ghostly figure emerged from the opposite side.

It was Known, one of the maintainers.

They looked exhausted—something Rune hadn't realized was possible. What had they been through during the assault on the towers? Could rancor hurt a . . . whatever they were?

"Rune." Their voice was softer, but still held an undercurrent of power. "I'm glad you've awakened."

"I've been awake," he admitted. "I just didn't want to talk to anyone."

"Excuse me?" Hanne crossed her arms. "I sat by your bedside."

"And you successfully kept the others away. Thank you." Rune forced his mouth into a smile, but it wouldn't fool anyone.

Hanne turned toward Known. "And who are you? *What* are you?"

"They're all right," Rune said. "They're the Nightre—" A wave of grief stole over him, rushing through his whole self. For a moment, he couldn't see or hear. The world tilted off-balance.

She was gone.

Trapped inside that nightmare weapon with Daghath Mal.

Forever.

When it passed and Rune could breathe again, he said, "They're her friend," and focused on holding back the flood of tears until everyone left.

Known sat beside Rune, quiet for a moment. Then: "I understand your grief. You've suffered many losses."

A distant part of Rune registered the fact that Known and Unknown had lost the Nightrender, too. They'd been her companions for thousands of years. This was a devastating blow to them, their mission, and the future of the Malstop. And when he could think again, when he could do anything but mourn, he should write laws, create protections—do something to ensure *this* Incursion was the last.

But that was for later.

He looked at Known. "I assume you came here for a reason. How can I help you?"

They tilted their head. "You should come with me."

His body felt too heavy, too weighed down, to move. Still, it seemed unwise to refuse them—because whatever they were, they were more powerful. Also, it was better than facing his generals and the other leaders. He'd get there eventually, but for now..."All right." He made himself stand. Slowly, he followed Known to a second door, one he hadn't noticed before.

"And you." Known looked over their shoulder at Hanne. "Wait here. I will be back for you."

51.

HANNE

In spite of Rune's reassurances that the ghost person was on their side, they'd locked the room's main door, and the second one—the one that had just appeared out of nowhere—had disappeared.

So she sat on the rumpled bed and reevaluated her entire life.

Things were going to be different now. Much different. She wasn't a princess or queen. She was no one now. Practically a pauper. Perhaps a prisoner.

But she didn't regret setting Rune free. It was for the good of Salvation. And if there was one thing Hanne still truly believed, it was that the three kingdoms needed peace. That couldn't happen with her at Rune's side.

It wasn't a nice thought—that the world was better off without her. She'd never felt *unnecessary* before, but she'd (unintentionally) helped Daghath Mal bring Salvation to its knees. She *should* be out there fixing it, but who would ever trust her to do so?

At least she wouldn't be alone.

Nadine was with her. As always. Hanne's ladies had promised to stay on with her for a while, as their families had also been imprisoned during the rebellion, but eventually, they would all need to make a decision about returning to Embria. Sabine as well, though no one had seen her in a few days....

And then there was Mae. She made Hanne's heart flutter. And judging by the way Mae bit her lip and blushed whenever Hanne entered the room—perhaps Mae felt the same way.

But like Hanne, she had much to atone for. She, too, had followed her ambitions to terrible ends—all under the influence of someone more powerful.

It was strange, thinking of Daghath Mal now. She'd seen him. In person. And he'd reached for her in those final moments, before he'd broken into a million tiny pieces and swirled into that horrible black dagger. For an instant—a very *fleeting* instant—Hanne had felt sorry for him. She'd given him hope in the end.

She wasn't sure how to feel about that.

For now, it was enough that he was gone. From her mind. From the world. That was a victory.

The second door appeared again, and the ghost emerged. Without Rune. Hanne stood. "What did you do with him?"

"That is none of your concern."

"It is very much my concern. I'm counting on him to rule—"

"He is fine." The door disappeared behind the ghost. "You're the one I want to talk about."

"First, who are you? Really, I mean."

"I am one of two maintainers. Nightrender called me Known, and my partner Unknown."

"Is Known your name?"

Known tilted their head. "No."

"Then what is your name?"

"Put that on the list of things that are none of your concern."

Hanne leveled her glare on the maintainer. None of this was going how she liked. "What do you want?"

"Close your eyes. Tell me what you see."

Obviously Hanne wasn't going to see anything but the backs of her eyelids, but if it meant exiting this conversation faster, she would do anything.

She closed her eyes to find that a pale blue spark had ignited within her. Crackling energy. Sharp. Deadly.

She gasped and opened her eyes. "What is that?"

"Ah. As I thought." Known's tone shifted softer. "You experienced Nightrender's power. A *lot* of it."

Like a half-remembered dream, Hanne could faintly recall lying on that altar, the Nightrender's sword pressed against her heart. That numinous power had flooded her, washing out every trace of the rancor king. "The Nightrender helped me," she said after a moment. "She had no reason to do it. But she did anyway."

"You absorbed immense amounts of energy."

Hanne went cold. "Is it going to kill me?" Of course the Nightrender would leave her with this strange, magical residue. It probably *was* dangerous. And now—

Known shook their head. "It will not harm you. But it does present an opportunity."

"What do you mean?"

"The choice is yours. You can ignore it, and it will fade away." Known turned toward the window—and the Malstop beyond. "Or you can use it."

"How would I use it?"

"In defense of Salvation, of course." Known motioned around them. "As you said, there are new malsites everywhere. Rancor. People in distress. And you, Johanne Fortuin, contain the last of Nightrender's power."

A chill slipped down Hanne's back. "The very last?"

"As far as I am aware, yes." Outside, the Malstop crackled.

"And you want me to use it."

The maintainer tilted their head. "I'm informing you of the option. Only you can decide what to do."

"But you think I should use it. Otherwise you wouldn't have said anything." Hanne dragged her fingers through her hair. "I don't understand. How would I use it? Would I— Would I become the Nightrender? Would I be summoned every Incursion? Would I spend eternity killing rancor?"

It sounded ludicrous to her ears.

Known sighed. "I cannot see the future, Johanne. Should you let it fade, the world will continue on. Perhaps your friends will be able to move entire malsites into the Malice. Perhaps they will not."

But the power shimmering inside Hanne could *destroy* the malsites.

If she'd had this power before, when she'd been trapped in the time slip, she would have used it in a heartbeat. She would have believed she was Tuluna's holy warrior, a sharp sword of the Numen of Ambition and Tenacity.

But now—she'd already affected the world. And she'd made it worse.

"It is your choice," Known said. "Already, the spark is dimming, so if you intend to use it, climb to the top of this tower before three days have passed."

The top of this tower? It disappeared into the clouds. She would spend three days heaving herself up stair after stair, only to die of thirst not even halfway to her destination.

But if she tried (and somehow made it up there), she would have power.

Real power. She would possess the ability to drive back the darkness as she'd always believed she could.

She didn't know what would become of Nadine, though. Or Mae. Or any of the others. But perhaps she could speak with them before. Nadine would tell her what was right.

"I'll leave you to consider," Known said.

Gradually, the room grew lighter again. The maintainer started to fade.

"Wait!" Hanne stepped toward them. "What did you do with Rune? Will he be back?" He could help her decide, too. He was one of the best people Hanne knew. And the power had belonged to his favorite person. "Where is he?"

The maintainer smiled. "You'll see."

52.
MEDELLA

She opened her eyes, discovering many things all at once.

First, most immediately: she was alive.

The last thing she remembered was using Light Eater. The midnight blade. The line of blood. The unraveling of the rancor king. His defeat; her victory.

And then Rune had been there, running toward her, his face twisted with horror as she, too, had begun to fall into the blade...

But she was alive.

Somehow.

Everything was muted. Indistinct. Muffled. Her senses, so strong before, were but shadows now, leaving lights and lines hazy, sounds distant, and odors faint.

Gasping, she heaved herself up—too far. Her weight was off. Her balance was broken.

And at the same time as she realized that pieces of her were missing, she registered the presence of another person. She wasn't alone. And she hadn't *known*. She hadn't heard or smelled anyone. She hadn't sensed anything.

Her heart kicked as she swung around, ready to fight. But it was Rune, rising from his chair. He took one hesitant step toward her.

"It's all right." His voice was gentle, calming. But how could she be calm? So she wasn't being attacked; she was *broken*.

"My wings are gone. My wings—"

His expression crumpled. Just for a moment. Then he smoothed it away. But it was enough to reveal he'd noticed—of course he'd noticed—and he'd been thinking about how to tell her.

"I know." Roughness hitched in his voice as he gazed at her. "I'm sorry. I wish..." He dragged in a breath. Swallowed. "It must be awful. Like losing limbs. That is, it *is* losing—" He shook his head and slumped. "Can I get you anything? Water?"

She hadn't moved. She wasn't sure she *could*. Her weight felt off, strangely heavy and too light all at once. Everything was wrong, including the fact that she was alive.

"I need answers."

"Yes, of course." He glanced at the mattress beside her. "May I sit by you?"

Carefully, she shifted to make space for him.

The bed bowed under his weight as he settled. "Known tried to explain it. I have to admit, I didn't understand everything. I was just so relieved that you're alive."

"Tell me," she whispered.

"They said some of you did fall into Light Eater." His gaze flickered beyond her shoulder—toward where her wings should have been. "The part of you that was the Nightrender. The fire. The flight. The never dying."

A cold dread burned deep in her gut. She would die one day. Like a mortal.

"And," he said softly, "the cut in your memories. It's gone, too. What you remember now is what you'll always remember—unless you forget the normal way, like the rest of us."

She lifted her fingers to her temple, as though she could probe the place in her mind. Nothing felt different, but perhaps that was a good sign.

Her hand dropped back to her lap. "I don't understand why the weapon did not take me."

"It tried to." He shut his eyes, remembered pain falling across his features. Muscles flexed in his jaw, an echo of his horror as he'd raced toward her—too late to stop her. "It nearly did."

"I didn't mean for you to see that."

"I know." He flashed a sad, hurt smile. "But I am your soul shard. I had to go after you."

She couldn't judge him for that.

"I will always fight for you." Emotion roughened his voice. "I would have done anything to save you. Anything. Traded places. Dragged the rancor king into the Dark Shard myself. I meant to stop you from using the weapon."

"You would have put the entire world at risk. For me."

"Yes." His hand covered hers, warm, protective. "For you, yes."

"But I'm not *me* anymore." Her shoulders flexed, but the muscles that had controlled her wings were gone.

"Yes you are." He squeezed her hand. "You've endured something trau-matic. Life will never be the same. But you're still *you*."

Her lips parted, but she wasn't sure what she wanted to say. She couldn't argue with his perception of her, but... "I was created for one purpose: killing rancor. I don't know what to do without that."

"Anything you want." He lifted her fingers to his mouth and kissed her knuckles, butterfly soft. "You're here. You're alive. Anything past that—we can figure it out."

It was an end to her endless fight, but not how she'd expected. She'd never considered that the fight might just... go on without her—that *her* part would end, but the struggle against the Dark Shard would continue.

"I asked Known," Rune was saying, "about why the dagger didn't take all of you. When I described what happened, they said it's because we're soul shards—that some of my soul filled what was taken from you. Or some of mine was taken instead. They weren't sure, either."

She touched her free hand to her chest. "I see."

"Do you?" He laughed a little—nervously perhaps. "Because I don't under-stand how something insubstantial could have been moved."

"You were touching me, caught up in the flow. And for weeks, you were channeling my power through the feather—" She bit off any further explana-tion. He didn't need that now. Only: "You saved my life."

He smiled faintly. "Perhaps you were made to fight rancor. But I was made for you."

"To connect me to humanity." That was what the others had been. Right?

"No," he breathed. "It's more than that." His gaze dipped to her mouth. "I was made for you. *Made yours.* From the very beginning. I am yours."

Hers.

Her summoner. Her Dawnbreaker. Her soul shard.

Heat bloomed in her chest. Perhaps this brief mortal existence wouldn't be so bad if she could spend it with him, but— "The treaty. You're already obligated."

The warmth in her faded. He wasn't hers.

Rune shook his head. "I'm not. Not anymore." He leaned closer, speaking quickly. "I can tell you the boring details of that particular clause of the treaty

341

if you want, but the shortest answer is that it's been annulled, and I'm going to work with Stephens and Abagail to form a new treaty, one that will unite the three kingdoms under the banner of peace, not war. So the treaty pitting Caberwill and Embria against Ivasland is off. Ivasland *does* need to answer for their breach of the Winterfast Accords, but we can't ignore the circumstances that pushed them into making the decisions they did. It's going to take a lot of work, but—"

She kissed him. It wasn't that she didn't care about what he was saying; she did, distantly. But she'd stopped paying attention the moment she realized she could kiss him without guilt, and without the looming threat to one of their lives.

With a faint, disbelieving laugh, Rune kissed her back. His hands were warm against her face, her arms, her hips. Heat raced through her as they pressed closer.

How strange to desire someone—to *be* desired. Loved. Not for what she did, but for who she was—wings or no wings.

She stilled.

Rune did, too. His voice was rough, but gentle. "Tell me what you want. When you want. And know that I want everything with you—at your pace." He touched her cheek, gentle and warm. "Come home with me. To Caberwill. You can have your tower if you like. The queen's chambers. Mine. The whole burning castle."

"I don't need a whole castle. But I will go to Honor's Keep with you." She forced a smile. She hadn't had time to think about where she would go after this. Surely Known wouldn't want her to stay here at the Soul Gate. And Winterfast Island was out of reach now. Her home—her real home—would surely fade into myth. Perhaps, in time, Honor's Keep would feel like home. "There is one thing."

"Anything."

"A voice on Incursions. On malice and rancor. On ways Caberwill, at least, can do better." She hazarded a smile. "I may not be all that I was, but perhaps I can continue my purpose in a different way."

He nodded. "The world needs that. The world needs *you*, Medella."

Medella.

For so long, she alone had stood between humanity and the unrelenting darkness. As Nightrender.

Now she would face that endless night in a different way. As Medella. And she would not be alone.

EPILOGUE

This is the world: a continent called Salvation, three kingdoms, and a peace so fragile that a breath might shatter it apart. But the people are trying, working to ensure that future generations never come so close to collapse.

It isn't easy. It will never be easy.

But in Ivasland, a young queen works tirelessly to rebuild an ashen kingdom—and the trust she lost. She's listening to her people, paying attention to the stars set in windows, and calling back the spies and assassins once sent to her enemies. She has so much to learn, but that has never frightened her.

In Embria, a new ruler forms a different sort of government, one the common people control, focused on feeding the hungry and ensuring everyone is safe from those with too much power. It's a different kind of ambition, one the majority is eager to embrace.

And in Caberwill, the king tends to the future of Salvation, restoring Dawnbreaker trials, organizing malsite containment, and drafting other practical policies that will protect generations to come. He does everything he thought his parents should do—and more—loyal to all the people in this world, not only his kingdom.

Nothing is certain in Salvation. Nothing but this: the portal to the Dark Shard remains. Until the passageway closes, the threat of another Incursion remains. And next time, they won't have anyone but themselves.

Unless . . .

Near the center of Salvation, in a tower at the Soul Gate, Hanne has been climbing. Her legs ache. Her head throbs. Her stomach is hollow. Beyond this pain, she has no idea how long she's been ascending.

But ahead, there's a light. Pale, electric blue. It's always just out of sight, around the bend of the spiral an instant before she can make sense of it.

Still, she knows it's what she's seeking. If she can catch it—

Hanne summons her strength. She pushes herself faster. She reaches out.

She *will* have the power she's always wanted.

And this time, she won't be anyone's puppet.

There's one more thing.

Medella wakes in the night, the darkness pressing hard around her. She can't see through it—not anymore. The unknown is so vast and overwhelming.

But she's not alone. Not anymore.

Rune stirs beside her. He takes her hand, and slowly her frightened breathing eases.

At last, she sits up and searches through the nightstand for the small item Rune had tucked there before. She hadn't wanted to touch it then. She couldn't bear to look at it. But now she closes her fingers around the feather's shaft.

A spark flares, snapping loudly in the quiet room.

Rune lurches up. When she turns to face him, his eyes are wide and round—worried. She can see them clearly.

He reaches for her. "What was that?"

Medella lifts the glowing feather between them. And she smiles. "You already know."

ACKNOWLEDGMENTS

The second book in a duology is hard. This is just fact. I'm eternally grateful for the folks who helped me survive this one, beginning with, as always, my agent Lauren MacLeod. Thanks for getting me through the crying days.

I'm so fortunate to have an amazing team at Holiday House. Mora Couch, my editor, continues to be an absolute star. Also, Sara DiSalvo, Terry Borzumato-Greenberg, Miriam Miller, Erin Mathis, Kerry Martin, Mary Joyce Perry, Any Toth, Chris Russo, Nicole Gureli, Lisa Lee, Judy Varon, and Della Farrell—thank you for all your hard work on *Nightrender* and *Dawnbreaker*.

YONSON, thank you for another striking cover! These books look so good.

Much love to my amazing friends and colleagues who supported me throughout the writing and production of this book, including Martina Boone, Cynthia Hand, Erin Bowman, Valerie Cole, Kelly McWilliams, C.J. Redwine, Cade Roach, Elisabeth Jewell, Aminah Mae Safi, Wren Hardwick, Leah Cypess, Kat Zhang, Fran Wilde, Erin Summerill, Alexa Yupangco, Katherine Purdie, Tricia Levenseller, Lisa Maxwell, Lelia Nebeker, Brigid Kemmerer, Kathleen Peacock, Mary Hinton, Nicki Pau Preto, Tanaz Bhathena, Robert Lettrick, Alexa Donne, Elizabeth Bear, Susan Dennard, along with everyone in the Zoo, #FantasyOnFriday, and Macaroni Knit Night. And, obviously, the Dawnbreakers server. Your support and friendship means everything.

As always, thank you to my family for enduring me!

And of course, thank you to the booksellers, librarians, and educators who champion books. Super extra special thanks to my friends at One More Page in Arlington, Virginia. I am, as ever, obsessed with you.

Finally, thank you—the person reading this book.